THE CHAIRMAN

Also by Harry Lee Kraus, Jr.

Stainless Steal Hearts

Fated Genes

Lethal Mercy

The Stain

THE CHAIRMAN

Harry Lee Kraus, Jr., M.D.

CROSSWAY BOOKS • WHEATON, ILLINOIS
A DIVISION OF GOOD NEWS PUBLISHERS

This is a work of imagination. None of the characters found within
these pages reflect the character or intentions of any real person.
Any similarity is coincidental.

Library of Congress Cataloging-in-Publication Data
Kraus, Harry Lee, 1960–
   The chairman / Harry Lee Kraus, Jr.
     p.   cm.
   ISBN 1-58134-038-9 (alk. paper)
   I. Title.
 PS3561.R2875 C48 1999
 813'.54—dc21   98-46847

15	14	13	12	11	10	09	08	07	06	05	04	03	02	01	00	99
15	14	13	12	11	10	9	8	7	6	5	4	3	2	1		

For all those waiting
for The Cure,
especially
Steve Heatwole

PROLOGUE

ABBY MCALLISTER'S voice cracked as she yelled her daughter's name for the second time, this time a little louder—"Melissa!" She paused from her frenzied packing and tilted her head, listening for the sound of little footsteps.

Nothing. Not the expected creak from the old stairs. No footfalls. Only the crooning of a country singer whose radio sonnet could never lighten Abby's mood.

She stuffed a worn sweater into a canvas suitcase and strained to zip the lid. She glared at the bulging suitcase, which groaned both from its contents and the memories they invoked.

"Mel-iiiissaaaa!"

She dragged the suitcase into the narrow, second-floor hall and began tugging it toward the stairs. Almost there, she detoured into Melissa's room.

A threadbare throw rug covered the cool, wooden floor. A single bed decorated with pink, frilly sheets was pushed against the wall. Its sole current occupant was an overstuffed gingerbread man named Willie.

"Mel—!" She stopped short when through the window she saw her daughter playing on the swing in the side yard. The swing, hanging from the largest oak in the neighborhood, topped the list of the five-year-old's favorite places. From the swing, a gift from her father, Melissa had a commanding view of the rolling country west of Fisher's Retreat. Whenever Melissa wasn't underfoot, it was a strong bet that Abby would find her right there.

"I should have known," Abby whispered to herself. "You're going to miss that old tree." She struggled with the heavy window, pulling it up only a few inches before it stopped. She yanked with an audible grunt and managed to coax it open another inch. She lowered her face to the opening.

The November air gave her a frigid greeting. Abby pushed back her long, dark hair and paused to listen as her daughter's voice rose and fell with the swing.

"My dad is the bestest dad," she giggled, looking back at her neighborhood friend, Tommy Evans. "Push higher!"

Tommy, apparently ignoring her, looked up to see yet another horse and buggy on its way out of town. "That makes twenty-one." He shuffled his feet in the leaves. "They're going to that funeral."

"What's a fooneral?"

Tommy squinted his eyes at the overcast sky and tugged on the front of his red coat. "It's a meetin' they have when you get dead." He nodded his head as if he really understood. "My dad said that boy took drugs. He killed hisself."

"Uh-uh! That's not what my dad said."

"Prove it."

"Don't have to. Besides . . . it's a secret. My dad told me hisself."

Tommy eyed the swing. "It's my turn."

Abby looked on silently for a moment longer. "Your father tells you secrets," she whispered. *If only he would talk to me like that, maybe it wouldn't have come to this.* "You're going to miss him too."

"Melissa!"

The petite child rolled forward off the swing in a reckless tumble. "What?"

"Come inside." She heaved a sigh, sending a frosty breath out through the screen. She raised her voice. "Now!"

Melissa looked at Tommy. "Want to watch *Rugrats?*"

"Alone, Melissa," Abby added emphatically. "We have to go."

Abby fought the window closed again. Moments later she heard the door slam, followed by light footfalls bounding up the stairs. Melissa appeared and threw herself in a heap onto the pink sheets. "Hi, Willie," she gasped, casting her arms around the gingerbread man.

Abby picked an oak leaf from her daughter's dark hair. "Come on, honey," she coaxed. "I want you to go to the bathroom before we leave."

Her daughter obeyed while Abby wrestled the suitcase down the wooden staircase.

Melissa's voice echoed from behind the painted door. "When do I get to see the rocket ship?"

Abby didn't answer. Instead, she twisted the rings from her left hand and dropped them into a side pocket of the old piece of luggage. She walked to the front door, again dragging the suitcase. There she paused, looking for a moment at the pictures on a small wooden hall table by the door. She picked up a framed snapshot taken at the Police Academy Ball. Nathan McAllister. Tall. Dressed in his formal blues. Piercing, honest eyes. The kind that could melt a lady's heart. Or make her look away because she knows he sees right through her.

The man I loved.

The man no woman in her right mind could love.

Her hand trembled as she placed the picture back on the table. Then, with determination, she grabbed a bus ticket envelope and shoved it into the back pocket of her faded jeans.

"Where is the rocket?"

Abby stared at Melissa, now at her heels. "What are you talking about?"

"Mom!" She spread her hands widely. "You told me! We are going together on a spaceship, remember?"

Abby knelt down and placed her hands on her daughter's slender shoulders. Her voice escaped as a sob. "Not a spaceship, honey." She smiled weakly. "Mommy said she needed some space. Not a spaceship."

Melissa frowned, then immediately brightened when she saw a deep blue Fisher's Retreat patrol car pulling into the gravel driveway. "Daddy's home!"

Abby whirled. *Nathan? It couldn't be—*

She leaned forward to look through the small dome-shaped window in the front door. Outside, police chief Joe Gibson climbed slowly from the familiar cruiser. Abby watched him step carefully toward the front of the vehicle, his eyes on the ground in front of him. He stopped once and pressed his uniform with his hands before continuing at a somber pace. His face, normally warm and full of expression, was stone.

"Daddy's home! Daddy's home!" Melissa pressed her nose to the window. "Dad?"

"It's not Daddy, honey. It's Joe."

Abby opened the door before he knocked. "Joe, why are you here?"

Melissa skipped forward and hugged his kneecap. "Hi, chief!"

Joe Gibson's eyes softened as they met Abby's. His chin quivered once before he cleared his throat.

Abby instinctively pulled back and reached for Melissa.

"Abby," he began, "it's Nate."

Her hand went to her mouth.

He looked at the clear sky. In the distance the chop of a helicopter blade was growing.

"I'm awful sorry," he said, dropping his eyes to the concrete steps in front of him, "but Nathan's been shot."

CHAPTER

1

NATHAN MCALLISTER sat in the chair, planning his future, trying to make some sense of the past, struggling to remember.

He looked from the double window onto the broad green lawn. Spring rain had started early, and the effect on the shrubs and flowers around Briarfield Manor was nothing short of splendid. The only one who seemed to mind was Jack, the yardman, who swore that the thick grass grew faster than in any year he could remember. Wide sidewalks crisscrossed the landscaping, and decorative metal benches dotted the lawn every few feet to accommodate old, tired feet and lungs incapable of endurance. Beyond the lawn, highway travelers hurried by, uninterested in the pace of nursing home life. Beyond the highway, just visible above the roofline of Ling's Chinese restaurant, North Mountain loomed.

Beyond the mountain, nestled in a quiet valley, the town of Fisher's Retreat beckoned, calling Nathan McAllister home. For Nathan to get there from where he sat involved more than just the forty-five minute, white-knuckled passage on Highway 2 that snaked between Brighton and Apple Valley. *To get there from here,* Nathan mused, *will take a miracle.* He glared at the distant mountain face as if the intensity of his gaze might somehow lessen the giant separating him from his goal.

Why does Abby seem so scared to let me come home?

Next to his chair, a computer monitor and keyboard occupied center stage on a long countertop covered with numerous books. The books, the writings of C.S. Lewis and other theologians, were not standing upright within bookends. They rested at the counter's edge, open and well worn, with broken spines. Beside the countertop, at a level awkwardly low for Nathan's rare visitors, a cluttered bulletin board whispered a story of pain and hope. Pictures of Melissa and Abby, vacation photographs, his daughter's artwork, and sympathy cards bordered an assortment of articles clipped from the *Apple Valley Journal* and the *Carlisle News Leader*.

In the center, a photograph of Nathan just prior to his graduation from the Police Academy accompanied an article entitled "Officer Critical After Drug Bust Shooting." Below it a second article— "McAllister Downed by Friendly Fire: Turner Suspended Until Investigation Concluded"—featured a picture of Officer Brian Turner, with his face partially shielded by his open hand. Below that, a single tack held an article updating the town's fund-raising push for Nathan's medical expenses, a voluntary effort spearheaded by Chief Joe Gibson.

On the board's lower right-hand corner, a Harley Davidson calendar marked the time since the accident—five months that seemed shorter because of his memory loss. Five months that seemed like forever.

The accident. In Nathan's mind it was: THE ACCIDENT. The sum total of his memory of the weeks surrounding the event was an isolated recollection in a sea of black nothingness. His doctor called it a memory island and explained the loss in terms of ischemic encephalopathy or other such fancy medical language that Nathan wished he'd never been forced to learn. Most of his thoughts of the event were gathered from his conversations with his fellow officers, especially his chief, Joe Gibson.

None of his visitors wanted to talk about it much, not even Joe, who had always been so talkative before. Now it seemed like Joe couldn't get beyond some deep sadness for Nathan. He would pump Nathan for his version of the events, then stay objectively distant, even mildly suspicious of Nathan, as if he needed to remain the unbiased detective in order to conclude the department's reports.

Abby wouldn't talk about it either. If she came by more than once a week, it surprised him. And when she did visit, she would simply talk about the weather or Melissa or a hundred other superficial items of small-town life, but never the accident.

He had brought it up to Abby only twice since he arrived at the nursing home. Perhaps before, at the University Hospital or during his weeks at the rehabilitation facility, it had been a multitude of times, maybe even a thousand. He didn't know. He couldn't remember anything from those first critical weeks. He could only imagine how he must've tortured her over and over with, "What happened?" When he talked of the accident now, she would shift uncomfortably, cry, and insist that they dwell on the future. She didn't say it, but Nathan could hear it anyway. *Ignore it. Bury it. Never bring it up again!*

Even Brian, who had been his closest friend on the force, couldn't seem to face him. He seemed overwhelmed by the investigation, and too guilty to sit for more than a moment or two before finding some reason to leave. Not that Nathan blamed him. Knowing what he'd been told about the accident, Brian ought to feel responsible, even guilty. Even if it was an accident.

Nathan's best information about his own shooting was from the small-town newspapers in the Apple Valley. He could recite almost verbatim from the phrases he'd read and reread. "Nathan McAllister was shot by fellow officer, Brian Turner, during a gunfire exchange with a drug dealer, Lester Fitts. Turner claimed to have responded to a distress radio call from the scene. Fitts was accosted by Turner as the dealer exited the front of a drug safe house carrying over a kilogram of heroin. Fitts retreated toward the front steps, drew a 9mm handgun, and opened fire on Turner, who returned multiple fire, striking his opponent in the chest. Turner did not see Officer McAllister in the doorway behind Fitts, and the second officer sustained a near-fatal injury in the altercation."

What really happened, God? If it's all so tidy, like the newspapers say, why won't anyone talk to me about it?

Nathan broke his gaze at North Mountain when he heard the door squeak.

"Hi, Nathan," Libby Summers chirped. "Lunch is served."

He turned around and inched slowly forward to position his legs under the table, where she had placed a tray of overcooked meat loaf and soft vegetables. He took a single glance at the plate before closing his eyes to offer a silent prayer. He *wanted* to be thankful, but what he really felt was a longing for Abby's homemade linguine with red pepper sauce.

He glanced at the tray again. All the food was cut into bites in the kitchen before he could see it. Another pet peeve of his—patient preference sacrificed in the name of efficiency.

I want to be thankful, Lord. But I'd like to see this stuff before they dice it up beyond recognition.

He looked again at the vegetables—instant mashed potatoes and creamed corn. He closed his eyes and dreamed of red peppers and garlic sautéed in olive oil, fresh basil, steaming pasta—

"Amen," Libby interjected, looking at the clock on the wall.

Nathan nodded and began to eat. Today he ate in silence. Although he longed for someone to talk to, he felt bad taking up Libby's time. He knew she had other people who needed assistance. If he talked, the others would have to wait, and she would get scolded by the patients at the end of the hall.

After a few minutes Libby fell into a boring routine. She seemed to be moving from one food to the next without thinking.

"I've had six bites of meat loaf. How about some smashed potatoes?" He used his daughter's words to soften the request.

Libby winced silently, and a hint of pink colored her full cheeks.

He watched her as he ate. She seemed young, maybe just out of high school. Her complexion was clear and her hair blonde, pulled back from her face in a braid he suspected she wore just at work. He could identify her by her hand lotion. Every day she smelled the same—a soft, floral fragrance. *Roses perhaps?* He fought the temptation to lose himself in an unreal fantasy, imagining the texture of her hair, the softness of her skin.

He closed his eyes and dispelled the thought.

After a few minutes he spoke. "Thanks, Libby. I've had enough."

She frowned. "You didn't finish."

"Can't do it."

"You really should drink more fluids."

"I know. But I can't. Maybe later?" A smile belied his thoughts. *You are paid to be my hands, not my brain. I've still got that!*

Libby shrugged and snapped a large yellow lid down over the tray. "Suit yourself." She headed for the door. She turned back when she reached the hallway. "Say, any word from Social Services?"

Nathan tilted his head from side to side. "Janice is doing a site visit in Fisher's Retreat today. Everything should be set. I should be going home."

"That's great." Libby spun on her heels and began pushing a dietary cart to the next room.

As she disappeared, Nathan added with a soft whisper, "If Abby agrees. If . . ."

◆　◆　◆

Paige Hannah stood with one hand on the open refrigerator door and the other on her lips.

"Don't just stand there," her mother urged. "Take something and close the door!"

She pulled a diet soda from the bottom shelf and shut the refrigerator. "It's too hard to decide."

"Come on, Paige," her mother laughed. "You act like it's culture shock just coming back home."

"It is culture shock," she protested. "You should see what my roommates live on. Tofu. Alfalfa sprouts." She gagged. "Wheat germ on bananas."

"Sounds simply scrumptious."

"Maybe to a rabbit." She wrinkled her nose. "What's up, doc?"

Barbara, her mom, heaved a sigh and opened the door again. "Here. Have some leftover lasagna. Or this pasta salad. Or curried chicken with rice."

Paige smiled sheepishly. "Couldn't we just order a pizza? I've been dying for a Tortina's deep-dish combination forever."

"I do all this cooking and—"

Paige caught her mother's eye. "Please? It's my last night home."

"Ugh." Her mother laughed. "You!" She lifted a phone book from the table. "You call."

Paige held up her hand. "I don't need the book." She picked up the phone. "82pizza. It's been the same forever."

Her mother rolled her eyes, then leaned forward. "Order some breadsticks too. And a side of ravioli."

Paige covered the phone with her hand. "Mom!"

"We might as well make it an occasion."

As long as Paige could remember, her mother was making "an occasion" out of something. Someone arriving. Someone leaving. A good grade. The first Monday of the month. A new baby in the neighborhood. A sale at Wal-Mart. Anything or everything provided an excuse for "an occasion."

Forty-five minutes later Paige watched as her mother greeted the pizza deliveryman by name and tipped him five dollars.

Barbara shut the door with her foot and carried a pizza box and a large bag to the kitchen.

"You know that guy?"

Barbara shrugged. "Everyone in this neighborhood knows him."

They sat and ate as Barbara talked excitedly about her upcoming trip.

"Mom . . ." Paige rearranged the crust remnants on her plate.

Her mother looked over her half glasses and lightly touched the corner of her mouth with a napkin.

"I've been thinking that going to see Dad might not be such a good idea."

Barbara took a deep breath. "Honey, we've been over all this before."

"But Dad's so busy. I'll just be in the way—"

Barbara didn't respond. She watched thoughtfully as Paige formed a triangle out of the crust fragments.

"He's always operating."

"You haven't stayed with him for the summer since you were sixteen."

"Mom, he's—"

"He's a very successful surgeon. And one who happens to love his daughter just as much as I do."

Paige began tearing off smaller and smaller pieces of crust, forming first an X and then a serpentine wave with the doughy nuggets. "Take me to Europe with you. I could do research, maybe even get credit for an independent study. We could sit in the little cafes, talk about your art—"

"Paige, you need to spend some time with your father."

"What will I do when he goes in for cases at night?"

"You're an adult. Go with him if you want."

"What if I can't find a job?"

"We've been over this before."

"Mom, he—"

"He's a driven man, but he's still your father. Besides, maybe it's time you saw what a jealous mistress medicine really is."

"And what's wrong with medicine?"

Barbara sighed. "Nothing. Everything." She paused. "Oh, Paige, you know my opinion." She shook her head slowly. "Medicine is a demanding profession."

"But so exciting."

Her mother turned away. "You'll see. It's not as romantic as you imagine."

Paige began to protest. "Mom—"

"You just go," Barbara interrupted. "Spend time with your father like you should. Maybe it will deter some of these pre-medicine notions you've gotten into your head." She shook her head to answer her own thought. "Knowing you, you'll just love it."

"Think I'll be able to get into the O.R.?"

"If you want to. Your father can work it out. He *is* chairman, you know."

"Of course." Paige pushed the crust pieces into a straight line along the edge of her knife, then lifted her nose in the air to speak. "Chairman of the Surgery Department, Brighton University."

Barbara started clearing the dishes. "You're a lot like him, you know."

Paige showed her straight teeth in a cheesy grin and closed her eyes in an exaggerated blink. "My fair face?"

"Your determination to be the best," her mother snapped. Then, softer, she added, "And your fair face, honey."

Her mother looked at the kitchen clock. "My oh my. Why don't you let me take care of these plates? Your plane leaves early in the morning, you know."

Paige nodded and kissed her mother on the cheek. "I know, Mom." She turned and started toward the den before pausing again. "I'll try to keep an open mind. About a career in medicine, I mean."

Her mother shrugged. "Fair enough." She lifted a pizza box from the table. "I called your father yesterday. He'll pick you up at the airport."

Paige nodded.

"And, Paige?" Barbara paused and reached for her daughter. "This summer will be important for him too. He needs a praying woman in the house again."

"He's too together to need anyone, Mom, not even God." She shook her head slowly. "He doesn't need me." Their eyes met. "He never listened to you."

"This is different. You're different."

Paige watched her. Her mother seemed to want to say more but somehow couldn't bring herself to do it. After a moment Paige nodded and walked silently to the stairs.

◆ ◆ ◆

Nathan eased forward through the doorway and turned right. He loved the wide hallway. Here he could move forward unrestricted, without the bother of bumping things or asking people to assist him. Here at Briarfield there were no pretenses, and no awkward labels. Everyone was here for a reason, and not many of their stories were happy ones.

Late evenings were his time. There was no one telling him when to get up or eat or move his bowels. No one doing his physical therapy, combing his hair, or brushing his teeth. No one making sure he didn't drown in the shower. In the evenings Nathan enjoyed the freedom of making his own choices, a liberty that seemed too rare for someone so smart and so young.

Nathan identified his first contact—Mrs. Ethel Bailey. Because she used a walker, she moved more slowly than Nathan, and he had no trouble catching her.

"Ethel . . ." He spoke quietly. "There's going to be a jailbreak at midnight. Are you in?"

Ethel smiled. "Hello, Nate," she chuckled. "I'm too old for that."

"Not you, Ethel."

They moved forward at a slow pace, comfortable with not speaking.

When they reached Mr. Smith's room, Ethel said, "This is as far as I go." They turned together and headed back up the tiled walkway. "Not quoting C.S. Lewis tonight? Or Bon—" Her head bobbed.

"Bonhoeffer?"

"That's him."

Nathan shook his head. "Not tonight. How's the hip?"

"I have a new one, you know. My sister is getting her knee done this week."

"Maybe that's what I need," he joked, tapping his legs with his mouthstick. "Couple new hips, couple of knees . . ." He looked up to see Jake Peterson carrying a power screwdriver in one hand and a collection of papers in the other.

Jake's tired face broke into a wide grin. An official brown hat with a Briarfield Manor logo topped his head, covering a scalp as slick as the floor.

Nathan smiled in return, as he did almost every time he saw Jake. Why anyone would want to wear a brown hat with the initials of Briarfield Manor embroidered on the front was beyond him.

"I got the stuff I was talking about. My boy got it off the Internet just like I said." He pinched the screwdriver under his left arm and started shuffling through the papers. "These boys in Miami are the best." He pointed to a picture. "Look at their logo. He's standing up!"

Nathan read the heading slowly. "The Miami Project."

"Yeah, just look at this stuff. Nerve research. Grafts. I tried to read it." He shrugged, shoving the papers toward Nathan. "You can understand it."

"Wow," he responded with more enthusiasm than he felt. He looked up at Jake. "Thanks." He nodded. "Thanks a lot."

Jake grinned.

"Can you put it on my desk? My door's open."

"Sure."

Nathan and Ethel watched Jake shuffle down the hall and listened as a whistled melody disappeared with him.

"The only thing bigger than that man's heart is his smile. If I was twenty years younger, I'd ask him out," Ethel announced with glee.

The duo maneuvered around a yellow plastic pyramid warning about a slippery floor. Ethel called into an open door, "Come on, Bob. Time for a walk."

Bob Price had his ear two inches from a blaring radio. He didn't look up.

Ethel shrugged and kept moving. "I've invited him for a walk sixteen days in a row. He hasn't heard me once."

"If there wasn't so much in the way, I'd go in there and ask him myself."

Ethel paused at the next doorway. Inside, Sam Miller snored on, oblivious to his restraints. "He hasn't recognized his wife in months." She nodded. "Some things make no sense at all. You and—"

Nathan eased forward. "Come on." He sensed Ethel's hesitation, but he wanted to move on. He and Ethel had bantered the why question around many times in the past months. He didn't feel like doing it again tonight.

She looked down at him and squinted. "Don't rush me. I know what you'd say anyway. Something about sovereignty—"

"Comin' to the rec room, Nate?" Tilly Swanson interrupted, smoothing out the front of her nursing whites.

She didn't wait for an answer. "Ella's volunteerin' tonight. You could play a game. She'll roll the dice for you."

"I want to stay in the hall. Janice might—"

Tilly frowned. "Have you ever seen her here this late before? She'll be in the Social Services office at 8 in the morning."

"She said she'd stop by after talking with Abby."

"In Fisher's Retreat?"

Nathan nodded.

"Hummph. That explains it. If I had to travel Highway 2 from the Apple Valley, I'd be ready for a drink." She unwrapped a stick of Dentyne. "She'll be in tomorrow, mark my words. Gum?"

"No thanks."

He watched as she deposited the gum on the tip of her tongue, which quickly retreated between generous, ruby lips. "It's cinnamon," she offered a second time.

"It gums up my mouthstick."

Tilly wrinkled her nose. "Of course."

Ethel spoke up. "I'll take some."

"Here, honey. I'm sorry." She handed Ethel an unwrapped piece and hurried down the hall.

"You leaving us soon, Nate?" Ethel started forward again.

"I don't know. That's what I'm waiting to hear."

"It takes time to make all the modifications you'll need."

"It's been over four months—first at Brighton University Hospital, then in rehabilitation, and now this." He shook his head. "I'm twenty-eight years old." His voice thickened. "I don't belong in a nursing home."

Ethel shook her head. "Nate, I—"

"When I first came to Briarfield, I thought it was just going to be a few weeks," he continued. "Seems like Abby always has another reason to put it off—"

Ethel interrupted him by placing a wrinkled hand on his shoulder. "She's afraid, Nate. That's all. Give her time."

"It's more than that." *She doesn't want me like this. It's time to face the music, Nathan. You lost more than your body. You've lost your family.*

"She'll come around."

"If anyone can convince her, Janice Marsh can."

"It's not Janice's job to convince her. She can make sure the health resources are available, but—"

Ethel pulled her hand from his shoulder just as the bedraggled social worker they'd just been discussing trudged into the hall.

Nathan and Ethel looked up at the sound of Janice's wooden clogs.

Janice stumbled forward. "Wait 'til you see what's cookin' in Fisher's Retreat!"

CHAPTER
2

JANICE SAT ON the edge of Nathan's bed and closed her briefcase. "Well, what do you think?"

"I don't like it."

"I just told you that Abby is willing to try it with you at home. I thought this is what you wanted."

"That is what I want," he sulked. "It's all the other stuff . . . the celebration—"

"Nathan, they *love* you! They just want to show their support."

"Nathan McAllister Day isn't exactly the homecoming I had in mind. I want to go home quietly, with no fanfare. I need a chance to adjust."

She checked her styled auburn hair in the mirror over Nathan's dresser. "I can register your complaint, but as far as I know, the plans are set."

"Un-set them then. I'm not a hero."

"You're a hero to them, Nathan. You've shown yourself to be a fighter. Look how far you've come. You're fighting against all odds to make a comeback. Let them enjoy this, for pity's sake!"

He winced at her choice of words, and their force. "Did you ever coach football?"

"Nathan—"

"Who's pushing this anyway?"

She didn't answer.

"I know it's not Abby. Have they checked this out with her?"

"Abby has given her consent. All that's left is setting the exact date."

"Janice," he protested, "I wanted you to line up a few people to attend my needs, walk through my house, make sure everything is suitable. I didn't ask you to arrange all this."

"I didn't arrange it. Fisher's Retreat did."

"Wait. You mean to tell me—"

"Look, Nathan, whether you want to believe it or not, your injury and Leroy Fitts's death are the biggest things that've happened in Fisher's Retreat in fifty years. Do you know how long it's been since they had a homicide? Seventy-two years!"

"I know. I am, uh, *was* a police offi—"

"And how long has it been since the last drug arrest?"

"Uh—"

"Fourteen months!" She paused. "We're talking Fisher's Retreat here, Nathan—a quiet country town—a haven for Old Order Mennonites. Your shooting still has the town buzzing."

"You've been talking to Joe Gibson. I should've known."

Janice folded her hands and rested them on her gray skirt. "It's really not that big a deal. They just want to know what day you're going to arrive. They'll put up a few banners to welcome you back. That's all."

"It *is* a big deal to me. I'm not a hero. They wouldn't want a Nathan McAllister Day if I had ducked."

"What?"

"They wouldn't celebrate if I was still on the job . . . if that bullet would've missed. But it didn't miss—I was shot. I didn't do anything heroic. I just got in the way. Don't you see? Just because I'm disabled, they treat me like a celebrity." He huffed. "The chief's behind this, isn't he? Joe goes out of his way to raise money for me. Has the high-school football team doing car washes. The Girl Scouts even sold barbecued beef sandwiches. You know why?"

She pursed her lips and shook her head.

"Joe Gibson." He picked up his mouthstick and pointed at Janice. "And do you know why he does it?"

She shrugged.

"Because he feels guilty. Responsible. It was an on-the-job accident. I'll tell you the statistic he didn't tell you. How many Fisher's Retreat police officers have been permanently disabled from injuries sustained in the line of duty?"

She responded meekly, "One?"

"Of course."

"He didn't tell me that."

Nathan stared into the mirror.

"He did tell me about the last officer to discharge a handgun in the line of duty . . . uh, before your accident, I mean."

He brightened at the memory, and after a minute's reflection he spoke again. "I killed Walker Thompson's wild bull right on the steps of the town Post Office. On Easter Sunday too. Little girls in pink dresses all gussied up for services at the First Presbyterian Church and little boys pullin' at their ties like they were being choked or something, scuffing their feet across the parking lot, when all of a sudden here comes Walker's prize-winner, the biggest bull I've ever seen, pawing the gravel and snortin' like the devil himself. Kids went screaming. Millie Brunk's Easter bonnet caught the wind when she hightailed it into the church foyer yelling, 'He is risen indeed!'"

Janice's hand went to her mouth.

Nathan started laughing. "Like if she yelled it loud enough, the bull might go away." Tears welled up in the corners of his eyes and started spilling onto his cheeks. "The bull ate her hat." His sentence dissolved into a chuckle. He looked helplessly at Janice. "I guess you just have to know Millie to see how funny it was."

Janice blotted his tears with a Kleenex.

"Thanks. Sorry."

"What happened after that? The chief didn't tell it this way, you know."

"Well, I was there. My version is the correct one." He smiled. "Well, next the old bull charged Mr. Tyson's yellow Cadillac and put a horn right through the front grill. At that point the situation turned into a standoff. Everyone was either sitting in their cars, too afraid to leave, or safely in the church waiting for the service to get started. The bull just snorted and pawed the ground, holding half the congregation at bay in their cars."

"Oh my."

"Then Wilda Boyers cranked up the organ and turned on the outside speakers. That bull took off across the street and down the road as if he had a true appreciation for Wilda's talent.

"I pursued him on foot, and just as he took a keen interest in destroying a public mailbox in front of the Post Office, I took him out. I hated to do it, really." He shrugged. "You do what you gotta do, I guess. It's the life of a small-town cop."

He paused for a moment. "Look, Janice, I just want to get home. If they want to have a celebration, so be it."

Janice looked at her watch.

"But I still contend that Joe is pushing these things because he feels guilty and doesn't know how else to respond . . . not because I'm a hero."

"Think what you want." She stood up and touched his shoulder. "*I* think you're a hero."

"Set the date then. Get me out of here."

"I have to line up some attendants. And I want you to interview them—make sure they're suitable to you. You're the one who has to get along with them."

"OK. Find 'em. I just want to go home."

"I'll need to talk to the home health nurses. They have the most contacts. I should be able to line something up soon."

Nathan nodded and watched as Janice picked up her briefcase.

"Janice . . . How did she say it? Abby, I mean. You said she's willing to try it with me at home. Did she sound excited?"

Janice sighed. "She's realistic, I think. Having you at home is a bit scary for her just now."

"Is that what she said?"

"Not exactly. It's what I *felt* when I talked to her. I've been trained to pick up on people's anxieties. I think she just needs some time."

"She clams up when I try to talk to her about what happened. It's like she doesn't want to even think about it."

Janice nodded and set her briefcase on the floor. "What did happen, Nathan? Do you want to talk to me about it?"

"That's just it, I don't *know* what happened. At least not exactly. All I know, I grabbed from the papers. They tell me I was so close to death that I didn't have a blood pressure for a while." He paused. "With a few exceptions, it's as if someone erased a month of my life. I can't remember a thing . . . from a few days before until just before I entered rehab. So every time I get a visitor from home, I see what I can find out. But the people in the know aren't talking. It's weird. Joe Gibson, Abby, Brian Turner . . . Well, Brian I can understand. He's the one who shot me." He stretched his neck from side to side and lifted his shoulders. "It's funny, Janice. I've spent over four months asking God *why*, and I don't even know the answer to *what* yet."

"Sometimes people don't want to talk about things that they're afraid might happen to them. They're so uncomfortable with your pain that they don't want to think about it. They deny their fear by not talking about it."

"Now you're sounding like a social worker."

"I am a social worker." She stood up again. "I hope you find the answers. Maybe getting back to Fisher's Retreat will be good for your memory."

"I've got to get home and find out. I've just got to."

CHAPTER
3

Dr. E. Ryan Hannah bristled at the ringing of the phone beside his bed. He looked at the glowing red numbers on his clock radio. *Five in the morning! Who's calling me at this hour?*

Restraining himself, he spoke his normal greeting, an efficient identification. "Dr. Hannah."

"Sorry to bother you, sir, but I thought you'd want to be the first to know." The feminine voice belonged to a third-year neurosurgery resident.

"Elizabeth?"

"Yes, sir."

Ryan rubbed the back of his neck. "What is it? You're not taking trauma call, are you? Griffin is the attending on call for trauma, not me."

"No, sir. I'm not calling about trauma. I'm full-time in the lab this year. *Your* lab, remember?"

"OK, OK," he chuckled. "I'm waking up now. Why are you calling?"

"Sir, Heidi moved her toe."

It took a moment to sink in. Suddenly he sat up, fully awake. "Sir?"

"I'm here, Elizabeth. Are you sure? It's not just reflex?"

"Dr. Hannah, I've verified it six consecutive times."

"Have you done the motor strip stim test?"

"Absolutely. The flexor on the left great toe is the only one responding now."

Ryan was on his feet, pacing, snapping on lights, looking for his clothes. "I'll be right there. Are you in the lab?"

"Of course. I've been with Heidi all night. Ever since I first noted a positive response."

"Ha-haah!" Ryan screamed, reaching for his electric razor and balancing the phone against his ear. "Who else knows about this?" He flipped on his razor.

"Only you and me."

"Great. I want you to seal the lab. I can't afford any leaks, you hear?"

"Dr. Hannah, you can trust me."

Ryan nodded. "Right. Okay, set up the video monitor with a split screen. I want simultaneous recordings of the stimulus in the cerebral motor strip along with a spinal cord reading and the toe movement. All on one screen. Got it?"

"Sure. I've been ready for this for months."

Ryan snapped off the phone and attempted to shave, but found himself barely able to concentrate on the task at hand.

"Heidi moved her toe. Heidi moved her toe," he sang, raising his Braun razor to his mouth as a microphone. Exiting the bathroom he jigged and pranced into his bedroom in a private moment of uninhibited celebration.

"Heidi moved her toe! Heidi moved her toe!" He came to a stop as he caught a glimpse of his silly display in his full-length mirror. His hands quickly moved to his sides, quieting the movement still present in his love-handles. He looked at himself, standing in only a pair of boxer shorts, and straightened his posture, attempting to regain a semblance of the debonair quality with which he normally carried himself.

He ran his fingers through his thick, gray hair and winked. He smiled for a moment before speaking.

"The boys in Miami are never going to believe this."

◆　◆　◆

Nathan's eyes were open wide, staring at the ceiling. Silently he focused on his last memory before the accident. It seemed a senseless island, with nothing around it to frame it or give it meaning: *A woman, her face nondescript, shaded by a dark bonnet that prevented his seeing her hair. She had melancholic eyes. The kind of eyes he'd seen before, during his work as a police officer. Eyes without luster, dulled by tragedy or loss. Eyes that scream their pain through silent tears. Eyes hardened by unknown calamity or blight. She wore a dark dress, and a black overcoat was gathered around her petite frame. In her hand she clutched fresh earth, the tight fist slowly loosening to spill the dirt through open fingers.* He strained to remember more and tossed his head back in frustration. Other than this memory, he last recalled putting Melissa to bed several nights before his shooting. He wondered whether the image was just a misplaced event, or something out of sequence from the past, or something dislodged by his own tragedy. But if so, why was it etched so forcefully in his mind?

He glanced at the clock. It was 5:30 in the morning, and he was fully awake, with no prospect of getting up for at least two hours. He studied his surroundings in the dim light. The screensaver on his computer pranced randomly, emitting a mystical glow that flickered against the back of his chair. In the corner, a small red light on top of his battery charger reminded him of a traffic signal destined to frustrate all who approached. It would change to green only when the batteries were fully charged. In his mind he sat at an intersection watching the signal, tapping his hand restlessly against the steering wheel of a 1964 Corvette. *Come on, light, change!*

In another corner, a humidifier hummed in a constant monotone, and in the hallway the squeak of a pharmacy cart chirped with a rhythmic tempo. *It must be Billy. Ms. Gifford never pushes it that fast.* Nathan took a mental ride on the cart's shiny surface, supervising and observing everyone's medications. *Careful, Billy. Slow down for the corner!*

Pock, pock, pock. Nathan listened as the sound of the night nurse manager's heels struck the floor. *Right on time, Katie. Don't you know those shoes are bad for your posture?*

Outside, the rumble of trucks from the highway was just picking up as early deliveries to and from downtown Brighton initiated the new day. Nathan imagined each one in exquisite detail, right down to the tattoo on the left forearm of a man named Ralph driving a Morning Harvest bread truck.

Sometimes he imagined the things he loved the most. The sound of Melissa giggling out a little song. The crack of his .38. The cool feel of its polished surface. Hours would pass as he remembered the fresh scent of Abby's hair, the feel of her arms around him, her breath on his neck, the way she made him respond . . . before. Before the accident that had changed everything.

Nathan sighed weakly. Sighing heavily was yet another thing of the past for him, a man whose life seemed separated into two segments by an ugly red scar—before and after.

He looked through the rails of his hospital bed. *As if I need the rails to keep me from falling out. What I wouldn't give just to be able to fall out of bed!*

Eventually he quieted his active thoughts and felt a gentle nudge on his conscience.

Not now, Lord.

In the silence, as he'd experienced many times before, he began to listen.

Please, God. I don't want to cry. I can't even blow my own nose.

Nathan squeezed his eyelids as a subtle conviction expanded.

Forgive me for trying to escape reality. But can it be wrong to treasure the life I had before?

Can it be true that you allowed all of this for a reason?

He thought of the books that had brought him so much comfort, and the meaning of his own pain.

Surely this can't be the abundant life the chaplain was talking about last Sunday.

One day I'll walk again. And you'll get the glory. That's your plan, right? I'm going to be healed.

He passed a moment in silence. There would be no audible answers today.

He thought of Abby and went back to praying. *Thank you for Abby, Lord.*

Please help her love me again.

Tears flowed, and Nathan licked his upper lip. *I've always been so jealous for her, God, never even wanting her out where she could be tempted to smile at another guy. It seems so stupid now. I didn't have a right to own her, Father.*

I should have given her to you.

Now I look at myself, and I know she deserves better. Maybe it would be best for her to leave. I can only be a burden to her now. I can never be the man she wants.

Oh, God, make me whole again . . .

Nathan sniffed and cleared his throat.

The door's movement caught his attention. Betsy Landis leaned through the opening, squinting toward Nathan in the semidarkness.

His voice cracked. "Morning, Bets."

"Good, you're awake. How about coming out with me to watch the sunrise?"

"Marlin usually doesn't come by until 7:30."

"Forget Marlin. I'll get Mikey and Tina, and we'll get you up." She pulled up her sleeve and flexed her arm. "I'll be right back."

He sniffed again. This time he prayed aloud. "Thank you, God. Thank you."

◆ ◆ ◆

His given name was Ernest Ryan Hannah, but for as long as he had been in control of his own life, and that had been as long as he could remember, he was Ryan Hannah—Dr. Hannah—to almost everyone, certainly to everyone important.

After a quick hour in his lab attending to a young female hamadryas baboon named Heidi, he arrived promptly in the neurosurgical intensive care unit, or N.I.C.U., for morning ward rounds.

There he was greeted by his chief resident, George Wingfield, who handed him a daily patient census.

"Thirty-one. Not bad. I'd better get going. It's going to be a busy day downstairs." He smiled and looked at the team. Three medical students, two interns, and a single resident from each year two through seven. "Is this everyone?"

"Yes, sir."

They walked to the first bed. The medical student, Nelson Billroth, needed a shave, Ryan noticed. The student picked up the bedside chart. "This patient is a seventeen-year-old Caucasian male who presented with a closed head injury sustained in a head-on motor vehicle accident. He was the unrestrained, intoxicated driver in a car not equipped with air bags. His initial vital signs were normal, and his glascow coma score was 10. Other than his decreased E.M.V. score, his physical examination was notable for a large scalp laceration and an open left femur fracture . . ."

Dr. Hannah interrupted by loudly clearing his throat as the chief resident cringed.

The student's face reddened.

Ryan squinted at the medical student's I.D. badge. "Student doctor—"

"Uh, Dr. Billroth, sir."

"You have a very distinguished surgical name. You are aware of the Billroth I and Billroth II gastric reconstructions?"

"Yes, sir. I rotated on the general surgery service last month."

"Ah, well, good enough then. If you've rotated on Dr. Neal's service, I'm sure you are also familiar with the term 'bullet rounds'?"

"Yes, sir."

"Good," he chuckled. "Please hand me the chart. You are doing a great and complete job, young doctor, but we have many patients to see before the O.R. begins paging."

Nelson Billroth passed the chart away and wiped his palms conspicuously onto the front of his white coat.

The chairman studied the chart for a moment before proceeding. "Seventeen-year-old male with a subdural hematoma and left femur fracture, post-op day number one from evacuation of the hematoma and O.R.I.F. of his left femur." He paused. "Stable first night, with no intracranial pressure problems."

He reached over and gently touched the patient on his chest. The boy opened his eyes. "Derrick? You're going to be OK. We'll get this tube out so you can talk a little later this morning."

Dr. Hannah looked at the third-year resident in charge of the I.C.U patients. "Timmons? Get this guy extubated this morning." Then, to the group he raised his voice. "Next patient."

The process continued through the eight-bed N.I.C.U. and out onto the ninth-floor med/surg ward.

Ms. Jones, an elderly patient with rheumatoid arthritis, was looking good on the second day after fusion of her cervical spine, but she wanted to have a bowel movement.

R. Potter had a routine lumbar microdissectomy complicated by a spinal fluid leak. His head still hurt in spite of the narcotics. "Another day flat on your back, Mr. Potter," they assured him. "It's going to get better."

Steadily they worked through the list—bulging lumbar discs, brain tumors, head injuries, spinal stenosis, and intracerebral aneurysms.

Finally, just before 8, Hannah excused himself and descended the stairs to his large office, situated at the end of a plush, carpeted foyer. Everyone at Brighton U. called it "the cranberry hall" because of the gaudy color.

He passed his administrative assistant's desk. "Good morning, Trish."

He hung up his white coat. "Where's today's schedule?"

She held up a daily planner. "You have a carotid endarterctomy at 8 in O.R. 4. Dr. Button wants your help with an acoustic neuroma at 10. You have to interview a new trauma attending at 2, and the dean wants your quarterly budget proposal on his desk by 5."

Ryan sighed and waved his hand. "OK, OK. Did Dr. Jeffries bring by the new Physician's Alliance fee schedule proposal?"

"Yes, but I've looked it over. It's only Medicare plus 10 percent. We'll never make it with that, sir."

"Put it on my desk. I'll look at it between cases." He started for the door.

"Dr. Hannah? There's one more thing." She held out a yellow sticky note. "Your ex-wife called."

He paused. "Barbara?"

"Your daughter's flight arrives at 9." Trish smiled meekly. "She called to remind you."

"Paige!" He struck his forehead and looked at his watch. "My carotid patient . . ."

"Why don't you ask Dr. Endean to do it? The vascular guys would be glad to—"

"Give a carotid to the vascular surgeons?" He shook his head. "It's out of the question. I'm sure they would never surrender a carotid to us. I'm not about to—"

"OK, OK, it was just a suggestion." She held up both hands.

He softened, looking at his watch again. "Look . . . Buy some flowers," he said, handing her his VISA card. "Put 'em on my desk. Get Elizabeth to pick her up. Bring Paige back here to my office. I'll see her after the acoustic neuroma case."

"Dr. Hopkins?" Trish tilted her head. "Your research resident?"

"Sure. I can't sacrifice one of the residents on the service. She won't mind."

"Sir, I could—"

He lifted his hand. "You need to stay here and man the desk. I'm expecting the Brighton Care people to bring an offer to counter the Alliance's figures."

"Dr. Hopkins isn't going to like it."

He retreated into the doorway. "Give her my VISA after you order the flowers. Tell her to put some gas in that guzzler of hers."

Trish shook her head.

The chairman nodded his head more forcefully and made his final departure into the cranberry hall.

◆ ◆ ◆

A large hair-net strained to contain Marty's long black hair. She pushed the last rebellious strand behind her ear before greeting her closest friend. "You cut your hair!"

Abby McAllister looked up from the dough she was kneading and smiled. "Well?"

Marty pranced in a circle, examining the cut from all angles. "Abby, it looks great!" She put a finger to her lips. "What does Nate think?"

"He doesn't know."

Marty raised her eyebrows and let the comment fall. "It's been great having you here, Abs."

Abby smiled again.

"I think it's just what this old place needed. Mr. Knitter says business at the cafe hasn't been this strong in years."

"It's been good for me too," Abby added. She continued massaging the dough for a moment before adding, "Nate's coming home soon."

Marty nodded. "I heard it from Brian. Where will you go? You want to stay with me for a while? I don't have much room, but Melissa could sleep on the couch and—"

"I'm staying at home." She caught her friend's eye. "I'm *staying* with Nate." When Marty didn't respond, Abby added quietly, "At least for now."

Marty sighed heavily. "But you—"

"I *know* what I told you." She plopped the dough into a large ceramic bowl. "But I can't leave him right now. You should see him."

"Now? Abby, you *left* him in November."

Abby dropped her eyes. "Not exactly." She rinsed the flour from her hands and began to pace around the cluttered kitchen. "I never really left, technically."

"That's because you didn't have to," Marty countered. "Nate left."

"Right. Sort of."

"Abby, you *promised* yourself. Remember all that talk about feeling confined? We must have talked about this a thousand times. Abby, you—"

"*Marty!* I never told him." She wrung her white apron in her hands. "At first I thought he would die. He didn't even know me for days."

"You never told him!"

Abby shook her head. "Eventually, once he was moved into rehab and then to Briarfield Manor . . . well, I just couldn't bring myself to do it."

Marty tapped her finger on the flour-dusted countertop and stared at Abby without speaking.

Abby busied herself by checking the large bread oven and arranging the loaf pans for the dough.

"So now instead of being married to a jealous, controlling able-bod—"

"Marty, don't!"

". . . able-bodied man," Marty continued even more loudly, "you're going to play nursemaid to a jealous, slobbering quad!"

"Stop it! You don't know what you're saying!"

Marty grabbed her arm. "Look at me, Abs. Nothing has changed." She shook her head. "Look, I'm sorry about what happened to Nate. We all are. But that doesn't change what needs to happen in *your* life. You were finally doing something for yourself, Abs. You were doing the right thing. Nate's accident doesn't have to change that."

Abby pulled free and began to cry.

"Look, Abs. I—I'm sorry. I—I shouldn't have said that about Nate." She sighed. "It's just that . . . Well, I think you deserve better."

Abby shook her head.

"You deserved better before he was injured, Abby. And you still do. How can he be a husband to you now?"

"I'm not going to be his nurse," she responded thoughtfully. "Nate specifically told me he doesn't expect me to do those things."

"You didn't answer my question. He can't be a man for you like Brian—"

Abby cupped her hands over her ears. "Don't say it, Marty, don't!"

Her friend threw her hands in the air. "I've got to check on things out front."

Abby watched her disappear, then turned, hung her apron on the back of the door, and fled into the narrow alley behind Fisher's Cafe.

CHAPTER
4

Gently George Wingfield lifted the cut edge of the patient's internal carotid artery, inspecting the inner surface. "It looks pretty clean."

"Let's make a final inspection," Dr. Hannah instructed. "If he wakes up with a stroke, you'll be thankful you looked again." He picked a final small fragment of plaque from the lining. "Flush."

The nurse responded and irrigated the surface of the artery with saline.

"There. Now it meets my approval. Six-O Prolene. Let's close."

The chairman watched each small stitch through his magnifying glasses. "Good, good," he encouraged his resident. "Let's take out this shunt before you get too far."

After a few more minutes, with the artery safely closed, Ryan handed his forceps to a medical student at his right elbow. "Help Dr. Wingfield close. I'm going to talk to the family."

He smiled behind his mask as he backed away from the table. "I'll be in O.R. 8 if there's any trouble. I'll be helping Dr. Button with the acoustic neuroma."

"Right, sir," George responded.

He smiled again, tore off his paper gown, and looked forward to meeting a thankful family.

◆ ◆ ◆

Paige strained to see her father among the crowd at her arrival gate. She looked for a gray suit, which was what he always wore.

A tall man in a sweat suit hugged his wife. A little girl ran forward yelling, "Grandma." A couple traveling together scurried toward the baggage claim area. A young woman kissed a man in a military uniform. A business traveler stopped in the middle of it all to use his phone. But no one looked like her father. No one even wore a gray suit.

After the crowd cleared, she thought she'd wait a minute or two longer by her gate, just in case her father had been delayed. She plopped onto a padded chair.

"Paige?"

She looked up to see a woman with a small framed photograph in her hand. "Yes?"

"Oh, good," she gasped. "I found you." She squinted at the picture in her hand. "You don't look anything like your picture." She looked up. "I'm Dr.—uh, Elizabeth Hopkins."

"Hi." Paige reached for the picture. "Oh, gag! Where did you get this? I must have been thirteen years old!"

"It's the picture Dr. Hannah has on his desk. His assistant gave it to me so I could find you."

"This should definitely be burned! I look fat. Ugh! Look at those braids!" She shook her head. "How did you find me?"

"Lucky guess." She shrugged. "You were the only one sitting at the gate."

"I'm going to get him a different picture." She slid the one she was holding into her carry-on bag.

Elizabeth smiled. "I guess we've all probably improved since we were thirteen. You certainly have."

Paige changed the subject. "So I take it my father isn't coming."

"He's operating."

"I should have guessed. You're a doctor?"

"I'm a neurosurgery resident. I'm taking an extra year as a research assistant in your father's lab."

They began walking to the baggage claim area as Elizabeth chatted on. "Excuse my appearance. I was up most of the night."

Paige studied her out of the corner of her eye. Elizabeth didn't look anything like any physician she knew. She was young, attractive, and looked strikingly similar to Sandra Bullock.

"Your father is working on a great project. Does he tell you about his research?"

"Not really. I've been taking pre-medicine in college. I'm hoping that this summer will help me know if medicine is really for me."

Elizabeth chuckled and imitated a ghoulish warning. "It's not toooo laaate to turn baaaack!" She laughed again at her own joke. "Where are you from?"

"L.A."

"Wow. City of the Angels."

"Lower Alabama," Paige corrected with a smile.

"You don't have the accent."

"I'm really local. I grew up just outside Brighton. Mom and I moved to Alabama five years ago."

Elizabeth nodded.

"That's my bag."

They waited for a minute longer until she claimed a second suitcase, then started for Elizabeth's car.

After lugging the bags across the parking lot, they paused at the back of a large, old, brown Buick. "Well, here we are," Elizabeth huffed, opening the trunk.

Paige stepped back and assessed the value of the car. "I thought you said you're a doctor." She heaved the bags into the dusty trunk.

"I *am* a doctor. A resident doctor. The financial rewards in this field come relatively late. Hop in."

Paige slid into the car, which although old was immaculate on the inside. The shiny leather seats and dashboard looked like Elizabeth must be infatuated with Armor-All.

"Do you remember your father as a resident?"

Paige shook her head. "Dad's been an attending as long as I can remember."

"Hmm. There's a lot about medical training you haven't seen then."

Elizabeth drove back to the University medical center in just under twenty minutes, telling Paige about her father's cases, his car, his clothes, and his eating habits. It was Dr. Hannah this and Dr. Hannah that, until Paige was convinced that Elizabeth was either obsessed with her father or just plain manic.

"Why don't I take you by the lab? I need to check on some stuff there anyway. Dr. Hannah will never be done with his cases by now, so you'd just end up sitting bored in his office."

Paige shrugged.

"Dr. Hannah is pretty secretive about his latest project. But you're his daughter. He certainly wouldn't object to me showing it to you."

◆ ◆ ◆

Marlin Clayborn moved Nathan's arms through a series of motion exercises. His left arm spasmed wildly. Slowly the physical therapist straightened the arm as the spasm subsided.

Nathan watched the process with interest. "Why does it just happen with my left arm? Gary doesn't seem to have so much problem with spasms."

Marlin shrugged. "Every quad is different, Nate. Some have no sensation, some have light touch, some have spasms all the time, some have them only in one limb. I'm not sure why exactly."

He continued working Nathan's fingers, wrists, elbows, and shoulders, each in turn, to maintain flexibility. Nathan watched his arms and felt exactly nothing. As a complete C3-4 quadriplegic, he had no motor function below his neck except for a weak ability to pull his arms across his chest, with virtually no sensation below his shoulders.

If only the bullet had entered his spine one or two levels lower, he would have had enough arm movement to operate a mechanical wheelchair with a specially adapted wrist splint, maybe even drive a special van. If only he wouldn't have been behind Lester Fitts. If only. For the most part he tried not to dwell on the if onlys. He preferred to be thankful that the bullet had not entered his spine one level higher,

which would have made it impossible to breathe without a mechanical ventilator.

"Do you want to ride the StimMaster today?"

"Sure, but let's do it this morning. Abby and Melissa are coming
by later."

"Suits me." Marlin looked up at the bulletin board. "Hey, what's
this?" He unpinned an X-ray film.

"One of the paramedics brought it by. He's preparing for a talk on
management of neck trauma or something. He was one of the guys in
the helicopter with me when I was injured."

"No kidding!"

"Really."

"It must be interesting seeing him again."

Nathan shook his head. "It was like meeting him for the first time.
I couldn't have told you I'd seen him before."

Marlin stared at the X-ray. "This is your neck?"

"Without the flesh."

He laughed. "How'd the paramedic get this?"

"He wants to use my case as an illustration, so he had the X-ray
department at Brighton make him a copy. I guess he thought it was
cool, so he took a chance to see if I'd want one too."

Marlin studied the film and pointed to the front of the neck. "Wow.
You had a trach?"

"Yep. For three weeks, so they say. I don't remember. I can see the
scar if I look in a mirror."

"This is wild. You can see the bullet and everything." He pointed
at the film. "What are these?"

"That's a row of staples that they closed me up with after surgery,"
he answered while leaning forward and scratching his nose against a
mouthstick that rested in a holder on his chair. "I asked the same
thing."

The physical therapist put the X-ray back on the bulletin board.
"Wait a minute. This is *after* your operation? Did they take the bullet
out later?"

"Nope. As far as I know, it's still there. Dr. Hannah told Abby that it'd be too risky taking it out. Seems like the damage had been done, and there was nothin' to gain by taking it out."

Marlin shivered. "I'd want it out of me."

"They said I could end up with further cord damage if they operated to remove it . . . maybe even be on a breathing machine forever."

"Don't the cops need the bullet for evidence or something?"

"Nah. I was shot by a fellow officer, so there's really no case pending."

Marlin tightened a Velcro chest strap around Nathan's torso. "You're a brave man, Nate."

"Being disabled doesn't make me brave."

Marlin didn't respond. He gently lifted Nathan's right arm and positioned it on the padded arm of his wheelchair, securing it with a second Velcro strap. He lifted Nathan's left arm. "Have you ever tried strapping this arm down?"

"In the beginning the physical therapists at B.U. tried it, but I had so many problems with the spasms that I always ended up leaning to the left. So it's just easier to let it rest without a strap."

"Let's go get you on the StimMaster."

"I'm with you." Nathan pushed his head gently against the right pad attached to the headrest on his wheelchair. One click, then two. His wheelchair obeyed and turned right. He then depressed the back headpad once to reset the chair's computer, and a second time to enter a command to go forward. With that, he glided straight out of the room behind Marlin.

◆ ◆ ◆

Dr. Hannah stood at the scrub sinks, just outside O.R. 8, quizzing the resident beside him. "What are the two approaches that can be used to resect acoustic neuromas?"

"The translabyrinthine approach and the suboccipital one."

"And which has Dr. Button chosen?"

"The suboccipital one. The translabyrinthine approach is only used if the patient has total loss of hearing."

Hannah smiled. "You've been reading. What is the biggest risk to the patient?"

"Facial paralysis."

"Correct. If we aren't careful, Mr. Johnson's smile will be as crooked as Highway 2." He dropped his scrub brush into the sink. "Show time."

◆ ◆ ◆

Paige got out of the car and stretched. "I don't want to sit down again for a long time."

"I hate airplanes too," Elizabeth confided. "If I can't get there by train, I usually don't go. Or I drink heavily first, and then go."

Paige shook her head incredulously. "What about my bags?"

"Leave 'em. You won't want them in there," she said, pointing at the ten-story University Hospital. "I'll bring 'em by Dr. Hannah's tonight."

Paige nodded and tried not to gag. *And just how many times have you been by Dr. Hannah's?*

The Brighton University Hospital sat diagonally across a large paved circle drive from the Dennis Foundation Research Facility. The medical and dental schools were housed in stodgy brick buildings located on individual spokes extending from the circle drive. In the center of the circular median, overshadowed by the research facility, a white statue of Hippocrates stood on an elaborate concrete pedestal. Hundreds of people walked in long, quick steps, with white coats and backpacks the normal attire. In front of the Dennis Building, a bicycle rack reminded Paige of a hungry, giant caterpillar with each leg grasping its metal prey.

Also in front of the research facility, harried students argued over open books and coffee on a dozen benches beneath a huge covered entrance. To Paige, the atmosphere seemed vibrant with excitement. Approaching a row of glass doors, she gasped when she saw a man with a red cloth bandanna tied as a gag around his mouth. He appeared to be in his young twenties and had long, blond bangs pulled behind his ears in thick, greasy strands. It was a style too unkempt to be unplanned. He remained silent except for an occasional emphatic grunt as he shoved white flyers into the hands of all who would receive them. Paige accepted a flyer from the odd man.

Elizabeth pulled her forward. "Ignore him. He and his buddies come down here about once a week."

She read the flyer. "DON'T HURT THE ANIMALS."

The young resident waved her hand in the air. "Some weird animal rights group."

"Why the gag?"

"They want to show us that animals don't have a voice," she explained as they stepped onto an elevator. "I'm glad for the gag. That way I don't have to talk to him."

Paige nodded silently and slid the flyer into her jeans pocket.

Since they were alone, Elizabeth continued, "What they wouldn't give to have access to the spinal lab!"

"My father's lab?"

She nodded.

They stopped on the sixth floor, then walked down the hall to a large door with a simple label: E. Ryan Hannah, M.D. Below that was a number on a nondescript plaque: 6-1121.

"It's best not to advertise some things," Elizabeth commented as she held her picture I.D. before a red sensor beside the door.

The door unlocked, and the duo entered.

"Welcome to Brighton University's Spinal Cord Research Lab."

The entrance to the main lab was a reception office, complete with a desk, a computer, and a cluttered bookshelf. "This is my station. The computer is on-line with the state's SCI database."

"SCI?"

"Spinal cord injury," she explained, donning a long white coat.

Paige looked through a large clear window into the next room.

"That's the main lab, although most of the preliminary work on our present project was done in the biochem and DNA labs downstairs."

Paige shook her short blonde hair. "Er, just what is my dad working on?"

"He hasn't told you?"

"Well, some," she muttered. "Dad doesn't really tell me specifics." She strained to see around a tall refrigerator. "We do talk. Well, E-mail mostly."

A little uncomfortable at the tack the conversation was taking, Elizabeth changed the subject. "Do you want to be a doctor?"

She smiled meekly. "I think so. A pediatrician probably."

Elizabeth shook her head. "No money there. Just a lot of snotty-nosed kids. Let me show you some real medicine." She led the way into a much larger room, complete with four long lab counters supporting a lattice of intersecting metal scaffolds, each holding what seemed to be a thousand different beakers, test tubes, and flasks. The scene reminded Paige of her organic chemistry lab back in Alabama.

"Over here we house the rodents." She opened a side door. Rows of clear containers lined three walls. On the far wall a large metal sink and a stainless steel counter bordered a rack holding an assortment of padded gloves.

Paige peered into the first container and winced. "Rats!" She squinted. "Oooh! What's *wrong* with him?"

"These are our Schwann rats. At least that's what I call them." She tapped on the Plexiglas container. "Hi, Freddy." She glanced back at Paige. "You've had human bio?"

"Two semesters."

"Good. Then you've heard of Schwann cells, the cells that line peripheral nerves."

Paige nodded and diverted her eyes from the rat, who had two egg-sized lumps protruding from his back.

"Is he in pain?"

"Not at all. Our animals are all well taken care of." She looked back to the first rat. "Aren't you, boy?"

Elizabeth continued, sounding as if she were lecturing a class. "These are patented rats—each with its own peculiar characteristics. They are growing benign tumors from the Schwann cells. I graft them under the skin of the rats when they're just a few days old." She motioned toward the door. "Come on, I'll explain it to you." She walked across the main lab into another smaller office lined with books and a large white, erasable marker board. A desk was barely visible beneath a large array of scattered papers.

"Your father's room."

Paige's hand went to her mouth. "Oh."

"Look here." She grabbed a marker to begin diagramming as she talked. "It has long been thought that the spinal cord, once injured, can never repair itself. But in the last few decades some significant things have taken place to challenge that dictum. In the eighties . . ."

Paige tried to keep listening but soon zoned out. *She's giving me a lecture.*

". . . researchers demonstrated that peripheral nerve grafts could be used to bridge a spinal cord defect . . ."

I'm starving. All I've had to eat today is airplane peanuts.

". . . try to bridge the gap by using only the Schwann cells, or support cells, to see if the cut axons of the spinal cord could regenerate through the open tubes. Are you with me?"

Paige nodded lamely, wondering, *Did you ask me a question?* Elizabeth's excitement was less than infectious.

Oblivious, Elizabeth droned on. ". . . what seems to hold everyone back is knowing the exact way to signal the injured spinal cord to heal again." She drew a diagram of a nerve cell.

Oh great. Now I know I'm back in school. I wonder if that's your real hair color. I might look good as a brunette too.

"Here on the cell surface, we believe, are chemical receptors that, when stimulated, will cause the axon to regrow. The problem is, the receptors seem to be switched off . . ."

I think my brain's switched off.

". . . Dr. Hannah thinks that the only time the receptors are normally up is early in the formation of the spinal cord, perhaps very early, during a stage when a person is only an embryo, during which the spinal cord is called the neural tube."

Paige brightened. She actually remembered the neural tube from embryology class.

"We need to provide the injured cord with the same chemical environment that was present at the formation stage."

"I read something about researchers using fetal spinal cords or something."

"That may be one answer, but your father has a different idea. There is another situation in which the body grows new nerve cells."

Is this a quiz? I'm losing my appetite.

"Paige?"

"Huh?"

"I'm almost done." Elizabeth put her hands on her hips in an attempt to persuade the daydreaming student to listen up.

Paige fought to focus, but the resident's dry monologue made it difficult.

"This is where your father's older work with brain tumors comes in. For fifteen years he focused on chemicals produced by brain tumors . . . tumor markers. In cancer cases, it seems that something has upset the biological clock, and the cells take on the characteristics of fetal tissue and grow uncontrollably . . . He kept trying different combinations of these tumor markers to see if any would stimulate an injured spinal cord to regenerate. Other researchers have scoffed at him, thinking that working with cancer chemicals might be somehow dangerous to the patients." She shrugged. "Sometimes you just have to run against the grain."

"Cancer chemicals?" The phrase pricked Paige's interest.

"They're just molecules that happen to be made by cancer cells. About two years ago Dr. Hannah discovered . . ."

Dr. Hannah—that's what they'll call me someday.

". . . a molecule present in the tumors we've been able to grow here in the lab. We have been able to repair rat spinal cord injuries using a bridge of peripheral nerve grafts that have been incubated with the tumor marker, a substance we call NTTF, or neural tube trophic factor."

"Wow," Paige responded, hoping to sound genuinely interested. "So this NTT . . ."

"NTTF."

". . . turns on the receptors of the spinal cord so they'll regrow."

Elizabeth squinted. "You were listening!"

"I got some of it," Paige responded defensively before adding, "Do you actually operate on rats?"

"Sure. They're cheap. And they multiply like rabbits."

"Yeah, but what works in a rat—"

"I'm not done yet," she responded, holding up her hand. "You've just gotten the intro." She stepped back into the main lab. "Time to meet Heidi."

"Heidi?"

Paige followed the slender doctor. Dr. Hopkins's brunette hair cascaded onto the back of her white lab coat. *You don't look like you've been up all night.*

They stepped into the next room. "This looks like a hospital," Paige observed.

"It is . . . of sorts." The well-lit room housed an array of blinking monitors mounted above what appeared to be a large incubator. Fluid bags and tubes were suspended like spaghetti above the patient, whose eyes immediately responded to Elizabeth's voice.

"Hi, Heidi. Hey, girl, it's OK," she added in a soothing tone. "It's just me. I've brought a visitor. Don't be alarmed."

Paige recoiled at the sight. The patient was a monkey! At least she thought so. Other than a few awkward chewing motions, it remained completely still, in spite of the lack of any physical restraints. The head was shaved, and a dozen colorful wires disappeared into its scalp, which had a large surgical scar. The animal made a few lip-smacking sounds in response to Elizabeth's touch, then snorted through an open tube exiting its neck. Another small tube entered a large nostril on the tip of a dog-like snout, carrying a beige liquid from a flexible bag hanging from a pole above the bed. Its tail was long and brown and fell limply from the end of the mattress.

"You can come closer. Heidi can't hurt you like this."

Paige edged forward an inch at most.

"Heidi's a young hamadryas baboon," she said, touching the thick, brown fur. "The males in this species have vicious teeth and a silver mane. The ancient Egyptians thought the hamadryas was sacred."

"W-what have you done to her?"

"Heidi is a C3-4 quadriplegic. In her case, her spinal cord was surgically divided at that level to simulate the same type of injury we see in humans."

A sickening dread began in Paige's stomach. "I think I've seen enough for today."

Click, click, smack. Heidi's tongue slapped the roof of her mouth, then protruded and explored the tube coming from her nose.

"Are you feeling okay? Maybe you should sit down."

"I . . . I'll be fine," she responded, retreating into the main lab. "I want some air."

Things began to dim, and Paige slumped to the floor and put her head between her knees.

"Are you all right? Would you like some water?"

Paige stared at the floor between her feet. After a few moments, she responded. "I'm OK. *Really*. The same thing happened to me when I saw my first cadaver in human biology lab."

"I'll get you a drink." Elizabeth quickly filled a paper cup from a water bottle in the corner of the room. "Here."

Paige took the cup without raising her head. "I want to see my father."

"Hey, I'm sorry about all this. I thought you'd be interested in—"

"I am interested." She blushed. "I guess I wasn't ready for Heidi, that's all." She shrugged. "Next time I'll know what to expect."

Elizabeth picked up the phone. "Let's see if your father is back from the O.R."

Paige listened as the resident talked cheerfully to the other party.

She hung up the phone. "He's on his second case, an acoustic neuroma."

Paige nodded as if she understood.

"Trish suggested that I take you by the personnel office and get you an official badge. That way you can come and go and the security guys won't harass you." She stopped and looked at Paige for a moment. "Actually, they'll still probably harass you. Anyone looking like you must have to deal with that all the time."

Paige looked up. Right now she felt anything but pretty.

"I know I do," Elizabeth added, crossing her arms in front of her white coat.

"Do . . . do you enjoy doing this sort of thing?"

Elizabeth stepped away from Paige. "I know it must seem gross, almost cruel, Paige, but if you look at the big picture, you can get beyond your emotional attachments to the animals in order to accomplish a larger good." She hesitated. "Heidi's not in pain, if you're worried about that. We have a full array of drugs to deal with that, just like we use in the human hospital."

"I don't think I could do it."

"Paige, there are 10,000 new spinal cord injury patients every year in the United States alone. What we are trying to do here could literally help hundreds of thousands of people."

"I know all that," she mumbled, feeling a little stronger. "I just don't think *I* could do it."

Elizabeth offered her hand. "Let's go get your badge. Then you'll have access to the lab anytime you want."

Paige struggled to her feet and muttered sarcastically, "Great."

Elizabeth shrugged. "You'll have to get used to it if you want to spend time with your father. I think he's here more than he's home."

Paige nodded as they started toward the door.

"Of course there *are* other benefits to working on projects like this," Elizabeth added at a lower volume. "Prestigious faculty positions in neurosurgery don't exactly grow on trees." She chuckled. "If we succeed, I'll be able to write my own ticket in academic neurosurgery."

Paige watched the young physician and quickened her own pace to keep up. *This is modern medicine? Oh, Lord,* she prayed, *what have I gotten myself into?*

CHAPTER
5

"DADDY, DADDY!" Melissa ran forward as soon as she saw her father through the doorway to his room.

Abby tried to restrain her. "Melissa, careful! You can't treat Daddy—"

"It's fine, Abby. Don't stop her."

Melissa put her hand on Nathan's leg.

"Here, honey. You can still sit here," her father told her.

"Nate, she's heavy, she'll—" Abby stopped when her eyes met Nathan's.

Melissa crawled onto her father's lap. She twisted around for a moment before pushing her face into his neck. "Hug me, Daddy."

Abby's facial expression softened as she watched. "Here, honey," she added, moving forward. "Your daddy can still hug . . . with a little help." She loosed Nathan's right arm and placed it around Melissa. Then she lifted his left, held it secure until a spasm passed, and placed it gently across his daughter's legs.

"Oh, Daddy, I've missed you!" She wiggled and grabbed her father's arms as they slipped from around her. "There, Daddy, I've got you," she added, clutching his arms in her little hands.

"And I've got you, little punkin."

"I brought you a picture for your board."

Nate nodded and looked up at Abby. She understood and began to dry his cheeks with a tissue.

"Why are you crying, Daddy?"

"You're not hurting me," he responded, pushing his face into her hair. "Sometimes I cry when I'm happy." He looked at Abby. "Honey, my nose—"

"I've got it," she responded.

"Do you see Mommy's hair?"

Nathan studied Abby's new look.

"Mom said you wouldn't like it."

"Melissa!" Abby blushed.

"Well, your mommy was wrong. I love it." He paused. "Turn around. I want to see the back."

She slowly turned a full circle.

"You told her not to cut it."

Nathan smiled. "Give your old dad a break, huh? He's had a lot of dumb ideas in the past, OK?" He studied Abby's face, perceiving a slight upward gesture at the corner of her full mouth.

All three heads turned in response to a firm knock. The room quickly filled with the afternoon staff. "Surprise!"

The shift supervisor, Colleen Smith, held out a set of keys and looked at Nathan. "We know you're leaving us soon, so we've planned a little outing."

She handed the keys to Abby, who protested, "No, I—"

"These are the keys to our van. We've called ahead to the Brighton Inn. They're expecting you for lunch."

Abby looked at Nathan without speaking.

Nathan looked at Abby and the nurses.

"Unless you'd rather just eat here. We *are* having creamed corn," Colleen responded.

"It's our treat," added another staff member. "Come on . . . It's your maiden voyage."

Abby turned the keys over in her hand. "I've never driven a van."

"You'll do fine," Colleen assured her. "Here," she said, touching her arm, "let's go out front, and I'll show you everything." She turned to Nathan. "Meet us in the parking lot in five minutes."

Abby sighed. Nathan smiled. "Let's do it."

◆ ◆ ◆

For the second time that day, Dr. Hannah scanned the crowded O.R. waiting room. "Ms. Johnson?" He walked forward and extended his hand to a woman with reddened eyes.

She pushed a Kleenex into the palm of her other hand, then reached for the surgeon.

"Your husband is fine," he reported softly.

She struggled to her feet. "Oh, thank you. Thank you. I was so worried."

"We were able to get all of the tumor."

"Thank God!" She lifted her fist to her mouth. "His face . . . will it—"

"His face will be fine. We were able to preserve his facial nerve There is no paralysis."

"Oh, praise the Lord!" Her face broke into a grin. "You doctors . . . you can do so much. Thank you, Dr. Hannah. Thank you."

◆ ◆ ◆

Abby looked up in response to yet another group arriving at the Brighton Inn. She leaned toward Nathan, who was seated closest to the door. "I wanted to sit up there," she said, looking toward the tables in the back, elevated on a two-step rim around the restaurant's perimeter. "They have a real view from up there."

"This is fine. Really. I'm just glad to be here." He looked at Melissa. "Here with you two," he added.

"Everyone sees us here."

"It's OK. It doesn't bother me."

A waitress arrived. "Have you all decided?"

"I want a hot dog," said Melissa.

"Very good. You're a very big girl," she added with a wink. "And what will he have?" she asked, looking at Abby.

Nathan looked up and interjected, "I'll have the sirloin, medium well, with a baked potato, and a dinner salad with blue cheese dressing." He looked at Abby. "And my wife will be having the chicken Caesar salad."

The waitress bit her lower lip. "Anything to drink?"

"I'll take iced tea."

"I want Coke," Melissa announced proudly.

"I'll have tea also," added Abby.

The waitress headed for the kitchen.

"Rachel Yoder stopped in before we left this morning," Abby reported.

"I rode in the buggy!"

Nathan smiled. "She took you for a ride?"

Melissa beamed.

"She heard you were coming home soon. She wants to bring us some meals, Nate. I didn't know what to say."

"Rachel?"

"She said over and over how nice it was for you to attend the funeral. I guess it's just her way of saying thank you."

"The funeral?"

"For her son Jonas." Abby stared at Nathan and wrinkled her nose. "You don't remember, do you?"

Nathan shook his head slowly. "Jonas is dead?"

"It was suicide." She paused. "The word around town is that he'd been hanging out with some of the Ashby High kids, that he'd gotten in with the wrong crowd, the drug users."

"That doesn't sound like Jonas. And why would an Old Order kid be hanging with the Ashby High crowd? They have their own school."

"I don't know, Nate. But Rachel doesn't dispute it. A lot of the Ashby High students even went to his funeral." Abby looked down. "Nate, his funeral was the day you were injured."

He let out a short sigh. "The very day?" Nate closed his eyes. *The woman in my memory. She wore a bonnet. An Old Order Mennonite perhaps? She was sifting dirt . . . turned up for a grave?*

"Nate?"

He focused on Abby.

"What should I tell her? Rachel, I mean."

He smiled. "I'm sure she's a good cook. The things they sell at the

Fisher's Retreat Farmer's Market are incredible," he added dreamily. "It would be fine. I'd like to talk with her anyway." *I'd like to know more about the day of my accident.*

Nate studied his wife. *Why does she feel she needs my permission? Have I really been that controlling?* "You know what I've been dreamin' about eating? Your linguine and red pepper sauce."

Abby wrinkled her nose.

"What? You know I love your cooking."

"I was just imagining trying to feed it to you. I'm nervous enough about trying to feed you steak. I can't imagine trying *that*." She snickered with a memory. "You always dropped the red sauce on your uniform."

He stuck his tongue out. "So it won't be anything new."

The waitress arrived with their drinks.

Nathan winked at Abby. "Here, start with a drink. Drinks are easy. Just use a straw and put it close to me. Melissa could even do it."

"I can do it," Melissa squealed, lifting up the glass of tea.

"Easy, honey. Not my nose."

Melissa giggled. Nathan looked up to see Abby smiling. "It looks like I could be out of a job," she said playfully.

◆ ◆ ◆

Ryan Hannah threw his scrubs in the laundry hamper and quickly donned a gray suit. He had exactly five minutes before his scheduled two o'clock interview with a surgeon seeking a new trauma attending position. He opened his daily planner. *Richard Hammond. I think Trish said he's from Baylor. At least he should be experienced in penetrating trauma management.*

He exited the O.R. doctors' lounge and turned right. He walked down the main hall, then took the elevator to the fourth floor. From there he needed only to pass the medical library before he entered the cranberry hall.

Trish stood with one arm outstretched, holding Dr. Hammond's C.V. Dr. Richard Hammond sat with his legs crossed in a small chair next to Trish's desk. He was pale, wore a gray suit two sizes too big, and had a military haircut. He jumped to his feet when he saw Dr. Hannah.

"Dr. Hannah?" He extended his hand. "I'm Dr. Hammond."

"Good. Good. Let's go in my office."

Trish touched his arm. "Sir, your daughter—"

"Paige!" He rolled the C.V. into a tight cylinder and slapped his hand. "I nearly forgot!"

"Sir, she's—"

He bounded through his office door, not heeding Trish's voice. Inside, a young woman, dressed neatly in a white blouse and designer blue jeans, reclined in an ornate chair with her feet on his desk. Her blonde hair was styled in two layers and fell just off the collar. From where Ryan stood, her legs looked longer than he remembered, identical to her mother's twenty years before. She wore almost no makeup, her freckles had disappeared, and she had four earrings in her left ear. Her lips were parted slightly to reveal white, even teeth. Her eyes were closed, and her breathing regular.

"Paige?"

She opened one eye, closed it again, then opened both with a start and flung her feet from the desktop. "Daddy!"

"Paige!" Ryan threw his arms around her in a bear hug before remembering his guest. "Oh," he said. "This is my daughter Paige. She just came in today. She'll be spending the summer with me." He smiled and looked at Paige. "This is, uh, Dr. Hammond."

"Hi."

"Boy, oh boy," he said, pushing his daughter to arm's length. "I can look you right in the eyes. I can't believe how you've changed."

"Daddy, it's only been six months."

He shook his head. "I'm sorry you had to wait."

"It's okay, Daddy. Elizabeth showed me around, got me an I.D. badge."

He looked at his watch. "Have you had lunch?"

"Two hours ago. Elizabeth took me." She wrinkled her nose. "She has your VISA card."

Ryan nodded without speaking.

Trish pushed her head through the doorway. "Dr. Hannah? Mr.

Bridges brought by the Brighton Care fee schedule. He said the neurosurgeons at McCue have already come on board."

He sighed.

"And, sir," Trish continued, "I still need those budget proposal numbers for the dean."

"I know, I know." He ran his hand over his scalp. "Look, honey, why don't you go on home? I know you must be tired from your trip."

Paige shrugged.

"I need to interview Dr. Hammond here, then pay attention to the dean, then make rounds, and—"

"It's OK, Daddy," Paige interrupted. "I can wait here."

"No," he said, reaching for his keys. "Take my car. Trish can show you where I park. I'll get a ride with Dr. Hopkins. I need to stop by my lab for a few minutes anyway." He smiled again. "I should be home by 8."

Paige didn't smile as Ryan dropped the keys into her hand.

"OK," Ryan said, turning to Dr. Hammond, "let's get to it."

Paige moved slowly to the desk and picked up her carry-on bag, then lifted a spring bouquet from the windowsill before walking to the doorway. "Thanks for the flowers, Daddy."

◆ ◆ ◆

Melissa stood in the hallway just outside Nathan's room. "Can I go play checkers with Mrs. Bailey?"

"Sure, honey," Nathan responded. "You know how to find her room?"

"I'm right here, Nathan," Ethel interjected, peering around the corner. "I'll show you the way," she said, looking at Melissa. "I'm the resident checkers champ, you know."

"I can beat you," Melissa boasted before disappearing down the hall.

"Go easy on her, Melissa," he called out after her before settling his eyes on Abby.

She sat on the hospital bed with her brown eyes fixed on the floor in front of Nathan's wheelchair. She smoothed the hem of her jean skirt before folding her hands in her lap.

"Thanks for taking me out, Abby."

She nodded without looking up.

"What's wrong, Abby?"

She didn't answer.

Nathan edged his wheelchair forward.

"What's *right*, Nathan?" she sighed. "How can you sit there like *that* and ask me what's wrong?"

"We can make it. I didn't die, Abby." He shook his head and added slowly, "I think that God must have spared me for a reason."

"Is that what you believe? That God spared you? Why didn't he just keep you from being shot? Some God that is."

Nathan let her words fall.

She looked up once to see herself in the mirror. She combed the edge of her thick, brown hair with her fingers before speaking again. "I've started working at the cafe, Nate. We need the money."

He watched her for a moment and longed to touch her, to put his arms around her like he used to do. The evening light from the sun seemed to lighten the natural olive tone of her skin. He loved Abby's skin. He always had.

He forced himself to respond to her statement. "Who watches Mel while you work?"

"Your mother, Nate, but I'm only working from 6 in the morning until 2, just after the lunch crowd slows." Abby sighed. "Nate, she offered."

"I spoke to the social worker. Between my disability income, the workmen's comp coverage, and the police benevolence fund, we should be able to make it."

"Maybe. But more likely, barely make it, Nate. I talked to Janice too. There are going to be other expenses, and—"

"It's OK, Abby. I'm glad you're working," he interrupted. "If that's what you want." He scratched his eyebrow on his mouthstick, now in its holder. "And you can keep the job after I'm home too," he added. "I'm OK by myself, especially once I'm in the chair."

Abby cleared her throat and nodded. "Thanks." She stood and walked to the window, shaking her head. "I was ready for a fight."

Nathan turned his chair so he could watch her. "Abby, I've had a lot of time to think these past months." He sighed. "Sometimes I think that's all I can do anymore. Before, uh . . . I stayed so busy that I never really took a good look at how I was running my life . . . running yours."

Abby's eyes met his. "Nate, you don't need—"

"Yes, I do," he responded, nodding his head vigorously. "I took you and Melissa for granted." He shook his head. "I'm not sure why you ever stayed—"

"Don't talk like that, Nathan," she reacted. She turned away, her eyes glistening. She stood with her back to him, facing the window and North Mountain in the distance. When she spoke, Nathan thought her tone was cold. Not mean, just casual, the conversational tone one would use with a stranger. Pleasant, but void of the emotion he expected in response to his attempt at an apology. "Well, we really must go. I don't want to drive Highway 2 in the dark." She put her hand on her hips. "The Subaru is getting a tire fixed, so I brought your pickup." She walked to the door after giving Nathan a quick peck on the cheek. "Please tell the staff thanks for lunch."

Nathan followed her out to say good-bye to Melissa, who had been hastily summoned from Ethel's room down the hall.

"Bye, Daddy," she responded. "I was winning."

"Bye, precious. I'll see you soon."

"Come on, honey," Abby urged, putting her arm on her daughter's shoulder. "It will be dark soon."

Nathan already felt the darkness in his heart.

◆ ◆ ◆

Ryan Hannah finished evening rounds with a lengthy consultation with the Darlene family. Mike and Cathy Darlene's ten-year-old daughter Linda had been admitted earlier that day in preparation for surgery in the morning. Linda had began complaining she couldn't see the television very well a few weeks before. After visiting her local eye doctor, a pediatric neurologist, and an endocrine specialist, and after extensive testing, she was referred to Dr. Hannah for resection of a rare tumor.

Dr. Hannah sat with the parents, his chief resident, George Wingfield, and two medical students in a cramped conference room just outside the pediatric intensive care unit. The Darlenes were huddled at one end of a long white table and stared at the brain surgeon in front of them. Their consultation with him had followed many similar discussions with a social worker experienced in neurosurgery, the referring physicians, and the chief resident.

"Any other questions?" he asked gently.

Mike Darlene spoke first. "Why didn't her pediatrician find this sooner?"

Dr. Hannah lifted a pen and drew an imaginary circle over his own head. "The tumor lies here, deep in the brain. For some reason children do not usually complain about their vision until they are nearly or completely blind in one eye. In that aspect, your daughter is unique. Most children will ignore the visual problems until the tumor is blocking off the flow of spinal fluid, which will cause headaches and vomiting. Your suspicions that something was wrong, based only on her complaints of not seeing well, may have saved her life."

Cathy's eyes met her husband's only briefly before looking back at Dr. Hannah. "How many times have you done surgery like this?"

"Many, many times." He leaned forward with sincerity and added, "I have the most experience south of Boston."

"That's what we've heard," Cathy responded, clutching her husband's arm.

"Help her, doc."

Dr. Hannah nodded. "The nursing staff will bring you a consent form listing the possible complications we've mentioned."

Cathy repeated them numbly, as if replaying a tape of what she'd heard over and over. "Bleeding, paralysis, personality changes, blindness, overeating, seizures, retardation, hormone imbalances, and death."

"Would you like me to talk with her?"

"You can tell her about the haircut," her father responded, "but not the things that could go wrong."

Dr. Hannah stood and shook Mr. Darlene's hand before walking from the room with the other medical staff.

He looked at the students. "This is the pinnacle, boys. The stakes are high, and so are the anxieties."

They nodded without speaking.

"The rewards are high too," Hannah added. He looked at his chief resident. "George, bump the girl onto the schedule first thing. I don't want to start this case in the afternoon." He turned to leave. "Run rounds in the morning. I'll be in the lab until you call. I want this girl asleep and prepped by 8."

"Yes, sir."

◆ ◆ ◆

Two hours later Ryan Hannah quietly entered the front door of his spacious home in the west end of Brighton. Nestled in the center of a two-acre wooded lot, in a development known as Mountain View Estates, his home looked like Williamsburg, with wooden shingles topping a two-story colonial brick and cedar-sided structure. Since his divorce, he had thought about selling and moving closer to the medical center, but he just hadn't found the time. Besides, there were certain expectations of the chairman of the department, and the hosting of professional parties and visiting professors couldn't be fashionably accomplished just anywhere.

He set Paige's suitcases down in the entry foyer and listened. The drone of a late-night newscaster and the smell of baked cheese and tomato greeted him. "Paige?"

He walked to the kitchen. The kitchen table was set for two. A casserole dish sat covered and cool on top of the stove. Ryan lifted the edge of the foil and saw the lasagna. *Looks like Barb's recipe.* "Paige?"

He found her in the den, asleep in his favorite leather recliner, in front of the TV. He touched her shoulder. "Paige."

She jumped.

"It's just me, honey."

She shook her head. "That's twice you've done that to me today."

"I didn't mean to scare you." He snapped off the TV. "You shouldn't have waited up."

"Dad, *you* have my suitcases." Her eyes widened. "You did bring my suitcases, didn't you? Everything I—"

"Yes, I brought your suitcases."

Paige pushed down the footrest and sat up straight. Lowering her voice, she asked, "Where's Dr. Hopkins?"

Ryan stepped back. "On her way home, of course. What do you mean, 'Where's Dr. Hopkins?'" he added imitating her question.

She huffed. "Nothing. I didn't mean a thing." She stood. "I made dinner."

"It smells wonderful, but . . ." His voice trailed off.

"But what?"

He responded quietly, "Honey, I had no idea you had this planned. I ordered a pizza down at the lab."

"You should have called!"

"Paige, I'm in a routine. I eat down there all the time. I didn't even stop to think that you would be waiting on me."

"Oh, that's cozy, isn't it?" She turned and started walking to the kitchen. "Just you, Elizabeth, and Heidi, huh? All having a nice little pizza party."

Ryan followed her. "Paige!"

She picked up the covered casserole dish, placed it in the refrigerator next to a salad she'd prepared, and slammed the door. "I'm not hungry anyway!" She faced her father. "Where are my things?"

"Paige, I'm sorry!"

She went to the front foyer and started dragging the largest suitcase toward the stairs. "So nice of Dr. Hopkins to drop by my things and give you a ride. Why didn't you invite her in?" She glared at her father. "Or did my being here mess that up for you?"

He stepped toward her and put his hands on her shoulders, pulling her to face him as she started to cry. "Is that what this is all about? You think that she and I are . . . ?" He shook his head. "It's not like that at all, Paige. You know me better than that. Elizabeth is a dedicated resident. Our relationship is very professional."

"Dad, she *adores* you. You should have heard her today. She couldn't stop talking about what a great man you are."

"There is nothing inappropriate about our relationship, Paige." He sighed. "I shouldn't have to tell you this." He wiped a tear from his daughter's cheek with the back of his hand. "Elizabeth is enthusiastic about everything. She could talk about the weather and give you the impression that it is of utmost importance to her." He shrugged. "I know she admires me, but it's only on a professional basis."

"You like being around her?" She sniffed.

He nodded. "There's nothing wrong with enjoying being around someone who admires you."

Her eyes met her father's. "But there's something wrong with *needing* it."

He didn't answer but just coaxed her into his arms. "I'm sorry for not calling."

Paige bit her lower lip.

"Come on, I'll help you with your suitcases." He lifted the largest one and groaned, "What's in here, bricks?"

"I'm here for the summer, remember?"

He nodded and smiled. "Maybe we can eat lasagna tomorrow night."

◆ ◆ ◆

Back in Fisher's Retreat, the sky was a canopy of black velvet. The rain had started gently just as Abby turned off Highway 2, right at Eddie's Exxon. By the time she'd wrestled their old pickup into the driveway and nudged Melissa awake, the wind had picked up, bringing heavy rain with it.

Now as she stood on her newly designed front entry, she squinted her eyes to see beyond the closest streetlamp and gathered her robe around her nightgown. Melissa huddled close to Abby, trying to stay beneath the overhanging roof. "Ooh, there's another."

Abby counted the seconds from the lightning flash until they heard the thunderclap. "One, two, three . . ."

"Let's play a game, Mommy."

"Mel, you need to go back to bed. I only said you could look at the lightning with me."

"Can I sleep with you?" Melissa concentrated hard to say sleep, not sweep.

Abby picked her up. "You are a big girl, but come on."

Mother and daughter snuggled into a creaky double bed with a homemade quilt covering.

The storm intensified, and lightning brightened the room for an instant before returning the room to blackness.

"I wish Daddy was here. He always prays during storms."

Abby nodded silently and listened to the rain pelting the window.

Boom! Lightning seemed to explode all around them as a simultaneous thunderclap shook the house. Melissa gasped and reached for her mother. Abby grabbed her and held her breath, then reached for the light switch. "It's OK, Melissa, we're OK." She sat up on the side of the bed. "Let's make sure the house wasn't hit."

She gathered her trembling daughter into her arms and ventured cautiously into the hall. The lights blinked once before staying off entirely.

"Mommy!"

"Melissa, you're choking me."

Melissa lessened her death grip.

"Let's find a flashlight."

"I have one in my playbox."

Abby inched along the hallway to Melissa's room, which was at the top of the stairs. "Show me where it is, honey," she said, setting her daughter down in front of a large wooden box at the foot of her bed. Mel lifted the lid and quickly retrieved a pink, plastic flashlight with a mermaid sticker on the side.

She snapped on the light and looked around the room. "Willie!" She grabbed her gingerbread man.

Abby picked up Melissa and Willie and started a slow search, room by room, though she wasn't sure what to look for. She sniffed the air and tested every light switch in the house. The lights didn't work, but everything else seemed all right. She even ran outside into the driveway to look at the roof but couldn't see any evidence of smoke.

"We're getting wet!"

She dashed back into the house. "It's OK, Melissa," she said again, as much to reassure herself as her daughter. "The worst of the storm seems to be over. And I don't see any damage to the house."

"It sure was loud."

Abby nodded. "That it was. Let's go back to bed."

"Can Willie come too? And my flashlight?"

"Sure."

They trudged up the stairs for the third time since retiring for the night and crawled back into what Melissa always called "the big bed."

Together they slept through the night as the storm lulled.

The next morning, when Abby ventured out for the paper, she discovered a large split in the trunk of their oak tree. The largest limb was severed from the thick trunk and lay in the yard, reaching for the house with its new spring growth barely touching the wall below Melissa's second-story window. Melissa's swing, tangled in a limb still connected to the tree, seemed to be some sort of lifeline thrown to the dying branch.

Abby remembered the lightning bolt. *So close to the house,* she thought. *Maybe God is on duty in Fisher's Retreat after all.*

CHAPTER
6

RYAN HANNAH hung a note for Paige behind a plastic refrigerator magnet shaped like a slice of pizza and headed for the door. He stopped and looked at himself in a gold-framed mirror located in the foyer. He straightened his tie and smoothed the front of his short, gray hair. At five feet, ten inches, he thought he was two inches too short for his present weight of 200 pounds. He touched the front of his leather belt. Too many pizzas in the lab. He smiled, forcing a dimple into his fleshy cheeks. *To think that Paige could even imagine Elizabeth falling for me.* He breathed deeply and studied the lines at the corners of his eyes. *Ahh, not so bad for fifty-three.*

He picked up his briefcase and left for the lab by 6, hoping to collect a fresh set of data recordings from Heidi before facing the O.R. schedule.

As he settled into his black Mercedes, he thought about his conversation with Paige. *What was it she said about enjoying being around those who admire you . . . that there's something wrong with needing it?* He tapped the steering wheel and turned on the radio. He yawned and checked his watch as his thoughts unwillingly drifted back to Paige's words. *Boy, she's sounding more like her mother every time I see her.*

By 6:25 he was walking into the Dennis Foundation Research Facility.

"Dr. Hannah!" Elizabeth hustled to catch him.

"Morning, Elizabeth."

"Coffee?"

"I had two cups before leaving the house."

She nodded. "Where's Paige? I thought she might come with you."

"Sleeping, I guess. I didn't check her room."

They exited the elevator and walked to his lab. The door was ajar, and the lights were on.

"Didn't you lock up last night?"

"I left when you did, remember?"

He pushed the door open with his foot.

Elizabeth's eyes widened. "My computer's on. I know I shut it down last night."

Papers were scattered on the floor, and a message was taped to the window leading to the main lab. The large, handwritten, red letters read, "HuRT ME."

"What's this?" Elizabeth lifted the paper off the glass.

"It's computer paper," the surgeon responded. "For a dot matrix printer." He pointed at the small holes at the edges of the paper.

"Right." She handed the paper to Ryan.

He looked at the smaller words at the bottom of the sheet. "Nathan McAllister, Jonas Yoder," he read. "Your handwriting?"

She nodded, taking the paper back. "Whoever wrote this message must have picked up the paper from my desk." She laid the paper aside and walked into the main lab, which was strangely quiet. The door to the rodent storage unit was open, and the lights were on. The two large chemical storage refrigerators were unplugged, and the doors were propped open with a chair.

Elizabeth cursed and looked at Ryan as they both sprinted for the animal intensive care room. Heidi's incubator was empty! Ryan placed his hands on the mattress, now cold.

"Heidi, Heidi," he mumbled, shaking his head.

"All our work," Elizabeth moaned. "Why would anyone do this?"

The professor of neurosurgery drummed his fingers on the counter and looked around the lab before searching through the rodent room and the operating suite. "Nothing else seems to be taken. Someone had to know exactly what we were doing here," he huffed. "And how valuable that animal was to our work."

"Maybe there's a ransom note."

"I don't see one." He looked at his hands. "I guess we'd better not touch anything. I'm calling the police."

Elizabeth cringed. "Maybe you'd better call Paige first."

"Paige? Why Paige? What's she have to do with—"

Elizabeth held up her hands. "I don't know exactly, but I have a bad feeling about this . . ."

"What are you talking about?"

"Yesterday she seemed so upset by the research—"

"You brought her here?"

"Sure, I—I thought she told you."

"She told me you showed her all around," he mumbled, shaking his head. "I never dreamed you'd show her *this*." He ran his fingers through his hair. "Very few people know about this. I told you I didn't want any leaks—"

"But she's your daughter. Surely you wouldn't keep this from her."

Ryan sighed. "No, no," he said softly. "I suppose I would have shown her myself someday, but . . . What happened anyway? She was upset?"

Elizabeth nodded. "She seemed OK until I showed her Heidi. Then she almost fainted. She had to sit down."

"Did she say anything?"

Color filled her cheeks. "She asked me if I enjoyed my work." Elizabeth shrugged. "I think the whole thing disgusted her, but she just blew it off, said she just needed some air."

"Great," Ryan added sarcastically. "And you got her a special access badge just like mine."

"Yes," she replied slowly. "One that would let her in everywhere you can go."

"But Paige wouldn't do anything this stupid. She wouldn't move Heidi."

Elizabeth grimaced. "I hope you're right. But maybe she decided to rescue Heidi from further torture or something."

"That doesn't sound like Paige."

"She's your daughter. You know her better than I do," Elizabeth replied. "But she was visibly shaken by what she saw in here."

Ryan closed his fist. "Maybe you're right," he said, picking up the phone. "Maybe I should call Paige first."

He put the phone to his ear after punching in his home number. "Hmmm. That's strange. She's not answering."

"Maybe she can't hear it. Maybe she's still sleeping."

"There's a phone right next to her bed."

◆ ◆ ◆

Wednesday mornings for Nathan always started the same way—the same way every Monday, Wednesday, and Friday began for a quadriplegic at Briarfield Manor—his bowel program. He despised the humiliation of not being able to care for himself in so many other ways, but this was one of the things he hated the most. He even hated the name. Why couldn't they call it something else? Why not just use the same words everyone else used for going to the bathroom? But no, he quickly learned. From now on his private toiletry needs would be the job of someone else, and at least for now everyone would call it his "bowel program." "Time for your bowel program," his attendants would say, carrying a fresh absorbent pad and a foil-covered suppository. To Nathan, it sounded like they were announcing a TV show or a children's play. "The Bowel Program will be showing at 8 A.M. Mondays, Wednesdays, and Fridays at a nursing home near you." He didn't share their lightheartedness on the subject.

Today he blocked it out just as he had so many times before. He ignored what was going on and listened to music on his headphones. He couldn't feel it, so pretending it wasn't happening wasn't so difficult. The smell remained the biggest reminder of what was really happening to him. He had asked them to let him use some scented candles, but as it turned out, candles were on the forbidden list at Briarfield Manor. Usually one of two day shift orderlies were assigned the job. Today, to Nathan's relief, it was Mike, a young man working his way through physical therapy school. When Henry, the world's oldest living orderly, got the honors, he always talked constantly and complimented Nathan on the job he'd done, much like a mother coaching a toddler through potty training. Nathan would either ignore his comments or sarcastically reply, "It was an excellent program, wasn't it?" Henry never got it but just kept talking until he left the room.

"Time for your bowel program," Mike quipped.

"Channel 5, I believe," Nathan responded.

"Right," Mike said with a laugh before positioning Nathan on his side by propping him up with some pillows behind his back. He slid a disposable, absorbent pad beneath Nathan's buttocks and adjusted Nathan's headphones. "What will it be today?"

"Just turn it on to WNLR. I want to hear the Huddleston morning show."

Mike peeled open a suppository and worked quickly at his task. "I'll be back in forty-five minutes."

"I won't go anywhere."

He smiled. "Right."

◆ ◆ ◆

Paige entered the cranberry hall just before 10 A.M. She smiled at Trish, who seemed to be juggling two phone conversations at once. When she saw Paige, she punched the Hold button and lowered her voice. Her tone was terse and strained. "Paige, where have you been?"

"Looking for a job," she replied in a matter-of-fact tone. "Is it possible to get another I.D. badge? I can't find mine anywhere and I've . . ." She suddenly noticed a police officer sitting on a sofa just outside her father's office. "What's going on around here?"

"Why haven't you returned your father's calls?"

Paige stepped backwards. "What calls? What's going on?"

"You don't know?" The phone rang again. Trish answered quickly and put the caller on hold. Now there were three blinking lights on the phone. "Someone broke into your father's lab last night!"

Paige put her hand to her mouth.

"Paige, Heidi's gone."

The officer stood to his feet. "Ms. Hannah, I presume?" The muscular officer appeared to be in his twenties, with jet black hair and a trimmed moustache.

"Yes, I'm Paige Hannah."

"I'm Keith Mansfield, with Brighton P.D. Could we speak for a minute?"

Trish stood, ignoring her phone. "Why don't you use Dr. Hannah's office? He's operating." She opened the door to usher them in, quietly explaining to Paige, "Your father was an hour late getting started in the O.R. because of all of this. He wasn't a happy man."

Paige felt increasingly defensive. "Why do you want to talk to me, Officer?" she asked as the two entered the office.

"I just have a few routine questions."

"Someone stole his lab monkey?"

"This is news to you, ma'am?"

"Yes."

"Why don't you have a seat?" He motioned to a chair. "Dr. Hopkins told us how upset you were after visiting the lab."

"Upset, yes, but . . . you don't think I had anything to do with this, do you?" Paige inquired anxiously, raising her voice. "I didn't steal anything!"

"I just need to ask you a few questions. You're not being accused of anything."

Paige sat down on the edge of a cushioned chair.

"Where were you last night between 11 P.M. and 6 this morning?"

"At my father's home, in my bedroom, asleep! Why are you asking me this?"

"What about this morning about 6:30 A.M. when the break-in was discovered?"

"I couldn't sleep, so I went for a jog. I wanted to run through my old neighborhood."

"Why didn't you return your father's phone messages?"

"I didn't know he'd called," she replied emphatically. "I didn't even listen to his messages. I figured they were for him."

"Paige, your father is missing a very valuable animal. A very, very, valuable animal, according to him. Do you have any idea why someone would take it?"

Paige stood. "Look, I've been in town less than twenty-four hours. I have no idea what any of this is about!"

Officer Mansfield shifted his eyes between Paige and Trish, still standing in the doorway of Dr. Hannah's office. "Look, Ms. Hannah, we know for a fact that you were upset when you saw the research facility yesterday. It would be perfectly understandable to want to protect the baboon and to even—"

"I had nothing to do with this!" Paige placed her hands on her hips. "I want to talk to my father! He knows I would never do such a thing in his lab."

The officer sighed. "He's the one who wanted me to talk to you." He extended his palm toward the chair. "Please," he pleaded, "sit down."

The teenager reluctantly obeyed.

"Only a few people have I.D. badges encoded with the access number to your father's lab—your father, several research assistants, Dr. Hopkins, the maintenance supervisor, the head of housekeeping." He locked on Paige's gaze. "And as of yesterday . . . you."

"My I.D. badge?" Paige shook her head. "I couldn't even find it this morning."

He nodded and made a note on a small pad. "You've lost your I.D. badge?"

"Maybe someone stole it from me. How do you know that someone broke in that way?"

"There were no signs of forced entry." He stopped and looked down as if reluctant to say more.

Paige stiffened. "I'd suggest talking to some of the other people who have those access badges. I didn't do anything."

Mansfield sighed. "The department is doing all it can, Ms. Hannah. I'd suggest that you quickly realize that cooperating with us is the best thing for everyone."

She dropped her jaw and held out her hands, palms up. "I am cooperating."

The officer shut his notepad and stood, signaling the end of the interview. "Let us know if you find your *lost* I.D. badge."

◆　◆　◆

Janice pointed excitedly at Nathan's Harley-Davidson calendar. "So Jim Over will come on Monday, Wednesday, and Friday mornings and on Thursday nights. Richard Ramsey will come on Tuesday, Thursday, and Sunday mornings and on Wednesday and Saturday nights. And Dave Borntrager will come on Monday, Tuesday, Friday, and Sunday nights as well as on Saturday mornings."

"How will this all work with Abby's work schedule?"

"Abby goes in early, at six o'clock. She'll be home by 2. Your attendants will only be around for an hour or two each morning. They'll help you get in your chair, take care of your bowel program, give you a shower, change your catheter, do your physical therapy, and give you breakfast. That means you'll be home in the chair by yourself for a few hours each day."

"That should work OK. I can eat lunch after she comes home from the cafe."

She nodded.

"I'm all right by myself, especially once I'm in my chair."

"And you can always use the speakerphone."

Nathan nodded. "So when's the big day?"

"Saturday." She smiled. "I'll have each of the guys come over so you can give your final approval, and so they can learn the specifics of your care."

"I've known Jim for years. He plays piano at church. And I played softball with Richard."

Janice blew her auburn bangs out of her eyes. "Ah, the beauty of a small town. I guess you know just about everyone there, don't you? What about Dave?"

"I've seen him around town, but I never knew he had an LPN license."

"He hasn't used it much since he started working in realty. But he seemed real excited about helping you out." She leaned forward and put her hand against the top of his knee. Nathan watched her pat his leg, feeling exactly nothing.

"It is very important that you trust your personal care attendants, Nathan. You will be giving them keys to your house and your ATM card number."

"I understand."

"If you have any doubts—"

"They'll be fine."

"They do *seem* fine. And they have worked with the Apple Valley Homehealth Network for a long time." She withdrew her hand. "Unfortunately, I have known of PCAs who took advantage of their disabled clients. As low as that sounds . . ." Her voice trailed off.

"Great," Nathan muttered. Thinking about being ripped off was more than he could deal with at the moment.

"I'm sure they'll be fine," she added with a nervous smile. "The town's really getting excited about your homecoming."

Janice had filled him in on their plans already, and he was less than totally thrilled. Before replying, he threw his head and neck forward to shift his body, a move he did several times each hour to slightly alter his weight distribution in the chair. "Nathan McAllister Day," he muttered slowly. "Catchy slogan."

The social worker frowned. "Be nice now."

"I'm going along with it, OK? I just hope the town knows it's not my idea."

"Oh, they know it. But they're excited just the same." She paused, then reached for his shoulder. "Can you feel me touching you there?"

He nodded.

She squeezed his shoulder gently. "Did you have a chance to talk to Abby about coming home?"

Nathan dropped his eyes to the floor. "A little. She's friendly to me, but . . ."

Janice squinted and leaned forward. "But . . ."

"Maybe I shouldn't say it, but she seems to treat me differently now."

"Differently?"

"Like I might break or something. She's nice to me, don't get me wrong, but . . . well, she doesn't treat me like I'm her husband."

Janice remained quiet and put her finger on her chin.

"More like a friend. We can't seem to get past talking about the weather." He paused. "Every time I try to talk about our relationship, it's like she just freezes up or something."

"She's afraid, Nathan."

"Have you talked to her?"

She nodded. "Just give her some time."

Nathan looked out the window. A low cloud obscured the peak of North Mountain. Jake the yardman was attacking the new growth on the long hedgerow running toward the highway. Nathan slowly shook his head. "It's weird how things change." He shifted his eyes to the floor again. "I've always been a jealous husband. I guarded Abby from everyone, including my friends. I always thought others couldn't help but be attracted to her beauty, just like I was . . . am," he corrected.

"Abby *is* very pretty."

"Now it's as if this whole accident has forced me to reevaluate everything. All I've thought about for months is getting back home, getting back to Fisher's Retreat, getting back to Abby."

"You're lucky to have a woman like her."

He raised his eyes from the floor. "But now that I'm on the verge of getting back home, I'm starting to think Abby would be better off without me. I can't really be a husband to her now. I'll be a burden."

"I've talked to her, Nathan. Abby is a strong woman." Janice leaned forward. "But she still has needs that you will meet. You are still her husband, and the father of her child. You belong together." Her eyes shifted to the open Bible on the counter beside Nathan's computer. "You're a Christian?"

He nodded.

"Then you know that being a good husband has little to do with what you are capable of doing physically. You can be a support to her in other ways."

"I try very hard to be in a positive mood when she comes around. I don't want to drag her down."

She spoke softly. "Perhaps you're trying to prove yourself worthy of her love?"

Nathan rubbed his eyebrow against his mouthstick. "Maybe."

"But underneath you don't feel so worthy."

"How could I?"

She avoided the question. "I think Abby might feel better if you start with a little honesty about how you're feeling." She paused. "From what she tells me, communication has never been your strong suit."

"I *tried* talking with her last night. About our relationship . . . about the way I used to treat her." He shook his head. "She just changed the subject and found some excuse to leave."

"Give her time, Nathan. This isn't easy for her either."

Nathan pushed his head back against the head-pad behind him. Holding sustained pressure caused his chair to move backwards. He stopped after moving a few inches, picked up his mouthstick, and pointed it at Janice. "I've heard that song before," he said, talking out of the side of his mouth.

"And you'll probably hear it again."

"I'm not sure time can heal the rift between us. Something bigger is eating at her . . . keeping her from accepting me—"

A sharp knock interrupted him. A tall police officer stood in the doorway. "Excuse me. I'm looking for a Mr. Nathan McAllister."

Nathan looked up without speaking and nodded.

The man backed up a step and stammered, "I'm sorry. I must have the wrong room."

"Wait," Nathan called after him before setting his mouthstick in its holder.

The youthful officer wrinkled his forehead.

"I'm Nathan McAllister."

The man shook his head, then took a slow step forward. "I'm with the Brighton Police Department. I'm investigating a grand larceny."

◆ ◆ ◆

Abby looked out from the kitchen into the front room of Fisher's Cafe. The breakfast crowd had thinned, and now only the owner, Ralph Knitter, and a single customer remained. The customer, a Fisher's Retreat police officer, Brian Turner, sat alone, drinking his third cup of coffee and busying himself with an assortment of papers. His hair was blond and wavy, and his shoulders square, much like Nathan's. When together, especially when they were in uniform, many thought they could be brothers. Brian was taller, and his features were chiseled, but his frequent smile softened his ominous stature, and he frequently had a joke or a story for anyone willing to lend an ear.

"I don't think he's going to leave unless you speak to him."

Abby whirled to see Marty, wearing her large kitchen apron.

"Talk to him, Abs. No one's around."

Abby sighed, picked up the coffeepot, and slowly pushed the door open. She worked her way to the front booth where Brian was working, straightening the salt and pepper shakers on several tables as she went. "More coffee?"

He looked up. "No thanks. I've had all I need."

Abby nodded silently.

"I hear Nate's comin' home."

She nodded. "Saturday."

He stared at her for a moment before asking, "How are you, Abby?"

"I'm OK." She looked out the front window, on which was painted the words "Fisher's Cafe."

Brian lowered his voice. "I never intended for it to turn out this way."

"How *did* you intend it to turn out?" Abby couldn't conceal the bitterness in her voice.

He reached for her hand. "I've never hidden the way I feel about you."

"Except around Nate."

"Abby, we *both* did." He sighed and dropped her hand. "In spite of what you think, not everything has changed. Not the way I feel. Not the way it could be if—"

"Brian, I can't!" she interrupted, more loudly than she'd intended. Then she softly added, "You know I can't leave him—not now."

Abby felt her eyes begin to sting. She bit her lip to keep it from trembling. She pointed to the writing on the front window, looking backwards from where she stood—ꟻISHER'S CAFE.

Brian squinted at the painted letters.

"That's the way my life feels. Like everyone else can see everything so clearly . . . but it all seems backwards to me."

"Maybe it's only your perspective, Abby," he said, standing and pushing past her on his way to the door. "Maybe if you'd stop feeling trapped on the inside, you'd see what everyone else is trying to tell you."

CHAPTER
7

"LET ME get this straight," Nathan responded. "You're investigating a break-in at Dr. Hannah's lab and you thought I might have helpful information?"

Mike Nelson nodded, his eyes darting around the room, finally coming to rest on Nathan's bulletin board. Nathan watched him as he scanned the news articles about his accident.

"And just what do you think I can tell you?"

The officer shrugged. "The case involves the theft of a valuable animal . . . a laboratory animal, a special baboon," he added. "Some evidence at the scene led us to believe that you may have been involved." He stared at the wheelchair. "A detective in our department remembered your name in conjunction with a charge of animal cruelty, so we thought since this case involved an animal theft there might be a link."

"You can't be serious," Nathan huffed.

The officer mumbled, "I—I didn't know you were . . . well, like this." He held up his hands.

"What did you think, that I live here by choice?"

"Look, I'm just—" He stopped. "I'm sorry."

Nathan pushed his head against the right head-pad twice to make his chair move forward and to the right. Then he pressed his head back against the backrest to stop himself directly in front of Officer Nelson.

"Look, I know all about following orders and following leads. But explain the reasoning to me."

Mike Nelson looked down at Nathan, studying him for a moment. "When your name came up at the scene, well . . . it seemed to be a meaningful link . . . animal cruelty and animal kidnapping." He coughed and shuffled his feet against the floor.

Nathan shook his head. "I'll help you out where I can. The animal cruelty accusation was frivolous and was brought by a man who was angry because I shot his runaway bull. There was never a formal charge." He paused. "Now you help me. Exactly what information linked me to the scene?"

"Maybe you should tell me."

"This is ludicrous."

The officer stroked his chin. Slowly he retrieved a paper from a small black notebook. He held the paper up for Nathan to read. "This is a copy of a note found at the scene."

Nathan read the note. "HuRT ME." His eyes fell to the names at the bottom of the paper. Nathan McAllister, Jonas Yoder. "This was left by the perpetrator of the crime?"

"It appears so. It was taped to a window leading into the lab where the baboon was located."

"The handwriting is different on the bottom."

"Hard to say. The names are in cursive. The words at the top are uppercase printing."

"On the original, were the names and the message in the same ink?"

"'HuRT ME' is written in red. The names are in black ink." He glared at Nathan. "You know all of this already, don't you?"

Nathan shook his head and met the officer's stare. "You can't believe that."

Mike asked the obvious question. "Any idea why your name is signed at the bottom of the message?"

He thought for a moment. "Hard to speculate. I was a patient of Dr. Hannah's when I was first injured." He moved his chair back a few inches. "But I can't think of a logical explanation."

The officer walked over to Nathan's window and looked out on the green lawn before turning around and focusing on the paper in his hand. "What about this other guy, Jonas Yoder? Any chance you know him?"

"Yes," he replied slowly, "I knew him."

"Knew him?"

Nathan rubbed his cheek on the end of his mouthstick as it sat in its holder before speaking. "He was buried the day I got shot."

◆ ◆ ◆

Elizabeth Hopkins was red-faced as she sat opposite Dr. Hannah in his opulent hospital office. "Sir, we have to make an appeal through the media. Heidi could still be alive."

Ryan tightened his fists. "You know I'm not crazy about letting anyone in on this."

"It's our only hope of getting her back alive. Just one rough movement, and all your nerve grafts could be pulled apart."

"I *am* aware of the risks of moving her." He sighed. "But we must think realistically. There is little chance that someone who doesn't know her condition intimately could keep her alive for more than a day."

She studied him for a moment. "What are you thinking?"

He raised his index finger in the air. "Who would have the most to gain from taking an animal like Heidi?" He paused and raised a second finger. "And why did the intruder only take Heidi? Why none of the other animals?"

"You don't think that a researcher would—"

"And why was your computer on? Was someone searching for more information about the project?"

"But how would anyone know about Heidi? The last time we presented our work, we only told about our success with rodents." She shook her head. "No one outside your lab knows anything."

"Leaks are almost inevitable." He sat in his leather desk chair and pointed at Elizabeth. "But to actually advertise what has happened on the news . . ."

"Dr. Hannah, it's the only—"

"What did you tell the detective?" he interrupted, picking up a copy of the paper that had been hanging in the lab. "Did he ask you about the names here?"

"He asked me about everything."

"And?"

"Don't worry. I didn't tell him what we're doing."

He stood and paced around his spacious office, stopping only to make fine adjustments at the corners of multiple framed awards and diplomas, lifting the corner of one, standing back, then lowering the corner of another. "Did you tell him the handwriting is yours?"

"Yes. I told him the truth." She shrugged. "That I had copied the names from a state spinal cord injury database, and that whoever had scrawled the other message had just picked up the paper from my desk."

The information satisfied Ryan. "As long as that's all you told him." He reached forward and pushed up a corner of a picture of himself standing beside the last Republican candidate for president. After moving it a millimeter, he nodded.

The door opened immediately after a sharp knock, and Paige entered without waiting for an invitation.

"Paige!" Trish called out from behind her, throwing her hands in the air.

Ryan caught his assistant's gaze and nodded. "It's OK, Trish." He looked at his daughter. "Come in, Paige."

Her eyes passed quickly over Elizabeth to her father, and her voice quivered when she talked. "Daddy, is it true that you asked the police to question me?"

"Paige, I was just trying to cover—"

"Daddy! How could you think I would have done something like this?"

Ryan read the disappointment and sincerity on his daughter's face. "Paige, I . . . I didn't really think you would . . . Well, uh . . . I knew you were upset by seeing Heidi, and I just . . ."

Paige glared at Elizabeth. "I was upset, but I would never pull a stunt like this."

"Of course," Ryan responded, his voice softening. "I'm sorry, Paige." He looked away, studying a framed diploma denoting his acceptance into the American College of Surgeons. "I merely wanted every possibility exhausted."

Paige picked up the paper on the edge of his desk. "What's this?"

Elizabeth's eyes darted to Ryan's before she answered. "It's a copy of a note left in the lab during the break-in, we presume."

Paige stared at the paper. "I've seen this somewhere before."

"What?" Ryan stepped away from the wall toward Paige. "What have you seen before?"

"This writing. See the way the 'u' is smaller than the rest?" She reached in her jeans pocket and pulled out a flyer. "I thought so. It's the same way it's written here." She pointed to the printing. "DON'T HuRT THE ANIMALS. See?"

Ryan frowned. "Where'd you get that?"

"This weird guy hands them out at the entrance to the research facility. This is the second day I've gotten one."

Elizabeth moved closer to study the flyer. "I didn't notice that before. Our villain is probably one of those animal rights jerks."

"How can you be sure?" Ryan responded.

"It's an acronym for Humans for Responsible Treatment of Animals, a radical group that frequently pickets this facility."

"The guys with the mouth-gags?"

"Exactly."

Paige brightened. "Since they used the same style on the note as on their slogan, I'll bet they were taking credit for rescuing your baboon."

"Let me see that." Ryan reached for the paper. "I'll admit, it does make as much sense as my jealous researcher theory." He drummed his fingers across the corner of his desk.

"This gives all the more reason to let the media get involved, Dr. Hannah. If one of these kooks has Heidi, there will be no way she'll survive more than a day or two at best. These weirdos won't know how to take care of her."

"I suppose an appeal on the news could be made as an emotional plea for Heidi's life."

"Then we won't look like the uncaring animal torturers they'll paint us to be," Elizabeth added.

Ryan chewed his lower lip. "But I don't want any specific information going out about the project. We cannot reveal what the nature of our research is."

Paige cringed. "Uh oh," she mumbled.

"What's the matter, honey?"

"I . . . uh, I talked to one of them yesterday."

Elizabeth raised her voice. "One of who?"

"One of the mouth-gag guys—the one who gave me this flyer yesterday morning."

"You talked to him?"

Paige nodded. "On my way out. After I left yesterday afternoon." She contracted her neck muscles to pull the corners of her mouth down in an exaggerated frown. "He tried to hand me another flyer. I argued with him, tried to tell him he didn't know what he was talking about. I told him you all treated the animals with great care and were doing a great work to help sick people."

Elizabeth's eyes widened. "You told him about our work? Did he know who you were?"

"I told him who my father is and defended what he does with the use of laboratory animals."

"You didn't tell him about Heidi!"

She cringed again before slumping onto a small couch that sat along a wall lined with books. "Yes, I'm afraid I did."

Ryan groaned.

"Daddy, it's all my fault, isn't it?" Her hand went to her mouth. "I wonder if that's when my I.D. badge disappeared."

Elizabeth glared at Paige and raised her voice. "You lost your I.D. badge—the one I got for you just yesterday?"

Trish's voice came over the intercom. "Dr. Hannah? You are wanted in O.R. 11. Dr. Wingfield has your patient prepped."

The neurosurgeon sighed. "OK, Trish." He looked at his daughter. "It's not your fault, Paige. Even if whoever broke in the lab entered using your badge, you could never have predicted this." To Elizabeth he added, "Call Detective Mansfield. Tell him our new thoughts about the animal rights group and their slogan."

He stood and checked his watch as he exited into the cranberry hall beyond Trish's reception area. At the doorway he looked back at his assistant. "Elizabeth, see what you can set up for a media release. I want to make a personal appeal for Heidi's kidnapper to return her to the safety of our lab."

◆ ◆ ◆

By the time Officer Mike Nelson had concluded his lengthy interview, Nathan sensed he had softened a little. In fact, he even agreed to let Nathan have a copy of the paper found at the scene containing Nathan's name. He left just before noon, with Nathan musing over Jonas Yoder and wondering just what possible link would bring them together on a paper in Dr. Hannah's lab.

Lunch was precut chicken breast, green beans, and a small salad with blue-cheese dressing that Libby dropped onto his shirt. She cleaned him up while Nathan breathed in the rose fragrance of her hand lotion.

"You're not very talkative today." Libby smiled.

"I have a lot on my mind, but not much I understand." He shrugged weakly before adding, "And I know the other residents are waiting for you to help them."

She nodded and began to straighten the items on his lunch tray. "I hear you're leaving us soon."

"That's the plan."

She picked up the tray and hesitated a moment before placing it on a cart just outside his door. She returned and wiped off the table in front of him before speaking again. "I just want you to know that I've enjoyed getting to know you." Her eyes fell, and she twisted the sponge in her hand. "You seem so together and . . . well, you've taught me a lot."

Nathan stayed quiet, not sure how to respond.

"'God screams at us in our pain.'"

He smiled. "You *have* been listening."

"C. S. Lewis," she countered with a shrug. "I had a good teacher." She stroked his forearm before retreating toward the door.

Nathan watched her leave, then turned his wheelchair to face his computer. He was about to check his E-mail when he heard a sharp knock on his open door. "Yes," he called before turning to see a familiar-faced woman accompanied by a shorter man with a large video camera in his hand.

"Mr. McAllister?" The woman wore a gray suit and smiled with a face covered with too much makeup. "I'm Judy Tanner, with Channel 4 news."

Nathan stretched his jaw and neck muscles without speaking.

"Janice did inform you of our visit?"

"No, she didn't." He put his mouthstick into its holder.

Judy sighed and glanced at her cameraman. "Steve did say he called, didn't he?"

He opened a small notepad and scratched his bushy mustache. "Yep. Nathan McAllister. One P.M. Confirmed."

She looked down at Nathan and lowered her voice. "I'm sure you're aware of the celebration in Fisher's Retreat this weekend—Nathan McAllister Day?"

Nathan nodded.

"We're from Carlisle. We hoped to cover the story, do a short interview with you, get your feelings about coming home." She glanced around the room and then back at Nathan. "Would that be OK?"

"I'm not a hero. I just want to go home quietly, without a lot of attention."

Judy stepped back. "Hmmm."

The cameraman set his camera on Nathan's bed. "Why don't you just say that? We can tell your story if you like. Or you can, if you're comfortable with that. Just tell everyone in the Apple Valley what you just told us."

"Would you mind answering just a few questions?" Judy pleaded.

Nathan positioned his chair in front of his mirror. "Will you at least comb my hair for me first?" He pointed his head toward the counter beside his computer. "My brush is over there."

"No problem." Judy picked up the brush and went to work. "Boy, you sure have thick hair." She looked at her assistant. "Dale, this will be fine. We can set up with Mr. McAllister sitting in front of his computer."

One by one, Nathan answered Judy's questions. Slowly, with precision, he proceeded to tell the account of his accident.

"I am a C3-4 quadriplegic, the result of an injury to my spinal cord between the third and fourth bones in my neck."

"It was an accident. I've talked to my fellow officers."

"I'm no hero."

"I harbor no bitterness toward Officer Turner."

"This was part of God's plan for me. He knows best." He added slowly, "I believe that someday I'll walk again."

"New research is being done every day."

"I'm no hero."

"I want to thank Chief Joe Gibson and all the people in Fisher's Retreat who have helped make the necessary changes to my house."

"I just want to come home quietly."

"I want to thank Abby and my daughter Melissa."

"I'm no hero."

"There are a lot of unanswered questions for me."

"I want to thank God."

"I'm no hero."

"I just want to come home."

Nathan watched Judy's eyes. *Is she crying?*

"OK. That's great." She looked away from Nathan, sniffling. "Thanks. I'm sure we have some usable material here."

The film duo chatted to themselves, seemingly ignoring Nathan for a minute. Then the cameraman, whom Nathan only knew as Dale, stepped forward to say good-bye. He fumbled with his hands for a moment before reaching down to Nathan's right hand. He squeezed his fingers cautiously.

"Hey, I won't break." Nathan offered a smile.

"Thanks, Mr. McAllister."

"Nathan."

"OK," he corrected himself. "Thanks, Nathan."

Judy edged backwards and did not offer her hand. "Maybe we can do a follow-up later, from Fisher's Retreat. Show people how you're getting along."

"One day at a time," Nathan responded.

Dale and Judy nodded. "Right."

They turned to leave. As they walked down the hall, Nathan could hear Judy talking. "Could you drive? I can't face Highway 2 again."

◆ ◆ ◆

That evening Nathan sat in his chair scanning the TV channels in the lounge. He deftly operated the TV remote using his mouthstick. He tried keeping the volume at a reasonable level, but every time he adjusted it down, a member of the over-eighty set would ask him to turn it back up again.

He couldn't get the Carlisle station that covered his hometown of Fisher's Retreat, so he settled for Brighton Channel 6 and watched with interest as they broke the story of the break-in at a Brighton University Hospital research facility. The story contained little information other than the fact that a baboon had been stolen and that its owners feared for the animal's life. There were a few suspects, but the Brighton police were tight-lipped. Most of the information came in the form of an appeal by Dr. Ryan Hannah who made a sincere plea for the safe return of the valuable animal.

The next story was about Brighton's elementary school teacher of the year, and then came the local weather. Nathan turned to leave as a dishwasher soap commercial blared at a level that even Nathan could feel. He looked at Bob Price, who stared intently at the screen with his hand cupped at his ear. Nathan smiled as he remembered Ethel asking him to go for a walk. *I think you need a new hearing aid, brother.*

Nathan spent the rest of the evening making his rounds on the hallway, moving beside Ethel as she exercised her new hip and musing about the extraordinary events of that day. "Can you imagine me being a suspect in a robbery?" Nathan snickered.

Ethel wasn't amused.

Later, after spending several hours with his books and the information that Jake Peterson had brought him about the Miami Project to Cure Paralysis, he went through his nightly routine. Mike, an aide on the evening shift, brushed Nathan's teeth, then transferred him into bed, where he undressed him and carefully positioned him for the night. He was required to sleep naked in order to avoid any clothing wrinkle, snap, or button that might initiate a pressure sore after a full night in one position. For Nathan, wearing socks was the only exception; they protected his feet and ankles from abrasions in case of leg spasms. After Mike hung Nathan's urinary drainage bag on the side of the bed, he propped his mouthstick on a folded towel beside Nathan's head. He brought the speakerphone within reach, covered Nathan with a sheet and blanket, and turned out the light.

"Night, Nathan."

"Good night, Mike. Thanks."

Nathan began to pray. For himself, for his healing, but also for Abby. *Help her to accept me again.* He couldn't verbalize it any further than that.

He thought about Jonas Yoder and wondered how he'd died. Abby said it was suicide, but she didn't mention how. She said he was spending a lot of time with the Ashby High drug crowd. That certainly didn't sound like any of the Old Order Mennonite boys he'd seen. They tended to stay to themselves, and he'd often seen them around Fisher's Retreat on their bicycles, carrying items in their baskets or saddlebags, always wearing simple clothing, and never without a hat. Not one of the baseball variety, and not broad-brimmed like the Amish, but short, with a dimple in the top and with a narrow rim, something Nathan imagined would have been at the height of men's fashion in the 1920s.

The ringing phone jarred Nathan from his thoughts. He turned his head to the right and lifted his mouthstick from the towel. Then he turned the opposite way and tapped the pickup button on his speakerphone. "Hello."

The voice was female, one he didn't recognize. "Is this Nathan McAllister?"

"Yes."

"Mr. McAllister, you shouldn't come here." The voice trembled.

"Come where? Who is this?" *Abby? It doesn't sound like her.*

"Doesn't matter. You followed me, didn't you? This is all my fault." The unknown voice sobbed with emotion. "Don't come to Fisher's Retreat!"

Nathan raised his voice. "Who is this?"

"It wasn't an accident. You should know that. Why did you say that on TV?"

"Accident? What do you mean? My shooting?"

Her voice was clipped and rapid, and she only babbled, "It wasn't an accident. Don't come to Fisher's Retreat" before gasping and hanging up.

CHAPTER
8

NATHAN LAY still in the darkness of his room for a moment trying to make sense of the phone call. *Who was that? Could it have been Abby?*

It must have been someone who saw me on TV. Someone in Fisher's Retreat?

What was it she said? "This is all my fault."

Why wouldn't she say who she was? Was she afraid?

After a few moments he looked at his clock. It was late but . . . *I've got to know if Abby's at home.*

Carefully, using his mouthstick, he punched the number of his home phone.

Abby picked up after three rings. "Hello."

Nathan concentrated on her voice. *Did she sound sleepy? Upset?* "Abby. Uh, it's me."

"Nathan? What's the matter? What time is it?"

"It's 10:30. I'm sorry. Were you sleeping?"

She sounded irritated. *From being rudely awakened? Or because she was already upset?* "Of course. I have to get up early. I'm almost always in bed by 10."

"I'm sorry."

"Nathan, what is it? What do you want?"

"Um . . . Did you see me on TV?"

"Yes, Nathan, I did. I didn't know you were going to be on, but Marty saw you and quickly called me. Melissa was excited."

"Oh. That's good. It wasn't my idea. I just went along with it because they seemed set on the story."

"Nathan? Can we talk about this some other time?"

"Sure, Abby. I'm sorry to wake you."

"It's OK. Good night, Nathan."

"Abby?" He hesitated. "Do you think I should come home again?"

Abby sighed. "You want to be at home, don't you?"

He was taken aback by the question. "Yes, I do."

"Then I guess you know what's best." She paused. "Can we talk about this some other time?"

"Sure, Abby," he responded slowly. "Abby?" he added. "I love you."

"Thanks, Nate. Have a good night."

Nathan clicked off the phone. *That's it, Abby? That's all you can say? "Thanks, Nate. Have a good night"?*

Nathan strained to look around his nursing home room. *I can't stay here, God. I don't care what's in store for me there. You opened the way for me to go home, didn't you?*

The caller's voice echoed in his mind. *"It wasn't an accident. Don't come to Fisher's Retreat."*

He tried to still his pounding heart. *Now I have to get back. I just have to get to Fisher's Retreat!*

◆ ◆ ◆

Ryan Hannah arrived home at 11 P.M. to find the house quiet and Paige's door shut. He sighed as he trudged to the kitchen and mindlessly pulled the leftover lasagna from the refrigerator. Not bothering to heat it up, he spooned a generous portion onto a plate and began to eat. With only the gentle buzzing sound of his refrigerator in the background, he sorted through his day. He reviewed the difficult, meticulous dissection of the crainiopharyngioma that he'd removed from the brain of ten-year-old Linda Darlene and tried to quiet his anxiety over whether her vision would return to normal. He remembered the look on the thankful parents' faces and the hug he'd gotten from Cathy Darlene. He mentally walked through his hospital rounds, formulating plans and treatment options. He thought of Paige and their strained communication. And, of course, he thought about his research, the years of trial and error, the success with NTTF in stimulating spinal cord regeneration, and now the great headache of the loss of his latest success, the baboon he knew as Heidi.

He fixated on the robbery, alternating between thoughts of other paranoid researchers who would stop at nothing to be the first to solve the critical gaps in their understanding of spinal cord regeneration and the interesting theory brought up by Paige, that the strange note had perhaps been left by a member of an animal rights group. Whoever his enemy was, he despised the interruption of his research, an obstruction to his progress just when he was on the brink of significant discovery.

He pushed away the plate of lasagna after eating only a few cold bites as self-pity, anger, and resentment robbed him of his appetite. He stood and poured himself two fingers of bourbon before walking into his den to collapse in a leather recliner. There, as on so many other tension-filled times in his life, he heard the tapes from his own demanding surgeon father.

"You'll never accomplish anything."

"Play the piece again, Ryan. This time, don't foul up the final chord."

"A B in organic chemistry? You'll never get into medical school."

He swirled the drink in his hand, unable to stop the negative flood. A memory from his surgery internship also haunted him.

"You gimped him, Hannah!" The chief resident on the trauma service was livid. *"Never, NEVER establish an airway in a head trauma patient without proper cervical spine immobilization!"*

"He'll never walk again."

"Idiot!"

"You should have done the cricothyroidotomy!"

"NEVER move the neck before you've seen the X-rays!"

Ryan fumbled with the TV remote, flipping rapidly between channels.

News. *Click.*

Full-time weather. *Click.*

Back to the news. *Click.*

ESPN. *Click.*

A cooking show. A man in a white apron showing how to read a liquid measuring cup at eye level. *Click.*

A black-and-white movie classic. *Click.*

Homer Simpson.

Ugh. Isn't there anything worth watching? He set aside his drink, dissatisfied after one sip.

He walked down the hall toward his bedroom, pausing briefly at Paige's door. He listened quietly for a moment before cracking the door just enough to hear her breathing. He paused, regretting that tension seemed to fill every moment since her arrival.

"There's nothing wrong with enjoying being around someone who admires you."

He remembered her eyes, locking with his. *"But there's something wrong with needing it."*

He closed the door, silently twisting the doorknob before pulling it shut. Then he padded down the carpeted hallway on heavy feet and entered his bedroom alone.

◆　◆　◆

No one seemed quite sure how Fisher's Retreat got its name. Some said it was named after a trivial battle in the Civil War when the North had been embarrassed at the tenacity of a group of Confederates and had pulled back from the mountains surrounding the Apple Valley. That explanation worked except that no one could find record of a Union officer named Fisher. Others claimed it was founded by Thomas Fletcher Fisher who made his money in the poultry industry before retreating into the alcove between North Mountain and the Misty range. This seemed rational too, but the early records were burned in a town hall fire in 1897, and speculation about the town's origin had harbored a mysterious tone ever since.

For police officer Brian Turner, there was little refuge to be found in the quiet town of 1,600 residents. Everyone he saw seemed to be staring at him, remembering the day of Nathan's shooting. Some hailed him as a hero, the one who rid their quiet streets of an unwanted drug dealer. Others silently dismissed him as a loose gun or worse, harboring private doubts about the events that left Nathan McAllister in a wheelchair. Oh sure, the people of Fisher's Retreat were nice. They smiled at Brian and talked about the weather. But he could sense the distrust. He could see it in their eyes, in the accusing way they looked back at him once they were past him on the sidewalk.

He stepped through the tall, wet grass at the cemetery bordering the First Presbyterian Church, following the beam of his halogen police spotlight, which cast tall, eerie shadows onto the trees beyond the fence. The headstones danced and shrank as his light moved closer, with each stone's shadow disappearing altogether as he passed. Finally, in the middle of the lawn, he stopped, taking a seat on the root of an old maple tree. He focused his beam on the closest headstone for a moment before turning the light off entirely. He didn't need it to remember the inscription. "Laurie Turner."

It had been a year since his wife's body was committed to the ground. A year that Brian was determined never to repeat.

"I didn't know I could feel this dark inside," he whispered to his wife.

"I never thought I could do the things I've done." He hung his head. "I'm sorry, Laurie. I'm sorry."

His hand went mindlessly to his revolver, a .38 caliber pistol. The gun felt comfortable to him. It didn't bother him that Fisher's Retreat P.D. seemed to be the last department in the state still using the .38. The others had opted for more modern, powerful firepower such as the 9mm.

He unsnapped the holster and held the gun in his hand as he recalled the events he'd been over so many times before.

"Get your hands in the air!"

Lester Fitts dropped the object in his hand and pulled a 9mm handgun from the waistband of his pants.

Everything moved in slow motion for him now. "Drop your weapon."

Fitts's gun flashed. Once. Twice.

His own hands were extended, holding his revolver in front of his face. One, then two rounds pinched off in a second.

The sound was like a snapping pop, louder than when he used the ear protectors at the range.

A third crack, his own gun recoiling in his hand.

A crumpled body was in the doorway.

The images were distorted now, his memory taking a haunting life of its own . . . Nathan standing in the doorway yelling . . . Brian's hand pointing the gun at Nathan . . . Nathan's blood on the doormat . . . Nathan breathing with the assistance of a ventilator through a tracheostomy tube . . . Nathan in his chair.

Brian snapped on the halogen lamp, dissipating his troubled thoughts.

He rose, brushed the seat of his pants, and returned his revolver to his holster.

CHAPTER
9

THE FOLLOWING morning, Ryan walked to the kitchen to find Paige eating a bowl of oatmeal. She was dressed in a pair of jogging shorts and a tank top, her hair wet.

"Morning, Dad," she said as she looked up from her bowl. "I didn't expect you to still be here."

"I told the residents to round without me. It's my clinic day, so I don't have any scheduled cases." He nudged the corner of the steaming bowl. "What is that you're eating?"

"It's called oatmeal, Dad. It's good for you."

You sound like Barbara. "Where's the coffee?" he grunted.

"Didn't make any."

He put the coffee in a filter and filled the top of his coffeemaker with water before reaching for the *Brighton Daily News*, which Paige had left on the table. He unrolled the rubber band.

He groaned. "Where did they get this picture of Heidi?"

"What? Let me see."

"Oh, great."

Paige crowded in at his right shoulder as he spread the paper out on the table.

MISSING LAB ANIMAL IN CENTER OF
ANIMAL RIGHTS CONTROVERSY

A valuable laboratory animal, a female hamadryas baboon named Heidi, has been stolen in the wake of allegations of animal cruelty made by the animal rights group, HuRT. A spokesperson for Humans for the Responsible Treatment of Animals, while not personally taking credit for the disappearance of the animal, applauded the action as an appropriate measure to expose the torture of the intelligent mammal. The animal, apparently used in an experiment studying nerve signals from the brain, was stolen from the laboratory of Dr. E. Ryan Hannah, the chairman of the Surgery Department at Brighton University . . .

"What is this? What allegations? Who wrote this junk?" Ryan slapped the paper onto the table.

His daughter pointed to the small print beneath the title. "Meg Givins, *Brighton Daily News*, staff reporter."

He scanned the rest of the report. "This is groundless. I was never told about any so-called allegations! And where did they get this horrible picture?"

He studied the picture of Heidi, a close-up showing the tube in her nose and her tracheostomy, as well as a prominent craniotomy scar and the wires disappearing into her shaved scalp. Beside her head, the edge of a cardiac monitor was visible. "This was taken in my lab!"

He picked up the phone. "I'm calling Detective Mansfield. I want to know the meaning of this."

◆　◆　◆

The phone began ringing while Nathan was eating breakfast. "I'll get it," he said, pushing his head back into the head-pad behind him. With sustained pressure, his wheelchair obeyed and moved in reverse.

Dylan, a nurse's aide, shook his head. "I'll get it for you."

Nathan raised his voice. "I'll get it."

The aide shrugged and let the phone ring and ring as Nathan manipulated his chair close enough to answer the phone.

He answered on the eighth ring. "Hello."

"Nathan . . ." Abby's voice came through the speakerphone. With anyone else in the room, there was no privacy for his callers.

Nathan looked at Dylan, who understood and retreated into the hall.

"Are you alone?"

"I am now. What's up?" He listened carefully to a buzzing noise in the background.

"I just wanted to call you back. You did call me last night, didn't you? Or did I dream it?"

"Yeah, I called." He tilted his head toward the speaker. "What's that noise? Where are you?"

"At home. I got Marty to cover for me at the cafe. Melissa isn't feeling well."

"Is she OK?"

"Just an earache. I'm takin' her up to see Dr. Buttz at noon."

"What's that noise?"

"The oak tree in our yard was struck by lightning in a storm the other night. Phil Bender and his brother are cutting it down."

Nathan sighed. "Oh man, not the oak. That must have been the tallest tree in Fisher's Retreat."

"I guess that's why it was struck. It sounded like the house was going to explode. It split so bad that Phil said it was a danger to the house." She paused. Nathan could hear Melissa in the background. It sounded like she was singing along with the chain saws. "Nathan, what did you ask me last night?"

Nathan stayed quiet. *Please don't ask me why I called.*

"You asked me whether I thought you should come home, didn't you?" She waited. "Nathan?"

"Yeah, Abs, that's what I asked."

"You know the answer to that, Nathan. I think you should be at home. Melissa misses you."

What about you, Abby? You're my wife.

"I told that social worker lady how I felt. She should have told you."

"She said you're afraid."

Abby sighed. "Of course I'm afraid, Nathan. Everything is different now. What if something happens to you? What if I can't help you? What if you fall on the floor or something?"

"We can make it together, Abby. Nothing's gonna happen that we can't handle."

Nathan listened to the chain saw noise. Abby was quiet.

"Abby?"

"I'm still here. Don't worry about me, Nathan. If you can adjust, I can adjust." She waited for a moment, then added, "But it doesn't mean I'm not afraid."

"I know. It's OK." He sighed. He hated the speakerphone. It made Abby sound like she was in a box. "Abby, tell me the truth . . . Did you call me last night?"

"Last night? What are you talking about?"

"Right before I called you, a woman called. She wouldn't say who it was."

"What did she say?"

Nathan hesitated. "It was a prank call."

Abby laughed. "And you thought it was me?"

He lowered his voice. "Not really." He looked at his cooling breakfast. "Are you coming over today?"

"It depends on Melissa. It might be best not to be exposed to any germs. I'm not sure you need a runny nose right now."

"I don't have to touch her."

"We'll see. I think your parents want to drive over. Your mom wants to go to the mall over there or something."

"Dad too?" He shook his head. *He never stays more than a minute or two before finding some excuse to leave.*

"I think so." Nathan could hear Melissa squealing in the background.

"What's going on?"

"I think the tree's coming down. I want to watch."

"See you, Abs. I love you."

"Good-bye."

Nathan struck the top of the speakerphone with his mouthstick. *That was my favorite tree. Now where will Melissa swing? And why just "good-bye," Abby? Why not "I love you too"?*

Dylan stuck his head in the doorway. "All done?"

"Yes." He looked at the hospital breakfast—cold eggs and soft toast. "Could you just leave my coffee with a long straw? I'm not very hungry."

◆　◆　◆

Two hours later, Ryan broke from his clinic for an unscheduled conference with a captain on Brighton's police force, Michael Sease, and Detective Keith Mansfield. The three sat in Ryan's office, with the neurosurgeon at his desk and the two officers sitting on chairs opposite him.

"We turned up the heat on the reporter at the *Brighton Daily News*. At first she gave us that baloney about never revealing a source," Mansfield said with a snicker. "But then I offered to talk to the magistrate about her obstructing justice and she opened up like a flower."

Ryan watched the detective, unsure why he felt a distinct unease around him.

The captain interrupted, "As it turns out, the person who faxed the Polaroid of your animal to her must have used the fax machine in your lab. The fax came in at 2:30 A.M., and the transmission was traced back to your machine."

Ryan shifted in his seat. "So do you know who did this?"

"We have a pretty good idea. He's a member of the animal rights group HuRT, a young punk by the name of . . . Richard Henry the Fourth." His eyes met with Ryan's.

"You're kidding. The philanthropist's son?"

The captain nodded. "The one and only."

"His father has given more money to this department than any individual I know. He practically paid the last chairman's complete endowed chair." He paused. "Are you sure?"

"Ninety percent. The kid admitted to sending the fax. But he tells us he didn't steal the monkey."

"I think he's scared," the detective added before pulling out a pocketknife to begin cleaning his fingernails.

"How'd he get in?"

"We found your daughter's I.D. badge on the dash of his BMW."

"You searched his vehicle?"

The detective flipped a fingernail fragment onto the Persian rug and shook his head. "Didn't need to. It was in plain sight, right in the driveway of his father's mansion." He paused. "When we went to talk to the boy."

"Can't you bring him in? Throw him in jail or something? He needs to tell us where Heidi is." He hung his head. "Even if she's dead, the autopsy of the animal could give me valuable information."

"It won't do any good to bring him in now. His father can post any bail a judge would set. It would be best to get more evidence, then charge him with grand larceny once we find the animal."

"There isn't much time," Ryan pleaded. "What else can we do?"

"We've got the kid under tight surveillance. We hope he'll lead us to your baboon."

Trish knocked at his open door. "Dr. Hannah?"

The trio looked up. "This is the third call I've taken from the team at Channel 6." She held up a message slip. "And a second from Channel 2. And here's one from WLTK-FM." She sighed. "They all want an interview about the treatment of animals in your lab."

The surgeon stood. "This is crazy! This isn't about how I treat animals in my lab! This is about robbery, grand larceny, kidnapping, murder!" He looked at the officers, who remained in their seats. Then to Trish he added, "Tell them I have no comment." He turned back, then stopped. "No, wait . . . Tell them I conduct animal research in order to find cures for human neurosurgical disorders, but that's all. Not a word about what my current project is about!" He felt himself blushing, so he retreated and plopped into his desk chair.

The captain cleared his voice. "Sir, you might need to make some sort of formal statement to clear some of the mud that's flying."

Ryan sighed. "Not yet. You guys just find my baboon! And turn up the heat on that Richard Henry the Fourth. I don't care how much money his father has. I want this kid prosecuted to the full extent of the law."

"Sir, I—"

"I want this kid brought to justice. And you can tell that to the state's attorney!" Ryan continued.

The captain nodded, then cleared his voice a second time. "With all due respect, I know this animal rights group, sir. They have the ear of the governor. If they raise enough stink about your lab, it could get very, very messy."

"No one in this country can get away with breaking and entering and grand larceny!" Ryan got up and straightened a framed award on the wall.

"Sir," the captain added softly, "just talk to your attorney. I suggest that you make sure you step very carefully."

◆ ◆ ◆

Mark and Sally McAllister entered their son's room just after supper, before Nathan's evening rounds.

"Hi, Nathan," his mother bubbled. "So good to see you." She pulled his face forward and planted a kiss on his cheeks.

He smiled weakly in return. She'd only started treating him this way since he'd gotten in the chair. She'd hardly ever praised him or kissed him before. "Hi, Mom." He nodded at his father. "Pop."

"Hi, Nate." He fidgeted with his large, callused hands for a moment before touching his son on the shoulder. "What're you readin'?"

"A book about suffering. A guy named Yancey." He pushed the book back away from the edge of the counter.

His father grunted.

He looked at his mom. "Could you break the binding in on this one? It won't lay open."

She nodded her head and began working the book over in a way that would make a librarian cry.

"Abby says you've been keeping Mel for her when she's at the cafe."

"It's been fine, Nate. We must have played a hundred games of dominos. And I'm letting her play the old piano," she gushed. "I found your old John Thompson books."

He smiled. "Oh, man, how I must have tortured you with those lessons."

"You weren't as bad as Larry," she responded, referring to his older brother. "He always pounded the keys so hard."

"He sends me E-mail once in a while."

Mark McAllister rubbed the sweat from his balding head. "Listen, Nate, I've been wondering if you shouldn't rethink your plans a bit."

Nathan moved his wheelchair to face his father, who continued to talk while looking out at North Mountain.

"You've got it made here. You have your computer, your phone, plenty of help, all the physical therapy equipment and personnel you will ever need." He paused, still not looking at his son. "I've walked Fisher's Retreat, looking at it from new eyes. I'll bet half the buildings don't meet Americans with Disabilities Act standards. And the only sidewalks are in the new section on the east side of town. How's a man in a wheelchair going to get around a place like that?"

"Dad, it's my home."

The older man shook his head. "It *was* your home, Nate." He looked at the floor. "I talked to that social worker, the one who came to our town for the site visit. She said that between your workman's comp, the National Police benevolence fund, and your disability checks, you should be able to stay here indefinitely."

"I don't want to stay here. I want to be at home." He turned his chair and moved another foot closer to his father. "The modifications to my place are done. I'm going back to Fisher's Retreat. Period."

"Why not come for a visit before making a final decision? I'll talk to the administrator about holding a spot here."

"Dad, I need to be with Abby and Melissa!"

"I just want what's best for you . . . under these circumstances," he added with a sigh. He looked at his wife. "Did you want to show him the ad?"

Sally pulled a small piece of newsprint out of her purse. "It's an ad for a healing crusade in Carlisle. We've heard so many good things about this Brother Stephen's miracle crusades." She held it up for Nathan to read. "We'd like to take you there."

Nathan bit his tongue. *You need to accept me like I am.* "I'll think about it."

Mark pulled up his sagging pants and tightened his belt a notch under his protruding abdomen. "Sal, we'd better get going before dark."

You just got here. You didn't even sit down this time, Dad. Why is it you don't want me in Fisher's Retreat? Is it really like you say—that you just want what's best for me?

His father was already retreating toward the door.

"I'll be home on Saturday. They're planning a little town celebration."

"So we hear," his father said quietly. "So we hear." He grabbed Sally's arm. "Let's go, Sal. Bye, son."

CHAPTER
10

ON FRIDAY morning Nathan felt a little like a puppy in the front window of a pet shop . . . exposed, a little anxious, but eager to see that someone was interested. The morning had been set aside for his new personal care attendants, or PCAs, to learn his routine.

Jim Over, Richard Ramsey, and Dave Borntrager looked on as the aides at Briarfield Manor instructed them on every detail of Nathan's day. Then they helped with his bowel program, a shower, changing his Texas external urinary drainage catheter, dressing him, physical therapy, and positioning him in his wheelchair.

Nathan didn't mind talking about his care, even the private matters. It was the actual physical exposure and the humiliation of allowing others to handle his toiletry needs and hygiene that bothered him the most. He often disguised his embarrassment with a joke or some self-directed humor, such as he did that morning when Jim changed his catheter. He watched helplessly as his body responded reflexively to being touched. Jim positioned the Texas condom catheter as Nathan cringed, realizing his inability to control his reaction. He glanced at his other caregivers, who had kindly diverted their eyes. "Looks like I'm ready for action now, eh, boys?" he chuckled nervously. "Where's Abby when I need her?"

Jim finished the job quickly. "Don't worry about it. We've all worked with spinal cord patients before. It's normal."

I know, I know, Nathan thought, *but it's not easy being the center of attention, especially when I'm completely naked and you all have your clothes on.*

A few minutes later, when they were positioning him in his chair, he cautioned them to carefully spread out the creases in his pants. "Even a small wrinkle can cause a slight increase in pressure and be the start of skin breakdown," he instructed. *I'm beginning to sound just like the staff here at Briarfield.*

After he was in the wheelchair, they reviewed the PCA schedule they'd agreed to and signed formal contracts of employment, something Nathan had originally thought was unimportant, but that Janice, the Briarfield Manor social worker, had insisted upon. Nathan signed each agreement with a felt-tipped pen in his mouth while Dave held the papers against a book.

"Whew," Nathan said, shifting the pen to the corner of his mouth like a cigar. "I think I'll have to change my signature to 'Nate.'"

Richard looked at the signatures. "At least it's neater than his," he said, delivering a friendly punch to Dave's arm. "What's this? Dave Buhmmmmer?" he mumbled. "All you can read is the *B* and the *r*."

Nathan laughed. "Just put the papers on the desk."

"Wait until you see your place," Jim said.

"Abby brought by some pictures last week."

Libby Summers appeared in the doorway. "Time for breakfast, Mr. McAllister."

Nathan looked at his new helpers. "Thanks a lot, guys—for coming over here this early and all."

"No problem."

He looked over at his calendar. "OK. It looks like I'll see Richard on Saturday evening."

Richard nodded. "I'll be there."

◆ ◆ ◆

Ryan stood beside Dr. Bill Timmons in O.R. 5 and pulled off his paper scrub gown and sterile gloves. He looked at the clock. "Good job, Dr. Timmons. I'm sure this guy will do better than Mr. Potter." Behind them, the nursing staff busied themselves with the business of moving a patient off the O.R. table and onto a recovery room stretcher.

The resident huffed and responded quietly, "Don't remind me. Potter leaked spinal fluid for so long, I thought you'd never let me do another lumbar disc with you."

"We've all seen 'em go bad." Ryan walked through the swinging operating room door with his neurosurgical resident on his heels. He began to wash his hands. "That's the irony of this business. It's incredibly rewarding." He stopped and looked at his resident before adding, "And incredibly humbling. And that goes for every one of us."

Timmons, the third-year resident, nodded.

Ryan's beeper sounded as he dried his hands. He pressed the button on the top of his pager, clipped to the waistband of his scrubs. "Hmm. Outside call."

He stepped to the hall phone as Timmons disappeared into the O.R. to write post-op orders. "Dr. Hannah here. I was paged."

The operator responded, "I have an outside call. Go ahead please."

"Hello. This is Dr. Hannah."

"Dr. Hannah, Keith Mansfield here. I hope I'm not bothering you. I thought you might like an update on your case. Is this a good time?"

Ryan looked at the busy O.R. hallway. "As good as any."

"We have some good news and bad news, I'm afraid." He chuckled. "Isn't that the way it always is? You never get only one or the other."

Just get on with it.

Mansfield continued, "A young lady animal doctor called last evening. She told us that she'd seen the monkey."

She's a hamadryas baboon, not just a monkey! "Someone saw her alive?"

"Yep. A Dr. Shippen. She said that a man matching the description of the Henry boy brought the monkey by her office before she opened yesterday morning. He practically begged her to take care of it. Said his name was Bob. That's all. Bob."

"What did she do?"

"She knew something was up because of the monkey's appearance. Evidently she never saw the top of the animal's head because the kid had it all wrapped up, but when she saw the trach tube, she wanted to know what doctor was caring for the animal."

"And?"

"The kid made up a story about just moving to town. She said he acted weird." He paused and cleared his throat into the phone.

Ryan shook his head and frowned. "Go on."

"She claimed not to have expertise in exotic animal care. She referred him on to the Brighton Animal Hospital. So that's where we went next." He sighed. "But the kid never showed."

Ryan rubbed the back of his neck and stretched. "Did the doctor say there was a tube in the baboon's snout? Heidi will dehydrate if she's not fed."

"Didn't say."

"Hmm."

"Anyway, with the vet's description of the boy, I twisted the magistrate's arm to get a search warrant for the kid's vehicle. We wanted to search the car for trace evidence that could firmly link the boy to the monkey. You know, hair fibers, that sort of thing."

"And?"

"Well, that's where the bad news comes in."

What you've told me so far was the good news?

"His BMW has disappeared."

"Disappeared? What do—"

"The father claims that his Aunt Lucy in Arizona needed a car. He said she left with it yesterday at noon." He sighed. "Between you and me, I think Dicky Trout, his attorney, warned him to get rid of it."

Ryan raised his voice. "That's an ethical violation!"

"Of course it is—"

"Can't you do something to him? That's got to be illegal!"

"Look, Dr. Hannah, I'm doing what I can. I'm going to talk to the Henrys' attorney this morning. Trout's pulled this kind of stunt before. I'm not going to let him get by with it this time. I'll see if the magistrate will give me a warrant against him for a tampering with evidence charge. He *had* to know we'd go after the kid's car. He's not stupid."

"And if the magistrate isn't convinced?"

"Doesn't matter," he chuckled. "I can still threaten Mr. Trout with it." He laughed louder. "But ol' Trout's a slippery fish. He's hard to catch."

Ryan didn't laugh at the detective's joke. "What about finding the car?"

"Since it involves a grand larceny, I'll get the Phoenix P.D. to look for the car. That is, if and when dear Aunt Lucy decides to show. And I don't need to tell you that the longer it takes to find the car, the harder it will be to find meaningful evidence."

Ryan nodded into the receiver.

"Dr. Hannah?"

The surgeon didn't answer.

"I need to tell you that the prosecuting attorney is looking over the pictures this Henry kid has been spreading around. His office is under a lot of pressure to do something about the animal cruelty allegations."

"That's ridiculous! Has any scientist in this state ever faced a charge like this?"

"No," he responded quickly. "But there's always a first time. And Richard Henry the Third is a powerful man. He may be stirring up the pot to take the heat and attention away from his son."

"This is crazy!" Ryan tried to stifle his voice as a patient was wheeled by on a stretcher.

"It may be crazy to you, Dr. Hannah, but if I was you, I wouldn't want to be in the courtroom when the prosecuting attorney flashes those pictures before a jury."

Ryan looked at his shoe-covers and scuffed them across the floor. He could feel cold sweat on his back. "You're not kidding."

"Not a bit." He hesitated, then added, "I wouldn't enjoy arresting you, Dr. Hannah."

The surgeon huffed, then mumbled, "I don't believe this."

"Do me a favor, doc. Take the advice Captain Sease gave you yesterday. It's time to talk to your attorney."

◆　◆　◆

Of all the activities Nathan could participate in at Briarfield Manor, his favorite of all was the program designed specifically for patients of spinal cord injury—namely, using the StimMaster Functional Electrical Stimulation Ergometer. It utilized space-age computer technology to give Nathan a cardiovascular workout similar to regular aerobic exercise.

Once Marlin Clayborn, his physical therapist, had Nathan properly positioned and attached to the StimMaster, electrical impulses carried into Nathan's legs by surface electrodes caused muscle contractions that were coordinated by the computer. The result of the functional electrical stimulation was purposeful pedaling motion by his legs. To Nathan, the StimMaster looked very similar to a semi-recumbent exercise bicycle. He had been working every other day with the StimMaster for over two months, and the reversal in his muscle atrophy was noticeable.

For Nathan, the psychological benefit alone was worth the effort. Just seeing his own legs move and pedal the StimMaster, even if he couldn't feel a thing, was a thrill he found hard to articulate.

After the workout, Marlin toweled down Nathan's hair as he again sat in his power wheelchair. "I sure wish I could keep this up. I think this is what I'll miss the most about this place."

"Other than your favorite physical therapist," Marlin added.

Nathan smiled. "Right."

"You could get one for home use, you know. I've helped at least three SCI patients get use of this baby right in their homes."

"I'll bet it cost a pretty penny."

"Not as much as you might think. All included, you could probably get set up between twelve and thirteen grand."

Nathan coughed. "See?"

"Compare that to the price of the high-tech powerchairs you guys drive. Up to eighteen grand and no turn signals or headlights." He chuckled. "The truth of the matter is, as insurance carriers get educated to the medical benefits of this technology, more and more are picking up at least part of the tab."

"Why?"

"They spend less money caring for pressure sores, less money on treatment of lower extremity blood clots—lots of reasons really." He began brushing Nathan's thick brown hair. "If you're serious, we should get your medical doctor to write your workmen's compensation carrier. What they need is a letter of medical necessity, detailing the medical benefits." He paused. "Most local docs really don't know enough about it to be convincing though." He held the brush in the air. "But I know that Dr. Hannah, your neurosurgeon, is familiar with the technology. He's written the letters for the other quads I've worked with."

"Hmm." Nathan nodded.

Just then an aide wheeled in an elderly patient. "Hi, Jack. Ready for the whirlpool?" Marlin asked.

Nathan controlled his powerchair, moving toward the exit of the P.T. department.

"Say, Nate," Marlin called from behind him, "you can always come back here for your workouts as an outpatient."

"It's a long drive from Fisher's Retreat," Nathan responded weakly without turning his chair to see him. "We'll see."

He traveled down the long hall past the recreation room and a small lobby, then stopped at the elevators. He slid his chair against the wall so he could reach the elevator button with his mouthstick. Once inside, it took him several tries of up and back motions to get close enough to push the first floor button.

Once down in his room, he ate lunch, the last meal he thought he'd eat from Libby's rose-lotioned hands.

"Thanks, Lib," he said as she put the yellow tray cover over his empty dishes. "Can you slide the phone to the edge? I'd like to make a phone call."

"Sure." She complied before leaving to continue her lunch duties.

Slowly Nathan dialed the number of the Fisher's Retreat P.D. It was time for him to find out more about Jonas Yoder—and his own shooting for that matter.

"Fisher's Retreat Police Department." The voice was unmistakable. Marge Twittlegate, owner of the Retreat's highest beehive hairdo, had worked as a front-office receptionist and secretary for twenty years. She had a heart of gold and was fiercely loyal to the department and especially to the chief of police, Joe Gibson.

Nathan smiled as he pictured Marge at her desk. *I'll bet you're wearing your blue sweater, aren't you, Marge.* She had worn the same thin, blue sweater every day, regardless of the temperature, for as long as Nathan could remember. "Hi, Marge."

He waited for her reaction. "Who's this?" She paused. "Nate?"

"Ah, you pegged me."

"Nathan McAllister! What are you doing? You're not back in Fisher's Retreat, are you?"

"Not 'til tomorrow morning."

"Well, I'll be," she exclaimed. He could hear her continue speaking, although it was more muffled. "It's Nate! Nate McAllister, guys!" Her voice became clearer again. "What can I do for you, Nate?"

"I just wanted to hear your voice again, Marge."

"Stop it, Nate. I know you better than that," she gushed. "Why did you *really* call?"

"OK, I'll admit it," he responded with a smile, "I want some information. I wonder if you can pull a few files for me. Maybe copy some information so when I get to town, I can review them."

"OK. What can I get for you?"

"I want the file of the investigation into my shooting." He paused, hearing only a quiet wheeze on the other end. "And I'd like to find out what I can about the death of Jonas Yoder. My wife tells me he was buried on the day I was shot."

"Oooh. Uh, that's true, Nate." She paused. She made a nervous clicking noise with her cheek. Nathan had heard it many times before.

"What's wrong, Marge? You can get me the info, can't you?"

She was silent for a moment, except for the quick, oscillating sound of air blowing in and out of her cheeks, another thing she did when she was under stress. "I'd better let you talk to Joe about all that. He's got a department-only policy we're trying to enforce here."

"Marge," he protested, "you're talking to Nate McAllister—Officer Nate McAllister. There can't be a problem with me looking at my own shooting investigation."

"Let me let you talk to Joe." *Click.*

Nathan stared at the speakerphone. *She put me on hold. This is definitely strange.*

In a moment the friendly voice of Joe Gibson boomed. "Nate! It's good to hear from you. Are you ready for the celebration?"

"I guess so." Nathan rubbed his cheek on his mouthstick, picturing his chief as he remembered him—the picture of neatness, his dark blue uniform without a wrinkle, beneath a weathered face, with too many lines on his forehead and too many chins underneath a warm smile. "Joe, we've always been straight with each other. What's this all about? I asked Marge for some info about my shooting, and she puts me through to you."

"Still searching for answers, Nate? How's the memory?"

Nathan sighed. "Not good. I still don't have any memory of my shooting. From what I gather from Dr. Hannah, it's not likely to ever return." He paused. "And you didn't answer my question."

"I know, Nate. It's just that we have unanswered questions too." He lowered his voice. "Are you alone? I know about your crazy speakerphone."

Nathan looked at his open door. "I'm alone."

"Look, Nate, I think it's best if you stay out of all this. I'm not sure you really want to uncover everything you might discover."

Where are you going with this, Joe? "I don't understand."

"Nate, just between us, I'd like to let this thing rest. We still don't know what was going on in that drug distribution house. You were there, apparently inside, with Lester Fitts. You weren't even wearing your gun. He comes out of the house, apparently in no hurry, and meets up with Brian." He sighed. "I don't know, Nate. I wish you had your memory back. Maybe then you could assure me that you haven't had something to do with all the increase in drug use we've seen in the area."

"I don't believe what I'm hearing, Joe. You can't believe that I was—"

"It's hard for me to believe too, Nate. You were a good cop. I would really rather not discover anything about you to make me think otherwise. The fact that you don't remember doesn't help me any." He paused again. "For your sake, I'd rather not look into it any further. I'm not sure any of us really wants to know why you were in that house unarmed."

"You're kidding, right, Joe?"

"I wish I was."

Nathan stared at the speakerphone, speechless.

"For the sake of keeping the investigation objective and third-party, I'm not going to be able to allow you to look at those files. I'm really sorry, Nate. Really I am. But you've got to look at it from my perspective. I have a department to run here, and if there is any suspicion of impropriety, however small, on the part of any of my officers, I'm the one who is responsible to see that those suspicions are handled in an unbiased manner."

"Joe!"

"I know, Nate. I'm sorry." Nathan heard papers rustling. "Hey, before I forget, I want to be the first to congratulate you on your coming home."

Nathan sighed with frustration and shook his head. He hesitated before adding softly, "I guess I owe a lot to you. Abby filled me in on all the fund-raising. I can't wait to see the house."

"You'll love it. The contractors really did a nice job."

He nodded slowly. "OK, Joe. I'll see you tomorrow."

He heard a click on the other end.

Nathan sighed with frustration. *How can I know if there's any real danger for me in Fisher's Retreat if they won't let me review the police reports?*

If only my memory would return!

He dropped his head forward in a prayerful posture and pinched his eyes tightly shut.

Help me remember!

CHAPTER
11

THE NEXT morning, as she did on most Saturday mornings, Elizabeth Hopkins slept in. It was one of the few luxuries she allowed herself, and one which she'd only enjoyed since rotating off the clinical neurosurgical service and into the lab. For the rest of her fellow residents, Saturday morning was the same as any other, making rounds and formulating a long list of work to be done for each patient.

She showered, ate, read the paper, and polished the interior of her brown Buick before meandering into the spinal lab by 10. At the door she was surprised to see two uniformed Brighton policemen.

"You guys making this your second home or something?" She smiled. "Didn't you finish all your fingerprint gathering last time?"

When they didn't reply, she realized they were different officers than she'd seen before. She held out her one free hand as the other clutched a large McDonald's coffee. "I'm Dr. Hopkins. Can I help you gentlemen?"

"Sam Jenkins, Brighton P.D." The taller officer with a large mole on his left cheek extended his hand.

The second officer cleared his throat and nodded. "Ben Seager." He cleared his voice again and began, "We're not here to investigate the break-in."

"Wha—?"

Sam Jenkins held up an official paper. "We've brought a search warrant."

"Search warrant? What for?"

Jenkins looked at the paper and read, "Brighton University Spinal Cord Research Lab, room 6-1121, Dennis Foundation Research Facility. These things are very specific. Have we found the right place?"

Elizabeth looked at the number on the warrant beneath the name E. Ryan Hannah, M.D. It matched the one on the door. "What's this all about?"

"Animal cruelty investigation."

"You're kidding."

The officers looked at each other. "No, ma'am," Jenkins answered. "Now if you'll let us in, we can get started. Otherwise, we'll get security up here to do it."

Elizabeth obeyed and put her I.D. badge up to the electronic sensor pad by the door. The door lock clicked, and she led the officers into the darkened lab.

Immediately the shorter officer, Ben Seager, pulled a camera from a large canvas bag and began photographing everything.

Elizabeth looked at the phone on her desk, wanting to call Dr. Hannah. Not wanting to be overheard, she slipped back into the hall to use her cellular phone. She punched the Recall button followed by the number 1. In an instant Dr. Hannah's home phone began ringing.

One ring. Two. Three. Four. *Come on, answer!* Five rings.

"Hello. Hannah's."

"Paige?"

"Dr. Hopkins?"

Her voice was pressured but soft. "Quick, Paige—I know it's Saturday morning, and I hate to interrupt, but I need to speak to your father now!"

"He's not in. He went down to Kensington. To the golf resort. He's giving a talk to a group of emergency medicine physicians at their state meeting. Management of head and spine injuries or something."

Elizabeth struck her left thigh with her fist. "Ugh! I forgot." She began pacing in the hall. "When will he be back?"

"I don't expect him until late. He said what with everything going on, he needed to get away, maybe even play some golf." She paused. "Do you know when my father last played golf?"

I don't really care. "No."

"The day my mother left for Alabama. My dad must be really stressed out to want to play golf."

Elizabeth whispered a curse.

Paige responded cheerfully, "Can I give him a message?"

She exhaled forcefully. "Just have him call me. The moment he returns, OK? It doesn't matter what time or how late it is." She hesitated. "He didn't leave the number of the resort, did he?"

"No, but I'm sure you could call Information. Or maybe you could page him. He usually has his beeper."

Elizabeth thanked her and hung up.

She watched helplessly as the two officers systematically removed the two computers, the videos, the incubator, a host of data books, and a Plexiglas cage housing a Schwann rat.

"What are you doing?" she cried for the tenth time. "At least let me have the original videotapes. I can make you copies! We need this for our research!"

Jenkins shook his head. "All of this stuff will eventually be returned."

"Eventually?"

"Yes," Seager responded, exiting the lab with his last armload of data books. "After the trial."

◆　◆　◆

Abby held out the small gift to Nathan. "Happy Nathan McAllister Day."

"What?" He edged his wheelchair backwards to allow Jake to pass with another box of books.

She shrugged. "Everyone else has surprises for you today. I wanted you to have something from me too."

"Abs, you didn't need to do anything," he protested.

"Here," she said, holding out the wrapped package. "You can open it." She turned the small box. "Just put your mouthstick here."

He followed her instructions and popped off the wrapping paper, held loosely by a short piece of tape. Abby made him push the top off the little box. "Look inside." She tilted it so he could see.

Inside, a little van, a child's toy, sat in the middle of some packing paper. He looked up at Abby and wrinkled his nose. *What on earth?* "Just what I always wanted?" he asked timidly.

"No, silly." She lifted the toy. "Keep looking."

Beneath the little van was a set of keys.

Nathan's eyes widened. He looked at Abby, unsure of what to say.

She lifted the keys. "Your carriage awaits, Mr. McAllister," she responded in a snobbish tone.

"Abby, the staff said we can use Briarfield's van to take me—"

"Before you protest, let me explain," she interrupted, raising her voice. "You know we need a special van now. We can't just strap you in the old pickup." She paused and put her hand on his shoulder. "Mr. Hartman practically gave it to me. He heard all about the celebration and called to help. It's not new, but it has the modifications you need."

"Mr. Hartman?"

"The owner of Carlisle Dodge." She smiled. "I traded the pickup for it."

Nathan sniffed. He could feel his throat closing and his eyes filling. "Oh, Abby."

She rescued him with a tissue to blot his eyes. He looked up to see a crowd of Briarfield staff, who had obviously known what Abby was about to do. He tried to say thank you, but his voice caught in a sob.

After a moment he collected himself and blew his nose into the tissue Abby held.

"Here," Janice Marsh said, pushing a small box of Kleenex into Abby's hand. "It looks like you're going to need these today."

"OK, OK," Nathan chided. "Let a man have some space." He moved his wheelchair forward. "Let's go see the van!"

A minute later he exited the front of the nursing home to see yet another crowd gathered around a light blue Dodge van with a low chassis and a foldout ramp extending from an open side door. Inside, behind the backseat, his clothes, books, and computer were already packed.

Ethel Bailey paced around the perimeter of the crowd, pausing only to rest on her walker after she had completed her inspection. "It's a doozie!"

Jake Peterson smiled beneath his brown Briarfield Manor hat.

Bob Price cupped his hand to his ear. "Is it running?"

Libby Summers wiped her eyes.

Janice tousled Melissa's hair.

"Let's go home, Daddy. Let's go home!" Melissa giggled as she ran up and down the ramp.

Abby blotted Nathan's eyes again. "Everything's ready."

He paused to say good-bye to each person before moving up the ramp. Once inside, he turned his chair toward the front and inched forward into the empty passenger space beside the driver's seat. He watched as Abby secured each wheel to the floor with straps. "All set."

Jake folded up the ramp and shut the side door. "You're off," he said, slapping the side of the van.

"I'm going home." Nathan heard his own words but could hardly take it all in.

◆ ◆ ◆

An hour later Officer Charlie Edwards checked his watch. His Fisher's Retreat patrol car was concealed just off Highway 2, where it straightened out after leaving North Mountain and led into town. "It's almost noon. They should be here by now."

"Relax," Brian Turner responded, checking his side-view mirror from the passenger's seat. "Abby will be driving slow."

Charlie, the newest member of the six-man police force, had been hired to replace Nathan. He was five-seven but had a forty-eight inch, iron chest that he punished daily at a gym in Carlisle. "You say the van is blue?" He pushed his mirrored sunglasses onto his nose.

"Sky blue, OK?"

Charlie nodded, studying his fellow officer for a moment before leaning out his window to see around a road sign reading "Runaway Truck Ramp."

"There they are." Brian grabbed the radio. "Joe? We've sighted 'em."

Charlie snapped on the overhead lights and siren and pulled onto the highway with a spray of gravel.

He watched as the taillights of the blue van flashed, then stayed on as it pulled onto the road's shoulder.

Brian and Charlie jumped out and approached together.

Abby already knew what to expect but played along. "Was I going too fast, officer?"

Charlie leaned toward the open window. "I'll need your driver's license and registration, ma'am," he said before breaking into a smile.

"What's this all—" Nathan started.

Charlie looked at the documents and frowned. "I'm going to need to escort you in." He motioned to his patrol car. "Fall in behind me." He paused. "And no funny stuff. I want you right on my bumper all the way into town."

With that, hearing Nathan's protests in the background, the two officers returned to their car and pulled in front of the van.

Slowly, with lights flashing, they proceeded forward, eventually joined by two other patrol cars and a Carlisle fire truck. As they pulled even with the First Presbyterian Church, they slowed even more and inched forward behind the Ashby High School marching band. On the sidewalks the town's children were waving flags.

Charlie glanced at Brian, who had been silent since they began the escort. "Abby sure seems like a nice lady."

Brian grunted. "She's a gem." He lowered his window. "She used to bring meals to us when Laurie was sick. She would even come by the house to help clean." He cleared his throat. "Laurie loved her."

Charlie nodded as their car passed beneath a banner hanging from Fisher's Retreat's only traffic signal. "WELCOME HOME NATHAN!"

He reached out and waved at a woman in a gray suit. "There's Judy Tanner." He pointed and nudged Brian. "She does the news on Channel 4 down in Carlisle."

"Huh? Oh."

A shorter man with a bushy mustache pointed a camera at them.

They stopped completely in front of the municipal building that the police department shared with the town government. There Joe Gibson and Mayor Lyle Jenson came out and spoke to Nathan. Charlie

watched through his rearview mirror as the mayor held a white envelope toward Nathan before stumbling around the front of the van and
handing it to Abby.

From there, with the band's music fading in the background, they
continued forward past the Fisher's Retreat Drug Center, where June
Gibson, the town's pharmacist and Joe's wife, stood on the sidewalk
waving. Past the town Post Office and the hardware store they traveled. Once he reached the Texaco station, Charlie turned on the siren
again and signaled to turn onto Cherry Street.

"Take the next street," Brian said forcefully.

"But it's straight through to their house if—"

"Take the next street!"

Charlie flipped off his turn signal with a huff.

"I didn't want to lead them past the old Allen house."

"Oh," Charlie mumbled as understanding hit him. "Where Nathan
was shot, right?"

He silenced the siren again and wove through the town until they
were sitting in front of the newly remodeled McAllister home. He
watched Abby pull the van into the driveway. Then, in accordance
with Joe Gibson's instructions, he pulled away to leave the McAllisters
some privacy.

Nathan McAllister was home.

CHAPTER
12

ON SUNDAY morning Ryan heaved himself from bed, feeling more exhausted than when he'd finally fallen into a fitful sleep three hours before. He threw on his robe and plodded to the kitchen, lured by the smell of fresh coffee.

Paige was up and dressed. "Morning, Daddy."

"Morning, sugar," he grunted, pausing to kiss the back of her blonde hair.

He poured two mugs of black coffee and headed for the table.

"Oh, none for me, Daddy," Paige responded, looking up from the Sunday comics.

"These are mine." He plopped onto a kitchen chair.

"Up late?"

"Couldn't sleep," he said, nodding his head. "I guess Elizabeth told you about my lab."

"On one of the dozen calls she made here looking for you."

"Sorry about that," he responded quietly. "She was pretty upset, as you can imagine." He managed a weak chuckle before adding, "She finally reached me on the seventh hole at Kensington. She sent out a man in a little green cart with a phone." He shook his head. "I just quit and came back to the U. Didn't matter really—I'd already shot over a hundred."

"If you'd play more than once a decade it would help."

It's not really fun doing something I'm no good at anyway. There's no reward in that. He took a large swallow from a mug with a picture of a moose on the side, a souvenir from an old family vacation. "I can't believe it was an accident those guys came on a weekend. They had to know I wouldn't be around to raise a fuss."

"I'm going over to the early service at Grace Fellowship this morning. I thought it'd be fun to see my old friends." She paused. "Wanna come?"

"I have to meet with Hal Ferguson this morning."

"Your attorney? I think he's usually in church."

Ryan snorted. "I think he understood the importance of my situation." He took another sip of coffee. "Maybe next week, Paige," he mumbled. "Maybe next week."

◆   ◆   ◆

Thirty minutes after Abby left for the cafe, Nathan heard the front door unlock. After a moment Richard Ramsey appeared in the doorway. He was wearing a Navy sweat suit and a Dallas Cowboys hat. In his hands he had two Styrofoam containers of coffee. "Awake, Nate?"

"Sure. I've been awake since 5."

"Coffee?"

"A sip would be great. Abby gave me orange juice before heading out."

Richard lowered the cup beside his head and folded over a jointed straw.

"Thanks."

"Let's get you washed and dressed," he said, putting the coffee aside. "Ready?"

They chatted as Richard used a large sea sponge to do a bed bath, dressed Nathan, and did his range of motion exercises.

"Abby has to work Sundays?"

"Just two a month."

Richard looked over at a small monitor by Nathan's bed. Nathan followed his eyes. "You can turn that off now."

Richard turned the dial. "What's this?"

"It's a baby monitor." Nathan paused. "So I can get Abby during the night if I need her to adjust my covers."

He nodded slowly but didn't speak.

"Abby says she wants to stay upstairs so she can be close to Melissa's room."

Richard gave him another sip of coffee. "Not exactly the sleeping arrangement you had in mind, I take it?"

Nathan stared up at the ceiling. "Abby thinks this room is too small for our double bed."

"What was this, your dining room?"

Nathan nodded. "Rich, this room is two feet wider than our bedroom upstairs."

"Oh." He hesitated.

"She's still my wife, even if—"

"Give her some time, Nate." He pulled the side arm up and off Nathan's chair in preparation for transferring Nathan. "These are big adjustments for her—"

Nathan followed Richard's eyes to the doorway, where Melissa had just appeared.

"Morning, Daddy!" She clutched her stuffed gingerbread man by one leg.

"Hi, honey. How's Willie? I haven't seen him for a long time."

She scampered over and crawled up on his bed before planting a kiss on his nose.

"Hey, not so fast," Nathan protested. "I didn't get to kiss you!"

Melissa giggled and placed her cheek against her father's lips. "You need to shave."

Richard responded, "It's on my list, young lady. Just as soon as we get him up." He looked at his watch. "Do you want me to take you to church?"

Nathan shook his head. "I don't think so. One new thing at a time." He paused. "I want to go with Abby," he added slowly. *If she'll agree.*

◆ ◆ ◆

An hour later, in the privacy of his home office, Ryan met with his longtime friend and attorney, Hal Ferguson.

"Sorry about this mess," Ryan said, pushing a stack of papers and a slide carousel to the side of his teak desk. "I didn't get in until late." He paused, then lifted a slide from the circular container. "Yet another one of my concerns," he sighed, holding the slide up to a banker's lamp on his desk. "Do you know how much money the U.S. government spends on caring for spinal cord injury patients every year?"

Hal shifted in his chair. "Uh—"

"For everything, disability, medical costs, all included." He paused. "Eight billion dollars."

The attorney opened his briefcase.

Ryan lifted a second slide to the light. "And do you know the total amount they spend on spinal cord injury research?" He didn't wait for an answer. "About fifty million dollars. A fraction spent on cure, a mountain spent on care."

Hal looked at his watch and pulled out a notepad.

"And do you know how many NIH grant applications concerning SCI were given money this year?"

"Ryan, I have no idea."

"Hmm," he mumbled. "This is an old slide." He squinted and pointed at the slide. "Well, in 1996 they funded less than 20 percent." He pushed the slide back in its slot and sat down. "Something is wrong with this picture."

"What's wrong with this picture is that you and I are spending valuable weekend time on legal matters rather than doing something else we'd both enjoy." He looked up at Ryan and held his hands up. "Now, can we get to it?"

Ryan nodded.

"OK, let's go over the situation as I see it now. After you called last night, I visited the county prosecuting attorney, Byron Whiteside, for a little chat. As far as I can tell, the decision for the Brighton P.D. to search your lab came directly from pressure from his office."

"That rat!" Ryan huffed, striking his desk. "He should be busy prosecuting that Henry boy for breaking into my lab."

Hal held up his hand. "Easy. I agree, but let me help you understand." He stood and began to pace. "What Whiteside won't say directly, but I'm confident will happen, is that if you drop your charges against the boy, the accusations against you about animal cruelty will quietly be forgotten."

Ryan sighed. "That's crazy. I've done nothing. The real evidence is against the boy."

"Ryan, so far all they have against him is a confession that he entered your lab and took some pictures—all in the interest of protecting innocent animals from needless torture."

"That's a crock of—" He stopped himself. "What about the eyewitness who saw the boy with my baboon? The veterinarian?"

"She gave a description of the boy that matches the Henry boy, that's all."

"So why doesn't the P.D. bring the kid in and put him in a lineup? I'm sure she could pick him out."

"The kid has already shaved his head. He looks nothing like he did two days ago. I can promise you, the lady veterinarian isn't going to be sure. And that's not going to convince a jury."

Ryan shook his head. "You're not encouraging me, Hal."

"I'm just trying to tell you the status of the playing field, OK? The other side is definitely playing dirty. I'm sure there's enough Henry money around to buy any kind of advice they want."

"But that's unethical! Why should this Whiteside want to come after me?"

"It's not you he's coming after. I suspect he's got political aspirations. His name has already been thrown around as a possible candidate for governor."

"I don't get it."

"He wants to prosecute the cases that will make him look good in the public eye. For some reason, the animal rights people seem to have a lot of public sympathy right now. I think he realizes that." He shrugged. "And it can't hurt that a major supporter of his party is none other than . . ."

"Richard Henry the Third."

"Now you're getting it," he said, shaking his finger at Ryan. "He's not vindictive against you personally."

"I just got in the way."

Hal sat back down and reopened his notebook. "Part of what I need from you is an explanation of what you're really doing in your lab. With you refusing to talk to anyone in the media about it, you look guilty. I'm sure you have good reasons for what you're doing, but . . ." His voice trailed off.

"But what?"

"But no one's seeing it. All they see are those horrible images of that baboon with the wires coming out of its head and all those stitches and that tube thing in its neck."

"A tracheostomy."

"Whatever." He shook his head at Ryan. "Ryan, what *are* you doing?"

"It's a secret."

"Ryan, don't do this to me. I can't help you if you won't cooperate."

"OK. It's not really a secret. At least not for long if anyone can decipher all the data they took from my lab." He paused. "Are you sure this is only about animal rights?"

"What do you mean?"

He lowered his voice, even though they were alone. "Look, I'm on the edge of making a significant discovery in spinal cord regeneration."

"Regeneration? Wha—"

"Teaching the damaged spinal cord to heal itself." He continued when he saw Hal frown. "*Curing* paralysis, Hal. Making the lame walk."

"Really?"

"Yes, really."

"Cool."

"Maybe you couldn't make the connection without knowing what I'm doing, but I suspect that someone in the scientific community might be behind what is going on against me."

"Why?"

"Jealousy. Maybe they know I'm on the edge of something that will change all the dictums about spinal cord injury being permanent."

"Come on, Ryan. Doctors aren't like that. Scientists work together—"

"Then why just my baboon? She was the first higher mammal to have signs of a successful reversal of motor paralysis after acute SCI. And now why all my tapes and data storage books and my computers?"

Hal took a deep breath and blew it out through pursed lips. "I don't buy it." He shook his head. "Who knew what you were doing?"

The doctor shrugged. "Almost everyone in the neurosciences that is anyone keeps up with the progress in this area. But no one knew about my baboon study. No one except Elizabeth Hopkins."

"Why the big secret?"

Ryan leaned forward. "'Cause I want to be the first." He sat back. "There, I've admitted it. Sounds pretty foolish, doesn't it?"

"Maybe not. I'm sure making the discovery carries a certain prestige, not to mention recognition for the university and access to grant money." He nodded. "That's very understandable, I'd say."

I also have some old debts to pay. Mistakes to erase.

"Could this Elizabeth you mentioned be behind this? You said she was the only one who knew about the baboon study."

"I don't think so. She was into the study, perhaps even more so than I. What would motivate her to trash it?"

"Did she have access to Paige's I.D. badge? Could she have given it to the Henry kid?" He paused. "Could she have sold the baboon to another research team and pinned the rap on this animal rights group?"

Ryan shook his head. "Not Elizabeth. She's a great neurosurgery resident. She's not that kind of manipulator."

"Then we're back to this being only an animal rights thing." He tapped his fingers on the top of his briefcase. "And they picked your lab simply because of the type of higher animal you were putting through this torture . . . uh, experiment." He winced. "Sorry."

He stood to pace again. "Would you be open to explaining in general terms what your goals of research are? Or let me make a statement about your totally humanitarian ideals of restoring movement to the paralyzed? How mad could people be at your experiments if they knew what they were for?"

"I just don't think it's time for everyone to know. I had hoped to have more data before springing this at the next academy—"

"You don't have that luxury now." He spun around to face Ryan. "I have another idea. One that even old Whiteside might respond to." He smiled.

"What?"

"Do you have any paralyzed patients we could work with?"

"What do you have in mind?"

"Envision twenty or thirty wheelchair patients jamming Whiteside's office to protest his decision to interfere with research that might put them on their feet again. It could be a media frenzy! It would look like a March of Dimes telethon . . . so many wheelchairs in there, he couldn't get in or out."

Ryan chuckled.

"Believe me, that would be an event Whiteside would do anything to avoid. He doesn't want to look like he isn't a friend of the disabled community. He'd be dead in the water politically before he ever entered the game." Hal laughed. "You haven't even been formally charged with a crime, Ryan," he added. "I think if the prosecuting attorney finds out what you're really doing, he'll find it beneficial to stop harassing you—regardless of the money Mr. Henry must be throwing around."

"Now I'm feeling better." He stretched and yawned. "What about the chances of getting the Henry boy on the grand larceny charge?"

"Without the body of the baboon as proof? Very slim."

"I seriously doubt he could keep it alive."

"I said 'body.'" He put his foot on the leather seat to tie his shoelace. "Of course, if they can find definitive trace evidence that the baboon was in the boy's car, that would strengthen the case against him, even if they never find the baboon."

"And I suppose there's little chance that dear Aunt Lucy will turn up with the car."

"I think you're starting to understand how Mr. Henry operates," Hal responded with a nod. "Young Richard Henry is using the dark side of our legal system, I'm afraid. Wealth can always buy legal advice, but it won't always be ethical."

"So what's the next step?"

"Let me have another chat with the prosecuting attorney. I promise not to give away the secrets of your research, Ryan, but . . . I will make sure Mr. Whiteside understands how loud the voice of the disabled community will be if he takes this any further."

◆ ◆ ◆

Abby checked the oven at the cafe while Marty made more coffee.

"You should have seen Nathan when I gave him those van keys." She shut the oven door. "He almost cried. I kept wiping his eyes. He was sniffing, all choked up." She paused. "He seems different, Marty. He never cried before."

"You'd cry too if you were paralyzed."

Abby shook her head. "It's not like that at all." She smoothed the front of her white apron. "He never wallows in self-pity or cries about his accident while I'm around. This was different. He cried because he was touched by what I did."

Marty rolled her eyes.

"Why did you do that?"

"You know what I think."

"What?"

Marty sighed. "Don't make me say it."

"I don't care what you say—Nathan's different. Softer. Like he values what I'm doing."

"Stop it, Abs. Listen to yourself. I didn't blame you for hating him before, OK? I applauded you, remember? Don't let your sympathy blind you into thinking he's different."

"But he—"

"What is it with you, Abby? Do you feel guilty? Is this your penance . . . taking care of poor ol' Nate?"

"No! It's—" She stopped. "That social worker said something that hit me pretty hard. She said God wants families to stay together." *Something you would know little about.*

"What does she know about your situation? It's her job to get Nate back home, don't you see?"

Abby felt her eyes moistening. "I'm *trying* to do the right thing. Maybe for the first time."

Marty bit her lip. "That's real nice," she said with an edge to her voice. She turned toward the swinging door leading to the dining hall. "I'd better count the breakfast receipts for Mr. Knitter."

CHAPTER
13

THE CLIP-CLOP of horse's hooves broke the quiet Sunday afternoon. Melissa skipped to the front window. "It's Chestnut!" She pressed her nose to the window. "He's stopping here!"

"Chestnut?" Nathan backed his chair around to face the front door.

"Rachel Yoder's horse!"

He moved forward to see the black buggy in the driveway. He watched as Rachel quickly tied the horse to the mailbox post before reaching back in the buggy for a large basket.

"Are we having a picnic?" Melissa asked hopefully.

"It looks like it."

Rachel knocked.

"Open the door, Mel."

She pulled the door open with a grunt. "Hi, Mrs. Yoder."

"Come on in, Rachel," Nathan encouraged.

Rachel was dressed in a light blue dress with a solid black sweater. On her head she wore a deep blue bonnet over a white covering, according to the Old Order Mennonite tradition. "I brought you some dinner." She stepped timidly forward, her eyes on Nathan.

"That's real nice of you." He shifted his wheelchair to the left with a tap of his head control. He followed this movement with an exaggerated stretch of his chin and neck, pulling the corners of his mouth toward his ears.

Rachel stepped back, staring at Nathan's face. Silently she mimicked his facial grimace.

"I'm OK, Rachel. Just stretching a little." He offered a smile. "Why don't you put that stuff in the kitchen? It's just through there," he added, nodding his head forward."

"Uh, sure." She disappeared for a minute as Melissa gathered her papers from the floor.

When Rachel returned, Melissa held up her construction paper. "We had Sunday school right here!"

She took the paper and smiled. "This must be . . ."

"Noah's ark! See the lion? Daddy drew that part." She plopped to the floor to continue her project.

Nathan spoke quietly. "I could have done better if Melissa had held the paper still."

Rachel squinted. "You drew this?"

He nodded.

"He draws wif his teef." Melissa colored the lion with a brown crayon, making quick, heavy strokes as if she were scratching the lion's back.

Rachel looked around. "You're alone?"

"Abby should be home soon. She had to work in the cafe."

She looked down, diverting her eyes from his chair.

"I'm really OK once I'm in my chair. I'm pretty independent this way."

She nodded and began to retreat to the front door. "Abby may want to heat the casserole up for a few minutes before you eat it."

"Thanks a lot, Rachel. You really didn't have to do this."

"I know." She reached for the door.

"Rachel?" He waited until she turned back. "I'm sorry about Jonas. Abby told me that he—" He hesitated.

"Killed himself."

They paused for a moment, the silence between them broken only by the sound of Melissa's brown crayon.

With his voice just above a whisper, he asked, "What happened, Rachel?" He tried to capture her eyes, which were concentrating on the floor in front of her. "Rachel, I—I don't remember that day. My injury robbed my memory," he explained. "I think that finding out what happened to Jonas . . . Well, it might help explain what happened to me."

"I don't see how that could be. My son is gone. How could that relate to your accident?"

Nathan shook his head slowly. "I'm not sure, Rachel. Maybe it's only coincidence that his funeral was the day I was shot. But I have a feeling there's more . . . a link I can't explain just yet." *I can't tell her about the note in Dr. Hannah's lab. Not until I understand it for myself.*

"I have faith, Nathan. Some people think it's too simple, but I believe God has his purposes and I don't need to understand them. My boy is dead. As much as I would like to know why, I know there may not be answers for that." She lifted her eyes to Nathan. "Just as there are no answers for your whys." She paused. "Brother Showalter says my job is to trust, not to understand."

Nathan didn't know how to respond. "Would you be comfortable just telling me about his last week?"

"Jonas had a hard life. He constantly struggled with his sugar diabetes." Her eyes began to mist. "If that wasn't enough, now I have to listen to the rumors about drug abuse." She pulled open the door. "If that's true, I'm not sure I want to know. Let's just let my son's memory rest!"

Nathan watched the door close and shook his head. He looked at Melissa, who had run to the window to watch Rachel and her horse. She watched with wide eyes as Rachel took the reins and steered the horse-drawn buggy back onto the street. As the clip-clop noise receded, she turned to her father.

"Why didn't you tell her our secret?"

"What secret, Mel?"

She put her hands on her hips in a defiant pose. "That her son didn't kill hisself." She knelt down to admire her artwork again. "That's what you told me, didn't you, Daddy? It was our secret."

◆ ◆ ◆

Ryan Hannah sat in a corner table at Luigi's, studying his daughter's face while she ate. "If I ate as much as you, I'd be . . . well, heavier than I am now," he chuckled.

"Dad, I *run*." She paused and stabbed a forkful of dressing-laden salad. "You should get out there with me."

"Right." He looked at his watch.

"Do you have to go back to the hospital? It's Sunday evening!"

"It's always good to pop in on the residents on the weekend. It keeps them on their toes." He shrugged. "Besides, I told Elizabeth I'd help her with the calculations for the insurance claims."

"Why do you drive yourself so hard?" She paused, enjoying another bite of warm bread. "You have everything—tenure, respect, money, a great job, intelligence . . ." She glanced at him before throwing in, "A *relatively* handsome appearance for an old man . . ."

Ryan coughed.

". . . and a wonderful daughter," she said with an exaggerated smile. "What more could you want?"

He ignored her question. "Why do you smile like that?" He imitated her, widely displaying his front teeth. "You have such a pretty natural smile when no one is looking, but as soon as someone says 'Smile,' you pull out all the stops as if they wanted to see your molars or something."

"Dad!"

"I'm serious. I have a whole collection of my beautiful daughter in every elementary school picture going—" He imitated her smile again.

"Like that stupid picture you had on your desk."

"It isn't stupid. I love that picture."

"You'll have to find another. I confiscated that one."

Ryan shook his head and laughed quietly. "It was a cute stage."

"Thirteen-year-olds do not want to be *cute*." She opened a packet of crackers. "You didn't answer my question. Why are you so driven when you already have everything?"

"You're really wondering why *you* are so driven."

"Just because you cut people's brains up for a living doesn't mean you can psychoanalyze my question. I'm asking about you."

"I don't cut people's brains up. Neurosurgery is a meticulous art—"

"You're avoiding my question."

Silence hung between them for a moment as Ryan took a deep breath. Paige balanced three crackers against each other as a small teepee.

"I'm not sure how to answer, Paige. We all have our insecurities, things that keep us striving for perfection. You're old enough to know that."

"Even you? You're practically the best-known neurosurgeon in the state."

"Even me."

Paige looked down and rearranged her teepee. "Mom says I'm a lot like you."

"I know." He smiled. "Sorry." Before he could stop himself, he added, "Has she tried to cure *you* yet?"

She huffed.

"I-I'm sorry, Paige." His eyes fell.

"*Mom* understands this stuff. Not that you would value what she thinks I need to hear."

He sighed and continued staring at the floor. "OK, OK. I *do* want to know what she says."

"The only cure for having to be the best," she added softly, "is understanding God's unconditional love." She added a fourth cracker to her tent.

"Hmmm." He took a cracker from his salad plate and slid it across the table. "Sounds like you've been listening."

She ran her fingers across her left ear, hesitating slightly as she touched each of four earrings.

"It's OK to be the best, Paige."

"But it's not OK to feel bad about yourself if you aren't perfect."

He made a face. "How old are you?"

"Nineteen."

"Going on forty." He looked up to see the waiter approaching with their entrées. "I know one thing you're best at," he said, pushing aside his salad plate. "You're the best daughter for this old perfectionist."

"Stiff competition too. I'm your *only* daughter."

◆ ◆ ◆

Back in Fisher's Retreat, Nathan looked through the new automatic glass door that exited off his remodeled kitchen. If he moved within a few feet of the door, an electronic eye caused the door to open, giving him access to the back patio and sidewalk. "Should I call Mel?"

"Let her play. She hasn't shown much interest in being outside since the tree was cut down." Abby dried her hands on a dish towel. "She can eat later."

"OK." He manipulated his chair around to the kitchen table. "It sure smells good."

"I told you Rachel could cook."

Abby busied herself with final table preparations while Nathan told her about his conversation with Rachel and Melissa.

She put a steaming casserole dish on the table. "I think you're making too much of this 'secret' thing. You have no idea whether what Melissa remembers is significant." She began filling water glasses. "I've heard you tease her a hundred times in the past about letting her in on a top-secret bit of official police information. You played that game with her all the time."

"Maybe you're right." He used his mouthstick to chase away a fly on his leg. "But why would I tell her *that*?"

"Nathan, none of us wanted to believe Jonas committed suicide. He seemed like a decent enough kid when I saw him in town." She shrugged. "I suspect you were just voicing your doubts, the same ones we all secretly harbored. The only difference is, you shared it with Mel."

She threw her shoulders back to imitate Nathan. "Come here, sugar. I've got top-secret police information—for your ears only." She flashed a quick smile before turning serious again and continuing in a low, sinister growl. "I'll bet you twenty-five Beanie Babies that Jonas Yoder didn't die like everyone said. He didn't kill himself, oh no." She squinted and looked slowly back and forth. "Did anyone else hear? Now don't you tell. This information could change the course of history."

He smiled at her imitation. "I don't act like that."

"Nathan Daniel McAllister, you act *exactly* like that."

Abby filled their plates and began eating and feeding Nathan. She tried at first to keep their forks separate, but every time she tried to talk, she became distracted and would eat from Nathan's fork or vice versa. "Oops. I did it again."

"Don't worry about it," he responded. "It doesn't bother me. As long as it's you, I don't care."

Abby nodded but still attempted to keep the forks straight.

"I think you need to consider Rachel's desires for privacy in this whole quest of yours. I doubt that their little community would be too happy about you stirring up a lot of skeletons."

"I knew that boy, Abby. He was always a quiet, polite kid." He paused to sip from a straw that Abby pushed toward him. "And I've spent enough time with the Ashby High kids to know a drug user when I see one. I think if Rachel has questions about the rumors circulating about her son, a little research might help clear the air rather than confirm her worst fears."

"Maybe. But you can't dig where she won't let you."

Nathan nodded. "And maybe I owe her an apology. She seemed a bit upset when she left this morning. Maybe I can talk with her when she comes for her dishes."

Or maybe I can get one of my PCAs to take the dishes and me to her farm. Perhaps I'll get more information if I talk to her on her turf.

◆ ◆ ◆

Elizabeth looked at the figure Ryan had circled on his marker-board: $52,385. "We'll never get that much out of these guys. Not without better documentation of our expenses." She sighed. "I'll call this Perkins guy at the insurance center again in the morning," she said, shaking her head. "But he's never going to believe this figure."

"Elizabeth, the price of the NTTF alone in this one animal was over six grand."

"I know that, and you know that. But you should try talking with this guy. It's kind of hard to expect him to want to cough up that kind of a payment without knowing the significance of an animal like Heidi."

"And next to impossible to document our expenses without our data books or computer records. Thank you, Brighton P.D.," he added sarcastically.

"It'd be easier to find the baboon than to get the university's insurance to cover the loss."

"I'm afraid at this point, we both know that's next to impossible."

"I have a different idea," she said, sitting on the edge of Ryan's lab desk after brushing aside a few papers. "Sue Richard Henry for the loss. He's loaded."

Ryan shook his head. "I've talked to my attorney. It sounds like there's little chance he'll ever be convicted of robbing the lab."

Elizabeth crossed her legs and tugged at the edges of her skirt. "I know that. But isn't there a difference between being guilty of a crime and being responsible for restitution? What was that O.J. Simpson thing . . . the difference between reasonable doubt and absolute guilt or something?" She made a snapping noise with her lips. "You know, didn't he have to pay the Goldmans because of a preponderance of evidence but wasn't guilty of the murder because of reasonable doubt?"

"Perhaps." He circled the figure again, this time in red. "But I doubt that anyone could get anything out of the Henrys with the law firm they've hired." He walked around his desk and sat down, trying hard not to be distracted by his colleague's legs, now dangling near his knees. "Honestly, I think our best approach is to start over. We did it once before—we can do it again. New animal. Different lab. Tighter security. I'll see if the dean will give me some space in the subbasement."

"We can't begin to reconstruct this project without the records."

"What about our backup data?"

"I have all the data in three separate folders on my computer, backed up on your computer, and all of that backed up on floppy disks, and all of that backed up by hand on our data books. But it's all with the Brighton P.D. now, pending the completion of their investigation, remember?"

"I'd been meaning to load it in my home computer . . . one of the many things I've never found time to do."

"Face it. Without our data books or our baboon, this project is dead in the water."

CHAPTER
14

PAIGE TRAVELED a hundred yards past the elaborate brick entrance before edging her father's Chevy Suburban off the road and onto the soft shoulder. *There,* she thought, shutting off the engine, *if I jog back in through the normal exit, that guy at the guardhouse will never even see me.*

She stepped out of the vehicle into the night air, thankful that the clouds had at least temporarily obscured the moon. She stretched for a minute before tying the Suburban's keys into her shoelaces. Then slowly, staying next to a line of trees, she jogged back toward the exclusive development known as The Woods. At the estate's entryway, a small guardhouse sat next to the road. This was flanked by two other curving entrance and exit roads, which met the highway at a gentle angle. Home owners could enter through the curving entrance road, after stopping to raise the barrier with their gate passes or come in on the main road by the guardhouse. People exiting The Woods would use the curving exit road if they were turning right onto the highway. People wishing to turn left would use the main road that passed the guardhouse.

Paige paused in the shadow of a streetlamp, hunching along the long brick wall that was part of the decorative entrance. She waited until a green Mercedes pulled to a stop beside the guardhouse. Then, with the guard's attention on the driver of the car, she casually resumed her jog up the curving exit road.

She jogged along the quiet, well-lit street that wound around the forested development. The houses were expansive, and all had brick-walled entrances that appeared to be smaller versions of The Woods' main entryway. The houses, each having three- and four-car garages, emitted soft lights that sprayed into the surrounding trees and created eerie, tall shadows. Her heart quickened as she heard a car slow down behind her and then creep past. She watched as a white Bonneville gradually moved ahead. The driver, silhouetted briefly by a streetlamp, had a phone to his ear.

Why are you driving so slow? She slowed her pace to increase the distance between her and the car. She saw the brake lights flash. *What is this guy doing? Should I turn around?* She hesitated for a moment, then continued jogging as the car pulled away.

She squinted at each home as she passed. *I should have known there wouldn't be any names posted here. How will I know which one is the Henrys' place? I should've done my homework.*

As she jogged deeper into the development, the houses were spaced further and further apart. *These must be at least five-acre plots. Larger than my father's anyway.*

Paige winced as she heard another vehicle. This time, to her relief, the vehicle did not slow down. A red BMW convertible, with a license tag reading "RH III," sped on.

RH III? That has to be Mr. Henry! She quickened her pace and squinted at the car as it disappeared around a corner. *Faster, Paige,* she chided herself, *or you won't see where he's going.*

With her heart pounding, she rounded the corner. Ahead, at the end of a large cul-de-sac, she saw brake lights flash and then stay on. *He's stopping!* She watched as the convertible pulled into a long drive. She kept her pace until she was within a few hundred feet of the driveway, then slowed to a walk. At the brick entryway, she stopped and peered over the wall. The red BMW was in a four-car garage that had the door up. Paige gasped. The house was huge and sat at least fifty yards from the road. She focused her attention on the garage, where a man lifted a large box from the backseat. He hoisted it up by a handle on the top and placed it on the trunk of the convertible. Then the man bent forward and appeared to rest his head against the end of the box. Paige squinted again and pulled her upper body onto the top of the brick wall to see more clearly around a holly tree. *It's an animal carrier. Like people use on an airplane!*

He's looking into it! That has to be Heidi!

Paige jumped down onto the pine needle mulch on the other side of the wall, wincing as a branch snapped beneath her feet. She stayed still for a moment, not daring to look around the holly tree again. *I need to get a closer look.* She peered around the tree, relieved that the man seemed occupied with the large box in front of him. She was just about to make a dash for the cover of another tree when she heard another car approaching. She pressed her body against the brick wall and listened as the vehicle slowed, then moved on. She waited a full minute, trying to still her racing heart, before daring to look again. The man, whom she assumed was Richard Henry III, carried the container across the front of the garage and to a separate, adjacent building that appeared to be a small guest house. There he disappeared from view.

Paige heaved a sigh and pondered her next move. *I need to see inside that building.* She moved from the shadow of one tree to the next bordering the long, paved driveway. When she was twenty feet from the house, wondering how to cross in front of the garage, she saw the man again. He was empty-handed and whistling the *Jeopardy* theme song. He walked into the garage behind the BMW and paused to shut the car's trunk before the garage door shut and he disappeared from view. Quickly she dashed to the corner of the smaller building and knelt between two bushes. She quietly moved along the front of the building and around the side, where she was shielded from the light coming from the main house. She had just pressed her face against a darkened window when she heard a snapping sound behind her.

She turned, and a spotlight blinded her. "Hold it right there! Brighton police!"

◆ ◆ ◆

Nathan wiggled his head, trying to get comfortable against his feather pillow. It seemed like the more he moved, the deeper his head sank into it, smashing his nose against the pillowcase and making it harder for him to get his breath. "Ugh," he grunted, shrugging his shoulder against the soft mound. The pillow didn't budge. He bit at it with his teeth, trying to drag it into a new position, but to no avail. It was too tightly stuck under his shoulder to move that way. Next he placed his face into the depression left by his head and pulled up the pillowcase, but the feathers in the pillow didn't move with it.

"Abby," he whispered, "are you awake?"

He stared into the darkness.

"Abby?"

In a moment he heard the creak of the old bed upstairs, followed by footfalls on the stairs.

Abby appeared in a moment and turned on the lamp by Nathan's bed. She had a smirk on her face and was wearing one of Nathan's T-shirts.

"What's funny?"

"I was just laughing at myself." She shook her head. "I forgot this monitor was only for listening." She smiled. "I answered when you whispered my name. Like you could hear me. Duh."

Nathan smiled. "You're cute."

She touched his hair. "You didn't get me up to tell me that."

"You're right," he confessed. "I need a new pillow. This one's killin' me. My face sinks in so far, it covers my nose."

"I have a foam one upstairs."

Abby disappeared. Nathan followed mentally as he heard first her steps on the stairs, then in the hallway upstairs, and then the sound of the hall closet opening and shutting.

"Here," she said moments later, entering the room again. "Let's try this one." She pulled the feather pillow out and replaced it with the foam one.

He bounced his head against it. "Seems better. Thanks, Abs."

She held the feather pillow up before pushing it into her face. "Hmm. I like this one. Maybe I'll use it."

She snapped off the light. "Night, Nate." She paused at the door and spoke as she leaned against the doorway. "Nate?"

"Yes?"

"I was thinking about what you said about apologizing to Rachel Yoder. You meant it, didn't you?"

"Well, uh, sure I meant it. Why?"

Abby paused. "I don't know. It just struck me as different for you, that's all."

"Different?"

"Unusual." She stepped back into the room, clutching Nathan's pillow in a bear hug. "I never remember you apologizing to anyone before . . . before your . . ." Her voice faded.

"My accident?"

Abby's voice sounded thick. "The sh-shooting."

Nathan thought for a moment. "I hope it's a good change."

She squeezed the pillow tighter. "It *is* a good change, Nathan." She retreated into the living room.

Nathan listened as she whispered the phrase again before beginning to climb the old stairs. "A good change."

◆ ◆ ◆

Ryan pulled back the curtain from the window in time to see Paige jump from the Suburban and run for the house. Behind her vehicle a white Bonneville sat with blue lights flashing atop the dashboard. As Paige opened the door, the Bonneville exited the Hannah driveway, its tires squealing.

Paige pushed past her father and into the den, where she collapsed onto the leather couch.

"Paige?" Ryan approached his daughter. "You're trembling."

She nodded forcefully and pressed her fist against her closed mouth.

"What's going on? Was that a police escort? Are you OK?"

"I'm OK, Daddy," she gasped before dissolving into tears.

Ryan paced in front of the couch. "Paige, it's late. I was worried about you."

Slowly, between sobs, she told about her ordeal, starting with her harebrained idea about seeing where the Richard Henry III mansion was, and then hoping to collect some evidence that might help prove Heidi was hidden there. She told of seeing the red BMW and the animal carrier and of being caught by Detective Mansfield. "I saw how frustrated you were," she cried, "and how little the police seemed to be doing." She wiped her eyes. "Daddy, I know it was a stupid idea."

Ryan shook his head and muttered, "I can't believe this! How could you do such a thing? Why would you do this?"

"I wanted to help. This whole thing is my fault! I told Richard Henry the Fourth about your lab, and he used my I.D. to get in. If it weren't for me, none of this would have happened!"

Ryan protested, "It isn't your fault." He paused. "Did the officer arrest you?"

She shook her head. "He just told me to leave the investigation to the police. He said they already had the house under surveillance. Once he realized it was me, he just followed me home. Daddy, he wouldn't listen to me. I told him Mr. Henry had Heidi, but he just kept staring at me and telling me he'd check into it."

"Did you actually see Heidi?"

"Not exactly. But it was an animal carrier. Why would he be coming in so late with another animal?" She shook her head. "I think the police are afraid of him."

"It's not like they can just break in and search the house."

"Dad, Heidi's in there! I know it!"

Ryan looked at his watch and sighed. "It's late, Paige. I'm going to talk to my attorney tomorrow. Maybe he can convince the police to search the house."

Paige shuddered. "I've never been so afraid."

He understood. "Paige, did the detective tell the Henrys he caught you trespassing on their property?"

She sniffed. "No," she said. "Right away he practically dragged me to his car, like I was some criminal or something. Then he took me to the Suburban. I had to ride in the back of his car and everything. Then once we were at the Suburban, he demanded I show him my driver's license." She paused to think. "No, he didn't report me to the Henrys."

Ryan stood, feeling too nervous to sit still. "Be thankful for small favors." He looked at his daughter's face. Her eyes were red and her hair in disarray. *Yes, be thankful for small favors, Paige. I don't think the Henrys need another excuse to lambaste our family.*

CHAPTER
15

Oɴ Mᴏɴᴅᴀʏ morning Nathan awoke before the sun rose. He had been positioned on his right side for the night, and because his clock was behind him, he had no idea if it was early or real early.

Mentally he reviewed his last few days. There was an answered prayer—his return home. But many unanswered questions still bombarded him.

He wondered about Jonas Yoder, about the timing of his funeral and Nathan's own shooting. He questioned why Jonas's and his own name would appear together on a sign stating, "HᴜRT ME." *Were the names written by the perpetrator of the lab break-in? Why? Was it a warning? A threat?* He thought about his conversation with Abby and the secret he'd shared with Mel. *Am I making something out of nothing? Or is this another clue telling me to dig further?*

His thoughts drifted to his mysterious caller and the strain in her voice. *Was the message for real, and one to be heeded?*

He sorted and resorted the information he'd deduced from the call: *The caller was female. Sounded young. Sounded upset, worried, even afraid.* The emotion of the caller was not difficult for him to read.

The reason behind the emotion was another matter altogether. *She feels responsible in some way for my shooting. What was it she said? "This is all my fault." How could anyone except Brian be responsible? Is it an associate of Lester Fitts? A drug pusher, or a user perhaps?*

The identity of the caller was just as much a mystery. *She must have been from around here. She saw me on a Carlisle TV station on Wednesday night, didn't she?*

Could it have been Abby? He didn't think so, but he wasn't ready to rule out anyone. In fact, ever since the call, he found himself listening carefully to every woman's voice he heard, including his mother's and Rachel's. So far, none sounded like the voice he'd heard.

And what did the caller know about Nathan's shooting? *Was she there? Is that how she knows something . . . or thinks she knows something? She said, "You followed me, didn't you?" Does she mean I followed her to the house where I was shot? Or some other time?*

Nathan heard footsteps coming down the creaky staircase. *Abby's up. Must be 5:30. Should I share any of this with Abby?* He knew the answer to his own question. *Not now. If Abby thinks I'm in danger, she'll want me to go back to Briarfield Manor where I'll be safe . . . and alone.*

Abby's silhouette appeared in the doorway. She squinted into the dim light of Nathan's room.

"Morning, honey," Nathan said.

She walked forward and sat on the edge of his bed. "You're up early." She ran her fingers through his hair. "Can I get you anything?"

"Some water would be good."

She touched his forehead. "You're sweating."

"It's just this quilt. Could you pull it off my shoulders?"

"You should have called me," she responded as she folded back the patchwork comforter.

"I thought you'd be up soon. I didn't want to wake you."

Abby frowned. "I wouldn't mind. I want you to be OK."

She left and returned with a tall glass of cool water. "Here."

"Thanks."

"I need to run."

Nathan nodded. "Just leave the lights on. And could you flip on the radio?"

"Sure." She pulled up the window shade and turned on the radio. "Jim Over should be here soon. I'll see you around 2." She leaned forward and kissed the corner of his mouth. "Bye, Nate."

"Bye, love."

◆ ◆ ◆

After morning hospital rounds, Ryan breezed into the cranberry hall and nearly into his administrative assistant, who stood directly in his pathway, holding up his daily planner. "Here."

"Thanks, Trish. Where did I leave this?" he asked, opening the little black book.

"On your desk in the lab. Dr. Hopkins brought it over first thing this morning."

"I'd be lost without it," he mumbled, moving to the side to get into his office.

Trish moved into his path again. "Not so fast. Let's look at your day." She lifted the planner from his hands. "I've pushed your eight o'clock case to 10, so you can—"

"No," he interrupted. "I told Dr. Wingfield to get that case on early. I don't like starting crainiotomies late."

"I know that, Dr. Hannah," she snapped bluntly. "I've been scheduling your O.R. cases for six years." She pushed her oversized glasses higher on her face and glared at her employer.

He looked at her and attempted a weak smile. His assistant's golden hair was pushed behind her ears, unwashed and unstyled, something Ryan had never seen before. Her stature was short but trim, and her body was well muscled, reflecting the hours she spent at the local YMCA. He pushed past her into his office. "OK, what's going on?"

"The dean's office called. He wants to meet with you as soon as you arrive this morning."

"Pritchard?"

She nodded. "His secretary has already called three times this morning, asking if you're in."

"Great. What does he want?"

Trish sighed before erupting in a loud voice, "What does everyone want around here?"

Ryan frowned and sat down. "Take a seat," he said, pointing at a chair. "Please."

His youthful assistant obeyed, then slumped forward.

"This isn't like you, Trish."

She stared at the folder in her hands. "I know. It's just—" She halted. "The robbery—"

"Yes, the robbery. And the four phone calls I've taken this morning from news reporters seeking comments from you. And the police in my office." She sighed deeply again. "I came in at 6 this morning just to try to get all the work done that I can't seem to do because of all these interruptions."

"This will pass," he said, holding up his hand. "My attorney has a plan to make some of the aggravation go away."

"It won't be soon enough for me."

"What else needs attention?"

She opened the folder in her lap. "We are under budget in capital expenditure requests for O.R. instrumentation."

"That should make the dean happy."

"That's great if that's your goal, but if we don't ask for more money, they will redo next year's allocation for equipment to match what we asked for this year. If you ask for more this year, you will likely be able to get more next year. So . . ."

"What a game." He pinched his eyes tightly shut while he thought. "OK, ask Dr. Griffin's secretary to come up with a figure for the stereotactic biopsy equipment he's been bugging me to get. Add that to the request and see what we come up with."

Trish made a note. "Mr. Bridges from Brighton Care called and said the grace period stops at the end of the month. After that, any patient covered by their plan will be going over to McCue for all neurosurgical care."

"Unless we agree to their fee schedule."

"Bingo."

"What percent of our business is with Brighton Care?"

"Currently they have 22 percent of the local market, but I hear rumors that Quincy Foods is about to sign. They have 2,000 employees."

"I'll survey the department." He paused. "What else?"

"Dr. Kennel turned down your request for another surgical intern. He says his boys are already doing too much time on neurosurgery."

Ryan stiffened. "I'm the chairman, and I—"

"But he's the director of the general surgery residency program, and he says he has to follow the national guidelines or risk losing the accreditation of his program."

Ryan stood to pace. "What else?"

"Just these phone messages." She handed him a list before pushing another letter into his hand. "And this. Sign at the bottom."

"What is it?" He scrawled his signature.

"A letter of medical necessity for a StimMaster for one of your quad patients. I just used our standard letter and filled in the blanks." She pointed at the specifics. "Nathan McAllister. C3-4. Complete. His date of injury is cited here. All the routine."

"Hmmm. I remember this guy now. Nice fellow. C3-4 complete, eh?" His rubbed his chin. "Just like Heidi." He nodded his head before adding, "Unusual to be complete, you know. Most quads have some preservation of function below the injury—some sensation or something."

"Thanks," she said, taking back the letter. "Now, should I tell Dr. Pritchard you're in?"

"Just like Heidi," he mumbled before looking up. "Huh? Sure, let him know I'm in."

◆ ◆ ◆

Brian Turner laid the manila folder in Marge's in-box just as Joe Gibson entered.

"Hi, Chief. How's the back?"

Joe nodded. "Better. Joan fixed me up with some of that heat cream of hers."

He smiled and brushed past him. "One of the perks of being married to the town pharmacist, huh?"

"Hey, could you take my car up to Ned's? He called and said the tires are in."

"Sure thing, Chief." Brian nodded and left.

Joe looked at Marge. "Morning, Marge."

"Morning, Joe." She motioned to the coffeemaker. "Just made it. And there are biscuits by the microwave."

"Mmmm." He sipped the fresh brew. "I've been thinking about Nathan."

She looked up.

"I think maybe I'm wrong about keeping him from looking at the case file concerning his shooting." He shrugged. "I have questions about the case, but maybe I shouldn't jump to conclusions. I don't have any concrete evidence that Nathan did anything wrong."

"I would never believe wrong about that boy," Marge chimed in. "He's always been a straight arrow."

"As long as Nathan is on a search, maybe it would help him to look at the file . . . as long as he can handle it if we turn up something he doesn't want to hear."

"It doesn't seem like he could lose much more than he already has." Marge lifted a biscuit from a napkin on her desk. "I'm glad you changed your mind. I think you're makin' the right choice, Joe."

"Give him a call. He can inspect the file here in the office."

"There aren't any pictures of him in there, are there? I'm not sure he could handle that."

"No. The helicopter picked him up before we photographed the place."

"Do you think he'll be able to come here?" She frowned. "How does he get around?"

"They have a special van for him. But I suppose I could take the file to him. As long as I stay with him, there shouldn't be anything wrong with that."

Marge stood and went to a file cabinet. She hummed as she looked. "Where did that file go? I thought I'd just put it—"

"It's right here." Joe lifted an expandable file from Marge's in-box.

"Hmmm." She pulled her blue sweater tighter around her. "Would you like me to get the other file he wanted? The Jonas Yoder file?"

The chief of police sighed and studied himself for a moment in the small hand mirror Marge kept on her desk. He was heavy but muscular, and his dark brown hair belied his age of fifty. He had dark, penetrating eyes that didn't quite focus in the same direction—the kind of eyes that were an advantage to a lawman because the people around him were never exactly sure where he was looking. He brushed his hair with his fingers before setting the mirror down again and answering Marge's question. "I guess not, Marge. I know the Yoders, and they want to put this whole thing behind them. Just because the Yoder boy's funeral was on the day Nathan was shot is probably not sufficient justification to open the file to him." He shook his head slowly. "I want to do right by Nate, Marge. Really, I do. But I think it's enough to let him see the records about his accident."

"He'll appreciate that. I'll let him know."

Joe nodded. "Thanks, Marge. Tell him I should be able to bring them by later this morning if that's all right with him."

◆ ◆ ◆

Ryan sat next to Dean Alan Pritchard at a large conference table. Opposite him, a university hospital attorney, Greg McLaughlin, sat tapping his pen against his briefcase.

The dean squinted when he talked, accentuating the abundant wrinkles around his eyes. He straightened his tie and smoothed it out over his pin-striped shirt before pushing another newspaper article toward Ryan. "I suppose you know the AP wire has this stuff. I saw a similar article in the *Washington Post* this morning."

Ryan nodded. "I've already consulted with Hal Ferguson, my attorney, about this. We have a plan to help quiet the waters." He hesitated. "I really don't think the university needs to get into this—"

"We *are* into this," the dean snorted, "whether we want to be or not." He slapped the paper. "They mentioned the university hospital six times in this article alone." He looked over his half-glasses. "I don't need to tell you what that kind of publicity can do in a competitive market."

"It's all distorted. They have no idea what's going on in my lab."

"Neither do I, apparently. Did you run this study through the proper channels? Does the institution review board know about this?"

"Sir, the review board is only concerned with studies involving human patient trials. You know—"

"Just what *are* you doing up there, Ryan? I thought you were growing tumors in rats or something. And now the first time I get wind of your new project is when I see it on the evening news."

"I'm working on the same thing I've been trying to accomplish for the last decade, in one form or another. Spinal cord regeneration."

Ryan watched the other two men exchange glances. "So Dr. Hopkins is not the only one around here with delusions of grandeur," Dr. Pritchard added.

"You've spoken with Dr. Hopkins?"

"She responded to my call right away, Ryan."

"So you already have the information you've requested." Ryan pushed back from the table. "What do you want from me?"

"Cooperation, Ryan," the dean responded. He looked at the hospital attorney. "Greg, why don't you tell Ryan about our arrangement?"

The three-piece-suited consultant opened his briefcase and cleared his throat. "Dr. Hannah, I'm sure you know that we haven't been just sitting around while the media throws mud at the university. We've been taking steps to deal with this situation since it first appeared on the news last Wednesday." He nodded to Ryan and continued, "I've spoken with the prosecuting attorney, Mr. Byron Whiteside, and with several attorneys of Richard Henry the Fourth."

"I am capable of handling my own legal affairs," Ryan responded before adding, "with all due respect, Mr. McLaughlin."

"This is a university matter, Ryan," the dean cautioned, checking his watch. "Cut to the bottom line, Greg."

The attorney shrugged. "Today at four o'clock Mr. Whiteside's staff will release a memo stating that your lab has been thoroughly investigated and that the animal research, while unusual, was presented in a distorted light. He will also state that serious questions regarding the authenticity of the photographs remain and that concern exists over the way the photographs were obtained." He paused. "Mr. Henry will not dispute this and will cease any public finger-pointing over the activities in your lab. Subsequent to the prosecuting attorney's announcement, the university will assure the public that they are conducting a thorough internal audit of all animal research, including the activities in your lab."

Ryan felt his cheeks redden. "What's the catch?"

"You will agree to not press any charges over the breaking and entering. And you will not pursue the matter of your stolen animal any further."

"But the kid is guilty! And I've done nothing wrong. I've talked to my attorney . . . I think we can silence the prosecuting attorney's office and go after the kid."

"Ryan," the dean responded, "we've talked to Hal Ferguson too. We know all about your little plans. Believe me, if I thought it would work, or if there was another way . . ." His voice trailed off.

"There *is* another way! If we give out some generalities about my project and get the disabled community to support us, the public perception of what is going on around here will radically change."

"We need this problem to go away today, Ryan. Now. Not tomorrow. We don't have time for your plan to work. We need to squash this ASAP. And Mr. Whiteside is ready to put this problem to rest this afternoon . . . if you'll cooperate."

"I'm supposed to roll over and let this kid go scot-free so the university can save face?" He pointed at the dean. "Why don't we just show the media we have a little backbone, that we won't put up with this sort of mess?"

McLaughlin folded his hands. "The only thing people will remember is those photographs, Dr. Hannah. If the university pursues a case against the kid, I can promise you, we'll end up looking like the giant coming down on a poor defenseless kid who was only trying to do what he thought was right."

The dean pointed a finger back at Ryan. "So do the right thing, Ryan."

"And what about my baboon? And my lab computers, all my data?"

"The police will return the confiscated materials. They won't be needed if there isn't going to be a trial." Pritchard paused and added quietly, "And your loss will be compensated by a private contribution."

The deal felt oily. Ryan didn't need to ask where the contribution would come from. Likely from the same pockets who would finance the next campaign for Mr. Whiteside. He stood up.

"Do we have an understanding?" the attorney asked.

"Oh, I understand all right. But we don't have a deal, Mr. McLaughlin."

The dean squinted and wiped the sweat from his forehead. "I don't think you understand, Ryan. You will not press charges against the Henry boy. We've already negotiated this deal."

Ryan retreated to the door. "I'll talk to my attorney."

"Do that, Ryan. I think you'll see things differently then."

The neurosurgeon headed for the door. Behind him he heard the dean make a final comment. "Don't make a mistake that could jeopardize your career. We wouldn't enjoy sacrificing one of our best."

Ryan clenched his teeth and kept walking, needing to be somewhere, anywhere except that room. *I built this surgical department. No one speaks to me like that!*

◆　◆　◆

For an hour Nathan carefully examined the material that Joe Gibson had spread out on the table in front of him. Nathan moved the pages around using his mouthstick, and Joe sat close by to help and to explain what Nate was seeing. Everything was as he expected. He read descriptive reports of the house, including detailed reports of the amount of heroin found and other drug paraphernalia present, and a scale drawing of the front of the house and the front yard, where the shooting had taken place.

"What's this?" Nathan pointed to a photograph with his mouthstick.

"The wall just inside the front door, showing the location of a bullet mark." Joe sighed. "Later the bullet was removed from that spot and was shown to have originated from Brian's gun."

"How about this? That's my car!"

"No, it's Brian's. The windshield was essentially destroyed by Lester Fitts's 9mm," he chuckled. "Fortunately for Brian, Lester was a terrible shot." He pointed at the scale drawing of the front yard. "See? Brian's patrol car was here. Yours was here. Brian was here, on the sidewalk, when Lester exited the house. When Lester started shooting, Brian advanced to this location, near this tree. Lester's bullets all went past Brian and into the car . . . except for this one," he added, pointing to another photograph of a tree trunk.

"And what's this? Syringes?"

"Yep. Regular syringes. Two cc type. They appear to be a generic syringe from an American medical supply house. My wife sells 'em at the pharmacy just like that."

"Where were they?"

"Upstairs bedroom, if you can call it that. The only thing up there was an old mattress on the floor. These were on the floor beside the mattress."

"And this?"

"The same room, with a little wider angle. Here are the syringes on the floor."

Hmmm. Syringes on the floor under the window. The window is open. Unusual for November.

"What's this?"

"The floor inside the front door."

Nathan winced. "My blood."

Joe nodded. "A lot of it."

"What's in the envelope?"

"Photographs of Lester Fitts's autopsy and a medical examiner's report on your injuries."

"Can I see them?"

Joe opened the envelope and showed the contents to Nathan, who noted the autopsy findings and a full set of photographs documenting his injuries. He'd had two bullets recovered, one from the left ventricle of the heart and one from the upper abdomen, both of which were shown to have come from Brian's .38.

"What about the narrative scene summary?"

"It should be there. Marge usually paper-clips it inside the front folder cover." Joe reached over, slipped out the document, and laid it in front of Nathan.

For the first time Nathan read the official play-by-play description from the viewpoints of both Brian and Joe. As he read about himself, he felt a vague discomfort. "Brian first saw me after he ran to check for a pulse on Lester Fitts."

Joe nodded. "Lester fell backwards, and his hand was lying on your left foot."

"Could it be that a bullet went through Lester and into me?"

"I wondered the same thing, but the medical examiner's report suggests no exit wounds."

Nathan read the report slowly a second time. "You heard my 10-33 call too?"

Joe nodded. "Brian responded first because he was assigned to direct traffic at the intersection of Main Street and Spring Creek Road at the conclusion of the funeral. I got there second, after the gunfire, as I was coming from Spring Creek Church."

"The Yoder funeral?"

"Yeah."

"You mentioned before that I was unarmed."

"We found your piece locked in the case on the floor of your car."

"Why?" he whispered. "I always carried my weapon. Why?" He pulled a paper toward himself with his mouthstick and stared at the report. Silently he read the vivid account of their fight for his life. "You did CPR on me?"

Joe nodded again. "Until the EMT crew came from Carlisle."

Nathan swallowed hard. "I think I've seen enough."

The police chief cleared his throat. "Did this help? Did it jog your memory?" He glanced from Nathan to the file and back again before coughing into his hand. "I need to know what you remember, Nate." He drummed his fingers against the tabletop. "What were you doing in that safe house?"

Nathan attempted to follow Joe's gaze and pulled his head slightly to the left, trying to tell if the lawman was actually looking at him or a spot just above Nathan's right ear. "I—I can't remember anything, Joe. Looking at these reports is like reading a story about someone else. Not about me."

Joe gathered the papers and spoke with an exaggerated country accent. "I'd better get."

When he was at the door, Nathan spoke again. "Thanks."

"Sure. I should have opened the file for you sooner." He shrugged. "Maybe even at Briarfield—"

"No, I don't mean about the file. I mean about saving my life. You kept me from dying, Joe."

Joe met Nathan's stare for a moment before looking down, away from the wheelchair. "Sure, Nate," he said quietly. "Sure."

CHAPTER
16

"Afternoon, Abby." Thomas Yeager plopped onto the cafe stool and smiled. "How's Nate?" He lifted his cap, emblazoned with a corn seed emblem, to reveal thinning, white hair. His face, weathered and brown from too much sun, seemed to open up when he smiled. A smile for Pastor Yeager began at the tip of his chin and traveled through deep dimples on his cheeks, expanding like ripples in a pond to the corners of his eyes, which pulled down in a spray of wrinkles to meet it.

"He's getting along fine." She poured the pastor a glass of water and wiped the counter in front of him.

"It's been a few weeks since I saw him at Briarfield." He shook his head. "I hope I can see him a bit more often now that he's home."

"You were one of the few people who made the trip to see him. I know he appreciated it."

"I'm amazed at his attitude through this whole thing."

Abby agreed. "I don't think *I* could stay up like he does."

Mr. Yeager lifted his eyes from the menu in front of him. "How are you handling all this, Abby?"

"I'm fine," she quipped, hoping the slight tremor in her hands wouldn't betray her thoughts.

He nodded quietly.

You know I haven't been in church since Nathan's shooting.

"We've missed you over at Community, Abby." He took a sip of water before adding, "We have a ramp in the front. Shouldn't be any trouble for Nathan, the way he gets around."

Is my head transparent? You seem to know what I'm thinking.

The pastor lowered his voice, even though, with the clatter of activity in the cafe, no one could hear them. "I know an injury like Nate's can be pretty devastating for everyone in the family. The same thing happened to my brother's boy, Ray. He was injured in a diving accident." He paused. "It practically put my brother under the first year."

"I didn't know."

Mr. Yeager lifted his eyes to capture hers. "Do you have family you can count on? Someone to talk to?"

She shook her head. "My folks have been dead for a long time." She paused. "And Nate's parents . . ." Her voice trailed. "Well, you know Mark and Sally. They're having their own troubles adjusting."

The pastor nodded. "Abby, Doris and I would love to talk with you if you'd like to come by."

"I'm fine," she repeated, looking away to avoid his piercing, blue eyes.

"I'll have the vegetable plate. Brown beans, kale, and the cheddar mashed potatoes."

"Just like always."

"And to drink . . ."

"White milk. Two percent," she predicted.

"I'll have the sweet iced tea." He smiled again.

"What?"

"Never, never too old for a change, Abby."

She walked back to the kitchen, tearing off the paper from her notepad before hurrying into the employee rest room. There she locked the door, scrutinized her reflection in the mirror, and cried.

◆　◆　◆

Nathan sat at his computer, studying the Bible text displayed on the screen in front of him. His keyboard had been adapted so that his numerical keypad replaced the mouse. When he depressed the 7 key, in the upper left corner of the numeral keypad, the cursor on the screen moved up and to the left; when he depressed the 3 key, in the lower right corner of the keypad, the cursor on the screen moved down and to the right. The 5 key was click, and the plus key was double click.

He had never been a real student of the Bible before his paralysis. Now it seemed like his accident goaded him forward in a search for solace—and answers. Today he went to his computer to escape. The images of the drug safe house where his shooting had occurred, the images of Lester Fitts, and the written description of how his fellow officers worked to save his life seemed too much to process all at once. He needed to fill his mind with something else.

Because regular books were difficult for him to manage, he preferred the computerized text of the Bible and turned, as he often did, to familiar chapters speaking of future hope and help.

"Jesus Christ is the same yesterday and today and forever."

The verse from Hebrews 13 seemed to stand out. *What does that mean for me? The same. Never changing.*

Nathan thought back to the Gospels, the accounts of when Jesus walked the earth. *You healed then, didn't you, Lord? Even the lame.* He felt his heart quicken.

He read the verse again, this time aloud. "Jesus Christ is the same yesterday and today and forever."

Does this mean you heal today? He nodded his agreement. *Why didn't I pay attention to this before? You are the same Jesus today.*

Nathan searched through the Gospels for examples of Jesus' powerful touch. He stopped in John 9, fascinated by the discussion between Jesus and his disciples.

As he went along, he saw a man blind from birth. His disciples asked him, "Rabbi, who sinned, this man or his parents, that he was born blind?" "Neither this man nor his parents sinned," said Jesus, "but this happened so that the work of God might be displayed in his life."

Is this the answer? Was I injured so your work could be displayed in my life? He read further the account of Jesus' healing the man born blind. *Certainly you can work this way in my life too.*

Melissa walked into the bedroom where Nathan sat. "Daddy," she whined, "I'm bored."

He frowned.

"Can I call Tommy and see if he wants to play?"

"Tommy Evans?"

"From across the street. We can play in my sandbox."

"OK. Bring me the phone book."

Melissa opened the book. Slowly Nathan explained which pages to turn. "Good, now one more page. There," said Nathan. "I'll tell you what to dial."

She picked up the phone and followed her father's instructions. Nathan listened to his daughter's conversation.

"Can Tommy come over to play? . . . No, but my daddy's here."

Melissa stood there, shuffling her feet against the floor, then plopped on the bed and began a rhythmic bounce.

"Um, I need to ask." She looked at her father. "Can I go play at Tommy's?"

Nathan imagined the phone conversation on the other end. Ms. Evans didn't approve of him watching her son. He hesitated. "Sure. I guess so. But tell Ms. Evans that Tommy can come here the next time."

"I can come," she said excitedly into the phone. "Bye."

"Melissa, I want you to eat your lunch before you go. Mom made you a sandwich and put it in the refrigerator."

"I already ate it." She laughed. "Bye."

Nathan followed her to the front door and watched through the window as Melissa scampered across the street. He observed as Ms. Evans opened her door and stood for a moment staring across the street at the front of the McAllister home. Her saddened face broke into a grin when she looked down at Melissa.

Feeling his throat tighten, he fought the impulse to cry.

◆　◆　◆

"I finally talked to the veterinarian, Dr. Shippen," said Elizabeth as she sat down in Ryan's office. "Seems she's been vacationing in Saint

John's for a few days," she huffed. "That's why she wouldn't return our calls."

"Convenient timing for a trip," Ryan responded.

"I'm sure the baboon she saw was Heidi."

"And?"

"She didn't realize Heidi was quadriplegic. She interpreted her lack of movement to listlessness and dehydration."

"Come on."

"She didn't even really examine her. The guy with Heidi was acting so weird that she said she just wanted to get him out of her office." Elizabeth drummed her fingers on Ryan's desk. "I don't blame her. I would have been pretty spooked myself."

"She thought Heidi was dehydrated?"

"Her eyes were dull and sunken," she responded. "I asked her about the nasogastric tube. She said there wasn't any tube in the baboon's nose. She specifically said she would have remembered that."

"That's why Heidi was getting dehydrated."

"She said her lungs sounded junky."

"The kid is probably trying to feed her. Heidi probably chokes and aspirates." Ryan pulled a small desk calendar closer. "I don't think it's possible she survived this long."

"I E-mailed just about every specialty-oriented animal hospital in the country, just in case Heidi shows up at one of them."

He studied the resident across from him for a moment, trying to make an accurate judgment. *There's no way you had anything to do with this, is there?* To Ryan, his attorney's question about Elizabeth as a possible subject seemed out in left field. *If you sold the baboon, the veterinarian wouldn't have seen her . . . unless you just arranged for this lady to call, posing as a veterinarian, then lied about your conversation.*

Ryan shook his head slightly so as not to betray his thoughts. *No way. You're getting too paranoid, Ryan. You've always been a good judge of character, and Elizabeth has never given you any reason not to believe her.*

"Look," Elizabeth said, breaking into his thoughts, "I know how important you feel bringing this Henry kid to justice is . . . but I also know you don't really want to slow down our research." Her voice was strained but soft as she continued. "You should do what you feel best.

You're the chairman, right? But if I can throw in my two cents, since I'm in on this research too . . . well, I'm weighing in with the dean. Make the deal the prosecuting attorney offered. Then we can get our data back and get this research back on track."

Ryan slouched forward over his desk. "Maybe you're right. I'm probably delaying the inevitable." He looked up and met the gaze of his resident. "I'm talking with my attorney at 2. I'll see what he says."

◆ ◆ ◆

At 1:30 Sally McAllister knocked on the door and immediately let herself in. "It's just me!" she yelled.

Nathan maneuvered his chair from the bedroom and out into the den. "Hi, Mom."

She came over and greeted him with a kiss, her routine since Nate's injury. "How's my boy?"

"I'm fine, Mom."

Her eyes shifted around the room. She tilted her head. "Where's Abby?"

"She'll be home any minute."

"Melissa?"

"She went across the street to play with Tommy Evans."

"Where's your attendant?"

"Jim Over was here this morning." Nathan watched his mother wrinkle her forehead. "Mom, I'm OK for a while by myself. Even Melissa helps me out once in a while. It's OK, really."

Just then Abby walked in. "Well, hi," she said, looking at Sally. Then to Nate, "How was your day?"

"Interesting. I talked to Joe Gibson. He showed me the file about my accident."

The women exchanged glances. Abby frowned. "I doubt your mother wants to hear about that."

Sally grunted, then took out a tissue and stepped toward Nathan. Before he could respond, she moistened her thumb with a flick of her tongue and applied it to his cheek. "Goodness me," she said, "I got lipstick on you."

Nathan grimaced.

Sally obviously wanted to think of something other than the accident details. "I'm concerned about you, Nathan," she proclaimed, setting her large frame down on the old sofa. She directed her next comment to Abby. "You shouldn't leave him alone like this."

Nathan spoke before Abby had a chance. "It's my decision, Mom. I'm OK by myself. I'm an adult, remember?"

His mother shook her head. "When we learned you were coming home, we had no idea you'd be staying by yourself. I thought you'd have full-time help."

Abby walked to Nathan's side and put her hand on his shoulder. "We can't afford full-time attendant care."

"And I don't *need* it."

"You are also caring for Melissa?"

"Yes."

Sally huffed. "Be realistic, Nate. What if she were to need something? Can you fix her lunch? Put on a Band-Aid? Pick her up if she falls on her bike? You can't do anything!"

"Stop it!" Abby snapped.

Sally pulled her head back as if she'd been slapped.

"Mom," Nathan responded in a soft voice, "I'm still her father. I can give her advice, set limits on her behavior, even play with her." He shook his head. "There are things I can't do, like you mentioned, but there are ways to make up for all that."

"Nate, as much as I love you, honey . . . you're just not being realistic." She looked at Abby, who hadn't moved from Nate's side. "If you *have* to work, Abby, I can care for Melissa *and* Nate. I did it before, didn't I?"

"That's not an option, Mom. I do not need someone twenty-four hours a day. And if I need help, I can use the phone anytime."

"Melissa is not safe in this house alone. Anyone could come in at any time using your automatic door."

"The door is secluded in the back of the house, Mom. And it's not like this is New York City or something."

"I don't like it. She's my granddaughter."

"And she's our daughter," Nathan responded. "Besides," he added, "in the fall Melissa will be in school while Abby is working."

"That will be even worse for you." Sally stood and shook her head. "Your father isn't going to like this one bit."

◆ ◆ ◆

Ryan stood and shook hands with Hal Ferguson as he entered. Hal had large, meaty hands, like the rest of his body, a frame Ryan thought would have looked more at ease in a football uniform than a business suit. "Please tell me you have some good news."

"I do." He didn't smile. "Of sorts."

"Well?"

"Aunt Lucy showed."

"Aunt Lucy? The Henry boy's BMW?"

"The one and only. I just talked to Detective Mansfield. The Phoenix P.D. called this morning. They found the vehicle. The I.D. numbers match and everything."

"They did a search?"

"A limited one. There's only one glitch. The car's interior has changed."

"Changed?"

"It seems that precious, old Aunt Lucy has a penchant for red. She stopped and had the car redone at a shop in Dallas."

Ryan sighed and shook his head. "I told you to tell me good news."

"I did my best." He looked up at Ryan. "I hear that you met with the dean and Mr. McLaughlin."

"You guys don't keep any secrets, do you?"

"Not when it's not in our client's interests."

"What's that supposed to mean?"

Hal seemed to ignore the question. "Ryan, you and I have been friends for a long time. I've seen you and Barbara through some tough times."

Ryan sat in his desk chair. *Get to the point, Hal.*

The lawyer continued, "You asked me to provide legal counsel because you were being investigated on animal cruelty charges."

"Right."

"And now you have the opportunity to silence those allegations and get your lab equipment back."

"And you think I shouldn't press charges against the boy."

Hal nodded.

"Even though he's admitted to breaking into my lab? What if we find the baboon? What if the police come up with more evidence linking the baboon to Richard Henry?"

"If you're even thinking about urging the P.D. to search the Henry residence, you can forget about it," he huffed. "I heard all about Paige's little escapade last night."

"You heard that—"

"I heard all about it. I talked to Detective Mansfield, remember?"

"But Paige says she saw Mr. Henry carrying an animal container and—"

"An animal container," Hal interrupted loudly. "But not your baboon! Mr. Henry was returning home with a new golden retriever. He breeds champion dogs, Ryan. He had just bought a new dog from another breeder over in Carlisle. Mansfield checked it all out after telling Mr. Henry about Paige."

Ryan felt sick. "He *told* Mr. Henry about Paige? Why—"

"Ryan," he interrupted again, "the officer is legally obligated to do so. If an officer doesn't notify a landowner about a prowler, he can be held accountable in a civil court should anything ever happen with an intruder in the future."

"But she wasn't even arrested!"

"She's very fortunate. The way I read the law, she could have been in violation of three separate codes—trespassing, playing Peeping Tom, and stalking. Believe me, she was very lucky to get off with a warning."

Ryan sighed. "I was hoping that what Paige saw would be helpful," he said, shaking his head. "But it looks like her trespassing could be another lever the Henrys can use to divert attention away from my case against them."

"Exactly. Actually, even if you agree to drop the charges against

Richard Henry the Fourth, you have no assurance they will overlook this."

"Tell me the truth—is there any way you see the Henry kid being held responsible for stealing my baboon?"

The attorney paused before speaking. "I'm afraid not. This whole scenario with Aunt Lucy is just another example of the kind of hassle working a case against this boy is going to be for the Brighton P.D. And even if by some miracle the baboon turns up, or enough new evidence surfaces to convict him of grand larceny, it's unlikely that a jury will hold Richard Henry the Fourth to the fire. All his lawyers will have to do is flash a few photographs of Heidi and claim that their boy was acting out of conscience. And I imagine that his legal representation would let everyone know what great emotional turmoil you have caused the Henry family, stooping even to stalking them on their own property."

"That's ridiculous!"

"I'm just telling you the games they'd play."

"What are my options?"

"You can hang on, refuse to give in to their agreement, and suffer the consequences." He held up a finger. "But your name will continue to be bashed as an animal torturer." He held up a second finger. "Your research will be stalled until after a lengthy trial." He held up a third finger. "The dean might see fit to side with your legal opponents and claim ignorance and shock over the brutality of the research being done in your lab. Or you can drop your charges against the boy, get back your confiscated equipment, and get on with your life."

"What about rallying the disabled community to support us?"

"That is a possibility, Ryan, but one that would simply hold Whiteside to the public fire, and you wouldn't get your research back on track anytime soon." He held up his hands. "You wanted my opinion."

Ryan snorted. "I *paid* for your opinion."

"Well?"

The chairman of the surgical department stood and gazed at his ego wall. "I've fought hard to be where I am, Hal. And now I'm sitting on the edge of the biggest scientific achievement in medicine in this century."

"Fighting the kid isn't going to propel you further."

"I know," he sighed. "I know."

Hal stood and put a hand on Ryan's shoulder.

"Okay, Hal, call Whiteside and the Henry kid's attorney. Tell them I have regret over the loss of my baboon and the great price my research has paid, but because my concern is to return to my humanitarian research efforts, I will not pursue the case against Richard Henry the Fourth." He threw up his hands. "Uncle!" he shouted. "I give."

CHAPTER
17

THAT NIGHT Dave Borntrager arrived right on schedule. Although of his three PCAs, Nathan knew Dave the least, Dave seemed friendly, and Nathan looked forward to his visits. Dave, a forty-four-year old, had gotten an LPN through Apple Valley Technical School during high school but worked now as a realtor. The rumor around town was that he had sold and resold so much of the coveted valley land that he worked now just for fun. He was heavyset and had a light brown beard salted with white and looked like a young version of Santa Claus.

One of the modifications to the McAllister home was the addition of a bathroom suitable for Nathan, located just off his new bedroom. The bedroom had previously been a dining room, and the new bathroom extended into the carport, halving its former size.

Dave walked from the bathroom wearing a frown.

"What's wrong?" asked Nathan.

He held up Nathan's toothbrush. "I found this hanging within six feet of the commode."

Nathan didn't verbalize a response. *So?*

"I read in one of my nursing journals about how everyone's stool has a unique combination of bacteria, and that when you flush the toilet, that same bacteria is suspended into the air," he responded, waving his arms in a wide circle. "If your toothbrush is anywhere within six feet of the commode, the same unique combination of bacteria can be cultured off the toothbrush bristles."

Nathan raised the corner of his upper lip.

The PCA looked at Nathan. "My response exactly," he said, holding the toothbrush between his fingertips like it was poison. "I'd better wash this thing." He returned to the bathroom.

"You have too much time on your hands, Dave," Nathan called after him with a laugh. "Most of America has their toothbrushes within six feet of their commodes."

"You're right. Gross."

Nathan moved into the bathroom and situated his chair beneath the special sink that extended from the wall. Dave looked at his watch and began brushing Nathan's teeth.

After a minute Nathan pulled his head back and spat. "Thanks."

"I'm not done," he said, pointing to the watch face. "Studies show that at least two minutes of brushing are necessary to remove a day's worth of plaque."

Nathan reluctantly opened his mouth for Dave to finish the job. With that completed, Dave slipped on a pair of disposable latex gloves and pulled out a long string of dental floss.

"What now?"

"We missed this last night, didn't we?" Dave chided himself. "Gotta get the plaque from beneath the gum lines, you know." He paused. "My wife saw a twenty-year-old once. Not a single cavity in his mouth, but Dr. Green had to pull all his teeth because of gum disease."

"Your wife? She's—"

"Dr. Green's dental hygienist," he responded quickly.

I could have guessed.

"Open up."

Nathan obeyed, and Dave went to work, efficiently moving from front to back, top to bottom. Nathan tasted rubber.

"Yuk. Latex."

"I'm sure it's better than my fingers." He paused. "You know, if you culture the space beneath someone's fingernails, you'll find—"

"Dave!" Nathan interrupted. "I don't really want to think about it."

Dave shrugged. "Sorry."

Nathan moved his chair back beside his bed. "Abby wanted to watch you do the transfer."

Dave called to her. "Abby!"

Creaking on the stairs preceded her appearance in the doorway. "Ready for bed?"

"I'll show you how it's done. You could probably do it yourself with a little practice," he said, looking at Abby. "Or we could get a slide-board to help, since his chairback will recline." He looked at Nathan. "How much do you weigh, Nate?"

"One fifty-five," said Nathan. He watched Abby's eyes widen.

"I didn't realize you'd lost that much," she said, stroking his neck.

"Down from 187 before my accident," he responded. "The only thing that seems to be growing is my neck size. I'm up to a seventeen and a half, the last time they measured me at Briarfield."

Dave busied himself with removing the left armrest on Nathan's chair. "Ready?"

"Sure."

He loosened the Velcro strap from around Nathan's chest before picking up his feet and moving them well onto the bed. "It's helpful if you have the top covers pulled back first, so that after he's undressed, you don't have to get them out from beneath him," Dave instructed. "I just put his legs over on the bed, then pull his body forward, so his arms fall over my back. Then, with my arms around him, I grab his belt for a firm hold and pivot his hips onto the bed." He performed the motion as he talked, holding Nathan in a sitting position in the middle of the bed when he was done. "There."

Abby smiled. "Looks easy when you do it." She put her hands on her hips. "Now what?"

"Letting him down slowly can pose a greater strain to your back, so, as long as he's far enough down in the bed, you can just drop him." He pushed Nathan's shoulders back gently, initiating a free fall to the mattress.

"Whee!" Nathan imitated the delight of a child.

"Ooh!" Abby gasped.

"I'm OK, Abby. I won't break," he added with a smile. "Marlin used to treat me like this all the time over at Briarfield." He shrugged. "I'm still tough."

Dave raised a finger of warning. "Just don't hold him up too far in the bed before you let him go."

Abby nodded as the phone rang. "I'll get that in the kitchen."

Dave undressed Nathan and carefully inspected his skin for signs of breakdown, paying attention to pressure points over his buttocks and hips. After completing all his tasks, he positioned Nathan for the night. "Let's keep you on your left side tonight, OK? You were on your right side last night."

"Fine."

After a few minutes of work Dave excused himself. "See you tomorrow evening, Nate."

Nathan said good-bye as Dave left and Abby returned. "Need anything?"

"I could use some water." He clicked his tongue against the roof of his mouth. "I still taste those rubber gloves Dave wore when he flossed my teeth."

"That was your mom on the phone," she said, pushing a straw toward his mouth. "She said she was so flustered when she was here that she forgot the reason she came in the first place."

"She was too busy telling me what my needs are."

Abby set the glass aside. "Really," she said with a nod.

"What *did* she want?"

Abby sat on the edge of his bed. "She wanted to invite you to that healing crusade. Again." She drew a deep breath and blew it out slowly. "I didn't tell her no, but I told her that you hadn't been out much yet and that I'd leave it up to you." She brushed his hair with her fingers. "I wish she'd stay out of your business."

"She can be pushy."

"Pushy isn't the word I had in mind. She made me so mad today."

Nathan stayed quiet for a moment before speaking. "I think I want to go, Abby."

Her eyes met his.

"To the crusade, I mean." He told her about the Bible verses he'd studied earlier that day, about the man born blind that Jesus healed in order to show the works of God, and about the verse in Hebrews. "It says he is the same, yesterday, today, and forever, Abby." He paused. "I want to go to that crusade. God is going to heal me. I'm going to walk. I know I am."

"Nathan, you—" She stopped. Her eyes were sad. "Nathan, I don't want you to be hurt."

"Abby . . . Listen, we've been Christians for a long time, right?"

She frowned. "Sometimes I don't feel like a Christian. I haven't been—"

"Just because we've never seen God do something like this doesn't mean it doesn't happen," Nate interrupted. "We just need to have faith."

"Nate—"

"All things are possible with faith," Nathan countered. "If you ask in faith, you'll receive." He nodded his head. "I've been reading, Abby. It's all in the Bible. I just never saw it before. I think God allowed all this so I'd finally pay attention."

Abby sighed. "I—I want to believe, Nathan, but . . ."

"When is the crusade?"

"All this week. Down in Carlisle."

"I'll talk to Mom tomorrow." He turned his face to Abby. "Can you imagine, Abby? I *will* walk again," he said. "'Jesus Christ is the same yesterday and today and forever.'"

Abby stood and looked away. Nathan thought he saw tears in her eyes.

"Night, Abby." He paused, listening to her retreat to the door behind him. "I love you."

Her voice seemed strained. "I'll see you in the morning."

He heard the stairs creak, rapid footsteps in the hall, followed by a dull plop and then squeaking from the old bed.

◆　◆　◆

Ryan Hannah pushed the phone to his ear, listening to the nasal voice of the Brighton University Medical Center operator.

"Yes, operator. Dr. Hannah here. I'm turning my pager off for the night."

"Aren't you on for neuro trauma, sir?"

"No. Dr. Griffin is on neurosurgical trauma call. I'm only on for my patients who are already in the hospital. You can reach me at my home number."

"Yes, sir, Dr. Hannah."

"Call the chief resident, Dr. Wingfield, if you have any questions."

He looked at the top of his pager. 11:46 P.M. He flipped off the digital display.

Paige looked up from where she had collapsed on the couch two hours earlier. "Oh, man," she said, stretching, "I'm going to bed."

"Night, Paige."

He sat for a moment in his lounge chair, wishing for his mind to slow enough to allow him to retire for the night. "What a day," he muttered. "What a week."

He hated to lose. Losing meant failures. Failures that everyone remembered. Forever. At least Ryan did. And he was sure others did too.

Ryan had failed that day, beaten, in his own eyes, by a rich punk who had robbed him and gotten away with it. The failure felt heavy, like an injustice. And it unroofed the scab of an old wound in Ryan's soul.

Deliberately he stood, struck with an idea. "It's time for a barbecue," he whispered. "One that's been long overdue."

He walked into his study and over to a tall, wooden filing cabinet. He opened the bottom drawer. *It's in here somewhere.* All the way at the back of the drawer, from underneath a shoebox of canceled checks, he pulled out a musty folder.

I don't know why I didn't do this sooner. Maybe this will quiet some of the nagging feelings I have.

He lifted the thick file, now over twenty years old. Inside the folder was a copy of old patient records and legal communication surrounding the malpractice case of *Jones vs. New York University*, where an inexperienced Dr. Hannah had done his surgical internship. The case involved an intoxicated young motorist who suffered quadriplegia as a result of a cervical spine fracture sustained in a car accident. Though Ryan asserted that the man arrived in the emergency room already paralyzed, the University settled the suit because of one emergency medical technician's claim that he had seen the boy move his foot at the accident scene an hour before Ryan had evaluated him and placed a tube in his trachea for breathing. Since it was one man's word against another's, and since the patient had suffered such a devastating injury, the NYU insurers settled and allowed Ryan's name to be splashed over the newspapers for everyone to make their own judgments. Throughout his training his attendings supported him, but the accusations lingered—in the eyes of his senior residents, and in the mind of Ryan's strictest judge—himself.

In his moments of victory, Ryan dismissed the nagging doubts about his competence. But in his darkest hours he would wonder. *Could the EMT have been right? Was the spinal cord injury the result of my negligence and not from the accident?*

Ryan shoved the file under his arm and carried it to the kitchen, where he opened the refrigerator door and searched for a high-calorie answer to the tension in his gut. He selected two slices of leftover pizza and a diet soda, which he carried with him to the back deck. There he squinted in the direction of his nearest neighbor and pulled his gas grill around behind a redwood windbreak. Then he ceremoniously crumpled the contents of the file and loaded them onto the open grill. After a minute, with the paper mound still rising, he abandoned that idea and simply placed the whole folder in. He dropped the lid, turned on the gas, ignited the fire, and sat down on a metal deck chair to enjoy his pizza.

The fire almost immediately filled the grill, angrily licking through the lid. Smoke belched from the sides, rising into the night as a thick cloud. Ryan sat and watched, entranced by the display of heat and light. Slowly he lifted the pizza from the box and began to eat.

He wanted to condemn anyone who had ever challenged his importance. He wanted to scream his accomplishments, to bellow his worth. Instead he sat silently. Sat and stared at the fire and quietly cursed the emptiness of his own heart.

He sipped the soda and methodically chewed the pizza without appreciation for taste or hunger.

His thoughts turned to Paige and her comments at dinner the

night before. "Why *do* you drive yourself so hard?" he spoke quietly into the fire.

What was it that Paige said?

"The only cure for having to be the best is understanding God's unconditional love."

I'm on the brink of a fantastic medical breakthrough, one that will revolutionize the treatment of spinal cord injury forever. One that will make the world stand up and take notice.

Then why do I feel so empty?

Is it possible that Paige is right?

CHAPTER
18

NATHAN AWOKE, as usual, before hearing Abby stir. There in the silence he prayed. Since his renewed Christian search at Briarfield Manor, he'd made a habit of praying aloud. That helped him focus his thoughts and keep his mind from drifting.

He whispered, "Dear Father, it's Nathan. I know that you know what you're doing with me. Help me to have faith. Help me to trust you more."

Nathan's eyes were open, looking around the room.

"Thank you for letting me return to my home. Thank you for Abby and Melissa. Thank you for all the people who worked so hard to make this happen."

He thought about his accident, about what he'd read about Joe saving his life. "Thank you for sparing me. Thank you for Joe's being there to help." He paused. "Help me, God, to remember." He sighed. "I—I don't know what to make of the caller who warned me to stay away. What should I believe? Was she just trying to scare me, God? Or could it be true?" *It seems so improbable that I have a hard time even saying it.* "Could Brian have shot me on purpose?"

The thought brought a knot to his stomach. "If so, why?" He gently shook his head. *It makes no sense.* "Keep me safe.

"And help me to be a better husband, Lord. I want to be, but I feel so helpless like this." He thought about Abby. "I've never been a good husband for Abby. I've always held her too tight because of being jealous. Forgive me, Father. Forgive me."

Ask Abby to forgive you too.

"Help her to love me again." He sniffed. "Help her to have a good day today. Give her extra strength while I'm like this."

He thought about the healing crusade and the verses he had read the day before. He wasn't sure if he should quote the Bible to God, but he didn't think it would hurt to remind God of what he'd said and to proclaim his faith. "I believe what you said. You're the same yesterday and today and forever. Please heal me, God."

He imagined getting up and walking. He tried to wiggle his toes and looked down toward the foot of the bed. "I believe you will heal me."

◆ ◆ ◆

Upstairs, Abby awoke to the sound of a faint whisper. *Melissa?* She rubbed her eyes and looked at the clock. 5:20 A.M. As the whisper continued, her disorientation cleared. *It's Nathan. The monitor!* She crept out of bed, tilting her head to one side. She turned up the volume.

". . . me to be a better husband, Lord. I want to be, but I feel so helpless like this."

Nate's praying.

"I've never been a good husband for Abby. I have always held her too tight because of being jealous. Forgive me, Father. Forgive me. Help her to love me again. Help her to have a good day today. Give her extra strength while I'm like this."

She put her hand to her mouth. "Oh, Nate," she whispered at the monitor. "Could you ever forgive me if you knew what I've done?"

◆ ◆ ◆

Trish appeared back in routine form on Tuesday morning, with immaculate hair and dress. She held up the daily planner as Ryan breezed by. "You've got two laminectomies this morning, Dr. Hannah," she reported. "In O.R. 6 in ten minutes."

He nodded and fought off a yawn. "Any coffee around?"

"Just made some," she called from her desk. In a moment she reappeared carrying a large Styrofoam cup.

"Thanks." He swirled the cup beneath his chin to allow the aroma to penetrate his nostrils.

"That was wonderful news last night, sir," she bubbled. "I'm sure you're glad to have that monkey off your back. Er . . ." She blushed. "I didn't mean your monkey, sir—not Heidi—oh, sir, I just mean the pressure, not your monkey—oh, itwasjustafigureofspeech—" she babbled with increasing speed and a blush.

"It's OK, Trish. Forget it. I know what you meant."

"I saw it all on Channel 4. That sure was gracious of Mr. Whiteside, sir."

"I didn't see it." He sighed. "I was in the lab, preparing for a new data run." He pushed his chair back and put his hands behind his head. "Did you know that a researcher once earned a Nobel prize for showing that neurons are incapable of regrowth after injury?"

Trish nodded silently.

"It's true." He chuckled. "Stupidity never dies."

"Oh."

"And do you know what Dr. Pritchard said when I told him what I was working on?" He didn't wait for her reply. "He said I had delusions of grandeur." He puffed his cheeks out and stood up. "Shortsighted fools," he muttered.

"Yes, sir."

He slipped off his gray sport coat and hung it on a hanger behind his office door. "Room 6?"

"Yes," she said, glancing at the planner. "First is a Kenneth Raines, and after that, Beatrice Hyde."

He nodded. "I hope Dr. Wingfield has their M.R.I. studies handy." He turned to leave before adding, "Please call the Brighton P.D. You might just talk straight to that Detective Mansfield. See if you can facilitate getting my confiscated lab computers and other data back. Since they've called off their little investigation . . ." he said sarcastically. "And ask Dr. Hopkins to call the mammal supply house we got our last baboon from. I want to get my work restarted as soon as possible."

◆ ◆ ◆

On Tuesday mornings, because there was no scheduled bowel program or shower, Nathan could get in his chair much earlier. Today, after a little mental elbow twisting, he had even convinced Richard Ramsey, his PCA, to take him out for a maiden voyage. He wanted to surprise Abby at the cafe.

Richard didn't take much convincing, being quite adventurous. At twenty years of age, he was the youngest of Nathan's personal care attendants, and the only one who wasn't married. He was slender, with shoulder-length blond hair, and spent most of his time as a self-employed carpenter doing home renovations in and around Fisher's Retreat. Nathan knew him as a talented member of a church softball team and a man with a sense of humor that bordered on the absurd.

Nathan looked at the back of Richard's Ford pickup and shook his head. A red and white bumper sticker announced, "I almost had a psychic girlfriend, but she left me before we met."

Richard finished folding down the van's ramp and looked over at Nathan. "Like it? I could get one for your van."

"No, thanks." Nathan smiled, unsure if he would ever understand Richard's humor. "Could you grab that basket inside the front door? I want to take it by the Yoder place."

Melissa ran up the ramp. "Come on, Daddy."

"On my way." He steered the powerchair up the ramp and into the back of the van. Within a few minutes, Richard secured Nathan's wheelchair into the proper position in the right front.

"Let's go," Richard said as he jumped into the driver's seat.

"I'm hungry. Can I have pancakes?"

"Whatever you want, Mel." Nathan stared straight ahead. "I think I'll have biscuits and gravy."

"Not biscuits and gravy! Oh, man," Richard moaned with a heavy southern accent. "I can't feed you biscuits and gravy in public on your first time out."

"How about grits?" Nathan laughed.

Melissa giggled at Richard's exaggerated whining. "Get the gravy, Daddy."

"Don't you start too." Richard tapped the horn in a greeting as they met a car.

"Wave for me, Mel. That's old Elmer Harper." Nathan smiled. It was amazing how much fun a simple drive around town could be after all those months away.

Richard pulled up in front of the cafe.

"You'll have to pull into the side lot," Nathan instructed. "There isn't enough room here for the ramp."

"You're right, chief." Richard pulled the van around the side.

A few minutes later the trio entered the front of Fisher's Retreat's favorite watering hole to a rowdy reception as steaming coffee cups were held up in greeting.

"Welcome back!"

"Well, look who's here!"

"Hey, Nate!"

"Ease up. Let the man through," Richard cajoled.

They selected a table in the center, and Richard moved a chair out of the way so Nathan could pull in properly.

A table full of teens, dressed in black leather and T-shirts, stood to leave just as Nathan stopped his chair. He met the stare of a young man he recognized.

The teenager, Dion Smith, was flanked by two other young men and a girl with black lipstick and short, white hair. Her mouth dropped open as her eyes fell on Nathan and his chair. She stepped back and slipped behind Dion, clutching his arm.

"Morning, guys," Nathan responded. "Time for school, isn't it, Dion?"

"Once a cop, always a cop, huh, Mr. McAllister?"

Nathan smiled. "It's in my blood."

"We were just leaving." The teens exited, giving Nathan a wide berth.

Nathan looked up to see Abby holding an order pad. "Nice to see you out, Mr. McAllister," she said formally.

"Mommy!"

"Just thought we'd have our breakfast out this morning."

"Just don't bring him the gravy. Anything but the gravy," Richard groaned, placing his head in his hands as Nate looked at the menu in front of him.

"I'll have . . ." He looked at Richard. ". . . two eggs scrambled with sausage and wheat toast."

"Thank you. Thank you," Richard smiled.

"What about you, Ms. McAllister?" Abby looked at her daughter.

"Mommy, I'm Melissa."

"Well?"

"Pancakes!"

Mr. Knitter walked up and touched Nathan on the shoulder. "Nice to have you back, Nathan." He looked at Abby. "This one's on the house."

"I'll be sure and tip her well then," Nathan joked. "Thanks, Mr. Knitter, but you really don't have to."

"I know." He backed away. "You're welcome."

Richard pointed at the menu. "I'll have the biscuits and gravy." He looked at Nathan. "Just kidding, Nate. I wouldn't do that to you. I'll take French toast."

"Coffee?"

Abby received two nods before disappearing into the kitchen.

Nearly everyone who came into the cafe came over and greeted Nathan. Some were timid and offered only a concerned stare before looking away. A little boy hid behind his mother's skirt.

An older woman came over with the advice, "It's not so drafty in the back."

"We're just fine here, Ms. Miller," Nathan replied.

She opened her eyes wide. "Well, Nathan, I didn't recognize you."

"I've lost weight." He offered a smile.

"Yes, that's it," she said before moving toward the counter.

They sat quietly for a moment. "It's nice being out again." He winked at Melissa. "Next time I'm gettin' the gravy."

◆ ◆ ◆

An hour later Richard drove the McAllister van down Main Street and then headed West on Route 752 out into the Old Order country bordering the town. There, with farming the predominant occupation, the Mennonites pursued a simpler life. To outsiders, they seemed backward and encumbered by the constraints put upon them by the church. There were no cars, though motorized farm vehicles were allowed and were used frequently.

Nathan filled Richard in on what he knew as they meandered along the winding stretch that led toward the Yoder farm and the Spring Creek Mennonite Church.

Rachel Yoder had been widowed for five years, since her husband, William, died from complications from AIDS, a disease he fought for ten years after contracting it from a blood transfusion. After William's death, Rachel continued living on the family farm, running a poultry house with the help of her brother and raising her three children, Jonas, Micah, and Stephanie. The previous November, after a rebellious foray outside the church community, Jonas, Rachel's oldest, had hung himself in his closet.

This much Nathan knew from talking to Abby. As he told the story, his heart was touched with empathy toward Rachel. When he told of what he knew about Jonas, he heard Melissa begin, "But, Daddy . . ."

He interrupted with just enough volume that Melissa knew to stop. "It's not time to tell secrets, honey."

As they crested a hill, Nathan nodded. "It's the next farm on the right."

As the van slowly moved up the long, gravel lane, Rachel straightened from her position in the middle of a freshly plowed garden plot. She walked toward the van to greet them. She wore a blue dress and knee-high, muddy farm boots. Her hair was up, partially concealed by a white covering.

Richard lowered Nathan's window. "Good morning, Rachel."

She smiled. "This is a surprise."

"I wanted to return your basket and dishes."

"I could have come down."

"I know. But it's fun for me to be out." He paused. "Thank you for your kindness. The food was great," he added as Richard hopped out of the van with the basket.

"We all help each other," said Rachel. "I've been on the other end a time or two."

"Rachel, I—I'm sorry for upsetting you the other day. I really didn't mean to—"

"Don't think another bit about it, Nathan," she said. "I can . . . well, be a bit too sensitive."

"Your son was a good young man, Rachel. I don't think badly of him."

"He wasn't a drug user." She shook her head rapidly and drew her lips together. "I won't listen to town gossip."

Nathan sighed, sensing her pain and her defensiveness. "I may be able to get some information . . . about Jonas, I mean . . . if you'd let me look into it . . . only if you'd want it. But I'd need to ask some questions."

"What could you do?" Her eyes began to tear. "I've talked to Abby, Nathan. She's told me about your quest for answers about your . . . problems." She put her hand to her mouth. "Do you have to drag my family through this just to find the answers to your own pain?" She took a step back and turned toward her garden.

"Please don't walk away, Rachel. I can't follow you."

Rachel bit her lower lip and looked down.

"I didn't come here to upset you. I came to apologize." He studied her for a moment. "I'm sorry, Rachel, really I am."

She took a deep breath. "Brother Showalter and I have spoken," she added quietly. "Nothing can bring my son back to me." She looked up. "Just leave this matter to us. Our community has dealt with it . . . and it is over. We don't need to have the world looking in upon us."

"Of course."

Richard started the van.

"Thanks again for the food."

Rachel nodded and waved.

Richard shook his head as they drove back down the gravel lane. "If you really want to know something about Jonas Yoder, just ask those kids we saw in the cafe today. I saw him with them a time or two, when I did renovations to Mr. Taylor's place in town."

◆ ◆ ◆

Paige stuck her head into her father's office. "Knock, knock," she said.

"Hi, Paige."

"Guess what?" She made an exaggerated smile.

He pulled his lips back to imitate her. "You're doing it again."

"I know." She kept smiling. "You didn't guess."

He looked at his watch. "I don't know."

"I got a job. Two jobs actually."

He put down his pen. "Really?"

"I'm going to work in the medical library."

"What? Here on this floor?"

"Yep. Right around the corner. Actually it's just shelving books, and only for two hours each morning. It's minimum wage, but at least I'll be in the hospital."

"You said two jobs."

"The other one is volunteer. The coordinator said I could spend two afternoons a week helping in the newborn nursery."

"That sounds good. Changing a few diapers might just challenge this pediatrician dream of yours."

"Dad, I know this may be hard for you to believe, but not everyone in the world thinks brain surgery is the highest call in medicine."

He raised his eyebrows and smiled. "Oh?"

Paige scuffed her foot on the rug. "Anyway, I was hoping that in my spare time I could spend some time in your lab."

Ryan tried not to sound surprised. "Hmm. You think you'd like that?" He put his pen to his cheek. "I seem to remember your reaction—"

"Dad, I know what you're thinking. I wouldn't get in the way. I could be a gofer, or feed the animals, anything you want." Her eyes were pleading. "I could pick up pizza."

He shrugged. "Some experience in modern research and statistics would look good on your medical school application."

"Then I can help?" She bounced on her heels.

Trish interrupted on the intercom. "Dr. Hannah, the dean's on line

1. And, sir? Your afternoon clinic started without you ten minutes ago."

Ryan held one hand toward Paige and picked up the phone.

"Hello."

"Ryan? Alan Pritchard," the dean said, clearing his throat. "I understand your resident is already searching for another primate for your research."

"Yes, sir. As soon as I can get my lab back in order, I want to get right back to work. Has your office been in touch with the Brighton P.D.? They still haven't brought back my stuff." *And how do you know what my residents are doing?*

"Ryan, I need you to slow down on this whole thing. I wasn't kidding when I told the media that we would be looking carefully at all animal studies in the future. I can't afford any more bad press."

"Sir, I appreciate your concern, but I'm sure if you see my data you will understand the necessity of moving forward. We're on the brink of a real—"

"Dr. Hannah," Pritchard interrupted, raising his voice, "you will not be continuing on this project until I've had a chance to conduct a thorough review. Now, is that clear?"

"Sir, I can show you the data as soon as I get my computer. Maybe even tonight if you'd—"

"Which part of the term 'slow down' don't you understand?" he huffed. "Put it in writing, Ryan. I want a complete justification in writing, on my desk, before you use one more primate in your research."

The phone clicked. Ryan stared into the phone and suppressed the urge to curse. "He hung up!"

Paige shrugged. "Some people have no manners."

◆ ◆ ◆

Nathan sat at his desk staring into the computer screen. After returning from the Yoders', his mother had stopped in and insisted on taking Melissa with her to Carlisle to shop, leaving Nathan alone for a few hours until Abby returned. He loved his computer even more now than before his injury. With access to E-mail and the Internet, he could communicate with others without them seeing his chair. At least then he was enabled, not disabled, and, except for his slower typing speed, he could communicate just like anyone else.

The phone rang. He moved his chair back and to the side, then advanced it so he could get near his phone. On the fifth ring he tapped the hands-free button with his mouthstick. "Hello."

"Hi, Nathan. I'm just calling to check in. How are you doing?" The voice was Abby's.

"I'm fine. My mom stopped by. She took Melissa with her to Carlisle to look for Depression glass."

"You're OK by yourself? Do you need anything to drink?"

"I'm fine. Mom set up a large container of iced tea with a long straw. I should be fine until you get here."

There was a pause. "It was nice seeing you in the cafe."

"It was nice for me too."

"I almost thought you were going to get mobbed. So many people wanted to say how good it is to have you back."

"Yeah."

"Well, I'd better run. I'm going to make dinner rolls before I leave."

"See you."

"Bye."

Nathan was just getting his thoughts reoriented to his computer file when the phone rang again. *Must be Abby. She must have forgotten to tell me something.*

He again manipulated himself into position to answer and tapped the phone. "Hello."

"Is this Nathan McAllister?" Immediately Nathan recognized the strained voice.

"Yes."

"Mr. McAllister, why did you come? I warned you!"

Mentally he asked himself key questions, hoping the woman would not hang up. *Young or old? Sounds young. Are there other voices in the background?*

"You should have listened to what I said."

"What . . . who is this?" Nathan pleaded. "Tell me who you are."

The girl's voice was low, and her breath sounds were loud. *She must have the phone right next to her mouth and nose.* "You know he killed Jonas. That's what you said," she sobbed. "But that was my fault too."

"Who *is* this? When? Who killed Jonas? When did I talk about Jonas?"

"When he shot you! Oh, Mr. McAllister, I tried to protect you. I don't want to be guilty anymore!"

"When I was shot? Please, who are you? I don't remember! I don't remember being shot!"

"I'm so sorry, I'm so sorry. I've warned you, so it's not my fault. I tried to warn you."

"Please help me. I don't remember! What are you talking about?"

There was silence for a long second before the girl grunted.

"Who are you?"

Click.

"No!" Nathan huffed. "Don't hang up! Hello? Hello?"

Silence.

The line was dead.

CHAPTER
19

NATHAN USED his mouthstick to depress the review button on his phone. Since he had a caller I.D. service, the last incoming call was displayed: 1:08 P.M. 566-6241. No name was listed, which meant it wasn't a privately registered line.

He dialed the number and waited. One ring, two, three . . . On the tenth ring, a man's voice finally came over the line. "Hello."

"Hello. I was just called by a party at this number."

"Could be, could be," the friendly, elderly sounding voice responded.

"Sir, where is this phone located?"

"This phone? Why, it's a pay phone outside the Ashby High School gymnasium. I was just walking by, and it was ringing off the hook."

"Is there a girl around, someone who perhaps just used the phone?"

"Sir, there was a whole group of students here just a moment ago 'cause they were changin' classes. But now these halls are empty except for me and Coach Smith."

"Did you see anyone using the phone?"

"No, sir."

"OK," Nathan replied numbly. "Good-bye."

He backed his chair over and then forward and to the left so he could reach his tea on the edge of the counter. Then he maneuvered his chair back in front of the computer so he could record as much of the conversation as he could remember.

He typed in all lower-case to save time, since to type a capital letter, he'd have to first depress the caps lock key followed by the letter.
For the same reason, he avoided using question marks. Slowly, using his
mouthstick, he began:

phone conversation number two

i tried to warn you. why did you come.
        you know he killed jonas. that's what you said. that was my
fault too.
        i'm sorry. i warned you.

*Was there anything else? It was all over so fast. She said, "He killed
Jonas." Who is "he"? The same "he" that shot me?*

Nathan read what he had written and made a raspberry noise
toward the screen. The absence of any upper-case keys made it difficult for him to read.

He looked at the computer screen until his screensaver blipped on,
reflecting inactivity for more than five minutes. He watched as colorful spheres formed, bounced around the screen, and dissipated again.

Am I in any real danger? He thought back to his interactions with
Brian Turner, especially those few times they'd visited since his accident. The interactions were uncomfortable, but Nathan thought that
was because Brian felt so responsible for Nathan's injury. He was bound
to feel uncomfortable and guilty around him.

But did he sense hatred or any reason to be afraid of Brian? No. He
hadn't felt that. Not in the visits they'd had at Briarfield Manor.
Nathan never felt threatened in any way, and certainly not like he was
in any danger when Brian was around him. Nathan had never been the
type to run scared at the hint of a conflict, and he didn't feel the need
to start now. If anyone sensed danger, it seemed to be the caller.
Nathan didn't feel the sense of fear his caller did at all.

*Every crime suspect must include an analysis of ability, proximity, and
motive. Let's assume I was shot intentionally. Brian had ability and proximity but no motive. It just doesn't make sense that way.*

Nathan scratched his ear by rubbing it against his mouthstick, now in a holder mounted on the arm of his wheelchair. *Could it be that the caller is someone who has a score to settle with Brian? Someone with a vendetta against him who wants to frame him or turn me against him? What would motivate someone to do that?*

The caller seems to think I knew something about Jonas's death, knew that someone killed him. I wonder which member of the Fisher's Retreat P.D. investigated his suicide?

Nathan maneuvered his way back to the phone and dialed the P.D.

Marge's voice boomed through his speakerphone. "Fisher's Retreat Police Department."

"Marge, how are you?"

"Nate?"

"You know it."

"Oh, Nate, I heard you were out at the cafe today. How are you?"

"No secrets in a small town, are there? I'm getting along."

"Joe's going to be sad he missed you. He's out on a call."

"Doesn't matter. I wondered about that Jonas Yoder file I'd asked you to pull, remember?"

Marge started her clicking cheek noise again.

"Joe showed me the file about my shooting. I'm sure you pulled it for him. But he didn't bring along that Yoder file, and I forgot to ask."

"Uh . . . He didn't bring it on purpose. I asked him about it, but he thought we'd better keep that one closed."

"But I thought that—"

"It's the family's wishes, Nate. Joe struggled with the decision. I know he wants to do right by you, but he needs to honor the Yoders too."

More clicking noises came over the speaker.

It's OK, Marge. No need for nervous tics. I'm not going to press it. "It's OK. I understand. I'll see you around, Marge."

"Do come around, Nate. I'd love to see you."

"Bye," he said as he tapped off the phone.

"It's OK, Marge," he muttered to himself. "I'll just check the patrol schedule to see who was on duty the night he died. That should tell me who did the scene investigation."

But what day did he die? It must have been just a few days before my shooting.

He moved back to his computer, accessed the Internet, pulled up a phone directory, and memorized the number for the *Apple Valley Journal*. He called the number and after talking to four different departments finally found someone who located the obituary he was investigating: Jonas Yoder, aged eighteen, died on November 15.

He moved into the family room and then into the kitchen to look at the calendar where he always recorded his patrol schedule. Unfortunately, it hung on a tack, just beyond his reach on the bulletin board above the phone.

Nathan sighed. The simplest tasks could now frustrate him. *I'll just have to wait for Abby. She shouldn't be away much longer anyway.*

◆ ◆ ◆

Ryan sat in the center of the B.U. Neurosurgery outpatient clinic listening as the medical students and residents presented the cases to him. From where he sat, in the large central staff area, he had access to six examination rooms to which patients were escorted through separate outside hallways. After the patients had been seen and examined by both a medical student and a neurosurgical resident, they were ready to be seen by Dr. Hannah.

Dr. Elizabeth Hopkins, the only person in the room without a white coat, stood at Ryan's side and gesticulated with obvious frustration. "Trish and I both have spoken to Detective Mansfield, and he just keeps putting us off," she snapped, placing her hands on her hips. "And I located another hamadryas baboon at the American Zoological Supply house, but the dean's office intercepted my request."

"Dr. Hannah," a second neurosurgical resident, Dr. Timmons, interrupted, holding up an X-ray, "I need to show you a new inpatient consult."

A medical student attempted to step in front of Dr. Timmons. "My patient has been waiting in exam room 3 for forty-five minutes."

Ryan held up his hands. The group of three fell silent, their eyes cast on the floor. He looked at Elizabeth. "What was the name of that

Brighton police captain? Crease? No, Sease, I believe. Get him on the phone. I'll talk to him myself. We'll get our lab back together." He took the X-ray from the resident's hand and held it up to the ceiling light. "Sub-arrachnoid blood," he said, pointing to the CT scan. "What's the date on this?"

"This morning, sir. The patient is a fifty-year-old female who presented to the E.R. with severe headache. She was admitted to medicine and—"

"The medicine service?" Ryan barked. "Transfer her to our service now," he added, shaking his head, "before they study her to death."

The resident started to retreat.

"Hold on, Dr. Timmons. What's your working diagnosis?"

"Ruptured cerebral aneurysm."

"Good. Get a four vessel cerebral angiogram, STAT."

Timmons stuffed the X-ray into its jacket and retreated another step.

"Take the angiogram to Dr. Wingfield, so he can review it and present the case to me."

"Right away, sir." The neurosurgical resident stepped toward the exit.

"Dr. Timmons!"

The resident froze.

"When is the highest chance of rebleeding?"

"The initial forty-eight hours, sir."

"Correct. When should we operate?"

"Tonight."

Ryan shook his head. "Common mistake, young man. This case demands a fresh team. I don't want to start this when everyone is tired. It's not worth the added risk to the patient. Post her for first thing tomorrow."

"OK, sir." He paused this time before trying to escape another question.

Ryan showed a thin smile. "Show the films to . . ." He looked at the medical student. "What's your name, Dr. . . . ?"

"Steadman."

"Show the head CT to student Dr. Steadman before you leave. It's a good teaching case." He motioned to the medical student. "Go ahead. Your patient can wait another minute."

Fifteen minutes later, Elizabeth motioned Ryan to the phone. "I've got Captain Sease on the line."

Ryan put the phone to his ear. "Captain Sease, I'm calling to see if I can straighten out this situation concerning my confiscated lab materials."

"As far as I know, everything should be ready for return."

"It seems that talking with Mr. Mansfield hasn't gotten my administrative assistant very far. He just promises to look into it and then—"

"That's because she was talking to the wrong person. Detective Mansfield is in charge of investigating the break-in at your lab, doctor. Officers Jenkins and Seager were doing the animal cruelty investigation. I'll talk to them for you and see what the hold-up is." He cleared his throat.

"I'd appreciate it. It is critically important that I get my lab back in order."

"I'm sure it is," Sease responded. "By the way, doc, I had a chance to look at that video myself. Just what *are* you doing over there?"

The last thing Ryan wanted was to explain his project to someone uninitiated in modern neurosurgical research. He decided for the snow technique. "I'd be glad to explain it to you," he began. "I'm studying the up-regulation of CNS neuro-receptors by neural tube trophic factor."

"Uh, er . . ."

"And the effect of NTTF harvested from schwannomas on the ingrowth of spinal cord nerve grafts for restoration of acute SCI. Quite simple, really." Ryan smiled.

"Uh, er, sure, doc."

"Just talk to your officers, captain. Patients' lives could be at stake if I delay this research much longer."

"I'll do my very best, sir."

"Thanks," Ryan added, terminating the call.

Elizabeth rolled her eyes. "Aren't you overdoing it a little?"

"Hey, if it gets my project back on track, I'll overdo it," said

Ryan. "Now," he added, looking into his residents' anxious faces, "who's next?"

◆ ◆ ◆

"Hey, Abs," Nathan said, "how about taking that calendar down for me? I want to see something."

Abby looked up from the kitchen counter where she was rolling out pizza dough. She clapped the flour off her hands as she reached for the calendar.

"Check out November 15, could you? Whose name is on for patrol duty that night?"

"Yours. You were on duty."

"I was?"

"No, wait," she added, looking again. "It's crossed out. Someone must have traded with you to work that night."

He sat silently for a moment while Abby returned to her work. "That was the night Jonas Yoder died. I just wondered who did the scene investigation."

Abby's eyes met his for a moment before she looked away. "I'm sure I wouldn't know."

"I don't remember doing it."

"It wasn't you, Nathan. Your duty was traded." She looked back at the calendar and studied it for a moment before nodding. "I remember now," she said contemplatively, pointing at the calendar. "Brian traded to do your call on the fifteenth."

"He wanted to do my duty on the fifteenth?"

"Actually, he wanted out of his duty on the following Friday, so he could play in a tennis tournament in Carlisle."

Nathan responded, finding it hard to hide the suspicion in his voice. "You seem to remember this pretty well. That was months ago."

She straightened and clasped her hands together until her fingers began to pale. "I remember just about everything that happened that week, Nathan. It was a hard week to forget."

Hard for everyone else to forget, but I can't remember anything . . .

except maybe a brief glimpse of Rachel Yoder at her son's grave site. "I—I guess I never paid him back for taking my duty."

"Joe covered it for him. I'm sure Brian's not holding it against you," she responded, her voice biting with sarcasm. Then, more softly, she added, "I took Melissa down to watch the tennis tournament. Brian took first place in men's singles."

"But, Abby . . ." Nathan spoke slowly as he figured out the days. "If that was the following Friday, I would have been in the intensive care unit at Brighton University, and you . . ." His voice trailed off.

Abby put her hands on her hips. "I know it might strike you as strange, maybe even cruel, Nathan, but put yourself in my place. You can't begin to know what I was going through," she added, her lower lip beginning to tremble. "I was camped out in that I.C.U. waiting room for days, not knowing if you were going to live or die, just wondering if you were going to wake up again." Her eyes were glistening. "Melissa was going crazy. They wouldn't let her in the I.C.U. to see you, and I wasn't sure if she could have handled it anyway," she continued, her voice thick with emotion. "There you were with all those machines and tubes keeping you alive. I couldn't even recognize you. Your head was so big with the swelling, you couldn't open your eyes."

"I—I'm sorry, Abby, I—"

She persisted, "Finally, after four days, Marty and Brian practically carried me out of there, just to get my mind on something else." She shrugged. "So I went to a tennis tournament in Carlisle while my husband was on life support in the I.C.U.," she sobbed. "Nathan, I felt so guilty. After your mother found out, she didn't let an opportunity go by to ask me about the tennis match. She acted like it was no big deal, but I could see it in her eyes—no decent wife would leave her husband's side when he was like that."

"Abby, don't cry."

"I'm *not* a decent wife, Nathan."

"Stop it, Abby. I don't hold it against you. You needed to get away. Don't kick yourself." He watched his wife sob as she put a dishcloth to her eyes. He huffed with frustration. He longed to be able to hold her, to wipe away her tears! How much he wanted to wrap his arms around her and comfort her like he should. He wanted to curse his injury, to curse his chair. Instead, he moved his chair forward, inching closer to his wife.

"Come here, Abby, come here." He felt his own throat tighten. "I want to hold you."

Abby gazed down at her husband for a moment before he coaxed her again.

"Come on." He began to cry, making quick gasps, like a child. "I want—to—hold—you—again."

She knelt on the kitchen floor beside the wheelchair before leaning in and placing her cheek against Nathan's chest. She gently placed her arms around his neck and shoulders.

They wept as Nathan nuzzled his wife's hair.

After a minute Nathan spoke, and Abby lifted her head and wiped away his tears, and hers. "I'm the one who can't be a decent husband. And I never was, Abby. I don't need to tell you how jealous I was. It was wrong. I'm sorry."

"It's OK, all right?" She gazed at him for a moment before returning her head to his chest. "Don't apologize to me." She paused before speaking just above a whisper. "I'm the one to blame, Nathan. I'm the one to blame."

He felt her shudder and then turn her face into his neck, where he could sense the cool moisture from her tears.

Nathan lowered his head and pushed his face into her hair, caressing her with his nose and lips. He kissed her quietly as his own tears began again. Then he whispered, "It's not true, Abs. I love you. You are a good wife. The best wife for me."

CHAPTER
20

THE NEXT morning, Ryan rose at 5 and made bullet rounds with the residents at 6 before stopping to see Elizabeth in the spinal lab.

When he arrived, she was sitting in the middle of an assortment of boxes, like a spoiled child at Christmas. But instead of smiling, she frowned and uttered a curse as Ryan entered. "This stuff is a mess. They could have kept it organized."

"At least they brought it back to us. And relatively quickly at that," he added. "I hate to imagine how long we would have been stymied if the prosecuting attorney had decided he had a case against us."

"Really."

He looked at his watch. "I have a case in a few minutes. I just wanted to make sure everything arrived."

"As far as I can tell," Elizabeth responded, "but I haven't looked at everything yet." She pointed to the rodent room. "You should have seen our Schwann rat. I don't think they fed it at all."

He smiled. "Maybe we should accuse them of animal cruelty."

Elizabeth didn't laugh at her chairman's joke.

Ryan turned to leave. "Elizabeth, Paige will likely be coming by later this morning. She's going to be spending some time in the lab, assisting with odd jobs."

He heard Elizabeth's audible sigh. He knew she wouldn't be bold enough to complain, too much.

"Could you teach her how to care for the rodents? You know, routine feeding, weighing, that kind of thing."

"Dr. Hannah, do you really think this is a good idea? The last time she—"

Ryan held up his hand, bringing an end to the resident's protest. "She's my daughter, and she'd like to help. She won't be in the way."

"Yes, sir," Elizabeth grunted.

"I have an aneurysm to clip," he said, looking at his watch again. "Wingfield should have that patient in the O.R. by now." He walked to the door of the lab before turning back. "Oh, Elizabeth? See if you can print out a copy of our hypothesis, and do a complete written project summary. Dr. Pritchard isn't going to let us go forward without it."

◆ ◆ ◆

Jim Over was forty-one, with thick, sandy hair and a likable round face that dimpled when he smiled. He was of medium height, but he had a posture so straight that it seemed to prompt everyone else to pull their shoulders back when they were around him. He was a father of four and served as a youth pastor and worship leader at the Community Chapel under senior Pastor Thomas Yeager. For the past eight years, since getting a nurse's aide certificate, Jim had supplemented his income by doing home health nursing through a private agency. Of Nathan's three PCAs, Jim was the most nurturing and, from what Nathan could tell, did not have the dental obsessions or bizarre sense of humor that characterized his other attendants.

Jim knew of Nathan's routine during his bowel program and brought a music CD for him to try. "Here," he said, lifting the earphone away from Nathan's ear, "I've brought something new for you to try."

"OK. What is it?"

"A new worship CD I've been using at Community."

Nathan nodded and closed his eyes. Jim lit a scented candle at Nathan's request before beginning "the program."

Nathan concentrated on the music and ignored the morning ritual. The melodies varied from soft and worshipful to fast and celebratory. It was tightly mixed with piano, keyboards, acoustic and electric guitars, bass, percussion, and even some brass. At the end of the CD, he wished he could listen longer. "This is great stuff! Where do you get this?"

"I subscribe to a worship leader's music service. They send me a collection of new music about every two months."

Jim lifted Nathan into his shower chair, a push-style wheelchair with a padded plastic seat that was open in the bottom, like a toilet seat. After balancing Nathan into position, he wheeled him into the bathroom, which had been built with a special shower area to accommodate the chair. There Jim used a handheld showerhead to wash Nathan down from head to toe.

After his shower, it was back to bed to dress and then an hour's worth of physical therapy before getting Nathan into his powerchair.

Once in the chair, he saw Jim looking over his electronic equipment—a CD player, a radio, and a TV. "You know, I went down with Pastor Yeager to visit his nephew a few months ago. He lives down at Tyler, just on the other side of the state line. He's been a quad for a long time, ever since a diving accident about twenty years ago now."

"I didn't know about him."

"He has a pretty neat setup. He has a remote that can operate all of his equipment. He keeps it in a holder on his wheelchair or positioned by his head when he's in bed." Jim looked around the room. "I bet we could get something like that rigged up for you."

"I have a remote for the TV." Nathan paused. "But I don't think I want to look into all that." He offered a smile and tried to sound confident. "I'm not going to need it for very long."

Jim looked down at Nathan and squinted.

Nathan continued, "I'm going to be healed, Jim." He went on to tell him about the verses he'd read in the Bible and the healing crusade that was going on down in Carlisle. "I've talked to my mom about it. My parents are going to take me down there tomorrow."

Jim took the CD out of the player so he could place it back in its holder.

"Surely in your line of work, you believe God can heal, don't you, Jim?"

He cleared his throat. "Yes, I believe God can heal," he responded slowly. "But I also know that God sometimes allows evil to touch us in ways we wouldn't have chosen, in order to accomplish his higher plan."

Nathan nodded. "Like the man in John 9. Jesus said he was born blind so God could show his power by healing him." Nathan paused and watched Jim turning the CD over and over in his hands.

"Well, I'll certainly be praying for you, Nate." He held up the compact disc. "You want me to leave this here? I have plenty at home."

"Sure."

Nathan watched his attendant as he put the CD back in the player and turned it on again. Jim shuffled to the door. "Ready for some breakfast, Nate?"

He doesn't seem to want to talk about the crusade, Nathan mused before calling out, "Coffee, here I come."

◆ ◆ ◆

Abby stood in the cafe's kitchen, gazing quietly at the activity in one of the front booths. There Brian Turner, dressed in his street clothes, sat opposite a young woman, dressed in a clingy white shirt that didn't reach low enough to cover an earring stud placed through her navel. She had short white hair, and her lips were outlined in black. She had a mature figure and, in Abby's opinion, was not unattractive at all, with the exception of her makeup and hair coloring. She had joined Brian a few minutes before, when Abby was out filling customers' coffee cups, but the girl had spoken in such hushed tones that Abby couldn't hear the conversation above the restaurant's clatter. *She's a little young for you, isn't she, Brian?*

She watched as Brian reached forward and gently squeezed the young woman's forearm. She played with a salt shaker before reaching for a napkin to dab at her eyes. She hunched forward with Brian briefly before sitting up again. Brian looked around the room, but not behind him toward the kitchen.

Abby watched as Brian closed his fist and leaned forward again. *She's crying. Maybe it's time to see if she'd like to order anything.*

Abby pulled out her notepad and strode across the room, arriving at the table just as the girl pulled away from Brian's grasp. "Don't talk to him again!" Brian said in an urgent, hushed tone before looking up to see Abby arriving.

The young woman slid quickly from the booth, her eyes wide and penetrating Abby's gaze for a moment before she pushed past her and ran from the cafe.

"Oh, er . . ." Abby stumbled with her words before looking at Brian. "I was just about to see if you needed something."

He stood. "Not today," he said politely, "not today."

Abby watched him leave and scout up and down the street before jogging out of view.

◆　◆　◆

Nathan called to Melissa when he heard a knock at the door. "Get the door, could you, Mel?" He looked at his clock. *Abby should be home soon, but she doesn't usually knock.*

He heard his daughter's excited voice. "Hi, Occifer, uh, Officer Brian," she giggled. "Daddy's workin' in his new room."

Nathan steered his chair around to face the doorway so he could see his old friend enter.

Brian nodded at Nathan. "Hello, Nate," he said, his eyes fixating on Nathan's chair.

"Hey, Brian. What brings you around?"

"Just thought it's time I showed my face, you know?"

Nathan followed his eyes as Brian surveyed the room. On the wall beside his computer, a large bulletin board had been reconstructed to mimic the one he'd had in his room at Briarfield Manor.

Brian cleared his throat. "How's it goin'? You like being back home?"

Nathan nodded. "I'm glad to be back, all right. I don't think I could have stood one more meal of that nursing home food."

"I'll bet."

Brian scuffed his feet against the floor.

"Sit down." Nathan pointed with his mouthstick. "Pull up that chair or sit on my bed. It's OK."

"Listen, Nate, I gotta ask you something. If you don't want to talk about it, I'll understand."

Nathan wrinkled his forehead but didn't reply.

"I want to know about the shooting. Uh, your shooting . . . when I . . . shot you." He leaned forward. "What do you remember? Certainly you remember something by now, don't you?"

Nathan studied Brian for a moment before answering. "I don't remember anything. Nothing. I have a partial memory, which I think is from Jonas Yoder's funeral, but nothing for a few days before that until I woke up at Brighton University."

Brian nodded. "Joe told me you were looking into your shooting."

"Yep."

He met Nathan's gaze. "I—I'm sorry about all this, Nathan."

Nathan thought about his attendant's words about how God can use affliction to accomplish a higher end. "You don't need to say anything, Brian. It's all right."

Brian frowned and began to pace, looking at Nathan's computer screen, pausing at the entrance to Nathan's new bathroom, looking over at the window and back at the bulletin board. "Come on, Nate. You remember something, don't you?"

Why all these questions? "Brian, I asked *you* what happened when you came to visit me in the hospital, remember?"

Brian looked down, away from Nathan's chair. "Yeah, I remember," he said, placing his hand against Nathan's bulletin board. His fingers ran over an article with his picture. "What a mug shot," he mumbled. He fixated on the X-ray hanging in the corner of the cork board. "This is yours?" He pulled it off and held it up to the light.

Nathan watched him closely. "You can see the bullet and everything."

Brian's fingers trembled slightly before he mumbled something beginning with "Holy . . . ."

"Brian?"

"Huh? Oh . . . what?" He looked at Nathan and put the X-ray on the counter.

"Did you do the scene investigation at Jonas Yoder's death?"

"Why?"

Nathan hesitated. *I'd better not mention the phone calls or the paper in Dr. Hannah's lab.* "He was buried the day I was shot. I'm just trying to find out about the day of the accident." He made a weak shrug, lifting his shoulders an inch. "I thought it might jog my memory if I studied the week before the shooting."

Suddenly Brian's face seemed to tense. "Yeah, I did the scene investigation. His poor mother found him hanging in his closet." He squeezed his eyes tightly for a moment. "It was a pretty straightforward case, from what I remember," he added, shaking his head. "Boy, that woman has had a hard life."

"Yes, she has." Nathan stared at Brian, who seemed intent on avoiding Nathan's gaze.

"Look, Nathan, it's best if you don't pry into these things," he said mechanically. "You know?"

"Not really."

"You're not in the department anymore, Nate. I think you should stay out of department business."

"Come on, Brian, you don't expect me to—"

He leaned down toward Nathan. "Take a look at yourself, Nathan. You're not exactly in a position to defend yourself, are you?"

"Defend myself? Why should I—"

Brian's voice was etched with strain as he interrupted. "Forget what I said, Nathan. Just forget it, OK?" He exhaled sharply. When he looked up, Abby was standing in the doorway.

"Hello, Nathan," she said, walking over to the side of his wheelchair. "Brian."

"Hello, Abby," he responded formally before dropping his eyes to the floor. "I was just leaving."

With that, he walked out, pausing at the doorway of Nathan's room. "Bye, Nate," he said without expression. "Good seeing you again."

Nathan heard the front door slam.

Abby looked at her husband. "What was that all about?"

He shook his head slowly. "I'm not sure. I asked him about doing the Jonas Yoder suicide investigation, and he just kinda freaked. He told me to stay out of department business and not to pry."

"That doesn't sound like Brian."

Nathan maneuvered his chair to follow Abby to the kitchen.

"I saw him in the cafe today," Abby began. "He was talking to one of the Ashby High students, I believe . . . a girl with white hair and black lipstick and a pierced belly button."

"Jennifer Hicks. I saw her in the cafe yesterday morning hanging out with Dion Smith."

"You know her?"

"I busted her before."

Abby's eyes widened. "Busted?"

Nathan nodded. "Heroin possession."

CHAPTER
21

BY LATE evening Ryan was done with the O.R., done with patient rounds, and done talking with a host of patients' families outside the neurosurgical I.C.U. By the time he headed for the lab, the sun had set and there was a slight chill in the air. He walked briskly between the main university hospital and the Dennis Foundation Research Facility, tipping his hat to the statue of Hippocrates as he passed. When he entered the building, he thought about the absence of the animal rights advocates. *I certainly haven't missed seeing them for the past few days.*

By the time he arrived in the lab, the pizza he'd ordered was cold and half-eaten, thanks to his daughter and Dr. Hopkins.

Paige smiled sheepishly. "Pizza's over there."

He held up his fingers and took an imaginary picture of his daughter. "There. Finally a smile to melt my heart."

She changed it to the overcheesy variety.

"Stop it."

"Couldn't help it. Where've you been?"

"Where else? Rounds, rounds, rounds," he responded. "The floors, the neurosurgical I.C.U.—"

Elizabeth poked Paige with a friendly jab. "Ahh, the vegetable garden." She used a term the residents often used for the neurosurgical I.C.U.

"Don't ever use that phrase around me," Ryan snapped. He winked at Paige before making an exaggerated frown at Elizabeth. "How's it look?"

"Better than I thought." She handed him a typed report, a summary of their project, and a proposal to continue.

"You've been working hard."

"I had a quick typist," Elizabeth responded.

Paige held up her fingers and waved them in the air across an imaginary keyboard. She imitated the phrase that her father often told the residents before an important operation. "Ten little ballerinas. Watch 'em dance."

"Hey," he said, looking at Elizabeth, "where'd you hear that?" He paused. "You can type?"

"Duh. I don't suppose you think I still write my papers by hand, do you?"

He spoke slowly with a heavy southern accent. "I thought everbody down in 'bama did."

"Cheap shot."

"Easy, you two," Elizabeth chided. "Look at this." She pointed Ryan's attention to a series of sensory evoked potentials graphed across a large data sheet. "These are sensory data recordings that I made of Heidi the evening before she was stolen."

"What's this?" He pointed to a small blip in the center of the line.

"It corresponds to a change in the position of Heidi's toe."

"A sensory evoked potential?" He leaned forward. "Why didn't we see this before?"

"I didn't have a chance to review the data. After Heidi was stolen, I spent all my efforts tracking down the veterinarian and talking to the police. Then they took our data away, so I couldn't look at it."

"You're sure about this?"

"Positive."

Ryan slapped his fist into his hand. "This is unbelievable!"

Paige wrinkled her nose. "Would anyone mind speaking English? What's so exciting?"

Ryan pointed at the small blip again. "This represents a measured response in the area of the brain responsible for position sense, the sensation we call proprioception. What this means is, not only did Heidi move her toe in response to stimuli that originated in the brain, but the brain also sensed that movement. In other words, movement messages were transmitted through the regenerated spinal cord segment, and a sensory message was transmitted back through the spinal cord all the way to the brain." He slapped his thigh. "The spinal cord is made up of thousands of minute tracks. In order to have success, we have to have the tracks match up in the correct order."

Elizabeth picked up his excitement and continued, "And this implies they were doing just that!"

"Just wait 'til I show this to old Dr. Pritchard. I'll show him delusions of grandeur!"

His pager sounded. Ryan looked at the number and groaned. "Ugh. Emergency room number."

He picked up the phone and dialed.

The chief neurosurgery resident, Dr. Wingfield, told of a nineteen-year-old with head trauma that needed an emergency craniotomy to evacuate a large epidural hematoma, a collection of blood between the skull and the tough lining over the brain called the dura.

"What's his E.M.V.?"

"Eight."

"Have the general surgeons seen him?"

"Yes. C-spine, chest, and abdomen have been cleared by the general surgeons."

"Does O.R. know?"

"Yes, sir. O.R. 2 will be ready in ten minutes."

"I'll see you there." Ryan hung up the phone and looked at Paige. "I'll be home late."

He picked up a piece of cold pizza and exited the lab with a light step. As he walked back to the hospital from the Dennis Building he ate and dreamed . . . dreamed of making the lame walk again.

◆ ◆ ◆

Brian Turner sat alone in the graveyard, underneath the old maple tree that overshadowed Laurie Turner's grave. He huddled within a blue police standard coat to ward off the night's chill. With the moon, a light yellow peach, overhead, there were no shadows tonight, except from the rare passage of a car down Main Street.

He sat with his legs outstretched toward a small bouquet of spring flowers he'd bought at Fisher's Retreat's only florist shop. Daffodils. Laurie's favorite. The kind she'd planted the autumn before she became ill. He'd bought her flowers more in the year since she was gone than in the five years they were married.

In this place, where many come to remember the dead with fond recollections of love, Brian returned to his tortured memories of his wife's last days, of love lost and love gained, of Abby, and of Nathan.

He squeezed his eyes tightly shut to remember the day that Abby promised to leave the man she no longer loved.

In his mind he also saw the old Allen house, the house in the heart of Fisher's Retreat where Nathan had gone down that day. A drug safe house that became the talk of the town. A distribution center, they'd discovered, that probably kept the likes of dozens of Lester Fitts active in the sale of illegal drugs.

In his mind he counted and recounted each agonizing time he pulled the trigger. He heard the sharp noise as Lester Fitts blew out the windshield of the patrol car, the sickening thud of a bullet striking the tree that shielded him. He was raising his gun again. *One, two . . . three.* He heard the wail of the siren and the rhythmic counting of Joe Gibson as he did CPR. He heard the chop of the helicopter blades as they sliced through the November air.

He recognized the irony. For Brian, it was a memory that would not die. For Nathan, it remained a memory forever lost, one that he desperately wanted to regain.

Brian sat forward and straightened the daffodils for a third time until he was satisfied. With that, he stood and shuffled away, alone except for the memories he loved.

And the memories he hated.

◆　◆　◆

Abby stroked Nathan's hair before leaving him for the night. Richard Ramsey had already come and gone, having positioned Nathan for sleep.

Nathan caught her eye. "Do you have any reason to think I may have been doing anything illegal when I was injured?"

"Illegal? What are you talking about?"

He collected his thoughts before speaking. "Joe tells me that I was unarmed when I was in the Allen house that day. He raised the question as to whether that indicated that I may not have been in there on official police business."

"That's crazy."

"I thought so too." He paused. "Then this afternoon Brian said something that made me think he may have similar concerns about me. He told me it was best not to pry into official police matters . . . and he told me I'm not really in a position to defend myself."

"What did he mean by that?"

Nathan shook his head. "I'm not sure. I can't believe that my dedication to the force could be in question. I may not be able to remember what I was doing in that safe house, but I can tell you what I wasn't doing."

"I doubt that anyone has real concerns about your reputation. You were the pride of Fisher's Retreat, Nathan." She rubbed his neck. "And you still are in many ways."

He watched her for a moment. "Good night, Abs. I'm lucky to have you."

"Night, Nate." She rose slowly, and he watched her as she walked away.

Nathan lay awake for a few minutes before whispering, "Abby, are you awake?"

He heard the bed upstairs squeak, followed by footfalls on the stairs. In a moment she was with him. "What do you need?"

"Did you deactivate the electronic door?"

She sighed. "Yes, Nathan. The automatic door is turned off and locked." She turned away. "Was that all?"

"I love you, Abs."

"You're just trying to make me feel better because you got me up."

"Can't hurt to try."

"Good night, Nathan."

CHAPTER
22

DEAN ALAN PRITCHARD wrinkled his nose as he entered the spinal lab. "What is that smell?"

"Rats, sir." Ryan offered a thin smile and observed the rotund physician, who obviously had spent most of the last fifteen years isolated from medical bench research. Ryan, however, prided himself on being one of the few physicians who balanced both a career as a true clinician, where his duties involved caring for human patients, and a second career in bench research, the pursuit of foundational medical knowledge that involved a host of test-tube and animal models but did not involve human trials.

Alan Pritchard, M.D., a cardiologist by training, spent little time with any sort of real medicine beyond his daily headaches with the administration of the B.U. Medical School, a task that he'd accomplished with great zeal and success for the past decade. He had thinning hair, a prematurely wrinkled face, and an annoying habit of squinting when he didn't understand something perfectly.

"This had better be worth it, Ryan," he began. "You know, I'll bet it's been six months since I've been in this building."

Doesn't surprise me a bit. Ryan bit his tongue. "Right this way," he offered, ushering the dean into his lab office, where Ryan made sure that Pritchard was seated in Ryan's own chair, and where Elizabeth handed him a warm mug of coffee.

"One package of Equal, no cream," she said. "Your assistant told me."

The dean raised his eyebrows and accepted the coffee with a nod.

Ryan pointed to the marker board in front of them. He gave a five-minute summary of the work and showed a video documentary of their research using the hamadryas baboon model.

Ryan watched Dr. Pritchard during the video as he squinted, shifted in his seat, and finally leaned forward and nodded.

At the conclusion Ryan handed a stack of paper to Dr. Pritchard. "It's all in this project summary and proposal that Dr. Hopkins prepared."

"You are confident this will work?"

"This is a significant step forward, sir. No one else has had this kind of success with a higher animal model before." Ryan cleared his throat. "I don't need to tell you how important keeping this project quiet is to me. I would like to present it to the neuroscientist community at the winter forum, if I can keep the research on track."

"But will it work again?"

"Absolutely."

"I'll give you my decision after reading the proposal." The dean stood and walked back through the lab's main work area, waving his hand beneath his nose as he went.

Ryan and Elizabeth watched him disappear.

Elizabeth slumped. "He hated it. Did you see him curl his lip when you showed the implantation of the cerebral sensors?"

"He seemed interested to me."

"And the way he wrinkled his nose at the smell." She shook her head. "He'll never go for it."

"I don't know. Pritchard is a man who cares about the bottom line—whatever will bring in money to support medical education."

Elizabeth shrugged. "This would be huge."

Ryan nodded before lifting his nose to the air. "The vivarium atmosphere in here is getting more noticeable. When *is* the last time the cages were cleaned?"

"I'll get it done."

"Good."

"Today."

"Better."

"This morning."

"Best," Ryan responded. "I've taught you well."

He looked at his watch and groaned. "I'd better run. I've got a cerebral aneurysm to clip with Dr. Wingfield," he said with a sigh. "He always gets so nervous doing these." He lowered his voice. "I think I'll recommend him to private practice. There he'll have his fill of lumbar disc surgery and can stay out of the brain."

◆ ◆ ◆

Brother Stephen's miracle crusade was held in a large outdoor tent that was erected at the Apple Valley Fairgrounds just outside Carlisle. It had been going strong for three nights, the paper reported, and they expected large crowds to continue through the weekend.

The floor of the tent was grass, which provided the first challenge for Nathan, whose chair needed an additional push several times to move through uneven areas. The second challenge was finding a location for his chair. There was a special area in the front labeled "handicapped," but Nathan did not want to sit away from his family. And when his father moved one of the folding chairs to make room for Nathan's chair, the usher redirected them to the area in the front, citing a vague fire code that prohibited Nathan from blocking an aisle. Finally Nathan settled on sitting in the back, behind the last row of chairs, and his father, in spite of a frown from an usher, moved a folding chair to sit by his son.

Nathan looked around. There were rows and rows of folding chairs beneath the tan canvas roof. The stage appeared to be wooden and could be accessed by stairs from either side. A woman sat at a grand piano that was center stage and surrounded by potted ferns. The melodies she played were familiar to him and were lofted into the tent's peaks by a powerful P.A. system.

Nathan's mom sat in front of them and to his right. Abby had politely declined the invitation and stayed home with Melissa.

Noisy feedback screamed from a microphone as a man began an

announcement. He tapped the head of the microphone and cleared his throat. "Ehh-uhh! Could I have everyone move to the center of the aisles please? People are still looking for seats. We're getting ready to begin." He tapped the microphone once more before leaving the stage.

After a few moments Brother Stephen, a youthful-appearing man in a double-breasted gray suit, carrying the largest Bible Nathan had ever seen, approached the podium. He wore a lapel microphone and paced as he spoke, waving his arms for emphasis.

Mark McAllister sat with his son while everyone else stood for singing and later for prayer.

They listened intently as Brother Stephen shared about the power of prayer, faith, and a miracle-working God. The atmosphere was electric, the singing enthusiastic, and the offering lengthy.

Finally Brother Stephen issued the invitation. "Come." He raised his voice and his hands. "Come with faith. Come expecting your miracle."

Mark wiped his son's nose for the tenth time. "Do you want me to come with you?"

Nathan nodded. "Help me get up the aisle."

Streams of people walked the aisle and onto the platform for prayer.

"I can't get up there," Nathan whispered as he edged his wheelchair closer to the front.

"He will come down here," his father said, laying a hand on Nathan's shoulder. "I'll make sure he does."

They watched as dozens were prayed for while the pianist played softly in the background.

Finally Brother Stephen approached the microphone and quickly dismissed the audience, inviting those who wanted further prayer to stay. The piano played on, and the audience began to disperse.

Nathan positioned himself in a line leading to the stairs at the right of the stage. "He's coming this way," Nathan said as the preacher prayed for first one and then another. Brother Stephen approached the edge of the platform, stopping again to pray for a woman holding a crying baby.

"According to your faith, be it unto you," the preacher said softly to a man standing on the stairs in front of Nathan.

When he arrived at Nathan's chair, he knelt and began a fervent prayer. Nathan could see the glistening sweat on the young man's forehead.

Brother Stephen prayed for peace, and for understanding, and for a special touch from God. He prayed for emotional healing and spiritual healing, for the healing of Nathan's relationships and for the healing of Nathan's self-image, and that God would use Nathan to further God's kingdom.

Mark McAllister cleared his throat and sighed audibly.

Nathan's vision clouded with tears. *Heal me, God. I believe.*

Brother Stephen continued to pray for faith and for God's timing. And finally he prayed that God would heal Nathan's body.

When he finished, he lowered his voice and spoke only to Nathan. "I believe God has something very special in store for you. He loves you. He created you." Nathan looked into the preacher's face. Brother Stephen's cheeks were streaked with tears as he reached forth his hand to grasp Nathan's shoulder. With his voice almost a whisper, he spoke one more sentence before moving to the next person. "You bear the image of God."

Nathan nodded as the preacher moved on. He tried to wiggle his toes. *Maybe if I concentrate real hard.* He looked down to see. *It's no use. I couldn't see my toes even if they were wiggling.* He turned to the left where his father stood. "Help me get out of here."

"Out of here? Your chair?" He reached for the Velcro strap around Nathan's chest. "You're going to walk?" He stared at Nathan. "You need some help?"

"No!" Nathan responded quietly but forcefully. "Help clear the aisle so I can move forward."

Mark cleared his throat and nodded. "OK," he whispered, touching the shoulders of the people in Nathan's way. "Let him through. Let him through."

"Sorry."

"Thank you."

"Excuse us."

Nathan followed his father down the aisle to the back of the large tent auditorium, where Sally McAllister stood with her eyes wide and her hand pressed to her lips.

"Let's go," Mark grunted and picked up the pace, moving on ahead of Nathan and his mother. He looked back for a moment before pulling away into the crowd. "I'll get the van warmed up."

Sally looked at her son and grabbed a Kleenex from her purse. "You're a mess," she said, wiping his cheeks. She pressed his hair against his head with her hand. "There."

Nathan submitted to his mother's grooming before tapping his headrest twice to travel on to the parking area.

"What happened up there?" Sally asked as she walked beside him.

"I'm not sure."

"Did he pray?"

"Oh, he prayed all right."

She placed her hand in Nathan's. "Go ahead, son. Squeeze."

Nathan sighed. "I'm trying."

"These things take time, son," she responded nodding. "And faith."

She moved her hand to the handle behind Nathan's chair and kept it there as she walked. "Maybe we can get Mark to take us up to Carlisle for ice cream."

When they got to the van, Mark appeared to be in no mood for ice cream, so Sally kept quiet. And after getting Nathan secured into position with straps, his father seemed determined to talk about anything except the crusade. Anything except his son or his son's disability.

"How 'bout them Packers?" he started in as he headed up the highway out of Carlisle. "That boy sure has an arm."

Nathan nodded quietly.

Mark prattled on about sports and fishing for fifteen miles, while Sally intermittently interrupted in a loud voice, commenting about this or that along the highway. "Let's go to that flea market sometime," she yelled.

Mark tilted his head and looked at Nathan. "Must be a lot of road noise in the back of this van. She talks louder than Emma Sue, and she's deaf as a post."

Nathan nodded again and tried to remember the exact words Brother Stephen had spoken.

Finally his father stopped talking as well, taking an appropriate hint from his son's silence. For the remainder of the trip up the Apple Valley to Fisher's Retreat, all was relatively quiet except for the road noise and Sally's commentaries.

Once they were at Nathan's, Abby greeted them warmly and invited them to stay.

Mark grabbed Sally's arm. "It's getting late, Sal. We'd better run."

Abby looked at Nathan.

"Not so fast," Nathan responded. "We gave my PCA the night off, knowing we'd be getting in so late." He smiled sheepishly, not wanting to admit he'd told Jim he wouldn't be needing him anymore. "I need you to help me get into bed."

Mark shoved his hands in his pockets. "Uh . . . Oh . . . sure."

Nathan started his chair toward the bedroom. "Abby can do most everything, except the transfer into bed."

Abby smiled and motioned to the couch. "Just give me a few minutes to brush his teeth. Make yourself at home. I made some tea. It's in the kitchen."

Once they were in the bathroom alone, Abby leaned close to him. "What's with him? He seems edgy."

"It's just Dad. He's out of sorts. He won't say it, but I think he's mad that I didn't walk out of that meeting tonight."

Abby nodded and opened the toothpaste before adding quietly, "What about you? You mad?"

"I don't know. Maybe. I've hardly had a chance to think about it. I think it was good, really." He shrugged and lowered his voice. "We can talk later."

Abby brushed his teeth. "Do I have to floss?"

"No way. Mr. Dental Obsession will be here tomorrow night."

Abby smiled, then leaned forward and kissed him full on the mouth. "Checking your work?"

She made a face. "Hey, I'm skilled at this sort of thing. I used to brush Melissa's all the time."

Nathan backed away from the sink and directed his chair into his bedroom. After he lined himself up beside the bed, Abby called for Mark to help.

With Mark lifting Nathan from behind, wrapping his own arms beneath Nathan's and around his chest, and with Abby moving Nathan's lower legs, they easily transferred Nathan into the center of the bed.

Gently, Mark lowered his son's head onto the bed. "There."

"That wasn't bad at all. You guys make a great team." Nathan looked up at his father. "Help me off with my pants, too, would you? It's a little tough getting them over my hips with me on my back."

"Uh . . . Er . . ." Mark looked at Abby. "Sure, I guess."

Mark fumbled with the button and zipper of Nathan's pants, then started tugging at the cloth around Nate's hips.

"Whoa. You're pulling me down."

"Sorry," he grunted. "There, they're coming off easier now." He grabbed the legs of the jeans and yanked.

Nathan heard a sharp, snapping sound.

His father winced and wiped his face. "What? Oh, for crying out loud!"

Nathan lifted his head to see his father holding the dangling tube leading to his urinary leg bag.

He dropped the tube and ran to the bathroom. Nathan heard water running. "Why didn't you tell me I was pulling . . . *that* ?"

"I couldn't feel it. I didn't know."

Abby put her hand to her mouth. Her eyes met Nathan's for a moment before turning away. She looked like she was trying not to laugh at her father-in-law's predicament.

Red-faced, Mark emerged from the bathroom.

"I can finish up from here," Abby interjected. "Don't worry about this."

Mark exited with a mumbled, "Thank you." Nathan listened as he tromped through the den. "Come on, Sal. Let's go home."

◆   ◆   ◆

Mark McAllister drove in silence after leaving Nate at his home. Sally eyed him with interest and contempt.

"Aren't you even going to tell me what happened up there with Brother Stephen?" Sally stared straight ahead at the yellow line in the road.

"Not much to tell."

"Not much? He prayed for Nathan longer than anyone else. What did he say?"

"I don't remember. He prayed about everything . . . I'm not even sure he prayed for a miracle!" He sighed. "All that preachin' but he didn't tell Nathan to rise up and walk or nothin'."

Sally didn't respond right away. After a minute, as they were nearing their own home just outside Fisher's Retreat, she spoke again. "It was nice of you to sit with Nathan. I know he appreciated it."

"I felt like punching that usher. Did you see him glare at me?"

"Oh, that would have been a pretty sight," she scoffed, her voice brimming with sarcasm.

"I'd have sent him to the healing line for sure," he muttered.

"Mark, Mark," she said softly.

He snickered. "I wouldn't have done it." He raised his voice. "But he deserved it."

He pulled the aging Buick into the driveway of their three-bedroom brick ranch. "What are we going to do with Nathan?" he asked, slumping forward over the steering wheel. "His life is over, Sal."

"It's not over, Mark."

She watched her husband's lip tremble. "He's my boy and he's ruined."

She touched the back of his shirt, damp with sweat. "He's our boy, Mark. And he's doing just fine." Sally slid from the seat and left her husband sitting in the car. At the front door of the house, she looked back and studied him for a moment before going in. "It's just going to take faith," she whispered to herself. "We just have to believe."

◆　◆　◆

Nathan talked Abby through the replacement of his Texas external catheter. As she worked, Nathan's body responded like it did during every catheter change.

Abby remained silent.

"I do that every time, Abby."

"Oh."

"It's just a reflex." He looked at his wife's face but could not capture her eye. "It still works, Abby. Not everything I have is broken." *You would know these things if you would've talked to the spinal cord injury counselors at the hospital like I wanted you to.* He cleared his throat. "We could even—"

"Do you want to be on your back tonight?" she interrupted. "I know you were on your side last night." She stood and fluffed his pillow under his head, still avoiding his gaze.

Nathan sighed. "On my back is fine."

She carefully smoothed the sheet beneath his legs and pulled his covers up to his chin. She flipped on the baby monitor and retreated toward the doorway.

"Abby," he called, "I'm still your husband. Not everything is the same, but there are still ways that—"

"Nathan," she interrupted, this time making eye contact with him. Her voice quivered slightly. "I'm not ready, OK?" She took a step toward him and stopped. "I'm sorry."

He watched her go and listened to her footfalls on the stairs. In a moment he heard the shower in the upstairs bathroom.

Nathan stared at the ceiling. *Abby's taking a shower. She touched me, but my body must repulse her now.*

He pinched his eyes shut as he listened to the water running through the old house's plumbing. He could see Abby in his mind. Showering, drying off. The thoughts of his wife's beautiful form both excited and frustrated him.

In the darkness Nathan began to sob. *She can't love me like this. She doesn't want to touch me.*

My father can't love me like this.

And I can't love me like this.

Who am I kidding? No one can love me like this.

He sniffed, helpless to stop his nose from running. He listened in the quiet as he heard the shower stop and soft bumping noises from Abby's closet, followed by the squeak of Abby's bed. Nathan's old bed.

He stayed awake for a long time, unable to sleep, attentive to every noise. Finally, in the stillness a peace nudged his soul. *I love you, Nathan. You bear my image.*

CHAPTER
23

ON FRIDAY morning Ryan looked up from the *Brighton Daily News* to see his daughter carrying a load of laundry.

Paige's eyes widened. "You're still here?"

He smiled. "Good morning to you, too, Sunshine."

"Morning."

"You're certainly industrious this morning," he said, eyeing the laundry basket.

She lifted a white blouse from the container, pinching it gingerly between two fingers. "I don't think I'll ever get that smell out of here."

Ryan sampled the air with a tilt of his head. "Smell?"

"Rat poop!" She dropped the blouse and pulled her hair toward her face. "At least after two showers I got that disgusting fragrance out of my hair." She wrinkled her nose.

Ryan stared at his daughter.

"Don't give me that blank look," the teenager responded. "You knew she'd get me to clean the cages, didn't you?"

He raised his hands in protest. "Please believe me," he said, unable to keep from smiling. "I had no idea Elizabeth would pass that job on to you."

"This is not exactly what I had in mind when I volunteered to work in the lab."

Ryan couldn't suppress a chuckle.

"What's so funny?"

"That a resident of mine could be bold enough to get the chairman's own daughter to clean out the vivarium." He chuckled again before looking at Paige, who pushed her lips into a pout. "By the way, I don't believe I thanked you," he added.

"You're right. Neither did Dr. Hopkins."

He stood up and bowed low. "Thank you so very much."

She responded by throwing the white blouse onto his head.

He waved it like a flag. "I surrender." He pulled it toward his nose. "It doesn't smell."

"It does too. It's all over it."

Ryan looked at his hands and the shirt they were holding.

"You're immune," she continued. "You *live* in that lab." She pulled the shirt from his hand and stomped off in the direction of the utility room. "By the way," she called back to the kitchen, "I thought by volunteering in your lab, I might just get to spend time with you and figure out whether I'm really cut out to be in medicine, but instead I'm cleaning rat cages!"

He sipped his coffee slowly. *You wanted to spend time with me?* He looked at his hands again. He rose and scrubbed them in the kitchen sink.

◆ ◆ ◆

After Nathan's Friday morning routine, Jim Over sat across the corner from Nathan at the kitchen table, each of them enjoying a second cup of coffee. Nathan was sipping through a long, jointed straw inserted into a Hardee's Winston Cup commemorative mug. Jim drank from a white mug with the town emblem and the words Fisher's Retreat Police Department on the side.

"I wasn't sure you'd show up this morning after what I told you on the phone yesterday afternoon," Nathan began.

Jim shrugged. "It's OK, man."

"After last night, I'm not sure I'm ever giving you the night off again." Jim's look of curiosity prodded Nathan to continue. "It was a disaster," he said, shaking his head. "I got my dad to help put me to bed and get me undressed." Nathan paused. "He pulled my catheter right off with my pants. Sprayed himself in the face and everything."

Jim laughed and set his coffee mug on the table.

"Believe me, my father wasn't laughing."

Nathan's attendant laughed even harder. "I can see Mark now."

Nathan chuckled too. "I suppose it *is* a little humorous—now that it's over." He looked at Jim and took another sip of coffee. "My dad was out of sorts over the healing crusade."

Jim looked up but didn't speak.

"I think he was upset that I didn't just walk out of there."

"What about you?"

Nathan shook his head. "That's just what Abby asked me. I don't know really. I thought about it some last night. I still believe God is going to heal me, but maybe I just need to seek his timing in this thing. Maybe he still has some lessons for me here." He looked down at the kitchen table. "Or maybe I just needed more faith."

"Hmmm. What happened at the crusade?"

Nathan gave the play by play of the evening, including the details of Brother Stephen's prayer and the quiet message he'd delivered only to Nathan.

Jim spoke contemplatively. "Sounds to me like this guy was pretty right on."

"How so?"

"Do you sense that God has work for you in the areas he mentioned?"

Nathan stayed quiet.

Jim prodded further. "Your relationships perhaps? You said he prayed for that." He paused.

Nathan looked out through the automatic glass door into the backyard. *Yeah, my relationship with Abby.* He couldn't say it.

Jim continued, "Your self-image maybe?"

"How could anyone feel good about himself when he's like this?"

Jim pinched his lips together and stayed quiet for a moment. "You tell me, Nathan. Tell me what Brother Stephen whispered to you again."

Nathan's voice was cold and mechanical. "He told me God loved me and that I bear the image of God."

Jim raised his eyebrows. "Sounds to me like ol' Brother Stephen has his act together more than I thought."

"I didn't want to hear that God loved me. I didn't want religious talk. I wanted to walk! I—"

Nathan quieted his voice as Melissa came in, squeezing Willie, her gingerbread man.

"Daddy, will you play a game with me?"

Nathan looked at Jim, then back at his daughter. "Uh, sure," he said quietly. "How about checkers? You can move my men too."

Jim reached over and squeezed Nathan's forearm. Nathan appreciated the gesture, even though he felt exactly nothing.

"I'd better run," Jim added. "We'll talk again."

Nathan nodded. "Bye." He looked at his daughter, who was setting up the checkerboard on the floor. "Oh no you don't, Mel. You always cheat when we play on the floor!"

◆　◆　◆

When Ryan exited the cranberry hall into his office suite, Trish immediately set the phone in its cradle. "Where have you been? You're not answering your pages."

He stopped and looked at his beeper. "Oh. It's still off." He shrugged. "I stayed at home for breakfast with Paige. I knew I didn't have a case this morning, and Dr. Cho is taking over ward rounds."

Trish pointed to a box of projector slides on the corner of her desk. "But you agreed to give Dr. Button's lecture so he could attend the Neurotrauma Forum in Detroit." She handed him the box. "You have to be in room M-301 in fifteen minutes. The medical students will be waiting," she added with sarcastic cheer.

"What am I talking about?"

"Pituitary tumors."

He shrugged. "OK."

"You have two hours to fill." She handed him a sheet of paper. "Dr.

Button submitted six test questions from the lecture. He wanted to be sure you covered these items."

"He did, did he?" Ryan muttered. "I've been giving this lecture since Dr. Button was in medical school. I think I can handle it." He looked at his watch. "Did the Physician's Alliance agree to change any of the neurosurgery fee schedule?"

"Not yet, sir. I have a feeling they're looking closely at the McCue surgeons to see how their negotiations go with the Brighton Care people."

Ryan sighed. "McCue . . . If those guys could operate their way out of a wet paper bag . . ." His voice trailed off. "Say, is there any way to find out what they're charging? Say, on the most common procedures . . . lumbar discs, carpal tunnels, you know."

Trish shook her head. "I talked with the hospital attorney, McLaughlin. I'm not sure I understand it all, but he says it's a very bad idea to talk about prices with any competing group . . . something about being in violation of antitrust laws. I think the Alliance could get sued if you do that."

"Kroger can look across the street to see what Safeway is charging for cabbage, can't they?"

"This is brain surgery, Dr. Hannah, not produce." She smiled.

He chuckled to himself. "I'm not sure I'll ever understand health care delivery again. When my dad practiced medicine—"

"I know, I know," Trish interrupted. "I've heard the good ol' days song from you before," she said, nudging him toward the door. "Better get going, Dr. Hannah."

He stopped at the doorway. "Did the dean call about my research proposal?"

"Not yet." She waved her hand. "I'll let you know."

Ryan smiled and began his trek to the medical school. A few minutes later he exited the University Hospital building into a warm spring day. He glanced at Hippocrates, then turned left onto a spoke extending from the circle drive. After walking a hundred yards, he climbed the steps to a large brick building that housed the Brighton University Medical School. Long white columns supported a balcony that overshadowed a wide bricked portico.

Ryan paused and looked at the old building, a seven-story structure that was the original science building used by the university, long before the formation of the medical school. The first floor was strictly administrative, the second and third housed classrooms and offices dedicated to the first two years of medical training, and the remainder were dedicated to the supporting sciences of biochemistry, anatomy, and physiology. The pharmacy and dental schools had long been crowded out of the building to sit on adjacent spokes extending from the main circle drive.

He shielded his eyes to scan the structure. On the very top floor, where the large human cadaver lab occupied most of the space, the windows were open for ventilation, as they commonly were during both summer and winter.

I should bring Paige here. She'd enjoy a tour of the old building. She could see what the rigors and joys of medical school are all about. He laughed to himself.

He entered, took the elevator to the third floor, and slipped into the back of the darkened lecture hall just as the instructor concluded. The lights snapped on, and bleary-eyed students begin to stretch. Several students in the back seemed immovable, with mouths agape and eyes closed. The images evoked memories of Ryan's own medical education—hours in lectures, nights cramming for exams, the cadaver dissection, his first real human patient.

He smiled, glad to be beyond the stage he was currently observing. "Take five minutes," he yelled from the back of the room. "Then we'll get started again."

He ignored the quiet groans and handed his slides to the projectionist.

In exactly five minutes the lights were lowered again, and Ryan showed his first slide. He carried the students on a journey through pituitary tumors, explaining their presentation and treatment, including the surgical approaches through the nose or under the upper lip, giving the neurosurgeon access to the base of the brain without leaving an external scar. After fifty minutes he gave them a break before resuming again for the second hour.

When Ryan showed his last slide, the lights came up fifteen minutes before his allotted time. He surveyed his audience. *Good. Less than a third asleep.*

"OK, in these last few minutes I want to bring another matter to your attention." He paused, hoping that his climb onto his soapbox wouldn't be completely lost on the students. "Unfortunately, today physicians are finding it more and more important to keep their political voice loud and clear, not only to protect our interests as doctors while the government is reaching into our pockets, but also to benefit the patients we serve." He wrote an 800 telephone number on the blackboard.

"How many people in this state sustain spinal cord injuries every year?"

Blank stares greeted him.

"Approximately 200," he said, answering his own question. "And how many permanent brain injuries?" He paused. "About 2,000."

Several students began shifting in their seats.

"And what is the cost in this state alone to take care of these patients in the first year?" He held up his hand.

"Four hundred million," he continued. "Two hundred thousand dollars for the first year after injury for each patient."

Two students stood and slipped out of the back row.

"The cost for surgical care for a pressure sore alone averages 50,000 dollars."

I'm losing them.

A male voice cracked from the back of the crowd, "Is this on the boards?"

The students laughed.

"Not everything that is important to know is on the boards." Ryan held up his hand again. "I'll be done in a minute." He leaned against the podium. "There is a neurotrauma initiative proposal before our state's general assembly. If this is enacted, every driver found guilty of driving under the influence would have to pay an additional fifty dollars to the state to help fund spinal cord and brain injury care and research. If you think that's a good idea, call this number," he said pointing at the blackboard. "Call the general assembly and express your opinion."

The projectionist handed Ryan his slides as the surgeon raised his voice for one last comment. "No, it's not on the boards," he added, lifting a finger, "but when you rotate through my neurosurgical service next year, I will be asking if you called." He flashed his audience a Paige-smile and retreated from the room.

It never hurts to start training them for the real world right from the start. Even if they can't see past their next exam.

◆ ◆ ◆

The cafe lunch crowd thinned, leaving only the Millers, who always had an extra cup of coffee before leaving, Mary Stutzman, who had stayed to read the paper, and Thomas Yeager, who was finishing a vegetable plate of brown beans, kale, and cheddar mashed potatoes.

"Can I bring you anything else?" Abby asked. *He'll say, "Not a thing, Abby."*

"Not a thing, Abby."

She smiled. *It's nice that some things in life are predictable.* She handed him the check.

He closed his eyes and picked up the tab. "Three twenty-one," he said before opening his eyes. "Right again."

Abby looked around before lowering her voice and asking, "Mr. Yeager, do you believe in healing?"

He tilted his head and looked at her with piercing blue eyes. "Is this about Nate?"

She sighed and nodded.

"Can you sit for a minute?"

She slipped into the booth opposite the pastor. "My shift is up," she responded.

"I believe in healing, Abby," he said thoughtfully. "Jim Over told me that Nate was going down to the healing crusade."

"He went last night."

"And?"

"Nathan was pretty quiet about it. When I talked with him this morning, he just told me that he still believed God was going to heal him, but he thought maybe it was going to be gradual. A process or something." She sighed. "I really think he believed he was going to walk last night."

"How'd he react?"

"He seems to stay pretty positive. I have a hard time getting him to complain." *I have a hard time getting him to talk to me, period.* "I think," she added, "that he feels like he didn't have enough faith, that if he'd have believed stronger, he would've been healed."

"Hmmm. That's a bad trap to be in. There's always guilt if you don't believe enough."

Abby nodded silently.

"Does he ever seem too up?"

"What do you mean?"

"I've talked to Nate, Abby—many times before his accident, and some over at that nursing home. He's not one to let you in on his feelings very quickly."

"You're telling me."

"Honestly, I think Nate is putting up some nice neat walls, only showing you and everyone else his best face." Pastor Yeager rubbed the back of his hand and pushed his empty plate aside. "Sudden, severe disabilities like Nate's are often devastating to a person's self-esteem. Most people take a long time to work out their feelings about themselves. I've seen this before. He might be afraid to be open up with you because he's insecure about the way you'll react to him."

Abby straightened.

"And it wouldn't be your fault at all. Some people with injuries like Nate's worry that they'll lose their families. They worry about being a burden." He shrugged. "So they act like they're up all the time, so they won't be a drag."

"Sounds like Nathan."

"And now he's talking about his healing. He may be reluctant to say anything that might reveal his fear that he'll never walk again."

"You said you believe in healing."

"I do, Abby. I've prayed for thousands of people to be healed. And some were." He looked at his plate. "And some died." He tapped the table with his weathered hands. "Jesus didn't heal everyone when he walked the earth. And I've come to believe that we twist the Scriptures to prove that he will heal everyone who asks now."

"But Nathan was so sure. He kept telling me, 'Jesus Christ, the same yesterday, today—'"

"'And forever,'" the pastor finished for her. "That Scripture is true, Abby."

"But . . ." she responded, unable to keep the sarcasm out of her voice.

"God will answer prayers that are in accordance with his will."

"It can't be God's will that Nathan was shot . . . that Nathan is like this!"

"It's not his will in the sense that he didn't cruelly design the accident to punish Nate. He's not that kind of Father." He paused. "But occasionally, in his love, he allows evil to come our way in order to fulfill a plan we can't understand or see."

"God couldn't have planned this." She shook her head, not wanting to cry. "Not the God of love you preach."

He reached his hand across the table, but Abby pulled away.

"*God* did not plan this for my husband," she said coldly.

◆　◆　◆

That night, after teeth brushing and flossing, Dave transferred Nathan into his bed for the night.

"Hey, Dave," Nathan began, as he watched his body being positioned, "can you take me through the old Allen house sometime? I saw an Apple Valley Realty sign in front of it last night when my parents were bringing me home. You still work with them, don't you?"

"The Allen house? You mean—"

"The house where I was shot."

"Well, I, er . . . Why do you want to go there? I mean, I guess so, if you really want." Dave looked down and scratched his salty beard before wrinkling his nose. "Do you really want to go in there?"

Nathan persisted. "Sure. If you can get me in."

"Oh, I can unlock the door."

"I know there are a few steps. I could go in my regular wheelchair.

It's not as heavy as my powerchair. You could lug me up a couple steps, couldn't you?"

"I guess so." He backed up a step and leaned against the long desk counter where Nathan's computer sat. "But you didn't answer my question. Certainly you're not interested in purchasing—"

"Of course not. Me? Live there?" Nathan shook his head. "There are a few things I want to check out, that's all. I saw the police sketches and diagrams. Now I want to see it with my own eyes."

"I don't know. Seeing it could bring back some pretty heavy memories, Nathan. Are you sure you want to do this?"

"That's just the point, Dave. I don't remember a thing about my shooting. I'm hoping that seeing the scene might just dislodge something up here." Nathan pointed to his brain by rolling his eyes.

Nathan could hear Dave pacing behind him. "I guess we could look. Why not?" Dave hesitated a moment, then added, "We could even go tomorrow morning if you really want."

"Thanks."

Dave pulled up Nathan's covers and arranged his pillow. "That OK?"

"Yeah." Nathan looked up. "Hey, could you plug in my powerchair? The battery charger is on the floor next to the trash can."

"Sure thing." He followed his instructions. "You want the light on or off?"

"Leave it on for now. Abby will come down for a minute, I'm sure."

"OK. Good night, Nate. I'll let myself out."

Nathan heard him pause at the doorway but couldn't see him because he was positioned on his side facing the other way.

"See you in the morning," Dave said.

"You know where I'll be."

CHAPTER
24

SATURDAY MORNING was overcast with occasional drizzle, the kind of weather a duck would love but Nathan despised.

"I don't know," Dave Borntrager said, walking through the automatic door onto the concrete patio. "It looks like this is going to continue." He turned back. "Are you sure you want to go?"

"I'm sure." Nathan looked at Abby. "You want to come with us?"

She kept her voice low. "I want no part of this. I don't want to see that house." She held a drink up for Nathan. "It's evil. I wish you wouldn't go either."

"It's just a house, Abby. I just want to see where it all happened."

"Personally, I wish you weren't so consumed with *it*."

Nathan cast an uncomfortable glance at Dave. He didn't want him to hear his argument with Abby. "Look," he said with his voice just above a whisper, "you'd want to know if it was you."

Her expression softened. "I suppose so, Nathan." She looked away. "I just don't want you to torture yourself. So you don't remember—so what?" She shrugged. "Why not just let it go?"

"I can't."

"Then go there, Nathan." She shook her head. "But don't expect me to go with you."

"It shouldn't take that long, Abby." He looked at Dave. "Let's go."

Dave pushed Nathan's wheelchair forward. In ten minutes they were sitting in the driveway of the Allen house. Just seeing the place for more than a fleeting moment had an eerie and unsettling effect on Nathan. He wondered if he looked as pale as he felt. With his mouth dry, he watched as Dave undid the straps securing the wheelchair to the floor of the van.

"Why do they call this the Allen house?"

"The last owner, Arnold Allen, willed it to his son about ten years ago." Dave shook his head. "His son doesn't even live around here. He just used it as a rental."

The yard was unkempt, and spring growth had begun to overtake the edge of the driveway. The house was a one and a half stories, with red bricks, green shutters, and a black roof with several missing shingles. Two dormers extended from the black roof like two conspicuous front teeth. Tall bushes were overgrown and nearly concealed the first floor from view. Several daffodils were blooming next to a mailbox labeled 17. The driveway was gravel, and that made for slow going for Dave as he pushed Nathan across to a cracking sidewalk leading to a small porch at the front door.

The drizzle had just begun again when Dave retrieved a key from a locked realty security box hanging from the front doorknob. The three steps leading up to the front door were manageable only because of Dave's strength and Nathan's relatively light weight. Dave pulled Nathan up in his chair, backwards, one step at a time. Once on the porch, Nathan said, "Made it," then paused and looked through the door Dave had opened. "That's where I fell," he said, nodding to the floor inside the doorway. He looked up at the wall just inside the entrance foyer. "They repaired the drywall here. The scene photographs showed a bullet entry right over there."

Dave grunted. "Where to?"

"Down this hall to the kitchen. I think this is where most of the drug cache was found."

The kitchen was empty except for a small vinyl-topped table with metal legs. Pale green painted cabinets lined the far wall on both sides of a window that was just above a single sink. There were gaps in the counter space, presumably for a missing oven and dishwasher. A brown spot on the yellow linoleum floor marked the spot left by a refrigerator.

"Turn me around." Nathan could see the front door from the kitchen and also the stairs leading to the second floor.

Dave walked around, leaving Nathan in the kitchen. "I think we're going to have a hard time moving this property." He looked at Nathan, who then quickly looked at the stairs leading to the second floor. "Oh, no. Don't even think about it."

"You go up there. You be my eyes."

Dave disappeared up the creaky wooden steps. He called down. "Now what?"

"Describe what you see."

"I'm standing at the top of the stairs, on a landing. There are only two rooms up here." Nathan heard a squeak. "Oh, make that three. Here's a half-bath."

"Look in the room on your right if you're facing the front of the house. Describe the room to me."

"There's nothing here. It's not a very big room. Wooden floor. Oak, I think. Two windows. One's a dormer. The other is at the end of the house in the middle of the far wall. White walls. White ceiling." Nathan heard another squeak. "Single closet with sliding door. That's about it."

"Can you open the window on the far wall?"

A grunt was followed by the sound of the window sliding. "Yep."

"Tell me what you see. Could you jump from that window?"

"Jump? Not me." His voice got fainter. Nathan imagined him talking with his head stuck out the window.

"Is there a ledge? Anything to stand on?"

"Yes. A two-foot roofline. I think it runs around from the front, as part of the same covering over the little porch."

Dave's footsteps descended again after he described the other room to Nathan. "What's this all about? Why all the concern about the window?"

"Let's go outside and look."

Dave shrugged. "You're the boss."

They exited through the back door, which only had one step down onto a small patio. "We should have come in this way."

"*Now* we find a simple way," Dave gasped.

Pushing through the long grass was not easy. The foot supports kept getting snagged on the overgrowth, so Dave tilted Nathan back on the two large back wheels and proceeded.

"There," Dave said, pointing up to the side of the house. "There's the window."

The front porch roof did wrap around the side of the house and dead-ended against a brick chimney. Beside the chimney on the side of the house was a wooden lattice, the sort used for climbing roses. *Or climbing people*, Nathan mused.

"Do you mind telling me what you're looking for?"

"I'm just playing with a hypothesis," Nathan responded thoughtfully. "What better way for a person to escape if they were in the house when the shooting started?"

"You think someone else was involved, someone else was in the house?"

"It's not something I want you repeating, OK? I have no solid evidence to back up my thoughts. But something I saw in the photos Joe Gibson showed me made me wonder, that's all." Nathan tried to catch his attendant's eye. "I'd really rather keep our little trip out here a secret. Every time I start asking questions, I keep getting the feeling that people don't want to talk to me about it."

Dave shrugged. "Don't you think that's just natural, Nate? I mean, nobody is going to feel too comfortable talking about your accident with you."

"Why not?"

"For the same reason you wouldn't want to talk about anyone else's illness or disability." He huffed. "I don't know how to explain it."

"You may have a point." Nathan paused as he felt Dave tilting the chair to begin forward movement again. "But I may just be on to something here, Dave. And finding out the truth might be pretty scary for someone who's hiding out there hoping I won't search further."

Dave huffed. Nathan could feel his breath on his neck. "Don't worry, Nate. I can keep a secret."

"Let's get out of here. I'm starting to get wet."

◆ ◆ ◆

When Nathan returned, he found Abby and Melissa embroiled in a checkers match.

Abby looked up at Nathan. "Well, how was it?" Her eyes widened. "You're soaked!"

"It's just a little rain."

"You hafta jump, Mom."

Abby went to the bathroom, retrieved a towel, and started drying Nathan's hair. "Your doctor said even a little chest cold could be serious for you," she scolded. "Because of your weak cough."

Nathan held his tongue. *Just because I'm in a wheelchair, everyone wants to treat me like a child.*

Melissa raised her voice. "You hafta jump me!"

"Ugh. Who taught you these rules?" Abby returned her attention to the game.

"Daddy."

Dave touched Nathan's shoulder. "Let's get you in your powerchair. I've got a client to meet."

Nathan looked ahead at the floor. "Better wipe off these wheels first."

Dave sighed.

"Hey, I saw you wipe your shoes on the welcome mat. This is just the same for me."

Dave took the towel that Abby had used on Nathan's head and rubbed it quickly over the wheels, edging Nathan forward a few inches at a time.

With that done, his attendant pushed Nathan into his room and transferred him into the powerchair. Behind him, in the family room, Nathan could hear Abby and Melissa.

"I want to watch TV."

"You've already seen two shows this morning. Why don't you color?"

"Maaahhhhumm! I'm gonna miss *Rugrats*!"

Abby's voice picked up in volume. "No. And that means no."

Footsteps were followed by Abby's voice again. "Here. You can use these. I need to do the breakfast dishes. Then you can go grocery shopping with me if you want."

Melissa whined again.

Nathan nodded at Dave. "That should do it. Thanks," he said before moving his chair back toward the kitchen.

There he saw Melissa bent over a coloring book on the kitchen table, and Abby closing up a box of Cocoa Puffs. Before his injury Nathan would have reached in for a handful of dry cereal. Now he couldn't do it, and he didn't want to ask for help. Besides, he didn't get hungry like before. *It's no wonder I lost so much weight. I hardly ever snack anymore. I used to be the snack king.*

"So what are your plans for the day?" asked Abby.

Same as every day, Abby. I'm going to sit in this chair until somebody moves me.

"I don't know. I think there's a Braves game this afternoon. I'd like to see if old John Smoltz will come through for me this time." He paused. "Maybe I'll go surfing later."

"The Net?"

No, I'm going down to the beach. He imagined himself strapped onto a surfboard. "Yeah. Jim Over gave me the addresses of some websites to visit. Did you know that some churches have their own web page, even chat rooms?"

Abby turned on the faucet over a stack of dirty dishes and rolled her eyes. "Cyber-church. It doesn't seem quite normal."

Nathan edged his chair a little closer to Abby. "Do you want to go to Community Chapel in the morning?"

"Oh, Nathan, I can't. I promised Marty I'd work her shift at the cafe."

"You worked last Sunday."

"I know," she replied, looking away from Nathan's gaze. "She wanted to go to Carlisle with Brian to a slow-pitch tournament or something." She picked up a dish. "But she'll work my Sunday next week. Maybe Richard will take you."

Nathan turned his chair around to look at Melissa, who seemed preoccupied with an orange crayon. "Are Marty and Brian . . . ?"

"They're just friends, Nathan." He heard Abby open a cabinet door. "Since Laurie's gone and Marty left Darryl, they've been hanging out together. Nothing worth gossiping about."

Nathan sat for a few minutes while Abby worked.

After putting away the last breakfast bowl, Abby spoke again. "You haven't told me about your visit to the Allen house."

He turned his chair to see her.

"Nothing to tell, really. It's like seeing a place I'd never been to. If it weren't for the pictures Joe showed me, I wouldn't have recognized anything." He watched as Abby wadded a dish towel in her fists. "I'm not sure I'll ever know exactly what happened there."

"Nathan, you know what happened there. You've read about it. Joe told you about it. What more is there?"

"I want to know what drew me there. Why did I go into that place? Why was I unarmed? What prompted me to send a Mayday 10-33 radio call?"

He had a thousand other questions that he didn't express. *Was someone else in the house? How does my shooting relate to Jonas Yoder? Did I know something about his death that somehow got me into trouble? Who keeps calling me, warning me, telling me I knew that Jonas was killed? Why does everyone seem to think I'd be better off not knowing?*

A clatter of dishes brought Nathan back.

"Oops. Nothing broken. I didn't mean to put them down so hard."

In a moment Abby was kneeling by his side. "Would you mind watching Mel while I get groceries?" She looked over at their daughter. "Unless you want to go with me, Melissa."

"I want to stay here."

"Go ahead," Nathan urged. "We'll be fine."

A few minutes after Abby left, Nathan, on his way to his room, heard the TV set. "Melissa," he called, "no TV. You heard Mom."

An advertisement for a sugary cereal blared.

Nathan stopped the forward movement of his chair and turned around. "Mel."

Melissa cast a furtive glance over her shoulder.

"No TV. Why don't you show me your picture?"

"No."

Nathan moved closer, until he was almost touching her with his chair. "You need to obey Daddy. Turn off the TV. Let's play checkers."

"I don't want to play checkers. This is my favorite show."

"Melissa, this is an ad. Turn the TV off."

He edged the chair against her foot. She pulled it away.

"Obey Daddy."

She faced her father. "You can't spank me."

He was shocked. "Melissa!" He moved his chair right up to the TV and strained to reach the on/off button with his mouthstick. No luck. *Where's that remote?* "I may not be able to spank you, young lady, but I am still your father."

"Daddy!" She began to cry.

Nathan hated crying. Especially the whiny-kid type that can be turned on and off at will.

Melissa snapped off the TV before running up the stairs.

Great. Another place I can't reach her. "Melissa?"

No response.

Nathan sat and sighed. Sat and waited.

After a few minutes he heard Melissa on the stairs. Her footsteps stopped.

She must be sitting on the stairs.

"Can Tommy come over and play?"

Nathan thought about the last time they'd invited Tommy Evans over. "After your mom comes home."

"Daddy!"

Nathan had an idea. "Come here, sweetheart. Look outside. I know something fun you can do with me."

Nathan heard her bump, bump, bump down the stairs, slow and deliberate in her progress. Finally she came into view, slipping down the stairs on her backside.

"Is it still raining?" he asked.

She opened the front door. "No."

"Good," he responded, heading for the front door. "The driveway may be a little slick, but it will be OK."

"What are we going to do?" she asked hesitantly.

Nathan smiled. "You know how you like to ride holding onto the back of Daddy's chair?"

Melissa nodded. "I don't want to do that. I want to watch TV."

"I think it's time you learned to drive this thing."

"Drive?"

He moved his chair through the front door, down the ramp onto a walkway, and onto the concrete driveway. "Let's practice here before going down the street."

Melissa's eyes widened.

"Climb on the back like you normally do. Just stand on the battery pack," he said. "Now reach your hand around and tap right here," he added, leaning his head toward his headrest."

"There," he added. "Hit it twice in a row, and it will put us in outdoor mode. It's faster that way."

Melissa giggled. "Whoa!"

"Now hit the side pad."

"We're gonna crash." She laughed and held on.

"You're doing fine."

"I turned us!"

Nathan glanced across the street at Ms. Evans, who scrutinized the activity from her porch. "Wave at Ms. Evans, sweetheart." He lowered his voice for Melissa's ears only. "She must have had a lemon for breakfast."

"Wait 'til I tell Mommy I can drive!"

CHAPTER
25

ON SUNDAY morning Ryan glanced through the newspaper, reflecting on how nice it was not to have to see headlines about animal cruelty. *Somehow,* he thought, *we seem to have gotten our priorities mixed up. We worry about spotted owls and lab animals and spend millions on the environment, but important medical research goes unfunded.*

Paige bounded though the front door, gasping. "Ugh! We don't have hills like this in Alabama." She gave her father a sweaty kiss on the forehead before opening the refrigerator.

"Morning, Sunshine."

"Do we have any bottled water?"

"Your mother always drank that stuff." He pointed toward the garage. "I just bought a whole case for you. It's in the utility room."

"Thanks," she replied. "That 'stuff' is good for you. Better than the pot of coffee you just drank."

Ryan shrugged as Paige walked away.

"Remember what you said last week?" Paige called from the utility room before returning with her water.

Ryan cringed.

"We still can make the 10:30 service at Grace." She paused to sip from the bottle in her hand. "You are off, you know."

"I was hoping to take you to brunch at the Sheraton downtown. Then I thought I'd show you the medical school. I was over there yesterday. It would give you a little feel for what it's like." He looked up to see Paige's frown.

"Dad, we can do all those things *after* church."

Ryan sighed. *You're just like your mother. And yet she says that you are just like me.*

"What do you have against going to church?"

"Paige, I don't have anything against going. It's fine for you. It's just—"

"Just what?"

"Well—"

Paige glared at him.

"They've just put their minds in neutral, honey. It's all faith, faith, faith. I don't fit in over there. I'm a scientist."

"All the more reason for you to believe," she countered. "You above all people ought to know that the complexities of the human brain are evidence of a Creator."

"I believe in God, Paige. I didn't say I didn't. I just don't know that I believe the way they do." He looked at his daughter. "Like you do."

"You were the one who took me when I was a kid."

"Paige, your *mother* took us both. I'd think you'd realize that by now." He paused and pushed the newspaper away from him. "It was one of the better things she did for you, actually." He smiled and tried to focus his attention back on his daughter. "I like the way you turned out."

"Go with me, Dad. It won't hurt you. We can sit in the back. No one will even know you're there. Then we can go to brunch."

Ryan's excuses were thinning. *I can't even use my lab as an excuse. That's where I normally spend Sunday mornings. Just me and my animals . . . and sometimes Elizabeth.*

He looked at the hurt in his daughter's eyes. "I'll go," he said, shaking his head. *Boy, if she has that effect on her boyfriends, I'm in trouble.*

She smiled.

"And, yes, we'll sit in the back. And the minute the preacher stands and asks us to introduce ourselves to everyone, I'm outta there."

"Dad, he won't do that." She smiled a gentle smile, just revealing the bottoms of her white front teeth.

He tried to return the smile. *Yep, I'm in trouble all right. I knew that when I first saw you in my office this time. You're going to break some hearts.*

◆ ◆ ◆

On Sunday morning in Fisher's Retreat, Nathan's attendant, Richard Ramsey, was an hour late. That was particularly worrisome to Nathan because Abby was at the cafe, and Melissa threw a fit because her mother had not left out the right kind of cereal. In addition, Nathan was thirsty, and his blankets were too high under his chin. The frustrations of physical disability!

When Richard arrived, Nathan found it difficult to be gracious.

"I'm sorry, Nate. My truck, er, I . . . Well, the truth is, I overslept. I was out at a ball tournament in Carlisle and—"

"Forget it, Richard," he snapped, barely able to control his anger. "Could you just get me some water? And check on Mel. She's been in a tizzy over breakfast."

Richard nodded.

Nathan listened as Richard chatted with Melissa and retrieved the kind of cereal she demanded. In a moment Richard came in holding a cool glass of water with a straw. "Here."

His attendant looked down. "I hope you weren't counting on making it to Community Chapel. They start in thirty minutes."

"Crud."

Richard started Nathan's limbs through a range of motions. Nathan studied his longhaired helper for a moment and forced himself to be civil.

"Say," Nathan started, "I know it's too late to make it to Community, but we could go somewhere else, if you can take us."

"Where?"

"Spring Creek Church. They don't start 'til 10:30."

"The Old Order church?" Richard huffed. "Oh, won't we be a sight! Those Mennonites don't even drive cars, and here comes Nathan McAllister in his 12,000-dollar powerchair." He paused. "Even I won't fit in there!"

"It will be fine, Richard."

"Oh, right. I'm wearing blue jeans. Those men wear black coats, every one of them."

"They don't mind visitors."

"Come on, Nate, you can't mean it! Have you ever seen the parking lot? It's nothing but hitchin' posts!"

"Richard," he countered, "they have a place for cars to park too. Just beyond the horse lot. It will be OK. Come on."

"You're serious."

"I'm serious."

Richard sighed. "Only because we're too late for Community Chapel. And only to make it up to you for my being late," he added shaking his finger at Nathan. "Why do you want to go there?"

"I'd like to talk to the pastor. Maybe he can help me understand Rachel Yoder's attitude better."

"I figured as much." Richard shook his head. "We'd better get you dressed."

◆　◆　◆

Nathan, Melissa, and Richard arrived at Spring Creek Mennonite Church just before the service began.

Melissa's eyes widened. "Daddy, there's no ladies on this side."

Nathan looked at the layout of the congregation. The division appeared simple enough—men on the right, women on the left.

"It's OK," said a man passing by. "Children may sit with their parents on either side."

The men wore black hats, somewhat like cowboy hats without dimples, and "plain coats," black coats without lapels, which were considered to be worldly. The women all had their hair up and topped with "coverings" made of white netting and also wore string tails tied under their chins.

The building had a simple design. Outside, it was made of white wooden siding. There were two entry doors, one for the men and one for the women. Inside was a single main room with two cloakrooms at the front, to the right and left of a plain wooden counter that was raised on a single step. There was no need for an abundance of other rooms for Sunday school classes because the children were expected to stay in the services with the adults. The benches were constructed of wooden slats. The center row of benches had a wooden partition in the center of the row extending to shoulder height. This partition, Nathan perceived, separated the women from the men. The floor was wooden, and the walls were plain white, with a double row of pegs on each side for hats or bonnets. The white ceiling was flat, about fifteen feet from the floor.

After most of the members were seated on their benches, Nathan maneuvered his chair next to the last row on the right. There was no place for a wheelchair except in the aisle, so that's where he planned to stay. Melissa sat on the bench next to him, and Richard sat next to her.

"I hope you know what you're doing," Richard whispered, "'cause I don't have a clue."

Nathan managed a weak shrug. The only other meeting he'd attended here was Jonas Yoder's funeral, and he had evidently left that meeting early to investigate the Allen house.

Four men sat behind the counter-like structure in the front and faced the regular members, the laity. A man stood and in a normal voice, without a P.A. system, began to speak. When he gave out a hymn number, Richard picked up black book from a rack on the bench-back in front of him and held it for Nathan. There were no notes in the hymnal, only words. No one stood or directed the congregation. A male voice from the audience started the hymn, which was sung very slowly and a capella.

After two songs a second man gave a short message from the Bible. *That must be the Brother Showalter Rachel often refers to.*

A silent prayer followed, with everyone turning and kneeling with their faces on the benches.

Richard glanced at Nathan. Obviously he wasn't sure whether he should kneel with the members. After a moment's hesitation, he knelt, leaving Nathan and Melissa the only two people in the room not on their knees.

After the prayer, another message by a second preacher, a second kneeling prayer, and two more hymns, the meeting was dismissed.

In all, the service lasted two hours, though it seemed longer to

Nathan because of Melissa's discontent. She'd wiggled and yawned and shifted restlessly until she finally fell asleep leaning against Richard's shoulder.

Many members who knew Nathan from his previous work talked with him on their way out. Most of the members were from the area immediately surrounding Fisher's Retreat. If they lived any farther than a few miles from the church, the trip by horse and buggy would take too long.

As the crowd thinned, Nathan moved his chair forward to speak with one of the preachers. "Brother Showalter?"

A white-haired gentleman looked over his wire-rim half-glasses at Nathan and clasped his hands, seemingly unsure of whether to shake Nathan's hand or not.

"I'm Nathan McAllister."

"Yes, I know. So good to have you here today."

"I wondered if I might speak with you. It's about a situation with one of your members."

He nodded. "Why don't you come over here?" He motioned. "I can sit next to you that way."

Nathan appreciated being talked to at eye level. "It's about Rachel Yoder."

The preacher nodded again. "She told me you'd been by." He paused. "Asking questions about Jonas."

"That's right." Nathan wasn't sure how to begin or exactly what this elderly man could do, but Nathan knew he needed to trust someone, and so far he had let no one in on his secrets about the mysterious phone messages. "I want to tell you some things," he started. He looked around and was relieved to see that Richard was taking Melissa out the back door. "And I need to tell you in confidence."

"It's OK, Nathan. I've been listening to this community's problems for a long time. The only place I take them is to the Lord." The elderly pastor reached for Nathan's arm.

The simple act of touch, although not felt physically by Nathan, warmed his heart and inspired trust in the white-haired man beside him. "I have reasons to believe that Jonas Yoder was murdered." He paused, studying the man's face. *No shock reaction so far.* "That his death was not suicide like everyone thinks. And I think that in some way Jonas's death and my shooting are linked."

"Rachel has told me of your amnesia. How is it that you have evidence about these things?"

"Brother Showalter, I have received two phone calls from a frightened young woman. She warned me not to return to Fisher's Retreat before I left Brighton. And since I returned, she has called again, this time asking me why I did not heed her warning, and saying something like, 'You know he killed Jonas. That's what you said.' When I asked when I said that, she just said, 'When you got shot.'" Nathan shook his head slowly, somewhat relieved to be telling his story for the first time, but still wondering exactly how the old man could help. "Anyway, I don't have any strong evidence, but the caller sounds so sincere that I don't want to discount her completely. She seems to indicate that I may have had information about Jonas's death that got me shot."

"Nathan, I understood your shooting to have been accidental."

"That's the story in the news and what everyone says . . . *except* my mysterious caller. She repeated over and over during her first call, 'It was no accident.'"

"I sympathize with your problems, and I will pray," Brother Showalter said before pausing. "But what did you expect from me?"

"Everywhere I go, people are discouraging me from looking into my shooting and into Jonas's death. When I talk to Rachel, she seems very hesitant to talk and would just like to let his memory rest. But if I'm going to make any attempt at making sense of this mystery and find out if I'm really in danger as my caller implies, I'm going to have to ask questions about Jonas."

"Ah," he said nodding. "Does Rachel know what you've told me? That you think that someone killed her son?"

Nathan shook his head. "No. I didn't want to say things I couldn't substantiate. And I didn't want to make her afraid." The preacher's brown eyes met Nathan's. "You're the only person I've told about the phone calls." Nathan adjusted his chair so he could see the women's side of the church. No one else was left in the auditorium. "Rachel implies that the Old Order community would rather not be looked in upon. It's as if she's afraid of bringing scandal on the church. She knows there are rumors about Jonas using drugs."

"Rumors that I never believed," the pastor responded. "But that is beside the point." He paused again, and Nathan noted a fine tremor in his head. "I believe I can explain Rachel's reluctance to talk about her son," he said slowly. "I don't really think it is what she says. We are not afraid of outside inspection. We are not afraid of the light of the truth."

"Then why won't she talk to me? Is his memory that painful?"

"This is the reason, Nathan. She has no confidence that her son is in heaven because we teach that killing is wrong, and to kill oneself is a situation that makes us question whether the sin is forgiven before death occurs." The old man shrugged and placed a spotted hand upon Nathan's. "This is the ultimate sorrow for a mother in our church, to lose a son in such a way."

"But I don't think he committed suicide."

"And that is the reason I think you should share with her your questions about his death. If Rachel can be convinced that her son was killed, I think a large burden will be lifted." He nodded again. "Leave this to me, Nathan. I will speak to her for you first. I suspect she will cooperate with your questions after that."

"Thank you, Brother Showalter."

The man smiled and stood, and Nathan made his way to the van in time to see his smiling daughter sitting on Rachel Yoder's horse.

◆ ◆ ◆

Ryan and Paige shared a corner table in the Cascades, a restaurant in the Brighton Sheraton so named because of a manmade waterfall located in the hotel's magnificent lobby. Ryan chatted on about memories of his medical school days and of his lecture to the students that he'd given. He spoke about his research and his anxiety over the dean's decision. He talked about the weather and the lawn, animal rights activists, and the injustices of the American legal system. He spoke about everything except the Sunday morning service at Grace Fellowship.

He watched Paige playing with a forkful of pasta salad.

He knew it was coming. She was going to ask about the church service. He preferred to talk about her pre-medicine studies or about going over to visit the medical school later that day.

"You haven't told me what you thought of the service this morning," she began, rolling a pasta noodle around the rim of her plate.

"It was OK."

"OK?"

"Yeah, OK."

"Did you see Hal Ferguson? He was sitting with another attorney from his firm."

"I saw him. Didn't have a chance to talk."

"Dad, you made a beeline to the door after the final amen. We didn't talk to *anyone*."

"The line gets so long here, especially when First Baptist lets out. I wanted to make sure we could get in right away."

"What about the message, Dad? I know it's stuff *I* needed to hear."

Ryan cleared his throat and looked around for a waiter to bring more coffee. He felt his temperature rising and tugged at his tie. *Is it hot in here?*

"Dad?"

Ryan sighed. "Why do they always have to harp on abortion?"

Paige looked around at the adjacent tables before leaning forward. "His message wasn't about abortion. If that's what you think, you missed his point."

"It sounded like an old tune to me." Ryan pushed his plate back and lifted his empty coffee cup in the air. A waiter quickly responded and filled his cup.

Paige shook her head. "Nothing for me." Her eyes bore in on her father. "Don't do this."

He pulled his head upright. "What?"

"You file people into neat categories so you won't have to listen to what they say. You think you know the tune, so you shut them out."

"Is this any way to speak to your father?" He leaned forward and whispered, "And lower your voice!"

His daughter looked off in the direction of the waterfall and stayed quiet.

Ryan tried a technique he practiced in the O.R. whenever a resident angered him. *One, two, three, four, five, six, seven . . . She makes me so mad . . . eight, nine, ten . . . She knows just what switches to flip . . . eleven, twelve, thirteen, fourteen, fifteen . . .*

After he reached 100, he sipped his coffee. "OK, Paige, I'm defensive. I know it."

He could see her eyes glisten. *Don't cry, Paige. Your mother used to do this to me.*

He leaned forward again. "OK," he said quietly, "I'm listening. I admit, I probably missed the whole point of the message." He hesitated, trying to capture his daughter's attention, which still seemed to be on the waterfall.

She looked back at him. "The message was not about abortion. It was about us, how God feels about us. It was a perfect message for us . . . for me."

"Perfect?"

"Just what we've talked about. About the way we feel about ourselves."

He shook his head. *Did I hear the same sermon?*

"His whole point, and the reason he read those verses about God loving the unborn, is to show us that babies are loved by God simply because he made them."

"Paige, everyone loves babies. This isn't new."

"But don't you see? Unborn babies have done nothing to earn God's love. They don't have to! They are objects of his love just because he made them."

Ryan started to speak, to change the subject, but Paige interrupted. "It's the same with us."

He looked at his hands, unsure of what to say. Paige's words made sense in their own way. He could hardly believe that she sounded so mature. This wasn't the same daughter he'd left five years ago.

"Paige, I . . ."

She sipped a Coke and stayed quiet.

Ryan cleared his throat. "It's good for you."

"It *is* good for me. Maybe that's why I'm so emphatic. It's what I need to hear." She shrugged and looked back at the waterfall. "When

I'm at home, Mom must tell me every day that I'm too driven, that I need to know that my life has value simply because of who made me."

"Oh. So this is a Barbara-message. I get it now."

"Don't do it again, Dad. What I said came from the sermon."

He looked at his watch. "Want to go see the medical school? Maybe I can even show you the gross anatomy lab."

"Cadavers? That *is* gross."

"Gross as in large. Not gross as in gross!" He made a face. "Let's see if I can get that waiter to bring our check."

CHAPTER
26

ON MONDAY morning Ryan breezed through the cranberry hall just long enough to be informed he'd been summoned to the dean's office.

"Do not pass go. Do not collect two hundred dollars," Ryan muttered as he plodded in to hear the fate of his research. He paused at the dean's secretary's desk, who motioned him to go on in.

"Sit down, Ryan." Pritchard was squinting.

Uh oh. He always does that when he's stressed. Ryan extended his hand. "Morning, Alan. I hope you had a good weekend."

"Just rosy," he snapped with sarcasm. "My son Tyler is up from Duke." The dean blew his breath out through pursed lips. "If he was half as interested in his medical studies as he is in basketball or those cheerleaders . . . Well, you're not interested in hearing about that, are you?" He pulled a stack of papers out of his briefcase and slapped them on the desktop. "This," he said with emphasis, "has consumed me, Ryan."

Ryan stared at his project proposal. The edges were turned up, and yellow highlightings could be seen along with handwriting in the margins. And that was just the top page. "Uh . . . consumed you?"

"How long have you been working at this?"

"Fifteen years."

"Right. It's all well documented in Dr. Hopkins's report, but somehow I . . ."

"Is this a quiz?" Ryan offered a sheepish smile.

"No, it's not a quiz." He threw his hands in the air. "When were you going to share this with me, Ryan?" He paused. "This may be the most important medical discovery in our lifetime."

"Sir, I only recently tried the neural tube trophic factor that I discovered in the schwannomas. It hasn't been that long since we hypothesized that this may be an important factor in turning on the receptors responsible for regeneration of central nervous system neurons. We were very lucky, sir. It could have been any one of hundreds of molecules. We just—"

"Ryan, you're being too modest. This data, if it is correct, is not to be tucked away under a rug. This is Nobel Laureate material," he added with a hushed voice.

"We've only just begun. Heidi . . . uh, our hamadryas baboon SCI model was the first attempt at testing our theories in a higher mammal."

Ryan had never seen Alan Pritchard this excited. In fact, Ryan had never seen Alan Pritchard excited. Stressed out, yes. Excited about research? Never.

Ryan pushed back his chair, preparing to stand. "It's great to feel your support, Alan." He hesitated. "But I trust we can keep our success from being broadcast until we have had a chance to reproduce our results and have the neuroscience community appropriately briefed."

The dean shrugged. "This is going to be very big for this school, Ryan." He shook his head. "I have to hand it to you. When I first heard what you were doing, I thought you were dreaming."

"I've heard it before, sir," said Ryan, clearing his throat. "It didn't bother me," he lied. "I will get right back to it. Elizabeth Hopkins has located another baboon similar to—" He stopped when he saw the dean's upraised hands.

"I didn't say I wanted you to resume, Ryan." He handed Ryan a folder.

Ryan leafed through the clipped articles, all adorned with screaming headlines about medical research overstepping normal animal treatment boundaries. "There must be a dozen articles—"

"Twenty-seven, Ryan. From Brighton, Carlisle, the whole Apple Valley. The AP even ran a story or two, just about one baboon theft and the controversy that ensued." Dr. Pritchard wasn't smiling. "These are from the areas that feed this university. I don't need to tell you that. And these are just the news items you can hold," he continued, pulling the folder from Ryan's hands. "There were countless radio spots, radio talk shows, and TV reports on the animal atrocities going on right here at good old B.U."

I should have known. The good news always comes before the bad news.

The dean squinted again. "The loss to the university with this kind of press is not just measured in dollars. It isn't hard for people to get their care elsewhere in this day and age. We lose patients, students, grants . . . just over public perception."

"But, Alan, you've looked at the proposal. You know we are sitting on the edge of something momentous. You just said this is going to be big for our school."

"It is."

"So we create even more secrecy than before, and we make sure that security measures are—"

"This isn't about needing more security. It's about public perception. You can't just launch back into creating primate quadriplegics! The public won't allow it." He twisted his nose. "I've seen your video, Ryan. The implantation of cerebral electrodes was not something I enjoyed watching—and I am an initiated member of the medical community. I'm on your side. And if I had a difficult time stomaching some of it, just think about the average Joe out there who thinks about the cute little monkeys he sees on TV or in the zoo."

"But if the public doesn't know what we're doing—"

"The public will eventually find out. You are going to report your results someday, aren't you?"

Ryan sighed. "Of course." He studied the dean for a moment. Dr. Pritchard filed the animal cruelty folder in a hanging file behind his desk. "Just what do you propose?"

"I've looked at your data. It's good, Ryan. Real good, in fact. I think you should push ahead into a human trial."

"Alan, I'd like to test this longer. We have many unanswered questions and—"

"So answer them with a human patient, Ryan," the dean interrupted. He returned Ryan's glare. "I happen to know that Dr. Hopkins has already been researching possible candidates through the SCI database."

"She told you that?"

He nodded. "She's a bit more loose-lipped than you are about the research."

"We were merely dreaming of the next stage, Alan. It wasn't like we were ready to proceed with a human trial any time in the near future."

The dean leaned forward and lowered his voice. "Think of it. Human quadriplegics would jump at the chance to walk—"

"Poor choice of words, Alan," Ryan said, interrupting. "We need more data."

"Exactly. And human quads can provide it. What do they have to lose? They can't *do* anything. What value is a life like that?"

"The institution review board is likely to raise a huge stink. We can't begin a human trial without their approval."

"Who do you think chairs that committee? I do." Alan Pritchard stood and began to pace around his spacious office. "What if you tried the procedure on a human quad and it didn't work? What would be the downside? Nothing. They'd be no worse off than before."

The neurosurgeon shook his head. "Very few quadriplegics are due to complete transection. Most of them have some function below the injury . . . some sensation, temperature sensation, partial motor function . . . something. We would risk losing the little they have."

"It's a chance I'd want if I was in a wheelchair. I'd do anything to get on my feet again. Just think about it, Ryan. What if you were suddenly paralyzed below your neck? Your life would be over, worthless." He paused. "You would risk anything to get your life back."

"That's a hypothetical argument. We can't let ourselves be swayed by nonobjective arguments like that."

"I've made my decision, Ryan. No more primate quadriplegics!" He closed his fist. "You think about your options," he added, pulling his door open. "I really hope you will be the one to carry on this next important step. It would be a shame to hand the ball to someone else once you've carried it so close to the end zone. I'll wait to hear from you."

Ryan could see the interview was over. He stood, stunned by what the dean had implied. *He wouldn't give my research proposal to someone else, or would he?*

◆ ◆ ◆

"Melissa, you're getting syrup on my nose."

The little girl giggled.

"Where'd you learn to make pancakes, Jim?"

"Corncakes, Nathan, corncakes." His cheeks dimpled with a smile. "Grandma Over's secret recipe." He lifted a pancake turner. "I make 'em for my kids every Saturday."

"I'm not ready. Slow down," Nathan cautioned his daughter, who held up another bite. He watched a syrup-laden mouthful fall on his shirt.

"Oopsie."

"It's OK."

Melissa retrieved the stray bite with her fingers.

"Oh no, you don't. I don't want it now." He looked over at Jim, who was obviously enjoying the scene.

"I need a bib."

Jim put a pancake in front of Melissa. "Here. I'll feed your pa. You need to eat for yourself." He finished the job and wiped off Nathan's face and shirt.

Melissa, apparently already full, ran off to her room to play.

"It's like a game for her right now. See how much you can get in the mouth before Daddy screams." He laughed.

Jim started cleaning up the kitchen.

Nathan moved his chair away from the table and closer to Jim. "Do you believe that someone who commits suicide goes to heaven?"

His attendant, though surprised at the abrupt question, kept rinsing a plate. "Why the sudden change to such a deep subject?"

"You're the pastor. You can handle it."

Jim looked at Nathan from the corner of his eye and kept washing. "You're not going to drive your chair into the lake or something, are you?"

"Me?"

"It happens, Nate. Quadriplegics and people with severe physical handicaps have a high rate of suicide."

"I'm not suicidal, Jim. That's not why I'm asking."

Jim leaned against the kitchen cupboard. "Quadriplegics have a high rate of drug and alcohol abuse, and suicide. And unfortunately some subtle discrimination comes in here," he added. "A quadriplegic commits suicide, and everyone says, 'Oh, I understand.' But if an able-bodied person kills himself people say, 'What a tragedy.'"

"You're not encouraging me, Jim."

"Sorry."

"I didn't ask because I'm feeling suicidal. I asked because that's what Rachel Yoder is worried about. You know about her son, Jonas?"

Jim nodded. "It rocked this whole community."

"Maybe that proves your point," Nathan responded. "Jonas dies, and everyone is shocked. But let me die and . . ."

"Some would say, 'I understand.'" He shook his head. "But I would say, 'What a tragedy.'"

"Why?"

Jim put down a dishcloth and sat at the kitchen table. Nathan shifted his chair around so he could see. "Remember the conversation we had on Friday? About what Brother Stephen told you?"

"Sure."

"What he said is the answer to your question. Your death would be a tragedy because a loss of your life means a loss of something very precious. You are loved by God and are stamped with his image."

"I hope God doesn't look like me."

"We have our concepts of self-image all screwed up in America. Ninety percent of the kids I counsel in youth ministry have problems with self-esteem. We depend on what we can do, how pretty we are, the grades we make, and the money or friends we have to feel good about ourselves."

Nathan nodded. "Jim, what about my original question? Can you commit suicide and still go to heaven?"

"Tough question, but my short answer is yes. I think Jesus' blood covers our sins past, present, and future. If a person is a child of God, he or she is held in his hand. Suicide doesn't change that."

"I don't think the Old Orders believe that. I think Rachel is worried about her son."

"Maybe she should be, Nathan. Some of the things I heard about him didn't sound like he had a Christian commitment. He was hanging around with a pretty tough crowd."

"I spoke to his pastor yesterday. He seems like a wise man. He doesn't believe the rumors about Jonas."

"Daniel Showalter?"

Nathan nodded.

"He's an honest man," he said reflectively. "I'd put some stock in what he says."

◆ ◆ ◆

Just before the local evening news, Nathan heard the unmistakable sound of horse hooves. He moved his chair forward to see. It was Rachel Yoder.

Melissa ran to the door. "Chestnut!"

Abby opened the door for Nathan, who maneuvered his chair onto their small concrete porch. "Evening, Rachel."

Nathan could see Micah and Stephanie in the buggy as Rachel stepped out to greet him.

"We're on our way back from the Farmer's Market," she began. "I just wanted to stop and tell you that Brother Showalter spoke with me about your conversation." She lowered her eyes to the ground. "He says you think Jonas was killed."

"I'm not sure, Rachel. That's what I'd like to find out."

"I'll help you." Her voice quivered as she added, "I want to know the truth about my son."

CHAPTER
27

THE NEXT morning, with Sally watching Melissa, and Abby at work, Nathan and Richard set off for Rachel Yoder's farmhouse.

"I can't believe I let you talk me into this," Richard groaned as he headed up Route 752. "First it's the Yoder farm and the cafe, then the Spring Creek Church, and now back to the Yoder farm." He looked at Nathan out of the corner of his eye. "Do you get your other attendants out this much?"

"Every chance I can," Nathan joked.

They pulled into the long gravel lane and parked as close to the white farmhouse as possible. The broad front porch was accessible by a wheelchair ramp, a modification that had served Rachel's husband before he died.

Rachel greeted them at the van and showed them into the house. "Can I get you anything to drink? I have fresh sun-tea."

"No thanks."

They settled into a large living room, with Rachel sitting on a plain wooden chair and Richard on a couch.

"I'm not sure what you expect from me," Rachel began.

"I'd like to hear about Jonas," Nate said. "I knew him from a distance, as I know most of the people in this town, through my work as a police officer. I know he was spending time with the Ashby High School youth. What was going on with him, Rachel? Why would your son choose to do that? It seems so out of character for a boy from your faith."

"Jonas was pulling away from our community, yes. He and I argued about this almost all the time." Her eyes stayed on the floor in front of Nathan's chair as she talked. In her hand she clutched a tissue, which she used to dab her nose and eyes as her story unfolded. She told of Jonas's concern for the kids in the community, how he insisted on trying to make friends so he could influence them. But in so doing, she explained, he had to endure the criticism of the church fathers who felt it was important that he stay separate from worldly behaviors.

Nathan questioned, "Did the Ashby kids accept him?"

"Not at first. It took him a long time to slowly break into their circles. Eventually he made a few friends, but not the type that I or the church approved of." She shook her head. "Their dress and conduct . . ." Her voice weakened.

"Did he bring them here?"

She nodded. "A few times. But I would not allow it when Micah or Stephanie was here." She paused. "Some of them attended his funeral."

"Did he act depressed? Suicidal?"

"Sometimes he was moody. He missed his father. He was withdrawn, especially at the end." She lifted her eyes from the floor. "I think something scared him." She leaned toward Nathan and put her hand to her mouth. "You never told me why you think my son was killed. He knew something, didn't he? He talked to you, didn't he, just before he died? That's why you are suspicious, isn't it?"

"He talked to me?"

She nodded. "You do not remember it?"

"No."

"It was at night, an evening or two before . . . before he died. He refused to tell me what was bothering him. I knew something was wrong." She wiped her eyes. "He said that he met you in the cafe." Her voice choked. "I don't know why he wouldn't talk to me." She shook her head. "Maybe I could have helped him."

"He talked to me," Nathan repeated slowly. "But why?"

Rachel sat in silence, having no answer. The question hung in the room, and in Nathan's mind, alone, uncoupled with any reasonable solution.

"Rachel, I know there were rumors . . . about Jonas using drugs. Did you ever suspect that might be true? Did Jonas act differently? Were his grades slipping? Were there any signs?"

"No," she answered with a definitive shake of her head. "He knew about drugs. It seemed to be one of the things he felt strongest about. I know he talked to his friends about it."

"He talked to them about drugs?"

"During his father's illness, Jonas became very focused on A.I.D.S. He was always very careful about handling his father's medical supplies and some of his personal grooming items, especially his razor." She pointed to the bedroom. "He became almost fanatical about disposing of his insulin needles in a protective container. William, my husband, was a diabetic too."

"And Jonas talked to his friends about this?"

"He would warn them about A.I.D.S."

"Were his friends using IV drugs?"

"Maybe. I'm not sure. They certainly looked like they could have been."

A thought struck Nathan. "Was Jonas ever tested? Is it possible he had the A.I.D.S. virus? He never used the same insulin needles as your husband, did he?"

"Never."

"Did you ever talk to the kids your son was hanging around with?"

"No. A few of them shook my hand at the graveside. But that's all. They don't come around anymore."

"Would there have been any reason for one of them to be angry with Jonas?"

"They were not friendly toward me, and not particularly so to my son. They would not stay here long, only for brief visits . . . but no one seemed to be angry with him."

"Did he have a relationship with any other officers in the Fisher's Retreat Police Department?"

"Not really close. He knew Chief Gibson the best. He used to bring medicines from his wife's pharmacy, especially for my husband, but occasionally diabetic supplies for Jonas too. He knew it was difficult for us to bring the horse and buggy downtown."

Nathan hesitated. "How about Officer Turner? Did Jonas ever mention him?"

"He saw him around town." She shrugged.

Nathan looked around the room. The room was neat, almost too neat. There was very little clutter and no pictures on the walls. "Could you show me his room? Is it on this floor?"

Rachel responded with a nod and stood. "It's just the way he kept it. I haven't been able to change it yet." She led the way down the hall, past a bathroom and into a spacious bedroom at the front corner of the house.

"It's big," Richard commented.

"It was mine and William's. I traded rooms with Jonas after his father died."

Nathan pulled into the center of the room and stopped. This room, unlike the other areas of the house, did have some decorations. A Michael Jordan poster adorned one wall, and there were several photographs of whitetail deer on a bulletin board above a wooden desk. There was a large walk-in closet in the near corner of the room.

Rachel opened the closet door slowly, as if afraid to look inside. A light went on in the closet as she opened the door. She took a deep breath. "This is where I found him. He was hanging by a rope from the bar in the back." Her voice was soft and her facial expression flat. "I came in to check on him just after midnight, to see if he was asleep. He wasn't in the bed, but his coat was lying in the center. I was always getting after him about putting his clothes away. But this time I decided to do it for him." She paused and looked down. "That's when I found him."

"Did you find a stool or anything he could have stood on?"

"This chair," she said, pointing at the desk, "was on its side in the back of the closet."

Nathan could see that the closet was quite deep, over six feet. "The light goes on automatically?"

"Yes. A nice touch added by my husband. He did the wiring in this room when the house was remodeled."

"Was the closet door open or shut when you came in?"

"Closed."

"You're sure?"

"Yes. Otherwise the light would have been on, and I wouldn't have checked to see if Jonas was in. He always kept the door cracked open for a little light in case he needed to get up during the night. With his diabetes, his vision was not good."

Rachel touched the tissue to her eyes again and excused herself. "Y-you can stay as long as you like. Everything here is just as it was before he died." With that, she swiftly retreated from the room.

Her footsteps accelerated and then faded into silence.

Nathan moved himself so he could look into the closet. The crossbar for clothes was high and sturdy, made from a metal pipe. He looked at Richard. "Could you do me a favor?" He paused as Richard shrugged. "Go into the closet and shut the door."

Richard did as he was asked.

"Can you see anything?"

"It's pitch black in here. Maybe just a little light coming under the door."

Nathan made mental notes. *It would be hard to see to hang yourself in a dark closet unless you were practiced at tying. And pretty hard to work in the light of the closet with the door open, and then be able to shut the door again when you're done. Maybe he used a flashlight.* "From the back of the closet, can you reach the doorknob?"

"No way. The closet's too deep."

Richard stepped out into the room again.

"Look in his drawers for me."

Richard frowned. "Are you sure this is OK?"

"She said she wants to know the truth about her son, didn't she? Let's find out what we can."

A search through the drawers netted only one interesting find— an abundant supply of insulin needles. Richard lifted two bags from a bottom drawer. One was from the Fisher's Retreat Drug Center, and another from a Revco in Carlisle. Both had boxes of syringes. "Wow, there must be two or three hundred syringes here."

"Look for a receipt."

Richard retrieved one from each bag.

"You can buy syringes without a prescription in this state if you have a medical need that justifies it. What are the dates on the receipts?"

"November 7 and . . . November 13."

"Hmmm. That's odd. Why would he buy so many insulin syringes when he had just bought them the week before?"

"Maybe his mother bought them for him, not knowing," Richard offered.

Nathan kept his thoughts to himself. *This would likely be at least a three- or four-month supply, maybe longer. Buying medical supplies like this doesn't seem like something that someone who was planning a suicide would do. Unless his death was a teenage impulse or accidental.*

But my caller didn't think so.

A detailed search of the rest of the room didn't reveal anything of interest.

As Nathan left the house, he asked Rachel about the syringes. She assured him that Jonas always bought his own supplies and that he typically used only two syringes a day. As far as she knew, he only bought supplies in Fisher's Retreat. He didn't drive a car, so it would be difficult for him to get to Carlisle.

"Did a medical examiner come to the scene?"

"Yes," she replied. "Officer Gibson insisted on it."

Nathan wanted to know more but wasn't sure how much Rachel could handle without breaking down completely. "Rachel, when you found your son . . . did you move him?"

"No. I knew he was dead. And I knew I couldn't lift him, so I went straight to the phone and called for help."

"Did you ever see the medical examiner's report?"

"No, but Chief Gibson talked to me about it." She seemed to hesitate. "He told me that Jonas would have been paralyzed if he would have lived," she said, clearing her throat. "Like you."

"He would have been paralyzed," he repeated, "from a neck fracture?"

"Yes. The chief said the medical examiner called it a hangman's fracture."

Nathan couldn't help wincing. "I'm sorry, Rachel. I really am."

He made a move with his wheelchair toward the ramp.

"Th-that's it?" she called from behind him. "Can't you tell me what you're thinking?"

Nathan stopped and turned his chair around. "I can only say that my suspicions for Jonas's murder have been solidified. Please don't make me say more. I'll tell you more when I can." He moved forward an inch. "Please understand when I ask you to keep this investigation quiet. If your son was murdered, the guilty party isn't going to be any too happy that I'm looking into this."

"What's next, Nathan? When will I know more?"

"I'm not sure. I'd like to locate some of your son's Ashby High friends. I want to talk to them before I decide."

She nodded, and they said good-bye. Nathan drove his wheelchair down the ramp toward his van. At the van's door he nodded to himself. *Jonas Yoder was murdered. But what was the motive? And by whom? And what did he tell me before he died? Something that got him killed?*

Something that got me shot?

◆ ◆ ◆

Ryan held his head in his hands. "Trish? Do we have anything stronger than Tylenol in this place?"

In a moment she appeared and set a bottle of ibuprofen on his desk. "I've got these."

"Thanks." As soon as she left, Ryan downed four ibuprofen tablets and two extra-strength Tylenol with a swallow of cold coffee.

He looked at his watch. Noon. He had an afternoon clinic starting in two minutes. After that, he needed to attend a neurosurgery resident journal club, and after that, a department heads meeting, and after that, go home.

Elizabeth knocked on the open door. "You wanted to see me, Dr. Hannah?"

"Yes. Sit." He motioned to the chair with one hand and massaged his right temple with the other. "I suppose you know about the dean's decision."

"Yes, sir."

He stood and stretched. "I bet I didn't sleep two hours last night." His resident stayed quiet.

"I want to know how you feel about this. This project's been partly yours, at least for the last nine months."

"I've thought about it, Dr. Hannah. I think there are very few options for me. You could go somewhere else if the dean won't let you conduct your research the way you want."

"Do you think we should do a human trial?"

"The data for our baboon model looks very promising."

"Promising, yes, but do we dare move ahead without some confirmation that Heidi's movement wasn't just a fluke?"

"It wasn't a fluke, Dr. Hannah. I can't believe I'd hear that from you."

Ryan straightened a framed diploma and waved his hand. "I know it wasn't a fluke, Elizabeth. It's just that I don't like being pushed. Dr. Pritchard implied that the work would go on with or without me."

"You are the one for this operation, Dr. Hannah. It's your procedure. The technique, the NTTF—it's all your brainchild. You can't let this go. You know you won't, too, don't you?"

He sat down and held his head in his hands again. "I can't leave the project to someone else. Pritchard knows that."

"So let's find a human subject willing to take the risk. A complete quad—as close to Heidi's model injury as possible—then be the first to make such a person walk again."

"It's a dream, Elizabeth. We have so much to find out yet."

"I'm sorry, but I have to side with Pritchard on this one," she responded. "Sure, we have much more to find out. But why not find out using a willing human subject, someone who can give an informed consent?"

He looked up to see Elizabeth's stare. "One animal success. Only one."

"And that's all they'll let us have. Now we're forced to go with a human subject. It's out of our hands."

That's exactly how this feels. Out of my hands. Out of my control.

"I stayed up half the night considering my options," he said. "Stay and proceed with a human subject. Leave, find a job elsewhere, set up a lab, resume animal studies . . . and watch as someone else takes my research here and runs with it. Or I could stay and refuse to cooperate with the dean's wishes."

"And how long would you be here if the dean wanted you out?"

Ryan sighed. "That's why my head is pounding. I don't have any good options."

"So take your best option and go with it."

He looked at his hands, then drummed his fingers against the desktop. After a moment of silence he leaned forward to speak. "Just think if we did . . . and if it worked just like it did in the baboon. This one operation could transform hundreds of thousands of lives."

"Making the lame walk. The cure is not just a dream. I've heard you say that over and over and over. I think I could give your 'Cure, Not Just Care' lecture by heart."

"So why, now that I'm on the verge of having the opportunity I've been waiting for, do I hesitate?" *Why am I suddenly plagued with self-doubt?*

He pinched the bridge of his nose. *I'm not fooling myself. These are the same battles I've fought a thousand times before.* He straightened. *Everyone will see the significance of my work. I will show everyone. I will show . . . myself.*

"Dr. Hannah?" The voice was Trish's. "The clinic is waiting."

He picked up the bottle of ibuprofen and tossed it in Trish's direction. "Tell 'em I'm on my way." He looked at Elizabeth. "Take the first step. Make a short list of people who have complete cord injuries," he said. "Then we'll talk again."

CHAPTER
28

Nathan sat in his chair slowly tapping out his thoughts on the keyboard. He sighed, both from frustration over his typing speed and because of a growing burden of loneliness.

The description "strong, silent type" might have fit him before his accident, but it would be sufficient to portray him merely as "silent" now. It wasn't that Nathan didn't have his own confidants, but he had mainly interacted with his fellow police officers before, especially Brian Turner and Joe Gibson, and now they seemed reticent to speak openly about his questions. And to share his anxieties about his shooting or a link with Jonas's supposed suicide with Abby would likely give her even more misgivings. As a result, he kept his musing about the mysterious calls and his concerns over Jonas's death to himself and shared his deepest questions only with his computer and with God.

What drove him was not a will for vengeance. He was not angry with Brian either. From the beginning, he'd understood his shooting to be an accident. But what if his caller was right? What if he hadn't been shot accidentally?

What motivated him was a desire to know the truth, and an increasing sense that his own life might still be in danger. A danger that grew out of something he had known, something that led to his "accident" in the first place and that persisted in the mind of his unknown caller.

He wrinkled his forehead, wishing he could retrieve some of his old criminology books from the shelves. From what he remembered from his classes on forensic evidence, people who die from suicidal hanging usually do not have neck fractures. They die from strangulation. *If Rachel is right about her son's autopsy report, there could be some real evidence that Jonas's death involved another party. A hangman's fracture results from judicial hanging, not from suicidal teens who end their lives in the backs of dark closets.*

Without the comfort of sharing his fears with Abby or his fellow officers, Nathan's sense of isolation seemed magnified. "I'm not sure who I should talk to, Lord," he whispered. "Something isn't right here . . . and I'm not sure where I should turn. I don't want to scare Abby. And Chief Joe doesn't want the Yoder file open to me. And Brian has told me to stay out of official department business. It's so frustrating, God. I can't put this together on my own. Is something amiss? Or am I just being misled by a high-school prankster?"

His screen faded into bouncing spheres.

He thought about the Allen house and the police accounts of the shooting. *What was I doing there in the first place? And why did I send out a radio Mayday call? Could I have accused Brian of murdering Jonas, and he shot me in return? Is that what my caller is trying to imply? That he didn't shoot me by accident? Is that why Brian warned me not to look into these things?*

He shook his head slowly. Things just weren't adding up.

"I need evidence, God," he prayed, "not just a bunch of crazy theories. Where is the truth?"

◆ ◆ ◆

Mr. Knitter shut the cash register and pointed at a bar stool. "Sit down, Abby. You've been going nonstop all morning." He smiled, and his cheeks dimpled.

His figure reminded Abby of the Pillsbury Doughboy—perfect for the owner of a small-town cafe. No one was a stranger as far as he was concerned. If he didn't know the name of a newcomer, it was only because it was their first visit.

He poured a cup of coffee and handed it to Abby. "Here, take a break."

"Thanks." She took the cup and sat down.

"It was great to see Nathan last week. How's he getting along?"

"Pretty well."

Mr. Knitter nodded and clasped his chubby hands together before leaning his elbows on the counter beside her. "And how's Melissa?"

"Fine."

The cafe owner wrinkled his forehead.

She detected his dismay. "Really. We're doing OK." Her eyes met his. "Really."

He slowly sipped his coffee. "If you need more time off or more flexible hours to watch Nate—"

"He's fine, *really.*" Abby firmly set her cup down, sloshing coffee onto the saucer. She blushed before continuing, "As amazing as it seems, Nate has coped with his situation without dragging everyone down around him. He stays very positive." She hesitated and dropped her gaze to the floor. "At least, he *acts* positive. Maybe he's afraid to complain."

"I admire him, Abby. I don't think I could cope."

"He has a strong faith," she added slowly. "We never talked about it much before. His beliefs were there, but never challenged, I guess." She lifted her cup. "But now that seems to be what he's leaning on."

Mr. Knitter smiled. "I thought so."

Abby looked around the cafe. The customers had all been served, and nobody seemed to need anything. She folded the newspaper that was spread out on the counter next to her. When she looked up, Mr. Knitter hadn't budged. He appeared to be staring at the writing on the large front window of the cafe. "You know, Nate seems more attentive to me and Melissa since his accident." Her face brightened. "The other day, when I left the cafe I found Melissa driving him around the driveway in his wheelchair. She was standing on the back, and Nathan was shouting to her about how to work the controls." Abby shook her head. "She seems happy just to have her daddy back." She paused, and Mr. Knitter chuckled. "She doesn't seem to care that he's disabled."

The cafe owner nodded his head.

Abby poured the coffee in her saucer back into the cup. "And you know what else? The other morning I overheard Nathan praying." Her lip quivered before she pressed her fist to her mouth. "He was praying for *me* . . . that God would give *me* strength."

"Wow." He looked away from the window and picked up the newspaper. "I think I'd be praying for myself."

"Oh, he does that too, but . . . Well, he's changed . . . The accident has changed him."

Abby watched Mr. Knitter's confused expression.

"It's not just the quadriplegia. He seems different . . ." She shrugged and put her hand over her chest. "Here."

Ralph Knitter picked up a damp sponge and wiped the already spotless counter. "I remember when you two used to come in when you were dating."

Abby smiled and pointed to the corner booth. "That was our spot."

"Yep. Nate always ordered a chocolate malt."

"He wore his academy uniform. He was so proud."

"And you sat over there staring at each other like no one else existed." Mr. Knitter chuckled again. "And *you* never ordered anything!" He held up the sponge as if he was going to throw it at her. "If Nate wouldn't have ordered, I'd have never made a dime. And you sat there for *hours*."

She stuck her nose in the air. "Ungrateful customers. How rude!"

Ralph laughed.

"There really isn't anywhere else to go in this town." She smiled smugly. "So we just had to settle for this."

"Agghh!" He feigned anger and raised his fist.

Abby looked at her watch. "Time to go," she quipped as she slipped off the bar stool. "I'll see you later, Ralph."

She quickly moved around the counter and paused at the swinging door to the kitchen before turning back. "Thanks," she added softly.

"Bye, Abby. Say hello to Nate for me."

Abby breezed through the kitchen, pausing only to talk to Marty. "Mr. Miller is on his fourth cup of coffee. Can you give him the tab?" Abby handed her the check.

"Sure. In a hurry?"

Abby shrugged. "Just want to get home, that's all."

She exited the back door into the alley with her head down, making a mental list of items she needed to pick up at the grocery store. She looked up and gasped when she nearly stumbled into Brian Turner. "Oh."

"Hi, Abs." He leaned forward slightly, his face only inches from hers.

She stumbled back. "You scared me."

"Sorry." He hesitated. "I figured you'd be getting off soon." He reached for her shoulder and touched her gently. "Can we talk?"

"Brian, I—" She stopped and shook her head. "I told you that we shouldn't be—"

"I've missed you."

She retreated another step. "I need to go. Nathan is expecting me."

He sighed. "Can't we talk? Just for a minute." His eyes bore in on her face. "Nathan seems pretty intent on dredging up old dirt, doesn't he?"

He paused, but Abby didn't answer.

"Abby, the chief conducted a thorough investigation into the shooting." He hooked his thumb in his belt. "I was suspended from duty for three months. I doubt if he can turn up anything new."

She looked down at the gravel in the alley. "I'm sorry if it's painful for you. He's only trying to find answers for himself. You know Nate. He needs to learn on his own."

"And he doesn't remember a thing?"

"No."

"Nothing?"

She studied Brian for a moment before shaking her head. "No." She moved to the right to go around him.

He moved with her and reached for her shoulder again. "Maybe you can help him find rest about all this. Encourage him to look forward. Looking back isn't going to change anything." He hesitated before adding, "I don't think the department will look kindly on an uninvited critique. He should give it up."

"It's Nate's search, not mine." She took another step to the side and began to walk toward a small employee parking area behind the cafe.

He called after her, his voice low but urgent. "Abby . . ."

She turned and faced him, his tall frame and wavy, blond hair high-lighted by the afternoon sun.

"I wish you'd reconsider . . . about us." He scuffed his feet in the gravel. "I can't seem to forget how it was."

Abby shook her head and pinched her eyes closed. "No."

"You met my needs when Laurie couldn't." He paused and added quietly, "Abby, now I can meet yours when Nate can't." He took a step forward.

"No!" She bit her lower lip. "What we did was wrong."

"Abby, love can make you—"

"*Love* doesn't treat people the way we did." She shook her head. "I'm not sure I know what real love is anymore."

He reached for her, but she retreated out of his grasp.

"I'm sorry, Brian. Really I am."

"Abby, I—"

"Brian, don't come around again! It's best if you stay away from me." She turned toward her car. "And stay away from Nate."

She fled as a sob erupted from her throat and her eyes flooded with tears. She blindly grasped for the door of her old, green Subaru wagon and collapsed into the seat before gripping the steering wheel with white knuckles. She didn't dare look back. She didn't want to see him. She fumbled with her keys, refusing to look out the side window. *I know he's looking in.* She stared straight ahead and punched the accelerator, sending a spray of gravel behind her.

"God," she sobbed, "I never thought it would end up like this."

◆ ◆ ◆

Elizabeth, intent on the screen in front of her, was undisturbed by Paige's noisy arrival.

"Hello," Paige repeated in a sing-songy voice.

The resident looked up. "Oh, hi, Paige." Tapping sounds flew from the keyboard.

"You type almost as fast as I do."

"I never said I couldn't type." She turned to the printer as it emitted an electronic chirp. "But someday I won't have to." She looked up at Paige. "Have you eaten? I feel like celebrating."

"I thought I might go over to my dad's clinic, maybe watch what he does over there."

"Ugh. I'm sure he's swamped." Elizabeth shook her head. "People come from all over just to get Dr. Hannah's opinion." She looked at her watch. "He'll be there until late. Why don't we grab a bite at Lonzo's first? You can go to the clinic after that." She paused. "My treat."

Paige wasn't so sure about Elizabeth's new friendliness. She hesitated a moment. "Sure. Why not?"

A few minutes later, as they walked out the front of the Dennis Building, Paige asked, "What are we celebrating?"

Elizabeth blew her breath out in a quick snort. "The next step in our research." She looked over at Paige and wrinkled her eyebrows. "You haven't talked to your father yet?"

"Not since last night."

She lowered her voice. "We're going ahead with a human spinal cord regeneration study."

Paige stopped and gasped. "You're going to make a human . . . like Heidi?"

"Of course not, Paige. We'll find a human who's already a quad."

Paige blushed at her own thoughts. "Oh . . . sure." She began walking again. "Of course." She looked at Elizabeth and attempted a sheepish smile. "Duh."

They walked along a brick sidewalk past the medical and dental school buildings. Across the street, on the corner of the main Brighton University campus, sat Lonzo's Deli, famous for fresh bagels, soft pretzels, and fast service. The lunch crowd had thinned, and the booths housed only a few undergrads who seemed more enthused with their books than with the food. Paige and Elizabeth selected a booth near the front window.

Elizabeth quickly ordered a beer. "Want one? They have their own brew on tap."

Paige wrinkled her nose. "I'll have Perrier." The waiter, a skinny man with his hair pulled back in a ponytail, nodded.

Paige leaned forward. "You drink while you're working?"

"I'm only in the lab this year, remember? Besides, I'm celebrating."

Paige studied the menu, which looked more like a newspaper than any menu she'd ever seen. "Just what are you going to be doing in the lab?"

"You know about your father's run-in with the dean?"

"A little. My dad wasn't very talkative last night."

"He's refusing to let your father go ahead with any more primate studies. He's afraid of another animal rights snafu."

"My father says the dean is an idiot."

Elizabeth shrugged. "Maybe so, but at least he's predictable. I knew this is what he would do." She paused as the waiter delivered their drinks. "And this is all going to work out to our advantage." She took a large gulp of her beer.

"How so?"

Elizabeth spoke quietly, her eyes focused on Paige. "He's forcing us to move ahead. We're way beyond any other group working on this problem. If I assist your father on the first successful surgery of this type—a procedure that I've assisted in developing—it will launch my academic career." She smiled. "I'll have cleaned out my last rat cage, that's for sure."

"But what if it doesn't work?"

"It will work." She shrugged. "And if it doesn't, at least we know the dean won't sink us. He's the one forcing the issue, not us."

Paige felt uneasy. Elizabeth seemed too cavalier about it all. *My father respects this doctor? Does he see her true colors? Or just her pretty smile?*

"So where will you find a willing subject?"

"That shouldn't be difficult. Your father has asked me to make a list of suitable candidates." She slowly rotated the glass in front of her. "I would think that anyone living the life of a quad would do anything to walk again. Just think about it, Paige. We're giving them a second chance at having a real life. At being somebody."

The disabled already have a real life, and a lot of them have a healthy self-esteem without you, miracle doctor. Paige bit her tongue and stared out the front of the delicatessen. The longhaired waiter took their orders. Paige didn't have much of an appetite now. She ordered a chef's salad.

Elizabeth spoke again. "You know what I'd do if I was in control of everything?"

Paige shook her head.

"I'd like to see young Richard Henry the Fourth as our first guinea pig." She raised her eyebrows. "Then we'd see how upset he'd be if we practiced on a few more baboons before we tried the surgery out on him."

Paige looked around for a rest room sign. "Excuse me," she said, slipping from the booth. "I'll be right back."

As she meandered toward the back of the deli, an image of Heidi smacking her lips flashed across her mind. Her hand went to her mouth before she glanced back at Elizabeth, who was looking the other way. An uneasy sense of foreboding gripped her.

◆ ◆ ◆

Nathan stared, unmoving, through the front window of his home. Without Melissa to occupy his time, and with Abby at work, he found the temptation of self-pity to be a powerful foe. He successfully fought the urge to cry, not wanting his nose to run. He blinked back a tear and sighed with a growing frustration. "Why me, God?" he muttered. "Why me?"

When he saw Abby's car, he swiftly maneuvered his chair to his back room. He needed a moment to refocus. For Abby, he would be up. He couldn't let her see his depression, his fear. Not yet.

He heard the door open. He turned his chair around again and was moving toward the front door when Abby entered, carrying two plastic grocery bags.

"Hi."

"Hi, Nate." She leaned forward and greeted him with a kiss, nearly losing her balance in the process and dropping one of the bags onto the floor. "Don't worry. The eggs are in the other bag." She retrieved the dropped bag and disappeared into the kitchen. "How was your visit with Rachel Yoder?"

He followed her. "Interesting . . . very interesting."

Abby began putting away the groceries. She paused with a box of cereal in her hand. "That's it? Interesting?"

He looked away for a moment, wondering just how much he should share. "I have even more questions now than before." He shook his head. "If I knew then what I know now, I can see why I might have told Melissa that Jonas didn't kill himself." His eyes met Abby's. For a moment he thought she was blinking back tears. "Abby?"

She stared into space for a second before answering. "Go ahead. I'm listening."

He studied his wife, who immediately turned her attention to the food items she was putting away. He watched as she placed first the milk and then a can of green beans in the refrigerator. He shook his head slightly before continuing. "There are a lot of things that just don't add up. If Rachel has her information correct, I'd venture to say it is very probable that the injuries that caused Jonas's death were not self-inflicted." He paused. "I wish I could talk to Brian. I know him well enough to know he wouldn't easily overlook the kind of information that suggests something other than suicide."

Abby blushed and retrieved the can of green beans from the refrigerator. "I think you should lay low." She locked eyes with him. "I know how you would have reacted if someone was challenging an investigation you'd conducted." Her lip quivered just before she turned away. "It's time to move forward. What good will challenging this old case do now?"

Nathan sighed. This wasn't exactly the response he'd anticipated.

Abby blew her nose and muttered something about her allergies. "Hungry?" she asked, turning around. "I'll make you a sandwich if you like."

CHAPTER
29

THAT EVENING in a large conference room just off the cranberry hall, the neurosurgery residents gathered for their monthly journal club. Each month, according to Dr. Hannah's instructions, the residents brought current journal articles gleaned from their assigned areas. First- and second-year residents were assigned to bring articles from general medicine, third-year residents brought general surgery articles, fourth-year residents brought current news from neurology journals, and the fifth-, sixth-, and seventh-year residents brought articles from neurosurgery.

The medical students who were rotating on the neurosurgical services also attended, but most of them seemed more interested in the food than the articles. Tonight the food was Chinese, take-out from Ling's Restaurant in south Brighton.

For two hours the residents ate, presented articles, ate more, answered questions by their attendings, and ate still more, while their hospital ward duties were neglected, and nervous interns worried about whether they'd ever get it all done before the early morning. When Ryan finally dismissed the session, he was late for his own department heads meeting and exited into the cranberry hall at a hurried pace.

"Dr. Hannah," Elizabeth called from behind him.

Ryan slowed slightly and turned to see Elizabeth jogging to catch up.

"Here's my short list." She held up a piece of paper.

"Already?" He took the paper. "I just asked for this list this morning."

"I've been planning this list for a lot longer than that." She shrugged.

He folded the paper and slipped it into his suit pocket. "Always pushing the proverbial envelope, aren't you, doctor?"

"I'll take that as a compliment. Should I go ahead and contact any of these patients to screen them for interest in our project?"

"Let me look over the list. I'll need details about each one. And I need to set up a meeting with the hospital attorneys to be sure we have the informed consent issues covered since we are embarking on an experimental surgery venture. It's really hard to know what to tell our prospective clients. For that reason, we'll need to have all the legal issues covered before we start." He continued striding at an accelerated pace.

Elizabeth clipped along stride for stride with her mentor, looking very attractive and professional in a blue blouse and skirt and monogrammed white coat. "I think our top prospect is going to be a quad who has minimal muscle atrophy, someone who was recently injured or who has been working with functional electrical stimulation."

"That would certainly lessen our rehabilitation problems." He lowered his voice, even though they were alone. "That's assuming this whole thing works."

"It'll work."

They turned right into a second hallway and stood still for a minute in front of a wall of elevators.

Ryan assessed her for a moment. "Dr. Kenney is trying to get out of doing an extra year in the lab. He seems anxious to get into private practice," Ryan said, shaking his head. "I had hoped that he might want to get involved in my project."

Elizabeth shrugged. "Maybe you could leave him on clinical rotations and let me have his lab year."

"You want to do another year?"

"If it means seeing this project through, yes."

Ryan nodded with understanding. "Perhaps I can talk to the academic dean over at the main university campus. We should be able to get you a Ph.D. out of the extra year if you're serious."

"Let's see," Elizabeth responded with a sigh, "four years college, four years medical school, six years neurosurgical residency, and two additional years in research . . . I'll be *ancient* by the time I'm through."

"Being the best takes time, Elizabeth." The elevators opened, and Ryan got on without her.

As the doors began to close, he heard her last comment. "You should know."

❖ ❖ ❖

The next morning, after Nathan's bowel program, shower, and breakfast, he sat at the kitchen table drawing pictures with Melissa. He used a pencil taped to his mouthstick to allow him to reach the tabletop. For a while they just played tic-tac-toe, and then they started trying to make a Valentine's Day card for Abby.

"But it's over, Daddy. Valentine's Day is over."

"But I missed it this year, Mel. I was in the hospital, remember? Let's make a card for Mommy."

"You already gave her a card! It's on her dresser!"

Nathan squinted at his adamant little daughter. *Could I have forgotten?* "Maybe Mommy saved the one I gave her last year." He shrugged. "It can't hurt to make another." He nodded toward a stack of construction paper. "Do you know how to make a heart?"

"Maybe we should make a birthday card. You already gave her a Valentine's card."

Nathan sighed, his curiosity definitely pricked. "Melissa, could you bring the card on Mommy's dresser to me? I want to see it."

"Do you want to copy it? In Sunday school, Ms. Matthews let us copy an Easter card."

Nathan shrugged. "Maybe. Just go get it, OK?"

Melissa plodded up the stairs. In a minute she returned empty-handed. "I can't find it."

"It's not on the dresser?"

"Nope."

"Melissa, are you sure there was a card up there? A Valentine's card?"

"Yep. With a heart and everything." She put her hands on her hips. "But now it's gone."

"OK, let's make another one." He pointed at the paper. "I need you to cut out a heart."

Melissa struggled with the task for a moment before looking up. "Why don't we make it on the computer? It will be neat."

"Hmmm. We do have that card program that—"

A knock at the door interrupted his sentence. Melissa ran and pulled it open. Nathan followed.

Thomas Yeager smiled at Melissa. "Hi, Mel. Is your father—" He looked up. "Oh, hi, Nate."

"Come on in. Nice to see you again."

Tom removed his cap and gripped Nathan's unresponsive palm. "I've been meanin' to stop by. I've been hearing some from Jim and Abby." He nodded. "You look great."

"Will you throw the ball with me?" Melissa pulled on Tom's hand. "My daddy can't play ball with me anymore."

"Melissa!" Nathan looked at Pastor Yeager, who seemed unsure how to handle the situation. "I'm sorry, Tom. I—I've never heard her say that before." He moved his wheelchair toward his daughter. "Why don't you play with your dolls so Pastor Yeager and I can talk?"

Melissa struck a defiant pose, and Nathan felt his cheeks redden. He didn't want to have a showdown in front of Tom.

"How about watching a Veggie Tales video?" Nathan offered in a firm but quiet voice.

"I want to throw ball!"

The behavior puzzled Nathan. He cleared his throat, wondering what to say next, when Pastor Yeager spoke.

"It's a nice day out, Nate. Why don't we go out back and I can talk to you and play ball with Melissa too."

"Yeah!" Melissa ran for the automatic door.

"I guess there's your answer." Nathan moved his wheelchair forward and lowered his voice. "I'm sorry about this, Pastor."

"No problem. I love to play ball."

They went out to the back patio, and Nathan watched as Tom and Melissa bounced and tossed a miniature inflatable basketball around. After a few minutes Melissa saw some sheep grazing in the field adjacent to their back fence.

"Can I go see the sheep?"

"Sure, Mel. But stay in our yard." He watched as she scampered off.

Tom pulled up a metal patio chair and sat next to Nathan. "How are you getting along?"

"Fine."

"It must be a difficult transition." He paused. "How about Abby? Melissa?"

"They're pretty tough. They're going to make it." He looked out at Melissa. "I haven't seen much behavior like you witnessed out of that one," he added, nodding his head toward his daughter. "Though she is a strong-willed one, that's for sure."

"Like her father," Tom added with a chuckle.

"Like her mother."

Tom stretched and put his hands behind his head. "I talk to Abby down at the cafe now and then. She's told me some about your books . . . and your prayers."

"Can't blame a man for asking why, can you?"

"What have you come up with?"

Nathan spoke slowly. "Mostly that God does what he wants when he wants. He's bigger than I am. And I need to just trust him."

"Wow. That's a large lesson."

Nathan nodded and stayed quiet. He watched as Pastor Yeager moved his arms to his lap and rubbed an age spot on the back of his hand.

"I can't begin to explain why this happened to you, Nate. But I think you're right about the trust part. God loves you, and he has plans for you. But sometimes it's downright hard to understand what's on his mind."

"I've been praying for healing, Tom." He paused.

"I'm praying for you, Nate." He glanced over at Nathan and appeared to be studying his wheelchair. "But I also remember what you said first. God does what he wants when he wants. Our agenda is not always his agenda."

Nathan listened as he watched Melissa lean across the fence with a handful of grass. The sheep seemed uninterested in her offer.

"How long have you been a Christian, Nate? What's it been? Ten years?"

"Longer. Since before I left for college."

"You know what I've been seeing? Many of our church members, even those who have had a strong commitment for a lot longer than you have, have trouble knowing who they really are."

Nathan grunted his affirmation. "Hmmm."

"Jim has seen it in our youth group, and he told me you two discussed it. So many have trouble with self-esteem because they don't understand who they really are in Christ." He paused and leaned forward. "We are sons of a God who loves us desperately, Nate. That's what should determine how we look at ourselves. Not what we look like, not what we can do."

"Hmmm." Nathan watched his pastor. "You want me to love myself just the way I am, so that it will be OK if God doesn't heal me." Nathan raised his eyebrows. "Kind of gets God off the hook, right?"

"That's not exactly what I was trying to say. I don't think God's on a hook, Nate. I don't think he's obligated to do everything we ask."

"You believe God answers prayers that are in his will. Abby told me you said that."

The pastor nodded.

"And it is God's will that we have an abundant life. So . . ."

"So?" Tom's voice was gentle and compassionate.

Nathan snorted. "It has to be his will that I walk again, doesn't it? I just can't believe that life like *this* is what the Bible is referring to as abundant! Just look at me! I can't even throw a ball to my daughter! What kind of life is this?"

Tom reached over and stroked Nathan's arm. "I don't understand God's plan, Nate. I only know he loves you. He may have plans to heal you soon." He paused. "Or he might have reasons for keeping you in this chair, ways for you to bring him honor that we can't anticipate."

Nathan felt like crying. He'd never cried in front of Tom before. "I just wish I could understand." He shook his head. "I get so tempted to be angry at God for allowing all this. I start to feel sorry for myself, thinking about how it used to be . . ." He sniffed. "I'm sorry, Tom. I'm going to need a Kleenex." He cringed as Tom grabbed a tissue and helped him blow his nose.

"Have you ever shared how you feel with Abby?"

"Some." He looked at the patio in front of his wheelchair before conceding, "Not much."

"All of your feelings are normal and understandable. I think Abby would like to be in on them."

Nathan knew what Tom said sounded right, but he wasn't sure he was ready to be so open with Abby. *She seems to have enough trouble loving me like I am without me telling her about my own struggles.* When he spoke again, he couldn't look at Tom. "Right."

◆ ◆ ◆

Ryan looked at the list he'd crumpled into his pocket the evening before. He had discussed the list with Elizabeth that morning, after a cervical fusion that he'd performed on an elderly female with rheumatoid arthritis. One candidate stood out as an early choice for Elizabeth, but the final decision belonged to Ryan.

He stared at the name starred with an asterisk: Nathan Daniel McAllister. A C3-4 complete quadriplegic.

Trish had pulled the medical record for him to review. Ryan lifted the file from his desk and read the details of the workup.

"Yes, Mr. McAllister, you might be on the edge of making medical history," he whispered to himself. He seemed to be a perfect candidate on paper. His injury made him very similar to their primate quadriplegic model.

The only thing left would be an assessment of his psychological makeup. It would take a very special person to fit into the secretive experiment Ryan had planned.

"Will you be willing to take the risk?" he whispered again.

Ryan rested his head in his hands.

Am I?

CHAPTER
30

THAT EVENING, after supper, the McAllisters traveled to Carlisle to see the new theater complex. In spite of the fourteen screens to choose from, the decision for Nathan wasn't difficult. There was only one G-rated option, and for Melissa, that's all he allowed. The seating location posed a second minor problem. There was only one location for wheelchairs—in the very back beside a half-row of stationary seats. Melissa wanted to sit closer, but wheelchairs were not allowed in the aisles. Nate volunteered to sit in the back by himself, but that meant no popcorn and no soda for him. "It won't matter. You two sit up front. I'll be fine," he responded with a forced smile. As he watched his wife and daughter walk away hand in hand, he fought off a wave of self-pity. *Look on the bright side. At least I'm here. It seems like forever since I've been anywhere like this.*

After the movie they stopped at an ice cream shop and later laughed in the van while Nathan and Melissa sang the movie's theme song louder and louder.

Once they were home, Abby put Melissa to bed while Nathan waited for Richard Ramsey.

Nathan looked up to see Abby in the doorway of his room. "Check the schedule, would you? I'm sure it's Richard's turn."

"It is. Do you want me to call him?"

"I guess so. He's an hour late."

Abby picked up the phone. "Hmm. No answer." She smiled. "Maybe he's finally found a girlfriend."

"Instead of the psychic who dumped him before they met?"

Abby twisted her lips into a frown. "What?"

"That's what his bumper sticker says."

"Should I try Jim?"

Nathan shook his head. "I think he has youth group on Wednesday nights."

"How about Dave?"

He made a clicking sound and shook his head again.

Abby walked over and playfully pinched his chin. "What's wrong? Don't feel like flossing?"

Nathan chuckled.

"How about your father? I'll bet Mark would be glad to help get you to bed."

This time they both laughed.

Abby sat on the bed beside his chair. "I could probably do it myself."

"I don't know, Abby. Do you think you can?"

Her response was timid. "Let's wait a few more minutes to see if Richard will come." She moved closer to him and began massaging his head and neck. "Tired?"

"Yeah." He closed his eyes as Abby's fingers worked out the tension in his neck.

"Sounds like you and Pastor Yeager had quite a talk today."

"Yep." He sighed. "He seems to know how to cut through all the superficial stuff, that's for sure."

She didn't reply.

"Abby," Nathan began slowly, "I think I may have to face the possibility God might want me in this chair for a long time."

His wife tickled his ear. "Oh, I'll put you to bed if Richard doesn't show up pretty soon."

"Abs!" Nathan snorted. "You know what I'm talking about."

She was silent for a moment. "I know," she said softly. "I think we need to be ready to face that reality."

"It's hard for me to trust God's timing."

"Me too, Nate." She stroked his hair.

"It's hard not to miss the way it used to be. It's hard not to be upset with God."

"I know."

Nathan turned so he could see her. Her brown eyes were soft, searching his face.

"You know what I was thinking?" she asked.

He shook his head weakly.

"That tonight seemed a lot like it used to be. Having fun, just enjoying something silly like the songs you were singing." She shrugged. "It felt good to laugh."

He smiled.

"Remember how we used to go to the cafe when we were dating? You always ordered a chocolate malt. Just like you did tonight."

"And you always had a glass of water. Except tonight you had an ice cream cone."

"OK, OK, so it wasn't *exactly* like it used to be."

They heard Richard's Ford pickup in the driveway. Abby got up and let him in.

Nathan didn't feel too talkative.

Richard still had on his softball uniform. "Sorry, Nate. Extra innings." He smiled. "But we won in the twelfth."

He hurried Nathan through his nightly routine and carefully positioned him for the night.

"See you in the morning, Nate. I won't be late."

Richard disappeared from view just as Abby returned. "Night, Nate. I had fun tonight."

"Me too. I love you, Abby."

She combed her fingers through his hair. "Can I get you anything before I go?"

He shook his head silently. "See you in the morning."

He listened as her footsteps ascended the stairs and went down the hall to her room. After a few minutes he heard the old bed squeak. *She should find my valentine right about . . . now.*

◆ ◆ ◆

Abby pulled back the covers and slipped into bed, curling her arms beneath her pillow. Her hand rubbed across some paper.

What's this?

She sat up and turned on the lamp on the nightstand. She looked at the computer-generated card. The fold wasn't exactly straight. There was a big red heart on the front. *Must be from Melissa. Isn't this cute?* She unfolded it and began to read the typing.

> I dream of you, Abby, my only love. I only wish I could hold you like before. But know that I will always hold you in my heart.
>
> I love you,
> Nate

"Oh, Nate," she whispered. "Oh, Nate." She wiped her eyes and walked to the dresser. There she retrieved a valentine from the top drawer. She pulled it out and ripped it in half. Then she bit her lip and ripped the fragments in half again.

◆ ◆ ◆

Downstairs Nathan was intent on every sound coming from above. He heard a squeak of the bed followed by the sound of ripping paper.

His heart sank. *She hates it. She can't bear to think of loving me like I love her.* He choked back a sob.

Hearing footfalls on the stairs, he pinched his eyes shut. He didn't want to face her. Not now. Not like this.

She came to the side of the bed and sat down before speaking. "Nathan?" She lowered her face over his. "You can't be asleep yet." She pressed her mouth to his, lingering for a moment before pulling back again.

He opened his eyes to see Abby clutching his little card. She pulled back the blanket and laid her hand upon his chest. "This is what counts, Nathan. This is what counts."

◆ ◆ ◆

In the spacious kitchen of the Hannah home, Paige stacked dishes in the dishwasher after a late dinner. "Here," she said, throwing a dish-cloth to her father. "Clean the table."

Ryan looked up passively, letting the cloth fall to the floor. "Excuse me?"

"Hey, I'm here to spend time with you—it's not a slave labor deal."

"I'm not charging you rent. You should thank *me* for just having a place to wash dishes."

"You're my *dad!* I don't have to pay rent. You're supposed to provide for *me*, remember?" She made a cheesy grin. "And I don't have to thank you. You get enough of that in your clinic."

Ryan grunted and attempted to look back at the day's neglected newspaper.

"I wouldn't have believed it if I hadn't seen it for myself. Your clinic yesterday was like a little 'Praise Dr. Hannah' session." She continued her exaggeration. "Oh, Dr. Hannah, what would we have done without you? You saved our child!" She gasped and put her hand over her chest. "Oh, you're so wonderful, Dr. Hannah. You saved my father! Oh, Dr. Hannah, Oooohhhh!"

The chairman forced a yawn. "Are you finished?" He picked up the dishcloth and began to wipe the table. "I get the point."

He stared at her for a moment as she continued her portrayal of heartfelt anguish and gratitude. She dropped on one knee and reached out to him with her palms up before bending and clutching her chest again. "Oh, Dr. Hannah."

"Stop, OK?" He shook his head. "You get the Emmy. You can stop now."

She laughed.

"They don't act like that anyway."

"Well, maybe I exaggerated . . . but just a tad," she replied smugly. "But it did appear to be a heady time." She smiled a characteristic over-grin. "That's why I take it upon myself to make sure it doesn't get out of hand here at home. Otherwise we'd have trouble getting your head through the door."

"Funny, Paige. Don't you have some homework to do?"

"I'm off for the summer, remember?"

She finished loading the dishwasher as Ryan watched. She was every bit as pretty as Barbara had been at the same age.

"Say, Paiger, would you like to go visit a prospective research patient with me sometime?"

"A research patient?"

"A quad. For our project."

"I don't know. I'm not so sure how I feel about all this." She paused. "Do you really think you should be experimenting on people?"

Ryan studied his daughter a moment before answering. "I don't really have a choice, honey. So what I'm determined to do is spell everything out as it really is, including all the risks and the unknowns, and let someone—a human—make a free choice."

"I'll think about it."

"Good. I think you're a pretty good judge of character, really. The visit would be informal anyway, and it might be fun for you to see the patient both before and after."

Paige turned to leave the kitchen. "I'm OK with the before part, Dad. It's the after that worries me."

He nodded solemnly. "Sleep tight, Paiger."

"Night, Daddy."

◆　◆　◆

Nathan lay quietly in the darkness. The only sound was a quiet humming from his battery charger. No noise came from Abby's room above him. All he had heard since her departure was a single creak from the bed upstairs, and then nothing. Tonight there was quietness without but an approaching peace within.

Tonight he wouldn't yield to the temptation to escape into fantasy. Tonight he wouldn't dream of being healed or concentrate on moving his lifeless limbs. Tonight he was determined not to ask to be delivered or healed or even to ask why as he had done so many times before. Tonight he wanted to concentrate on the advice Pastor Tom had given him. He would try to align himself with the thinking of God.

OK, God, you said I'm your son, so I'm your son.

You said I'm loved by you, so I'm loved by you.

You said I'm a new man in Christ, so I'm new. You did say something like that, didn't you?

If you love me . . . then I guess I'll have to try to act like it.

◆ ◆ ◆

For Ryan Hannah there was no quiet peace, but only a haunting truth that his daughter seemed to know how to bring to the surface. He glanced at his outline in the full-length mirror as he undressed. *You're overweight.*

He donned a T-shirt and slipped into bed as his insecurities nagged on. *I'll never be the best. I failed at organic chemistry. I failed Mr. Jones. I failed at marriage.*

Is that why I strive so hard to be worthy of the compliments people pay me? Or am I driving myself just to get patted on the back again and again?

Is there anything wrong with enjoying being the center of attention?

He thought about his current project and tried to silence his discomfort about being pushed into speeding up the work. *For once at least I'm not the one driving ahead.*

Or is my desire to do what no one else has done preventing me from standing up to the dean?

He wished he knew.

CHAPTER
31

THE FOLLOWING morning, Officer Charlie Edwards looked at his reflection in the front window of the Fisher's Retreat Police Department and flexed his biceps. He pulled off his mirror shades and walked into the chief's office. "Here's the stuff you wanted, Joe. I got the state police info as well as the Carlisle Police data." He plopped the papers on the chief's desk.

"Hmmm." Joe frowned, accentuating a dimple in the middle of his double chin.

"I had a chance to review it last night myself." He pointed at a column of numbers. "It looks like heroin has become the new recreational favorite for a lot of high schoolers."

Joe turned to a page reflecting usage in the Apple Valley. "And look how all these parameters went up over the first eleven months of last year. Busts were up. Drug-related crimes were up. Usage among high schoolers and middle schoolers was up."

Charlie pointed a stumpy finger at the peak. "What happened here? Every parameter starts to improve."

Joe nodded. "November," he muttered.

"I don't get it."

"This is what I suspected. Something changed in November."

"November? The Fitts bust? You shut down a safe house right in Fisher's Retreat in November, right?"

"Yes," he answered after a moment of reflection. "And I hope that's what explains it."

Charlie poured himself a cup of coffee and sat down. "You hope?"

"We have to keep in mind that there may be other possibilities."

Charlie raised his eyebrows. "Wha—"

"You've seen it in your work in Carlisle, I'm sure. Close a safe house, the suppliers just open another one. Kill one pusher, another fills his place." He shook his head. "No, I'm not totally convinced that Lester Fitts or that one safe house could affect all of these parameters."

"What are you suggesting?"

"Think, Charlie. What else changed in November?"

He brightened. "I came on the force. You don't think that the drop has something to do wi—"

"Nice try, but I don't think so. I was referring to the loss of Officer McAllister."

Charlie blew his breath out slowly. "You suspect he was giving some inside information to the pushers?"

"I don't know what to think. It's very hard to believe that about Nate. But I also have to make some sense of the fact that he was shot unarmed in a drug safe house, and that since he's been out of commission, drug use has fallen precipitously."

The officer sipped his coffee. "I was considering asking Nathan whether he'd help me with a D.A.R.E. program down at Ashby High." He looked at Joe. "Do you think I shouldn't?"

Joe shrugged. "I'm neutral. I still have a lot of respect for Nathan. Just because I have a few unanswered questions and some circumstantial evidence . . . we can't declare him guilty without a trial."

"In my opinion he's clean. I never knew him before, but from what I've heard about him, he's laced pretty straight."

"I think you're right, Charlie," Joe responded, slapping his hand against the papers. "But his accident has softened him. He was always an instinctive responder. As a cop Nate operated on his gut reaction most of the time. Fortunately for him and for me, his instinct was almost always right."

"He's changed?"

"He's more thoughtful. Pensive." He put his hands behind his head. "But maybe that's because that's all he has left."

Charlie began to clean his sunglasses with a paper napkin.

Joe chuckled. "It might be a good idea to parade Nathan in front of the Ashby High crowd. A lot of them knew him before. Use him as an example of what can happen to them if they get involved in drug-related crime. That ought to scare a few of them straight." He got up and poured himself some of the morning coffee. "I'm for whatever might keep these kids on the right track. If Nathan can help you do that, more power to ya."

◆ ◆ ◆

After breakfast Richard agreed, reluctantly, to take Nathan and Melissa out for yet another visit to Rachel Yoder's farm.

As Richard lowered the van's side ramp, he issued a final protest. "Why can't you just call her? She might be at the Farmer's Market or something."

"If she's not at home, maybe we could check there," Nathan responded.

"I want to see Chestnut," Melissa added.

Richard sighed.

"The things I need to ask are best done face to face, Richard. It shouldn't take long."

"OK, but let's get going. I have a roofing job to do."

"Include this on your PCA time sheet. I'm not asking you to go for free." *And I'm not even going to mention the fact that I waited for you over an hour last night.*

Once Nathan was positioned and secure, they were on their way. As they crested a hill on Route 752, they met a Fisher's Retreat patrol car. Richard waved through the window at Brian Turner, who seemed not to notice them.

Nathan lifted his chin as the patrol car passed. It was the only wave he could offer. *I wonder what he's doing out in Old Order country. We usually don't have a patrol out this way.*

Richard turned right onto the Yoders' gravel lane. Rachel was, as usual, in the garden. She came over to greet Nathan at the van's window.

"Good morning, Nathan, Richard." She leaned into the window. "Hi, Melissa."

"Hi."

"Have you come with news about Jonas?" Her face turned anxious.

"No." Nathan shrugged weakly. "Only more questions than ever." He paused. "Rachel, I was wondering if you could speak to the police chief for me. He's not going to open Jonas's file for inspection without your permission. I'd like to see the medical examiner's report."

Rachel took a step back.

Melissa pulled open the van's side door and scampered across the lawn to a fence. "Here, Chestnut! Here, boy!"

Rachel watched Melissa for a moment before replying, "I've been rethinking this whole thing." Her eyes shifted from Melissa to the ground, to the sky, and back to the ground, looking at everything or anything except Nathan's eyes. "I've starting thinking that this isn't such a good idea, digging back through my son's death."

Nathan started to grunt a protest.

"I've not slept well for the past two nights," she added, shaking her head. "Having you out to the house and in his room just brought it all back."

"I'm sorry, Rachel, but I—"

"This matter has already been investigated by your department when the evidence was fresh. So what would be different now?" She clasped her hands together. "It's not going to do any good to rehash everything."

"But Brother Showalter thought you'd want—"

"He has nothing to do with this. This is my decision." She coughed nervously. "I've decided that my son's salvation is in the Lord's hands. I'm not supposed to worry about it. I'm supposed to trust."

"But what if—"

"I don't want you to look into this any further." Rachel interrupted again. "It won't do anyone any good."

Nathan looked helplessly at Melissa and at Rachel, who continued to look away.

His daughter continued to yell at the empty field. "Chestnut!"

Rachel watched her and finally turned to Nathan. "Can you stay long enough for Melissa to see the horse? He's in the barn."

Nathan looked at Richard, who seemed preoccupied with cleaning the dirt from beneath his thumbnail. "Sure."

Nathan watched as Rachel led Melissa off toward the barn. After a minute he shook his head. "I don't understand it. She finally seemed cooperative and wanted to know the truth about Jonas's death, and now she's completely flip-flopped again."

"It's a woman thing," Richard muttered. "I've seen it before." He began twirling his long blond hair with his index finger.

"I'm not so sure. Something's changed. Something's gotten to her." *Or is it someone?*

"It's a woman thing, I'm telling you. They flip-flop all the time. First they like you. Then they dump you. Then they want you again."

Nathan watched his attendant out of the corner of his eye. *Richard Ramsey . . . the voice of experience. When I was twenty, I knew everything, too.*

◆ ◆ ◆

Elizabeth arranged the X-rays on the viewing box for the third time.

Paige checked her watch. "Why don't we just go down to the cafeteria and find him?"

"The cafeteria? No way. Your father only dines with other faculty members down there. It's an unwritten rule. No residents in the faculty area." She shrugged. "Mostly he eats with the other department heads. It's kind of a prestige thing."

"Maybe he forgot."

"Not a chance. He seemed pretty anxious to go over these films. Besides, if he shows back on cranberry hall, Trish will bully him right back down here. She knows we're waiting."

Paige smiled. "I like her."

"Herculina?"

"Hercu—?"

The resident laughed. "That's what we call her."

Paige twisted her expression. "I don't get it."

"One of the residents saw her down at the Y last year. Underneath her office attire is a woman of steel. Dr. Henson said she has bigger biceps than he does."

"Whatever."

"I can't believe your father lets her push him around like she does."

"He needs it. To be pushed around once in a while, I mean."

Dr. Hannah's voice broke in. "I *know* you're not talking about me."

Paige looked up at her father, standing in the file room doorway. She smiled sheepishly. "Hi, Dad."

He walked over to the large, lighted view boxes. "Are these his?" He began a thoughtful examination of Nathan McAllister's films, punctuated with "Oohs," "Ahs," and "Hmms."

He pointed at a CT scan. "The bullet causes too much artifact distortion. I can't tell exactly how much cord has been destroyed."

Elizabeth nodded.

"It's amazing that his bone structure fared so well." He looked at his daughter. "Here, Paiger, look at this. The bullet path was from anterior to posterior, coming in from the right, taking out his internal jugular vein and external carotid." He moved his finger across the film. "It may have ricocheted off of the body of the third vertebra, but that didn't cause enough of a fracture to make his neck unstable."

"That explains why he was never in the halo," Elizabeth offered.

"The halo?" Paige queried.

"It's a metal external fixation device. We screw it into the skull," her father said, circling his finger around his own head to demonstrate. "It connects to a shoulder and body brace that keeps the head in one position and prevents any movement of the cervical spine."

Paige curled her upper lip. "That's disgusting."

"It's better than what we used to do. When I was a resident, we strapped these patients into a big Stryker frame and put tongs in their skull for cervical traction. There they stayed, rotating every few hours—faceup, then facedown, looking at the ceiling, then looking at the floor—for weeks on end until their bones healed or we operated to fuse the spine."

He looked back at the X-ray. "I'm not sure I like this, Elizabeth.

This bullet fragment is in the way, and without knowing exactly how much damage there is, we might be looking at quite a gap to bridge." He huffed. "If the grafts take too long, he may not survive without another source of blood."

"What about an M.R.I. scan?"

Ryan looked at his daughter. "Magnetic resonance imaging," he explained. "I'm not sure that would give us much better information. There's still going to be distortion from the bullet. And if it's anything other than lead, the fragment might shift while in the magnetic field."

He started pulling films from the boards and placing them in the X-ray jacket. "Let's go back to my office," he said, looking at his watch. "I have a few minutes before my next case. Let's brainstorm about the best research candidate before we make a decision."

Ryan broke into his surgeon's stride with Elizabeth beside him. Paige followed behind. Once in the cranberry hall, they breezed past Trish's desk and into the chairman's office.

"Tryouts for the Olympic walk aren't until next month," Paige gasped.

Ryan laughed. "Have a seat."

The women obeyed.

"Before we do any interviewing for possible candidates, I think we need to firmly establish what the characteristics of the best candidate will be."

Elizabeth nodded and took a piece of paper out of her lab coat pocket. "The patient should have a complete transection," she began. "That way the surgery will not risk a loss of function they already have."

"Good point."

"With minimal muscle atrophy, as we discussed before."

"Right."

"They should be well set financially," Elizabeth added slowly.

"What's that got to do with it?" Paige questioned. "They won't be paying for this, will they, Daddy?"

"No. It will all be covered by the university." He looked at his resident. "Why do you say that?"

"If they're well off, they're less likely to sue us if something goes wrong."

"Not necessarily. In fact, they may have better access to the legal system. Remember Richard Henry."

"Really," Paige responded.

"But your point is heard. It might not be a bad idea to do a background check . . . make sure the person hasn't sued another physician for something else. I could probably get Hal Ferguson to check on that for us." He paused. "Let's think about the patient's physical characteristics. Young? Old? Does it matter?"

"Young," said Paige.

"More years to benefit. I agree," said Elizabeth. "And easier to rehabilitate."

Ryan tapped his fingers on his desktop. "The gap in the spinal cord should be minimal. And there should only be one level of injury. We can't have someone who has had multiple fractures. The cord may be damaged in more than one spot."

Elizabeth looked up. "What about social status? Does it matter?"

"Probably not. But I do want a patient to have the ability to enter the study without a lot of fanfare. I want to do our initial work in a sealed environment. This must not be a media event. The family will have to be supportive and willing to keep a secret."

"Will the dean agree to keep it a secret?" Paige asked.

"I think so. If he won't, I'm not doing it." He stood up and looked at his watch. "He should realize the advantage of working behind closed doors until we have a success. If we make it a media event and something goes wrong, the whole thing could backfire on the university."

"Dr. Pritchard is going to milk this one for all it's worth, I can promise you that," Elizabeth added.

"He'd better be patient. And we'd better find a way to do the first case very quietly." He paused. "We should also choose a patient who is psychologically well suited for this kind of experimentation."

Elizabeth nodded. "What are you saying?"

"Someone well adapted to their paralysis. If not, they may not be able to accept the results if the surgery doesn't live up to their expectations. We don't want them too desperate to be made well or the surgery will never be good enough."

"But they can't be too content either. We need a fighter. Someone who is willing to do just about anything we ask."

Trish interrupted using the intercom. "Dr. Hannah? O.R. 4 is ready for you. Your patient's asleep."

◆ ◆ ◆

Abby groaned when she saw the patrol car parking in front of the cafe. *Great. I don't want to see Brian. He knows I don't want him—*

She looked up to see Charlie Edwards get out of the car. Abby looked around to see if her anxiety or relief had been noticeable to anyone else. Everyone seemed content with their food. *Good,* she thought. *It's only Charlie.*

He walked over to the nearest stool and took off his mirror shades. "Afternoon, Abby." He nodded at Mr. Knitter, who was sitting behind the cash register. "Ralph."

"How goes it, Charlie?" Abby smiled. "Can I get you something?"

"Just a glass of your mint tea."

"No lunch?"

He shook his head. "Actually, I just came in to chat."

She held up her hand toward the crowded cafe. "Plenty of ears out there."

She poured him a glass of tea.

"I wanted to talk to you."

"Me?" Abby glanced sideways at Marty, who was wiping down the counter.

"I wanted to bounce an idea off of you. I don't know Nathan very well yet, so I wondered if I could screen something through you."

"You've made me curious now." She leaned her elbows on the damp counter.

"How do you think Nathan would feel about helping me with a D.A.R.E. program next week?"

Marty stopped wiping the counter and looked at Charlie.

"Um . . ." Abby squinted. "I think he might like that." She nodded. "Yes, I think he'd want to help. I know he's still concerned about drug problems."

"Recruiting new help while the boss is on vacation, Charlie?" Marty intruded with a laugh.

"Vacation?" Abby hadn't heard.

"Joe is taking June to Hawaii for ten days." She laughed again. "While the cat's away . . ."

Abby raised her eyebrows. "On a Fisher's Retreat police salary?"

Charlie snorted. "More like his wife's salary from the pharmacy."

"Oh." Abby brightened. "Anyway, I think you should ask Nathan. Why don't you stop in sometime? He enjoys company."

Charlie lifted the tea and drained it in three gulps. He set the glass down with a clatter. "Ahh. Great tea." He laid a dollar on the counter and looked at Abby. "Thanks. I'll drop by."

◆　◆　◆

That night, after Jim Over had come and gone and Nathan was in bed for the night, the phone rang at the McAllister home. Nathan heard Abby pick up in the kitchen after three rings. "Hello, McAllisters' . . . Yes . . . Hold on."

Nathan heard footsteps, and an instant later Abby whispered, "It's Dr. Hannah. He wants to talk to you." She held up her hands as if to say, "What's he want?" She tapped the top of the speakerphone.

"Hello."

"Mr. McAllister? Dr. Ryan Hannah here. I hope I'm not calling too late."

"No, doctor. What can I do for you?"

"I'll cut to the bottom line, Mr. McAllister. I'd like to come to visit you, if I may. I'd like to talk with you about a promising new therapy for spinal cord injury patients."

"New therapy? Surgery?"

"Possibly," he replied. "I'd like to talk with you in person."

"Should I set up an appointment in your clinic?"

"No," the surgeon responded quickly. "I would like to interview you at your home, if I may."

Nathan looked at Abby and raised his eyebrows. "I, uh, sure . . . That'd be fine."

"How about Sunday afternoon?"

"I'll be here." He paused. "Just what kind of therapy are you talking about? Physical therapy?"

Nathan heard the doctor sigh. "No. Not physical therapy. It's experimental surgery to restore function."

"To make me walk?"

"Possibly."

"That's impossible, right? I mean, that's what you told me in the hospital. What do you mean, 'experimental'?"

Dr. Hannah chuckled. "Slow down, Mr. McAllister. I don't want to give you promises or details over the phone. This is merely to interview you to see if you might fit our needs for research."

"Research."

"That's right. We've been working at this for a long time, Mr. McAllister." He paused. "I have your address. Would three o'clock be OK?"

"Yes. Sunday afternoon, right?"

"That's right. And I would like to ask you to keep this confidential, just between us, OK? I don't want anyone else in on this just yet. It is experimental . . ." He cleared his throat. "I'm sure you understand."

Nathan looked at Abby, who was staring at the speakerphone with wide eyes. "Sure."

"I'll be bringing a few assistants, if that's OK."

"Fine."

"All right. I'll see you on Sunday afternoon. Good-bye." *Click.*

Abby tapped off the phone. "What was all that about?"

"That's what I was going to say. New therapy? Surgery?" He felt his face flush. "Abby, do you think this could be my healing?"

Nathan watched Abby pace. "I don't know, Nate. I don't know," she repeated as she walked to the door and pirouetted to return. "The doctor was pretty vague." She looked back at him with an electrified expression. "Oh, Nate, whatever it is, it's exciting."

"Great," Nathan mumbled. "That call was some stimulant. I'm awake now, just when I'm down for the night. I miss being able to get up when I want."

"Paralyzed on the outside but pacing on the inside, aren't you?"

He smiled. "I guess."

Abby sat on his bed. "Close your eyes, Nathan. Try not to think." She began to rub his neck and shoulders gently.

After a few minutes she left him and turned out the light again. "Sleep tight."

He tried to sleep, but his mind was busied with the details of the phone call. Finally, when he had almost drifted off again, another memory hit him. He thought about the news story he'd seen about the break-in at Dr. Hannah's lab. He remembered the gruesome pictures of the monkey in the *Brighton Daily News* too. He felt sweat beading on his forehead. *Ugh. I wonder if that's what Dr. Hannah's new therapy is all about.* He hoped not.

CHAPTER
32

SATURDAY AFTERNOON in Fisher's Retreat was hot. The kind of weather that was made for broad, covered porches and lemonade. For trips to the swimming hole or a trip up North Mountain to look at the view and feel the breeze.

Because Nathan could not sweat below his shoulders, he knew he had to be careful of overheating, and for that reason it was a day, like many others, that he would spend predominantly inside. It was nearly three o'clock when he heard a familiar rumble.

"Sounds like Richard's truck," Nate commented.

"I think he needs a new muffler."

"He's not due until tonight. Don't tell me he's *early*."

Abby laughed and looked out the window. "He's backing into the side yard."

Nathan turned his attention to the solitaire game on the computer screen.

"I'll see what he's up to," she offered.

Nathan clicked to move the queen of hearts before moving his chair into the den where he could look out the window. He watched Abby talking with Richard, who was throwing lumber from the back of his truck onto the lawn. *What on earth—*

He studied Abby's expression. She was smiling, then putting her hand to her mouth. Finally she reached out and touched Richard's shoulder before walking back toward the house. As soon as she was inside, Nathan asked, "Just what is going on out there?"

"He wants to build a swing set for Melissa."

"He wants to what?"

"He's been talking to the men up at the mill. Phil Bender gave them the wood from our tree, and they gave the lumber to Richard to use here."

He raised his eyebrows. "Cool."

Abby folded her arms across her chest as if she were giving herself a hug. "He said he knew Melissa missed her old swing, so he thought he'd build her a new one."

"Maybe he should've asked first."

Abby frowned. "What would you have said?"

"Yes."

"That's what I told him." She turned to go to the kitchen. "I'd better make him some tea. It's gonna be a scorcher."

"Still, I wish he would've asked me."

"Let it rest, Nate. He knew you'd say yes. He wants to do this."

Nathan followed Abby into the kitchen. "Is this the way it's going to be all our lives? People doing nice things for us because they feel sorry for me?"

She replied cheerfully, "I hope so."

"Abs, I'm serious. I don't like being the object of pity. I don't want them to look at me like that."

"He's not doing it because he pities you, Nate. He's a friend, and he wants to help." She softened. "I see your point though. But your time will come—a time when you can give as well as take." She looked out the back window. "I know you've already given a lot back to this community. Everyone I talk to down at the cafe says they've been encouraged by the way you've handled all this."

He sat silently, watching his wife. She seemed lost in thought, not meeting his gaze.

Finally she spoke again. "You've inspired me. I know that."

It was difficult for him to accept the compliment. He nodded his head and didn't reply.

When he did speak, he made a joke. "Maybe I should go out and help him." He chuckled. "He could use my wheelchair as a sawhorse or something."

She stirred a large glass pitcher of tea. "Oh, brother."

Nathan returned to his computer game as Abby worked in the kitchen. Melissa played in the yard "helping" Richard.

An hour later a knock at the door gave Nathan a good excuse to quit a game he was hopelessly losing. He listened as Abby welcomed Charlie Edwards.

Nathan moved his chair into the den. Charlie was stocky and well-built and had short, stiff blond hair cut in a flat plane on top and shaved on the sides. He had a ruddy complexion and a friendly manner.

Charlie lifted his hand in a wave. "Hi, Nathan. I don't believe we've been formally introduced."

Nathan smiled. "You escorted me into town."

"Oh, yeah."

"That was fun," Abby responded with a laugh. "I'll leave you two. Can I get you anything?"

The two men shook their heads.

"Have a seat." Nathan nodded to a chair. "Abby told me you'd be by. You want me to help with a D.A.R.E. program?"

"Yep. You were a D.A.R.E. officer before, right?"

"Not full-time. Like you, I did some D.A.R.E. work and some general police work."

Charlie clasped his hands and leaned forward. "What do you say? Will you help me with the program?"

"Why do you want *me*?" He studied Charlie's muscular features. "Do you want me because I'm disabled?"

The officer sat up. "Well . . . yes . . . and no." He hesitated, then added, "I want you to help because you were a cop, because you're familiar with D.A.R.E., and because you personally have suffered from drug-related crime. And because I think your courage would inspire the kids."

Nathan nodded. Charlie seemed sincere. "I—I didn't mean to sound so accusatory. I'm still working through how I feel about all this."

Charlie looked over at a bookshelf, at a picture of Nathan's parents. He pointed. "Is that your folks?"

"That's them."

"I may not know exactly what you're feeling, but my father knows all about discrimination against the disabled," Charlie responded while staring at the picture. "He's been in a wheelchair for fifteen years."

"Really? How'd he—"

"Motorcycle accident. He's a paraplegic. He works as a stockbroker in Carlisle."

"Hmm."

"He says the tendency is for employers of the disabled to overpraise them. You get patted on the back all day just for doing any little thing." He flipped over his palm. "On the other hand, some employers tend to be overly critical of a struggling employee if they're disabled. The employers seem to be so afraid of lawsuits claiming discrimination that they overstate their case against the disabled employee, criticizing everything they do, just to justify firing them." He sighed. "My father has seen both in his work as a disability advocate."

Nathan backed his wheelchair up and turned so he could look through the window. "I'd be glad to help you, Charlie. What do you want me to do?"

"It's just an assembly, actually. Over at Ashby High. I thought maybe you could tell your story, maybe talk about the fallout we see from drug trade." He moved so Nathan could see him. "If you want."

"Sure. How goes the fight anyway? Before I left, it seemed like things were just getting worse all the time. The kids at Ashby seemed to be having a real love affair with heroin."

The young officer squinted and looked away. "Things are some better. I'm not sure why. Maybe the safe house you helped close broke some sort of pipeline."

"I didn't do much." Nathan shook his head. "I don't remember anything about that day—what I was doing there, why I went there in the first place, getting shot—nothing." He made a weak smile. "So my story to the high schoolers might be a bit short."

"What's the last thing you remember?"

"I have a vague memory that I think comes from Jonas Yoder's funeral. I can see his mother dropping dirt from her hand onto the ground. Other than that, I don't remember anything from a few days before the accident until I woke up at Brighton University."

"I heard about Jonas. Joe tells me he was a troubled kid, maybe even into drugs himself."

"Maybe so. But his mother doesn't think so." He shrugged. "I have a feeling that Jonas's funeral has something to do with why I was at the safe house. Joe questioned me about it. Why was I in there unarmed? I'd like to know myself."

"That's when you were shot?"

"Right. My weapon was locked in the box in the car. All I can figure is, I must have taken it off and locked it up out of courtesy to the Mennonites. I've done that before when taking calls on their property. They seem a bit put off by the uniform, and removing the gun shows respect for their teachings on nonviolence."

"Oh. I haven't had too much interaction with them yet. They don't cause any trouble around here."

"I think I put the gun away when I attended the funeral. Then something must have alerted me to leave, and I just didn't take out my gun. Maybe I was in a hurry." He leaned his neck forward and scratched his eyebrow against his mouthstick. "Maybe I'll never know," he added reflectively. "But it was a mistake I'll regret forever. It was the mistake that put me in this chair."

◆ ◆ ◆

That evening at Abby's insistence Richard Ramsey joined the McAllisters for supper, not as an attendant but as a friend. "Oh, no," she joked. "I'm feeding Nathan tonight. You're not on duty until bedtime, pal."

Richard accepted and seemed to enjoy himself.

Nathan chided him. "What's wrong, Rich? Saturday night and nothing to do but hang around us married folk?"

"I've got plenty of things to do," he responded. "But you know women. First they love you, then they dump you."

"Really."

"All right, you two," Abby protested. "Where's this coming from?"

"Hey, it's a fact. But they say it's their *prerogative* or something like that." Richard pushed his hair behind his ears. "Just like that Ms. Yoder that Nathan has been up to see. First she says, 'Find out about my son.' Now she says, 'Don't.'" He took a bite of lasagna and folded his arms across his chest. "Women are fickle."

Abby's eyes met Nathan's. "Is this true? Rachel said she doesn't want you looking into Jonas's death?"

Nathan nodded. He could feel the "I told you so" coming.

"What did I tell you? What good will digging through all that do?"

Richard shook his head. "If you ask me, she's afraid to know the truth about her son. The kid must have been a dope addict. What else would he have been doing with all those syringes?"

"What?" Abby questioned. "What syringes? You never said—"

"We found hundreds of extra insulin syringes in Jonas's dresser. Most of them he'd bought the week before he died." He looked at Richard. "Have you ever considered that he might not have been using them himself? Maybe his dope-using friends were using him to get needles."

"Hmm." Abby scratched her head. "I'll bet you're right, Richard. I'll bet Rachel is afraid of finding out information about her son that she doesn't want to face. At least now, if she doesn't know, she can convince herself he was a good kid." She stood and began to clear the dishes. "As a mother, I can't say that I blame her. I'd want to preserve the memory of my kid any way I could."

The men looked at each other and shrugged.

Richard pushed back from the table. "I've got a game at 7:30, Nate. I'll be back after the game to help you out, OK?"

"Where's the game? Maybe we should go watch."

"It's in Lake Park."

"City league?"

"Yep. Blackstone Drywallers versus us mighty men from Reynolds Welding."

"Mel, Abby, you want to go?"

"Let me get these dishes done first."

"I want to go, Daddy."

Nathan smiled. "OK, Rich, I guess it's a plan."

Richard went to the door, then called back to Abby, "Thanks for the dinner. I'll see you guys at the game."

◆ ◆ ◆

Melissa restlessly and happily played under the bleachers with Tommy Evans. Nathan positioned himself beside the bleachers, next to Abby on the front row.

Nathan squinted toward the home-team dugout. "I didn't know Brian played on Richard's team."

She stiffened and stared ahead at the batter. "I didn't either."

The batter hit a hard grounder, and when the shortstop overthrew the first baseman, the ball struck the fence in front of Nathan.

"Oh!" Abby exclaimed, continuing to stare at the players.

Nathan made small talk with other spectators as Abby sat quietly, apparently absorbed in the game.

Nathan studied his wife for a moment. "Is something wrong? Or have you suddenly been captivated by men's softball?"

Abby shook her head and continued looking at the batter.

"Abby?"

"I want to watch him, Nate. What if he fouls a ball this way? It could hit you."

"I'll back up."

"Nate, you'd never be able to react in time." She heaved a sigh of frustration. "Why don't we move behind the backstop?"

"I don't want to. Everyone would be looking at me over there."

"At least you'd be safe."

"I'd rather sit here and take my chances." He nodded toward the plate. "Cheer for Brian."

"Go, Brian," Abby muttered obediently.

Nathan looked at his wife and rolled his eyes. She still refused to look in his direction. He raised his voice. "Come on, Brian, show 'em what you've got."

Melissa appeared from beneath the bleachers. "I want a hot dog."

"Mel, we just ate."

"I'm hungry."

"Get the girl a hot dog," Nathan responded. "I'll be OK."

Abby kept her eyes on the batter. "I'm not leaving you."

"OK, I'll go with her."

"I can go by myself."

"Whatever," Abby quipped.

"I can take her," their neighbor, Mrs. Evans, offered. "My Tommy will want something too." She stood and took the children by the hand.

Nathan shook his head and watched as they headed off to the refreshment stand.

Brian Turner hit a triple, and the Reynolds fans cheered. Nathan added an "At-a-boy!" and looked at his wife, who made no comment.

After the second inning Abby, staring through the fence, said, "We really should get Melissa home. She's filthy. She'll need a bath if we're going to make it to church tomorrow."

Come on, Abby, the game's just starting. What's eating you? "How about another inning? She can take a bath in the morning."

Abby grunted as Richard came to the plate. "Let's just hope this game doesn't go into extra innings. I don't feel like waiting on Richard tonight."

◆ ◆ ◆

That night, long after Melissa's bath and Richard's sweaty but timely return, and long after Nathan's nightly routine, Abby tossed in sleeplessness. The images of Brian playing ball prodded a memory she longed to bury—a memory that refused to die.

"Laurie's asleep," Brian whispered, taking off his baseball cap. "Thanks to the pain pills, I think she'll finally sleep through the night." Fear and concern were etched on his face. "Thanks for your help."

Abby reached for him and drew him close. "You're going to make it, Brian." She laid her head on his chest as she felt his strong arms surround her. He sobbed for a minute, and she wiped his tears with her hand. "It's going to be OK."

Their eyes met for a moment before he lowered his face to hers, and their embrace shifted from comfort to passion, from concern to a fire that neither resisted. "Abby," he gasped, pulling her against him.

She sat up in bed and clutched the sheet beneath her chin. "Oh, Nathan," she sobbed quietly. "I—I'm s-so sorry."

CHAPTER
33

ON SUNDAY morning Richard arrived right on time and assisted Nathan through his morning routine.

After Nathan was dressed and in his chair, he looked at himself in the mirror. "Oh man, I wish you could wash my hair before church." He frowned. "Jim does it on his mornings, but it's been since Friday and I—" He stopped when he heard Richard sigh.

Abby walked over and combed Nathan's hair with her fingers, then looked at Richard. Nathan watched their interaction in the mirror.

"I have a tournament in Carlisle."

Abby shrugged. "Don't worry. I'll do it." She touched Nathan's neck. "We can wash it in the sink." She looked back at Richard. "You don't need to stay. I'll do breakfast for him."

Richard retreated two steps. "Are you sure?"

"No problem."

Nathan called after him, "I'll see you on Tuesday."

Richard disappeared.

"Abby, this isn't going to work. The headset on my wheelchair will be in the way. I can't lean back over the sink."

"Oh." She scratched her head. "What if we lean you forward? I'll just move your chest strap down and lean you over the sink."

Nathan moved his chair so Abby could position him so his upper body would rest against and over the sink. Slowly, awkwardly, and with some hesitation, Abby accomplished the task, but not without getting water in his ears, down his back, and on the floor.

"I'm glad that's over," Nathan sighed with relief as Abby changed his shirt.

"Oh really?" she responded. "You only said, 'Careful' or 'Watch out' about a thousand times." She smiled demurely and turned on the blow-dryer.

He watched her in the mirror. Abby looked weary. "Thanks, Abs. I didn't want to go to church that way."

"There," she said with a yawn, adding a final brush stroke. "Handsome as ever."

◆ ◆ ◆

At Community Chapel an usher quickly moved some chairs so Nathan could sit in his wheelchair in the back row with Abby and Melissa. It was his first visit to his home church since November. He enjoyed the music and the sermon and, for the most part, the dozens of pats on the shoulder and the "Welcome backs."

Abby was noticeably quiet and kept her hands clasped in her lap. When it was over, she quickly leaned over to Nathan. "Do you think we can leave soon? I need to straighten the house before the doctors come over."

Nathan nodded and strained to see Jennifer Hicks on the far side of the auditorium. "I can't believe she's coming here now," he said softly, pointing with his head. The teenager was dressed more conservatively than when he'd seen her in the cafe but still sported her short, nearly white hair and dark lipstick. She looked up, and for a brief moment her eyes met Nathan's. Then she quickly turned away and slipped out of view into the adjacent fellowship hall. Nathan sighed. *I wish I could talk to her about Jonas. Maybe she'd know whether there's any truth to the rumors about his drug problem.*

Abby seemed to ignore his comment and headed for the exit. Nathan followed the path she cleared into the main foyer and then into the parking lot. As he paused next to the van, he heard his name.

"Nathan."

He looked over to see Emma McMillan, clutching the white bow of her blouse under her chin. A look of worry punctuated her already wrinkled face. She put her hand on his arm.

"Hi, Emma."

She shook her white hair slowly. "Oh, Nathan, you don't know how hard it is for me to say this," she began. "It's so horrible to see you going through this trial." She sighed and clutched her blouse even tighter. "I saw you down at the healing crusade in Carlisle. I prayed soooo hard that you would be healed. Praise the Lord."

Nathan edged his head away from Emma's face. Her breath smelled like fruity gum. "Thank you." He cast a glance over at Abby who was preoccupied with lowering the van's wheelchair ramp.

Emma hesitated, then cleared her throat. "Nathan, in times when our prayers for healing go unanswered, we must consider the difficult truth that sin might be blocking the flow."

He squinted. "Sin?"

She lifted her head and quoted piously, "'If I regard iniquity in my heart, the Lord will not hear me,' Psalms 66 and 18." She nodded. "Sin's a part of the curse, Nathan. And sickness is a result of sin. We need to find the spiritual cause of our illnesses before the Lord can heal us. Praise the Lord."

"You think I'm being punished for some sin?"

"Oh, Nathan," she gushed, "it sounds so horrible to say it that way." She winced and added timidly, "But I think so."

Abby stepped away from the van to Nathan's side and locked eyes with the older church member. "This is not Nathan's fault! God may have plans for my husband, but he *isn't* punishing him for sin!" She paused and lifted her nose. "Praise the Lord!"

Emma glanced around to see several other people in the parking lot turn their heads in response to Abby's raised voice. Emma made an exaggerated swallowing gesture and cleared her throat.

Nathan nodded his head and spoke in a quiet tone. "Thank you for sharing your concern." He started backing his wheelchair toward the ramp.

"Oh." Emma seemed flustered and pulled her hand away from

Nathan's arm. Her head bobbed, and she retreated a step. "Yes, well . . . I'm glad you could come."

Nathan drove up the ramp and positioned his wheelchair in the van. Abby folded the ramp and slammed the side door. He glanced pensively at his wife and stayed quiet as she strapped down his wheelchair with obvious vigor.

A mile down the road, Abby said, "I'm sorry for blowing up, Nate. She made me so mad, talking about you like that." She shook her head. "With all the other pressures . . . I just couldn't handle it."

"It's OK, Abs. I understand."

"It's not OK. I'm going to apologize. I can't believe I mocked her like that."

Melissa started singing. At first it sounded like a chorus they'd sung in church, but it quickly changed to the theme song from a movie she'd seen.

Nathan snickered and looked at Abby. "I can't believe you said that either, and maybe you should apologize, but . . . I think old Emma needed to hear what you said." He hesitated. "Maybe not in the exact *manner* you said it, but your message was on target just the same." He hummed along with Melissa for a moment before adding, "Thanks for sticking up for me."

He cocked his head back and teased, "Don't mess with me . . . or you'll have to deal with *Mrs.* McAllister."

◆ ◆ ◆

At a quarter past 3, a new Chevy Suburban pulled into the McAllister driveway. "He's here," Nathan announced to Abby.

She went to the door and smoothed her dress. "How's my hair?"

"You look fine."

Abby opened the door and smiled. "Welcome, Dr. Hannah."

"Hello, Ms. McAllister." Dr. Hannah looked beyond to see Nathan. "Hello." He lifted his hand. "This is my daughter Paige and Dr. Elizabeth Hopkins, a neurosurgery resident working with me in research."

"Come in, come in." Abby stepped back.

Dr. Hannah wore a gray suit with a dark maroon silk tie. The women were less formal, with Paige and Dr. Hopkins wearing dress slacks and blouses. Dr. Hannah squeezed Nathan's hand. "So good to see you again."

"Won't you sit down?" Abby lifted her hands toward the chairs in the den. "Can I get you something to drink? Lemonade? Coffee?"

They politely declined.

Abby offered a hesitant shrug and then sat quietly on the edge of a chair next to Nathan.

Dr. Hannah selected a chair across from where Nathan had positioned himself. "I guess you're filled with questions since our conversation."

Nathan smiled nervously. "I *have* been wondering what this is about."

Dr. Hannah leaned forward. "Let me just lay it out in simple terms, Mr. McAllister. What we are working on is spinal cord restoration or regeneration. We have been using special nerve grafts to restore the transmission of nerve signals through an area of previous spinal cord injury."

"You're already doing this?"

Elizabeth cleared her throat. Dr. Hannah looked in her direction momentarily before responding, "Not in humans. Only in animals."

"Hmm." Nathan scratched his forehead on the end of his mouth-stick. "And I suppose you're looking for a human to try this on?"

"Yes."

The surgeon's brevity left Nathan unsure how to respond. "Well . . . uh . . . what are the chances it will work?"

Dr. Hopkins brightened. "We have been quite successful in—"

"We have some data to suggest that it may work to restore partial function," Dr. Hannah interrupted, casting a sideways glance to silence his resident. "But we have never tried the procedure in a human before."

"Partial function?"

The neurosurgeon shook his head. "I won't be able to guarantee the amount of success we will have. All we can say is that in a higher animal model we have evidence of restoring both movement and sensation in a limited amount."

"A higher animal?"

"A baboon. We've had experience with the operation using a quadriplegic primate."

"What happened with the baboon? Did it walk again?"

Dr. Hannah's eyes shifted from Nathan to his assistants and back again. "We do not have the benefit of knowing whether the animal would have been able to walk."

Abby pushed herself back in her chair. "Why? Did the animal . . . *die?*"

Dr. Hannah sighed. "No. Our animal was stolen shortly after the operation. I'm afraid we'll never know just how successful the procedure would have been."

"I read about that in the Brighton papers," Nathan said. "I didn't realize that the experiment was on a quadriplegic."

"Mr. McAllister, I—"

"Call me Nathan."

"I really didn't come to get into specific details of our research. What I really wanted to establish was a first contact, to see if you would even like to be considered for this project. It would mean an extensive workup, and then, *if* we felt you were suitable, an attempt at restorative surgery." Dr. Hannah paused. "How have you been coping with your disability?"

Nathan looked at Abby. "Uh, OK, I think." He shrugged. "It's been a struggle, as you might imagine, but I have the support of my wife and of my faith."

"His faith is what has carried him," Abby interjected. "And the support of this community. Practically the whole town chipped in to help us with the modifications to our home."

"Wow," Paige responded. "That's great."

The neurosurgeon leaned forward. "Let me ask the question a bit differently—have you come to terms with being a quadriplegic for the rest of your life?"

Nathan looked at Abby again and paused before turning his attention to Dr. Hannah. "That's not an easy thing to accept, Dr. Hannah.

I've struggled with self-pity and have wondered, 'Why me?' I've spent hours praying that this situation would go away and that I would walk again." He looked at the floor. "I want to be strong in my faith. I hope it is God's plan for me to get out of this chair, but lately . . . lately I've begun to understand that it may not necessarily be God's plan to heal me before I die." He looked up and searched the faces of his three visitors. "If I spend the rest of my life in a chair, it must be God's will for me, and I will trust him because I know that he knows what's best."

Abby squeezed his shoulder. Paige pinched her mouth in a tight smile and nodded rapidly. Drs. Hannah and Hopkins looked quietly at the floor.

"That's awesome," Paige responded quietly. "Your attitude, I mean."

Dr. Hopkins changed the subject. "I saw from your medical record that you're classified as a complete C3-4 quadriplegic." She moved over and touched his knee. "You have no feeling at all? No temperature sensation? No deep pressure or pain? Nothing?"

"Nothing. No movement. No feeling." Nathan watched as the doctors exchanged glances. "Is that good?"

Dr. Hannah shrugged. "We don't want to try the surgery on someone who has only a partial cord injury, at least not initially. The surgery has the risk of further damaging the cord, so there's a chance of loss of function below the operative site. If you have no function to lose, there is less risk."

"Why not try it on another baboon so you can answer some of your questions first?"

Dr. Hannah drummed his fingers on his knee. "I won't lie to you, Nathan. Our research came under an incredible amount of criticism because we were surgically injuring a previously well animal before we operated to make it better again. The animal rights people went crazy when they found out what I was doing . . . or at least what they thought I was doing." He shook his head. "The whole project blew up in my face, Nathan. The university is under such scrutiny that the dean will not allow the research to continue using animals." He paused, choosing his words. "But the animal data shows so much promise of success that we feel using a human who can understand what he or she is risking is the next best step."

"A human guinea pig."

He frowned. "I don't like the term, but yes, that about sums it up."

"Hmm." Nathan looked at his wife. "What's in it for me?"

"The chance to walk again and—" Dr. Hopkins promised before Dr. Hannah interrupted.

"All of your medical care will be provided at no cost to you, and if there are any ongoing medical expenses related to complications from our procedure, they would be completely taken care of." His eyes were stern. "Your involvement, if you were found to be a suitable candidate after our workup, would be strictly voluntary."

Nathan raised his eyebrows. "Wow."

Abby shook her head. "But what about the risk of surgery? You mentioned that there could be—"

"I'd rather not discuss the specifics until after we've had a chance to fully examine Nathan's situation." Dr. Hannah looked at Abby. "But yes, there are risks. There are always small risks with any surgery—things like infection, bleeding, blood clots, that sort of thing."

Abby pressed the issue. "You talked about loss of function."

"There is only a slim chance of that in Nathan's case because he has no function below his cord injury, but certainly we would want to carefully test him to be sure." He paused and looked at Nathan. "Any damage to the spinal cord higher up could lead to a loss of your diaphragm innervation. In that case you would not be able to breathe without a mechanical ventilator."

"Oh." Nathan frowned.

Fear strained Abby's voice. "Could the procedure kill him?"

"Very unlikely." The neurosurgeon held up his hands. "I really don't want to get into all of that now. This discussion is premature at this stage. We are confident that the complications would be rare and that the potential benefit would outweigh them."

Abby stood and retreated in the direction of the kitchen before asking quietly, "Are you sure I can't get anyone anything?"

Nathan looked up. "I'll take some lemonade."

The doctors shook their heads.

"I'd like some too," responded Paige. "Can I help you?" she asked, following Abby to the kitchen.

While Abby was gone, Nathan gave the neurosurgeons a tour of his small home, showing them his automatic back entrance and his room.

After a few more minutes Dr. Hannah, Paige, and Dr. Hopkins stepped onto the front porch. Nathan followed them down the front ramp into the driveway.

Dr. Hannah looked down at Nathan. "Feel free to think about this as long as you want."

"Pray about it," Paige whispered to Abby loud enough for Nathan to hear. He looked over to see Paige smile and squeeze Abby's hand.

"I should mention that this project at this point is strictly secret. I'm sure you understand how sensitive this information is. I can't have the popular press getting hold of this and distorting the facts. I'd have an avalanche of people demanding an operation before we get all of our data examined. This process is going to take *a long time*." His eyes met Nathan's. "I'd really rather you didn't share this with anyone unless it's absolutely necessary to help you come to a decision."

"I understand." Nathan watched as Abby nodded her agreement.

"And again, we are not promising you that you'd be accepted as our first candidate for surgery. We are only offering you the chance to be evaluated to see if you would suit our needs."

"I understand."

Dr. Hannah nodded.

Dr. Hopkins shook Nathan's limp hand.

Paige smiled and waved. "Bye bye."

◆ ◆ ◆

Once in the Suburban, Paige frowned. "Why can't I drive? You never let me drive when we're together."

"Sure I do," her father countered. "But I want to drive, OK? This is a bad road."

Paige huffed and looked out the window. "This is a nice town."

Elizabeth snipped, "This is nowhere."

"Oh, it's beautiful. Just look." She pointed up toward North Mountain.

Ryan sighed. "So what did you guys think? What's your first impression of McAllister?"

"He's so together," Paige bubbled. She looked over to see Elizabeth's steel expression.

"He's made to order. Just what we're looking for."

"If he agrees to the evaluation, I'll give you *my* opinion," Ryan countered.

Paige looked at Elizabeth and couldn't suppress a frown. "Made to order?"

A thin smile cracked Elizabeth's lips. "Exactly what I ordered."

Ryan chuckled. "Right."

CHAPTER
34

MONDAY mornings at Fisher's Cafe were always busy. It seemed to Abby that the whole town had gotten into the routine of starting the business week with the cafe breakfast special with extra coffee.

Today was no different, and Abby sighed as she collected a quarter tip from a customer who had occupied a bar stool for an hour reading the paper. She scanned the crowded room. Marty and another employee, Kristine, were waitressing and busing. Mr. Knitter, the owner, was running the grill. Even though he could afford more help, he liked to cook and frequently assigned his help other jobs. Abby glanced in his direction and smiled. *The doughboy makes a great omelette.*

Marty slid up to her side and whispered, "What's with the fancy-suit guys?" She nodded with her head toward the corner booth where Officer Brian Turner sat opposite two men in dark suits.

Abby sighed. "Please don't ask me to wait their table."

"Oh no," she replied, shaking her head. "I've already claimed that one." She looked at the two mysterious men. "Besides, they look rich. And cute."

"Who are they? Fisher's Retreat doesn't really cater to the suit crowd very often."

"I have no idea. That's why I asked you."

"Looks like they're talking business." Abby watched as the men hunched together in serious conversation. The older-appearing man of the pair glanced briefly in Abby's direction before turning a stern gaze back at Brian.

"Did you see the watch on that guy?" Marty huffed. "I'll bet he stiffs me for the tip. Rich guys are like that."

"What are they talking about?"

"Beats me. Every time I get close enough to eavesdrop, they chill. I've topped off their coffee three times just to check."

"Probably just some police work."

"No way," Marty countered. "Not without the chief around. You know he keeps a tight rein on things. But they're definitely outsiders."

Abby nodded and stayed quiet.

Marty continued, "Yep, I'll bet old Joe is walking down a white beach right about now." She looked at her watch. "What time is it in Hawaii anyway?"

"I have no idea," Abby muttered. *And I don't really care.* As she watched the men, an uneasy feeling crept over her. She wasn't sure if it was because of Brian's presence or the two well-dressed intruders.

"A number 4 and number 6 are up," Mr. Knitter called, placing an order of french toast and a plate of biscuits and gravy on the counter.

Abby broke her stare. "I gotta get to work."

◆ ◆ ◆

That afternoon at the D.A.R.E. assembly at Ashby High, Nathan admired Charlie Edwards's easygoing manner and straightforward, no-frills approach. He spoke the truth about drug addiction and gave information about recreational drug use and the importance of saying no. His body build couldn't help but impress the students and tended to give him an automatic in with the student body, particularly the jocks.

Boy, it's no wonder the kids give this guy their respect. He looks like a compact Arnold Schwarzenegger. H himself and sighed. *I wonder how they'll respond to me after looking at* e looked at *Charlie?*

An important portion of Charlie's presentation dealt with the factors that lead kids into drug use and the importance of a healthy self-esteem. As he talked, Nathan cringed inwardly. *Great! The very things I'm struggling with, and I'm supposed to help these kids?*

Finally, when it was time for Nathan to speak, he drove his wheel-chair to center stage. Up until that point he had been offstage, only visible to Charlie and a few of the students in the front row. A murmur swept through the audience as he looked up helplessly at a solitary mike, which Charlie hadn't needed because of his strong voice.

Charlie worked for a moment trying to adjust the microphone, then abandoned that idea and just held the mike while kneeling beside Nathan.

Nathan slowly shared his story, relating the vague knowledge he had of the events surrounding his injury and what he'd gone through in rehabilitation and his fight to return to his home community. Knowing that many of the kids had contributed their time to fund-raising activities on his behalf, he thanked them for their help.

"Thanks for making this possible," he said with a weak voice. Nathan swallowed and sniffed. *Oh, Lord, I don't want to cry in front of all these kids.*

"In closing, I'd like to add a little bit to what Officer Edwards said about the importance of self-esteem. The irony about drugs is that many kids get trapped into it because they're searching for a way to be cool, for an escape from their own inabilities." He paused and searched the faces of his attentive audience. "But in the end you're left feeling worse about yourself than before. Drugs are a lie. You need to tell yourself the truth. I almost paid with my life to fight this problem. You need to do your part. You need to say no."

He paused as a slow rhythmic clapping started from the back of the auditorium. It spread until the whole crowd joined to give Nathan a standing ovation.

Charlie pulled the microphone away and cleared his throat.

Nathan looked up. "I'm not finished, Charlie."

The officer nodded and lowered the mike back to Nathan's face. The crowd hushed to hear his final comments.

"This is a tough problem. Self-esteem, I mean. Look at me, guys," he joked. "Can you imagine someone like me impressing a girl?"

No one laughed.

Nathan listened as an uncomfortable moment passed. "Let me share with you what I'm learning. I haven't arrived yet, so please realize that

I'm just like you. I'm struggling too." He paused. "I'm learning that a proper self-image comes from realizing that I'm loved by God. Not because of what I did in the past. And not because of what I can or can't do now." He looked the audience over from side to side. "And not because of how I look or whether I can impress a girl or anyone else."

Nathan looked up at Charlie, who had started to weave the microphone up and down. He looked concerned that Nathan had decided to share about God in a public high school. Nathan continued, "If I have any advice to give to students who are struggling with self-esteem or drugs, it's this: God loves you. You need to believe that. And don't believe the lie that drugs are the solution to how you feel."

A bell sounded, indicating the end of the period. The audience immediately started breaking for the exits.

Charlie stood up straight and touched Nathan's shoulders. "Man, I think you had 'em. That was great."

Nathan nodded. He felt good. He knew he had said the right thing.

Charlie started packing up his materials as Nathan moved his chair to the side of the stage. Below him, just in front of the stage, Nathan saw a group of students making their way to an exit.

"Dion," Nathan called. "Dion."

The teenager, dressed in a black T-shirt and a leather jacket, looked over and lifted his head in a silent greeting.

"Dion, can I ask you something?"

He shrugged.

Nathan recognized Jennifer Hicks, clinging to Dion's elbow and standing behind him. "I want to ask you about Jonas Yoder." He studied the teen's face for a response. "Did you know him?"

"Yeah. He was all right. It's too bad about him, you know?"

"Dion, was Jonas doing drugs?"

Jennifer gripped Dion's elbow. "Come on, Dion."

Nathan sighed as Dion stayed quiet. "Dion, I'm not a cop anymore. It's not going to get anyone into trouble if you answer my question."

"Jonas was clean, man. He talked like you."

"Do you know if anyone disliked him? Was he in any trouble?"

Jennifer pulled Dion back. "Come on, Dion. You don't need to talk to him. Let's go."

Dion hesitated.

"Don't talk to him. I'm leaving." Jennifer avoided Nathan's gaze.

Dion yielded to his friend's coaxing and started to back away. He looked up at Nathan. "I don't know, man. I don't know anything."

"Dion, Jennifer, I—" Nate watched helplessly as the two disappeared through an exit, leaving him alone on the stage.

"There's a ramp over here," Charlie called from the opposite side of the auditorium. "Come on down. I want to talk to the principal for a minute before we leave."

Nathan shook his head. *Why is everyone so reluctant to talk about Jonas Yoder?*

◆ ◆ ◆

That night after Dave Borntrager had assisted Nathan through his nightly routine and positioned him for the night, Abby appeared in the doorway. "Sleeping?"

"Not yet. My mind's too busy."

"Thinking about the research?" Abby sat on the edge of Nathan's bed.

He nodded. "What do you think?"

"It's so exciting, Nate." She paused and reached out to touch his cheek. "But you're the one who has to make the decision. You're the one taking the risk." She stroked his face with her hand. "What do you want to do?"

He clenched his jaw and searched Abby's eyes. "I want to do it. I— I at least want to go through the workup. They may not accept me."

She rocked back and forth. "I can hardly believe this is happening." Her eyes were shining. "Nathan, you might walk again."

"Maybe this is how the Lord will heal me."

"Maybe."

Their eyes met again before Abby leaned forward. She kissed him slowly and softly on his lips and cheek, moving to his earlobe and down onto his neck. Nathan closed his eyes and moved his head to respond to her gentle caress, the touch he had desired for so long. He breathed in the scent of her hair as he sensed his heart quickening. She lifted her head and accepted his kiss, then moved so she could cradle his face on her neck, her hands lightly massaging the back of his head.

Subtly he sensed her desire to pull away. She stiffened momentarily, no longer surrendering to the passion he'd felt only moments before. Her fingers ceased their wondrous probing of his hair, and a short gasp escaped her lips.

Abby sat up and turned her face away with her hand raised, but shielded by her hair. Was she wiping away tears?

"Abby, don't—"

A sob caught in her throat.

He watched helplessly. *She can't bring herself to love me like this.* "Abby," he whispered. "I love you."

She continued to look away. When she finally glanced back, her brown eyes were moist.

"Tell me what's wrong. Why are you pulling away? Is it me? You can't love me like this?"

She bit her lip. "It's not you, Nate."

Nathan searched her face for clues, a hint of what stirred beneath the surface. There was no glimmer of light that would indicate her true feelings. *Why won't you say, "I love you"?* He sighed. "Why won't you share your feelings with me?"

She sighed heavily. "I—I . . ." She hesitated. "I just can't. Not now."

"It's me." Nathan pinched his eyes closed. " I know it is. So just say it!"

"It's not you," she repeated emphatically as she edged away from him toward the corner of the bed.

"Of course it is. Just look at me." He shook his head as tears began to cloud his vision. He felt powerless, like a child, when the tears came. "Why would you want me now?"

"No!" Abby stood. "It's me, Nate." Her voice was thick and wavering. "No matter how things appear, it isn't you." She wouldn't look at him but just kept staring at the floor. "Once upon a time, before your accident, I would have blamed you in an instant. Blamed you for my own lack of commitment and passion." She wiped her eyes with the palm of her hand and sniffed. "But not anymore. You've changed, Nate. You're not the same man who used to patrol Fisher's Retreat."

He huffed sarcastically.

"I'm not talking about your body. I'm talking about your head. The way you act. The way you treat people. The way you treat me."

"What are you saying?"

"Something's happened to you, Nathan. Your jealousy has melted. You're more thoughtful, more interested in others." She looked up. "I think something happened during those weeks you spent in a coma." She showed the first hint of a smile. "It's like you forgot how to be impatient. You forgot how to be mean."

"Mean?"

"Well, not mean exactly, but. . . . well, controlling."

He thought about that for a moment. He knew she was right. "I'm not sure it was the coma, Abby. I think it was all the time I was forced to just lie there and think. Maybe God finally broke through to me when I couldn't run away." He watched his wife for a moment as she retreated one more step toward the door. How had she switched the conversation around to him?

She edged back another step, shaking her head.

"If it's not me, what is it?"

"I don't know." *I know, but I can't say it, Nathan.* She folded her arms across her abdomen. "I want everything to be like it was at first—when we first married. It's just that I—" Her voice trailed as she retreated.

"Don't do this, Abby. Don't shut me out. I can't chase you anymore."

"It's me, Nate. Just give me some time to work out my feelings. It isn't just you making adjustments. Everyone around you has been affected too." She turned away, and Nathan watched as her hands went to her face, apparently to wipe her eyes again.

"Abby, why—"

"Nathan . . . it's late," she said flatly. "I have to get an early start in the morning, and I just can't talk about this right now." She looked at him one time before turning out the light and hurrying from the room. "Not yet."

He followed her footsteps with his mind. The creaky stairs, the hallway upstairs, and a thump as she collapsed onto her bed. Nathan lay still in the darkness, not understanding her reaction, not wanting to cry.

Minutes passed. Sleep would not come easy tonight.

Why is she pulling away, God? Why doesn't she open up to me?

He stared at the ceiling, toward Abby's room, in the direction of the squeak from their old bed. *Abby must be restless too. I repulse her, but she won't leave me because she's afraid of hurting me even more, is that it? She's afraid of telling me the truth—that she can't love a man in a wheelchair.*

He thought about Abby's kiss, her touch. *She kissed me in her excitement about me walking again, didn't she? She can get excited about that, but not about life with a quad for a husband. She can't really believe I'll walk and . . .*

She says I've changed, God. I know that's true. And she seems to like the change . . . So why did she pull away? He couldn't put it all together, and the confusion felt like more than he could bear.

Nathan coughed weakly, frustrated by his inability to comprehend. He wanted to be patient, to be able to see things from Abby's perspective, but understanding seemed to float just beyond his grasp. He prayed, cried, and waited before eventually sensing a quiet peace, a calmness within his storm of anxiety. He recognized the Holy Spirit's prompting.

You must learn to trust her with your heart, Nathan. Communication is a two-way street. Try sharing your own feelings with Abby. Don't accuse her of shutting you out unless you're ready to admit that you're doing the same thing.

He clenched his jaw. *Me? I'm shutting Abby out?*

He thought about his shooting and the facts he hadn't shared with his wife. *Should I even share the anonymous phone calls with her?*

But she'll be afraid for me. And I'm responsible to shield her from worry if I can, right?

He frowned in the darkness. He knew he couldn't argue himself out of it. He was only holding back from sharing with Abby because he feared her reaction, afraid she would use it as a reason to move him away from Fisher's Retreat again.

I can't share everything with her. I'm supposed to protect her from some things, right?

The impression persisted. *Be open with Abby. Show her you love her by opening your heart.*

Nathan looked over at the baby monitor. The light in the corner of the monitor was off, indicating that Abby had forgotten to turn it on before she left. He verbalized his prayer, knowing Abby would not hear. But tonight he changed his prayer from "Help her to love me" to "Help me to love her the way you want me to."

CHAPTER
35

THE NEXT morning Nathan was awake before he heard his wife's preparations upstairs. He could hear her tiptoeing softly about, getting dressed, and running water in the bathroom. When she descended the stairs, she seemed to be going extra-slowly in an attempt not to wake him. Going slowly, however, still activated the creaking floorboards. He heard her moving about the kitchen, quietly preparing Melissa's lunch and setting out what she would want for breakfast. Finally, only moments before she was due at the cafe, she appeared in the doorway, squinting into the darkness in the direction of Nathan's bed.

She hesitated, not speaking.

"Morning, Abby."

"You're awake. You should be sleeping." She remained silhouetted against the gentle light coming from the front room. She looked at her watch. "I'm late. I'd better get to the cafe. Do you need anything?"

"I'll take a little water."

Abby nodded, disappeared, then reappeared with a tall glass with a straw. "Probably good to take a drink. It's Richard's morning, and he isn't always on time." She pushed the straw into his mouth and let him take a slow drink.

"Thanks."

She reached up to turn off the monitor and grunted when she found it already off. "Oops. I hope you didn't call me."

"It's OK, Abby. I didn't need you."

She retreated to the doorway again, not pausing to kiss him good-bye like she normally did. "I'd better get."

"Get?" He shook his head. "My country woman."

She glanced back and seemed to hesitate.

"Abby? Let's talk today . . . when you get home. I have some things I need to tell you."

With her eyes downcast, she nodded rapidly. Her voice was flat, and she looked tired. "Sure. I really need to go. Mr. Knitter wants me to run the grill."

"I want to call Dr. Hannah today," he called after her fleeing form.

She didn't respond, and he only heard her quick steps and the sound of the front door. It was obvious that her short visit was by design; she'd purposefully allowed herself little time to interact with him.

Nathan sighed with frustration. It just didn't seem fair. His disability affected everything. *I'm so dependent until I'm in my chair. I can't even talk to Abby unless she comes to me. All I can do is lie here and wait. Wait for her to come to me. If I get cold or hot, I wait. If I want to get up, I wait. If I want to rub my eyes, I wait.*

He whispered to the ceiling, "Boy, do I want to talk to Dr. Hannah."

◆ ◆ ◆

Paige bounded into her father's spinal lab to find Elizabeth at her desk, elbow-deep in neurosurgical textbooks. "Hi, Dr. Hopkins." She stopped in front of her desk and waited for Elizabeth to look up.

Elizabeth only grunted, closed her eyes, and mumbled something about the median age of patients with some sort of neurological condition.

"What? Glioblaster?" Paige curled her upper lip and tried to pronounce the words the resident had mumbled.

Elizabeth looked up and rolled her eyes. "Glioblastoma multiforme," she corrected, saying the words slowly and loudly, much as one would to a young child. "It's only the worst of all brain tumors."

As if I should know that. Paige looked on as Elizabeth returned her attention to the book in front of her. Paige cleared her throat and smoothed her scrub-top in another attempt to get the resident to notice her.

Elizabeth finally looked up at Paige as she hovered in front of the desk. "What?"

Paige grinned sheepishly. "Notice anything?" She pirouetted.

"You combed your hair."

"No! The scrubs!" She held up her arms. "What do you think? I'd look better in blue. This green clashes with my eyes."

"Oh, the scrubs. What's the grand occasion?" she asked sarcastically.

"Ms. Taylor let me off so I could watch my father in the O.R. He's operating on a man with an as-tro-cy-tom-a," she said, unable to resist imitating the way Elizabeth had just spoken to her. She babbled on, "It was *so* cool! I got to see the brain and everything."

Elizabeth placed her hands behind her head. "Nothing quite like the sound of the oscillating saw opening the human skull in the morning."

"Ugh. That part made me feel a little queasy."

Elizabeth shifted and pulled her textbook closer, an obvious attempt to get back to her work.

Paige looked down at an open box sitting on the floor beside the desk. Inside she could see several plastic dolls. She picked up the top one and snarled. "What is *this*?"

The doll she held was bald, with a red mark painted on the scalp.

Elizabeth smiled for the first time. "Oh, that. I call 'em my craniotomy Barbies." She lifted a second doll from the box. "I buy old Barbies at yard sales and modify them."

Paige couldn't hold her tongue. "Sick."

"I'm not doing it to *torture* them, Paige. I make them this way for the pediatric neurosurgery patients. One of the I.C.U. nurses, Ellis Heatwole, makes them little patient gowns and everything. Here . . . since you're bugging me, you might as well learn something." She pointed to a red mark running side to side in front of Barbie's ears. "This is a bicoronal incision." She picked up another doll. "This one had a suboccipital craniotomy. We use this approach to get to the posterior fossa." The doll had a red mark in the center of the scalp, running from the upper neck toward the top of the head.

Paige put her hand to her mouth. "Poor Barbie."

Elizabeth shrugged. "The kids love 'em. We even attach little IVs to their chest to simulate the chemotherapy ports."

"She looks like a punk rocker."

The phone rang, and Elizabeth picked it up. "Oh, hi, Trish." She covered the mouthpiece with her hand and whispered, "It's Herculina."

Paige listened to the one-sided conversation.

"Really? Three times . . . Huh . . . Uh huh . . . Great. Say, do you have his number handy?" Elizabeth scrawled the number onto a Post-It. "Gotcha. Bye, Trish."

The resident looked up. "It seems that Mr. McAllister has taken us up on our offer. He's pretty anxious to get started with the workup. He's already called the office three times, trying to get your father." She winked. "I guess I'll call him and try to get some of his tests lined up." She put her hands behind her head again. "I knew he'd say yes."

"That's great . . . I guess," Paige responded while turning the mutilated Barbie over in her hands. She looked down at her scrubs. "Well, I'll let you study. I need to change out of these so I can go to work."

◆ ◆ ◆

"What's with you today?" Marty nudged Abby on the shoulder. "You just keep staring out the front window."

Abby looked up to see her friend waving her hand in her face.

"Earth to Abby. Come in, please."

Abby shook her head. "Sorry. I just have a lot on my mind."

"Nate?"

Abby dropped her eyes to the countertop. "Yep."

Marty lowered her voice. "It's not as easy as you'd hoped, is it?" She leaned close and touched Abby's arm. "No one would look down on you if you found him a good nursing facility."

Abby could feel her coworker's eyes boring in on her.

"You'd be free, Abs. Just like you dreamed before."

"Don't start this, Marty." Abby pulled her arm away. "Nathan is happy being at home."

"Have you ever told him the truth? I'll bet he'd change his tune about staying with you then."

Abby's eyes began to sting. "I can't. He's been through too much."

"Maybe I should talk with him. I could—"

Abby's temper flared. "Don't you dare! He's *my* husband, and I'll take care of this situation myself!" She saw Mr. Knitter walking over from a corner booth. He didn't look too happy.

"Suit yourself." Marty busied herself with cleaning a table before returning to Abby's side at the grill a few minutes later. "Brian and I are going down to the new bowling alley in Carlisle tonight. You could come along. The break would do you some good."

Abby straightened. "I can't." She sighed. "Nathan needs me. Besides, he wants to talk, and I thought I'd take Mel up to her grandmother's place so I can be alone with him, maybe even go out."

"Whatever."

"I think he really wants to talk about us."

Marty raised her eyebrows. "So that's why you keep staring off into space."

"I guess."

"Be honest with him, Abs. It's better than letting things drag on forever."

"Staying with him is *my* choice. I'm finally doing what I'm supposed to do."

"If I spent my whole life doing what I was supposed to do, I'd be a miserable wreck."

Abby clutched the front of her white apron, gathering the cloth in her hand. She looked away from Marty and shrugged. "It's more than that, Marty. It's what I *want* to do."

"Don't tell me you're falling in love again." She shook her head. "With Nate?" She frowned and muttered just loud enough for Abby to hear, "I'll never understand the power that man has over you."

Abby smiled thinly and kept quiet. She looked over to see Mr. Knitter holding up two fingers.

"Two number ones and a cheese omelette, Abby."

"Two number ones and a cheese omelette," she repeated, glad to be able to turn her attention away from Marty and onto the grill.

◆ ◆ ◆

That afternoon Ryan whisked through the cranberry hall to find Elizabeth sitting behind his desk. She quickly stood and moved to take another seat. "Dreaming of greatness, Dr. Hopkins?"

"It's never hurt me before. Here," she said, handing him a piece of paper. "I was just leaving you a note. I thought you'd want to know."

Ryan scanned the note. "He said yes?" He broke into a broad grin. "So soon?"

"He called Herc—uh, Trish three times this morning. I called him back this afternoon to make some arrangements. I need to confirm the tests you want done."

He raised his fingers one by one as he enumerated the items in the workup. "Complete physical exam, especially the neuro exam, CT of the neck, EKG, CBC, and blood chemistries." He tapped the side of his head. "Did you have a chance to review his hospital chart?"

"Start to finish. With all his complications, the poor guy was here forever."

"For a while his spinal cord injury was the least of his worries."

"I think we ought to repeat his chest X-ray. He's certainly at risk for pulmonary complications because of his weakened diaphragm."

"Good idea. He had adult respiratory distress syndrome, didn't he?" He shook his head. "It's amazing he survived."

"He was on the ventilator for fourteen days before he made any kind of meaningful response like opening his eyes. His brain took quite a hit from the blood loss."

"He seems pretty sharp now. He must have made a good recovery. Maybe we should get a baseline EEG and CT his head while we're at it."

Elizabeth opened a small black notebook and began to write. "Anything else?"

"I think we'd better get an arteriogram. The trauma surgeons had to ligate his external carotid artery."

"That shouldn't affect us, should it?"

"It may," Ryan said as he settled into his large desk chair. "I've been thinking about ways to support our nerve grafts in case the spinal cord defect is too large. We may have to bring up an omental flap to provide adequate blood supply to the grafts."

"An omental flap?"

"Sure. Has he had any previous abdominal surgery?"

"I don't know. All the admitting intern's note said was 'history unattainable.' I'll have to ask."

"We would have to get a general surgeon, and one of the plastic surgeons to help too. The idea would be to dissect a tongue of the greater omentum from where it attaches to the stomach. In many cases it can be mobilized to reach all the way into the neck. It can be passed through the chest or under the skin. Once it's in place, we gently wrap our nerve grafts in it to provide extra blood flow to help keep them alive."

"What if the omentum won't reach?"

"Then we completely remove a small portion of the omentum, along with a feeding artery and draining vein, and have the microvascular surgeons attach them to new vessels in the neck."

"A free flap?"

"Exactly. That's why we need an arteriogram. We'll want to know the anatomy so they'll be able make plans for their blood vessel anastomoses."

"Wow. I scrubbed with those guys when I did my plastic surgery rotation as an intern. It takes *forever*."

"We have to be ready for anything. And we have to set aside a least a full day for this one procedure." He leaned back. "Did you check on the availability of research beds?"

"The research unit won't have any beds until next week."

"They're all full?"

"Dr. Blaisdale is doing some flu virus study. He has a group of medical students quarantined in the research unit until Sunday."

"What's he working on now?"

"Another high-dose vitamin C study. He gives the students a flu virus to see whether those given the vitamin will get better faster or will show more resistance to the virus in the first place."

"They willfully accept an injection of a live flu virus?"

"Come on, Dr. Hannah, you remember what it was like, don't you? Medical students will do *anything* for money." She stood and retreated toward the door before adding, "I know I did."

◆ ◆ ◆

That evening, after a quiet dinner at home together, Nathan moved his chair into position in front of the couch where Abby reclined. "There are some things I need to tell you."

Abby looked up without speaking.

"Last night I started thinking . . . Here I was, accusing you of shutting me out, of not being open . . . and I've been doing the same to you."

She put down her magazine. "What are you talking about, Nate?"

"There are some things I haven't told you. I've been afraid you might not want me to stay here if you knew." He hesitated.

His wife prodded again. "What? You can tell me."

Nathan took a deep breath and began to explain the reasons for his obsession to find the truth about his accident and for his questions about the supposed suicide of Jonas Yoder. He gave a chronological account beginning with the first anonymous phone call warning him not to return to Fisher's Retreat and finishing with the second phone call claiming that Nathan knew "he killed Jonas."

Abby's mouth had fallen open. "I can't believe you didn't tell me these things. The caller said you knew 'he' killed Jonas. Who's *he*?"

"I'm not sure. The girl said, 'That's what you said,' and when I asked when, she said, 'when he shot you.'"

"Brian?" Abby's hand went to her mouth. "You think Brian shot you on purpose? You think Brian had something to do with Jonas Yoder's death? Why didn't you say something before?"

"Whoa, Abby. I'm not saying that Brian shot me on purpose. And I'm not sure of anything. This girl, whoever she is, might be playing a nasty trick. Maybe she's just trying to scare me. Maybe it's all a hoax, a druggie I busted who's just playin' with my mind." He shrugged.

"Sure, it looks like Brian shot me, but it all looks like an accident. Brian didn't have any motive for shooting me."

"You should have told me this sooner."

"I didn't want you to be afraid. I've never felt any reason to fear, no sense of danger, no signs of trouble, except for the phone calls. If I'd been convinced I was in danger, I would've told you."

Abby began to pace, asking question after question about the phone calls and Nathan's theories that his caller could have witnessed his shooting and then escaped from the second story of the Allen house after the shooting started.

Nathan offered another possibility. "Maybe my caller actually is trying to get Brian in trouble, trying to manipulate me into making him look bad."

"I doubt that a high schooler could be so sophisticated. *If* your theory is correct about the caller being from Ashby High."

"That's where the second call came from. I guess it's possible that it wasn't a student."

"Did you tell Joe about the phone calls?"

He shook his head. "I thought it was best for me to just keep quiet and see what would turn up." He looked at the floor, unable to meet Abby's gaze. "I was so intent on coming home that I didn't want anything to jeopardize it. I knew that if I shared my feelings with Joe or you, my homecoming would have been delayed. Besides, I never felt any real danger. And later, after the second call, I thought I'd better sort through the situation a bit more before I told anyone else."

She pointed her finger at him. "That's been your operating procedure all along, hasn't it, Nathan? Hold it in. Figure it out for yourself. You're so independent that you won't let anyone else in on your problems." She huffed. "Maybe I was wrong last night, Nathan. Maybe you haven't changed. We talk about anything and everything until it comes to something of substance, something that affects our lives, and then *you* decide what to do . . . you *alone*, without any discussion with anyone, including me!"

"Come on, Abs, I—"

"It's true, Nate. I've been dying to know what's in your head, your heart, for years, but you just clam up. The only one you tell your secrets to is Melissa."

"Abby! Those aren't real secrets. I—"

Abby retreated to the stairs. "This is a perfect example of what's wrong in this relationship! You played the strong, silent role, making all the decisions, even how I wore my hair, whether I could work, while I sat idly by, the pretty little wife, never valuable enough to offer an opinion."

"Abby, that was before. I—" He halted. "You mean the world to me."

There was fire in Abby's glare. "You set me up like a prize. You only wanted me because having a pretty woman on your arm made you feel important. But you never trusted me, did you, Nate? You held me in your jealousy, hardly letting me out of your sight . . ." Her words dissolved in a series of sobs.

He watched as she turned to look up the stairs. "Don't leave, Abby. Please!"

She looked at him and then back up the stairs. After hesitating a moment, she sat down on the second step and buried her face in her hands.

Nathan was unsure how to respond. He expected Abby to be worried about him, but he hadn't anticipated uncapping such a flood of anger and hurt.

After a few moments he spoke softly. "Abby, I know what you say has been true. And I feel horrible about it." He hesitated. "And I've been trying to tell you that I'm sorry."

His wife remained silent and wiped her eyes with the back of her hand. When she looked up, the fire was gone from her gaze, and her eyes were moist.

"Abby, I love you. What you think is very important to me."

"What *has* changed, Nate? You value me now because you're in that chair, is that it? You *need* me now. Suddenly I'm important to you again—"

"No!" He edged his wheelchair closer. "It's not that, Abs. It's just that the shooting has forced me into a position where I had to take a critical look at my own life . . . at how I treated others . . . at how I treated you." He shook his head. "I know it must seem like I'm chang-ing because I need you. I can't get away from that. But it's not true, Abby. I finally took a look at how I was running things, and I didn't like what I saw." He watched as Abby blew her nose. "I'm sorry. Really."

"I know." She couldn't seem to meet his gaze. "I'm sorry too." She sniffed. "You *have* changed, Nate. I guess I know that." She paused. "But it does upset me that you didn't trust me with the information about the calls." She sighed heavily. "Nathan, you might be in danger. Someone might be afraid of what you know."

"That's the irony. Because of my memory loss, I'm not a risk to anyone."

"But they might not know that. Your caller seemed to think you knew something about Jonas Yoder." Abby chewed her lower lip. "Didn't you tell me that Brian was asking about what you remembered?"

Nathan nodded.

"Did he seem worried? Suspicious?"

"No." He thought back to his last visit with Brian. "He did ask me about what I remembered. And he told me that I shouldn't pry into department business . . . that I was defenseless . . . whatever that meant."

Abby knitted her eyebrows, and her hand went to her mouth.

"I didn't take it as a threat. I think I have a pretty good read on Brian. It just doesn't fit to think he would deliberately shoot me. I don't buy it. There's no motive."

Abby looked away before standing and walking to the front win-dow. "Here comes your mom with Mel. It looks like she's been shop-ping again."

◆ ◆ ◆

That evening in the luxurious Hannah home, Paige played an imagi-nary guitar while she listened to a DC Talk compact disc. She cleaned up the kitchen and strummed a spatula while her father looked on.

"You call this Christian music?"

She looked up. "Of course. These guys are great."

Ryan lifted a saucer from the table and put it into the sink. "I guess you heard the news about Nathan McAllister."

Paige stopped strumming for a measure and nodded. "He's so neat. I hope it will work out for him." She put the spatula into the dishwasher. "He seems to have such a simple trust in God." She shook her head in amazement.

"Maybe it's all he has left, Paiger." He shrugged. "Or maybe it's an act."

"I don't think so. He seemed real."

"How could a quadriplegic be satisfied with life? He can't do anything."

"Because *doing* doesn't necessarily equal contentment. *Being* a child of God does."

"Not necessarily."

She frowned. "It's a good start."

Ryan watched his daughter for a moment before speaking. "Maybe. I'm going to turn in."

Paige called from behind him, "Thanks again for letting me watch you in the O.R. It was so cool."

"Cool," Ryan muttered as he smiled. *Well, there you have it folks. Paige Hannah sums up modern brain surgery with one word: "Cool."*

CHAPTER
36

LONG AFTER Dave Borntrager had come and gone and Nathan was positioned for the night, Abby lay awake, staring at the ceiling. Finally she got up, went to the bathroom, and checked on Melissa. She picked up Willie the gingerbread man and placed him on the bed next to her daughter's silent form before reaching to lower the window shade. She paused, searching the street in front of the house.

A gasp escaped her throat when she saw a Fisher's Retreat patrol car slowly pass, then circle and stop. *Brian! Why is he sitting there? He's looking at my window!*

She stood in the darkness of the room, confident he could not see in. She squinted to confirm the presence of Brian's silhouette.

He's watching the house.

Watching me?

Wanting me?

Stalking me?

Or is it Nathan he wants?

She felt her heart quicken. She moved back to her room and opened the closet door. There, from the top shelf, she retrieved a locked box. With trembling hands she pulled the key from the middle dresser drawer and unlocked the lid. Slowly she lifted Nathan's pistol, not the one he used as a police officer, but a .45 caliber semiautomatic that he'd used at the target range.

She loaded the gun and set it on the nightstand before checking the street again, this time by gently lifting back the curtain from her own front window. *Still there!* Terror gripped her as she dared to take another glance. Although his figure was dark, she imagined him straining to see her window. *As if he doesn't have all of Fisher's Retreat to think about tonight.*

Self-consciously, she clutched the neckline of her nightgown and whispered, "Oh, Nathan, he did have a motive. His motive was me."

She picked up the gun, her palms wet with sweat. "And it looks like he's not going to stop until I'm his."

◆　◆　◆

Nathan heard the floor squeaking above him. *Abby's up again.* He looked at the clock. *She must be worried about me.*

Maybe I shouldn't have told her about the phone calls.

He looked around his room, wide-eyed in spite of the early morning hour, his sleep chased away by Abby's restlessness and his own anxieties.

I'm worried about my wife, Lord. She seems to have so much bottled up inside. She has such strong feelings about the way I've treated her. Help me to understand. I want to be a good husband. Nathan closed his eyes tightly. *I want to be the husband Abby needs and desires.*

But how can that be possible with me like this? Will she ever be able to love me again?

He listened carefully to the sounds of Abby returning to bed.

"Abby," he spoke softly in the direction of the baby monitor, "thanks for talking with me tonight." He paused, hoping she wasn't bothered by his intrusion. "Are you having trouble sleeping? I hope you're not worried about me. Everything's going to work out OK."

He paused before continuing his one-sided conversation. "I love you, Abby. Try to get some rest. Everything's going to be fine."

Nathan wrinkled his nose, feeling a bit self-conscious about talking to the baby monitor.

Everything's going to be fine? I wish I believed that myself.

CHAPTER
37

FOR THE rest of the week Abby wrestled with a growing load of guilt, afraid to admit her unfaithfulness to Nathan, yet also afraid that concealing the affair might have more serious consequences. Her head swirled with the possibilities. Could Brian have shot Nathan on purpose? Was it an accidental shooting . . . or a convenient way to eliminate his lover's husband? Or could Brian have shot Nathan to silence him for something he knew . . . perhaps the truth about Jonas Yoder's death?

For months Abby had justified her silence, her unwillingness to confess her sins to Nathan. *It would only hurt him more,* she told herself over and over, *and he's been through so much already. It just wouldn't be fair to tell him, would it?*

Now, after hearing about Nathan's phone calls, Abby's guilt was magnified. Every time she saw him in the wheelchair, she fought to maintain composure. *It's my fault. Brian shot him because of me. I'm the one who put my husband in the chair.*

On top of feeling responsible for Nathan's quadriplegia, she carried the added sense that not bringing the truth to light was perhaps endangering Nathan's life again, and possibly even hiding critical evidence of other crimes.

When Abby saw Pastor Yeager on Wednesday and Thursday in the cafe, she avoided his gaze, ashamed to speak, feeling as if he could discern the darkness of her heart. By Sunday she was relieved to have to work, relieved not to endure sitting under the pastor's eye during the morning service.

When she was home during the day, she busied herself in the kitchen or in her room and successfully avoided serious conversation with Nathan.

At night she slept in fitful bursts or not at all, checking the window intermittently for the presence of a Fisher's Retreat patrol car or Brian's old Camaro. On two additional nights she saw him there, parked just beyond her neighbor's house, two doors down, barely visible from her bedroom window.

By Monday she trudged to work in weariness and begged for Marty to cover for her. With her friend's reluctant blessing, she left the cafe by noon to meet Joe Gibson in his office.

Joe, sporting a new Hawaiian tan, extended his hand. "Morning, uh, afternoon, Abby." The concern on his face was evident.

I must look awful, Abby thought. "Thanks for agreeing to meet with me on your first day back. I know how hectic it is after vacations." She glanced at his open door and frowned.

Joe nodded. "Go ahead, shut the door, Abby. What's on your mind?" He wrinkled his brow. "Everything OK with Nathan, I hope?"

"Maybe," she began. "I need to tell you some things in confidence. I didn't know exactly where to turn, but you've been so good to Nathan and me . . . Well . . ." Her voice trailed off.

"It's OK, Abby." He leaned forward. "What is it?"

"It's Brian." She looked down at her hands, conscious that she was gripping the arms of the chair. "I think he tried to kill Nathan. It wasn't an accident, Joe." She paused. "And it was all my fault."

She confessed her secret relationship with Brian and punctuated her story with tears, pausing only to lower her voice when she saw the silhouette of Marge Twittlegate's beehive hair pass the office window.

Eventually Joe interrupted, but not until Abby had used three facial tissues and had carefully expounded the details of Nathan's quest to solve the puzzle of his shootings, the anonymous phone calls, and the possible link with Jonas Yoder's suicide. "Why didn't Nathan tell me these things himself?"

Abby shrugged. "You know Nathan. He's so independent. He

always keeps things to himself until he has it figured out. I think he thought you'd be offended if he questioned your investigation."

Joe yawned. "He should have told me. He may be right. The phone calls may be pranks, but nonetheless he should have let me know." He looked up and cleared his throat. "I take it you haven't told him about Brian?"

She shook her head. "I haven't been able to bring myself to do it."

"So why tell me, Abby? Why confess it to me?"

"I feel so guilty, Joe. Every time I see Nate in the wheelchair . . . it's like I put him there. I've been so ashamed of myself all along, but it's only since I learned of the anonymous phone calls that I was able to put it together." She studied her open hands. "Brian shot Nathan on purpose. He had a perfect opportunity to make it look like an accident. And he thinks no one knows." She paused. "But I think someone saw him. Someone who feels responsible." She hesitated again, searching his questioning face. "Why tell you? Because you're the law in this town, and I don't have anywhere else to turn. Besides Nate and his parents, I have no family. And I knew that if anyone could help, it would be you."

Joe tapped his desktop with a pencil. "Do you really think Brian would harm Nathan again?"

"He's been watching me, watching the house. I see him parked just down the street from our house at night." Abby pleaded, "Joe, he's starting to scare me. I think he's obsessed with having me back. He can't accept the fact that I've taken Nathan back."

The police chief sighed. "This is touchy, Abby. Without a collaborating witness, it would be very difficult to prove anything you suspect. And without the bullet from Nathan's neck as evidence, we couldn't even convince a jury that Brian shot Nathan at all, much less convince them that it was premeditated attempted murder." Joe stood and began to pace around his little office. "Do you want me to help you get a restraining order against Brian? Has he ever assaulted you? Physically?"

"No." She took a deep breath. "No, I don't want to do that. I don't think he would harm me." She paused. "It's Nate I'm concerned about."

Joe shook his head. "I really don't think Brian would harm Nathan now. What's there to gain from it?"

Abby replied meekly, "Me?"

"It doesn't add up, Abby. Why would Brian have tried to kill Nathan in the first place? You said you were ready to leave Nathan before his accident. So why would Brian have to get rid of him to have you?"

"I was so confused. I would promise to leave, then feel guilty or scared, then flip. Maybe Brian saw an opportunity to eliminate the competition and couldn't resist." She swallowed hard. "I've thought of another possibility too. Maybe he purposely lured Nathan to the Allen house, using one of the Ashby High druggies as bait. He shoots Nathan there and blows Lester Fitts away in the process, coming out looking like a hero. Meanwhile, his accomplice begins to feel guilty for her part and makes the phone calls to Nathan to warn him not to return. Obviously, the caller felt responsible in some way. At least that's the way Nathan tells it."

"Hmmm." Joe reached for his cooling coffee mug before sitting down at his desk again. "We'd better walk pretty softly here. If anything you suspect has bearing in truth, I don't want to tip our hand to Brian. I don't want him to run."

"He's too confident for that."

"I'll tell you what—I'll deepen my investigation into the shooting. I'll look for the possible witness. And hopefully Nathan's little caller will clue us in again." He lowered his voice and looked at Abby. "And I think you need to be honest with Nathan about Brian. If any of your suspicions are right, and I can come up with the witness, this whole thing is going to blow up. You don't want Nathan finding out that way. It'd be best if you told him. Give him a chance to work through it before all of Fisher's Retreat finds out."

Abby hung her head. "The only other person who is aware of the affair is Marty. I don't really want anyone else to know."

"I'll not betray your story, Abby. But if we find a witness to the shooting, someone who claims Brian shot Nathan on purpose, it's bound to come out."

"Right," she mumbled.

"And I'd be careful to keep Nathan from talking to Brian again. As long as Brian thinks Nathan knows nothing, there's no reason for Brian to act. There should be no reason to be afraid."

Unless he wants to punish me for turning him away.

Joe wrote down a number. "Here's my private cell-phone number," he said, handing her the paper. "I'm never far away if you sense any danger."

◆ ◆ ◆

That night Dave Borntrager positioned Nathan on his left side, with one pillow beneath his head, one behind his back, one crossways beneath his legs just above the ankles, and one in between his knees. It was all part of the necessary routine to prevent him from getting skin breakdown.

He covered him with a sheet and blanket and excused himself. "See you again tomorrow night, Nate."

"I won't be needing you tomorrow, Dave. I'm going over to Brighton University Hospital for a few days. Dr. Hannah wants to run some tests."

"Nothing serious, I hope."

Nathan shook his head. He didn't want to elaborate. "I'll be back on Friday. See you then?"

Dave shrugged and took the hint not to ask questions. "You're the boss."

Nathan listened as Dave let himself out the front door. He could hear Abby putting Melissa to bed, and he traced the sound of her footsteps into his old room where the bed groaned as Abby flopped onto it. After a few minutes he heard her blow her nose, and then her footsteps again, descending the stairs. In a moment he heard her in the doorway behind him. "Abby?"

"I'm here, Nate," she said, walking around the bed to where he could see. She didn't sit on the blanket like she usually did but pulled a second chair up beside the bed. Her eyes were red. He knew she'd been crying.

"What's wrong, Abby?"

"There's something I need to tell you, Nate."

He searched her eyes. Something was eating her. Anxiety? Pain?

Her words struck like a hammer. "I'm not the faithful wife I've pretended to be."

No, not this! He didn't want to believe, but he could see the truth in her expression. He felt his mouth go dry and found it hard to concentrate on her words. He heard the confession in a blur, catching snatches of phrases as his heart ascended to his throat.

"I never intended for it to be this way . . . Brian Turner . . . It started long before this trouble in the police department . . . when Laurie was alive, and I wanted to help . . . over a year ago . . ."

My best friend! Abby wiped her eyes.

"I've hated myself . . . It was so wrong . . ."

The room was spinning. Nathan felt flushed. "Take this blanket off."

". . . I didn't want to hurt . . ."

Brian!

Abby's voice cracked and faded into the white noise in Nathan's mind. *She fell for him before my accident!*

Her sobs grew louder.

His mouth fell open. There were no words to say. This was the very thing he had feared the most. Another man had stolen his Abby's beauty away.

". . . I'm . . . so . . . sorry . . . Please forgive me, Nathan . . ."

He touched his tongue to his teeth. He felt parched, unable to respond. He watched her crying, her head in her hands. And he felt powerless to comfort her.

She fell for Brian when I was whole.

And look at me now.

Long seconds passed before he finally found his voice. "This is why you won't say, 'I love you.'"

"Love doesn't treat people the way I did."

"This is why you pull away when we kiss." He stared at her, but she would not meet his gaze. "You're thinking of him."

She nodded. "Yes. But it's not what you think. I'm tortured by the memory of what I did. Kissing you only makes me remember." She looked up with tears on her cheeks. "But it wasn't because I didn't want to kiss you. It was because I didn't want to think of what I'd done . . . done to you . . . done to us. It tortures me to remember."

"It wasn't torture when you kissed *him*!" The words slipped out before he could stop himself.

"Can you ever forgive me?"

"Why are you telling me this now?"

Her voice was strained, broken by her weeping. "Don't you see, Nathan? This whole horrible mess, your shooting . . . it's all my fault," she sobbed. "The girl on the phone was right. It wasn't an accident. Brian shot you . . . because of me."

Nathan closed his eyes. He could see Abby's pain, but he needed time to think, to sort through what she was saying. In the old days he would have stormed off, looked away, found someplace to be alone. But now he could only close his eyes to shut the world away.

He opened his eyes as Abby continued to weep. "Please go now, Abby. I need to think. I want to be alone."

She obeyed and rose slowly, pushing back the chair and walking to the door. Then she slapped the light switch and left him alone in the dark.

CHAPTER
38

THE NEXT morning Abby came into Nathan's room just before she left for the cafe.

"Nathan?"

He kept his eyes closed. He heard her walk around the bed.

"I'll see you on Friday, OK? I'm coming to Brighton to get you." She paused. "Just like we planned."

Nathan opened his eyes and studied her. He wished the night before had been a dream, but Abby's worried face confirmed his fear. His wife had had an affair with his best friend.

"I've got to go to work, Nate. Will you be OK?"

He nodded silently.

"Richard will take you to the university this morning. Dr. Hannah is expecting you by ten o'clock. Just drop Mel off at your mother's. I'll get her after work." She hesitated, then leaned forward to kiss him.

He turned and received her kiss on his cheek.

"Bye, Nathan." She retreated to the doorway behind him.

"Abby?"

"Still here."

"My bags. Where are—"

"All packed, Nate. You just need to have Richard put in your toiletries. I put them on the floor in the hall."

"Uh . . . Thanks." He paused. "Bye."

◆ ◆ ◆

The following afternoon, Charlie Edwards sauntered into the chief's office and took off his mirror shades. Joe looked up. "Any luck?"

The officer shook his head. "I've talked to every person living within two blocks of the Allen house, and no one admits to seeing or hearing anything. The best info I got was from Mabel Newsome next door. She says she's seen kids climbing the latticework on the side of the Allen house in the past." He shrugged. "She can't say when or what they looked like, only that they were kids. And to Mabel," he added with a smile, "that's anyone under sixty-five."

Joe twirled a pencil in the air. "I don't suppose she heard anything."

"Not a thing. But you practically have to scream in her ear just to talk to the dear woman."

"Great."

"How about you? Anything turn up over at Ashby?"

"*Nada.*" He shook his head. "And the girl that Abby saw with Brian at the cafe would hardly talk to me. If she knows something, she's not about to tell it to a cop."

"Did you ever confirm Abby's story with Nathan?"

"Tried to. But he's away."

"Away?"

"All Abby will say is that he's gone to Brighton for some tests. She's pretty vague about it." He squinted. "Something's going on with them, and she's being secretive. I'm not sure what to believe anymore. And I think Abby is so wound up with guilt over her past with Brian that she's unable to think objectively about him anymore. We may be researching a crime that was never committed."

Charlie mumbled. "Maybe. But when you're sure of that, let me know. I'm tired of looking for witnesses that may not even exist." He turned to the door. "Speaking of Abby, have you had lunch? I think I'll go to the cafe for a late one."

"No thanks. I'm going to eat with June at the pharmacy." He looked at his arm and frowned. "Maybe I should pick up some of that special lotion. My tan is already fading."

◆ ◆ ◆

Wednesday afternoon Ryan scurried through the cranberry hallway and nearly ran into his administrative assistant. Trish held up both hands and mouthed, "The dean is in your office."

"My office?" Ryan whispered. "What's this all about?"

She threw up her hands. "Came by twenty minutes ago," she responded in a hushed tone. "Which is when I told him you were due." She extended her hand toward his door. "He said he'd wait."

Ryan prepared himself for the worst and pushed open the oak door. "Alan? What brings you by?"

"I want to meet him. Where are you hiding our quad?"

Our quad? And how do you know about that? "Our quad, sir?"

"For your research." He smiled. "I happened to talk to Dr. Blaisdale at lunch today. He was whining, as usual. Seems he wanted to inject another group of medical students with some sort of flu virus, but he said you'd booked the research unit for the next three days." He raised his index finger. "And I knew what that meant. You've found a candidate?"

Ryan wasn't happy to know that his attempts at secrecy were so easily thwarted. "Maybe." He walked over to Alan Pritchard, sitting behind Ryan's desk. "Excuse me," he said, reaching for his top drawer.

"Oh, of course." The dean stood and cleared his throat before moving around to another chair.

"We've been running some tests. But it's premature to introduce our potential candidate."

"We should get some pictures. Maybe a shot for the press release." The dean sat down again.

Ryan felt his hair stand up. He touched his neck. "No."

"Ryan, this is going to be big. We have to market our progress in the right way."

"I am not *marketing* anything. There will be no press release and no pictures." He pointed his index finger at the administrator for emphasis. "I will *never* agree to that." He leaned forward over his desk toward the man sitting across from him. "We can release our story to the press only after we've made history—not before the first attempt. It would never look good if we tried and failed."

"Failed?" The dean made a clicking noise with his lips. "I've not heard that word before, Ryan—not from you. Caution perhaps, but failed?" He shook his head. "Your data is too good."

"I'm serious about this, Alan. I'll take my research elsewhere if you send this to the media before I'm ready."

The dean held up his hand. "OK, OK. I think you're right—it would be smart to wait a little longer." He put his hands behind his head. "That's not really why I came by anyway." He leaned back, and for a moment Ryan thought he might put his feet on his desk. Instead, he crossed his legs like Ryan's mother always had.

"Well?"

"Ryan," he responded smugly, "your funding problems are over. A private contribution has come through." He smiled. "And it's twice the worth of your stolen baboon."

Ryan felt his heart quicken. "Twice the amount?"

"Actually more."

"I don't suppose I need to guess. Richard Henry?"

The dean shrugged. "Let's just say he was relieved to hear that the state's attorney is no longer interested in prosecuting his son for grand larceny."

Ryan grunted. The deal felt oily. *Oh well, research money is so tight . . . I guess I should be glad that Mr. Henry is willing to push forward the very project his son almost destroyed.*

◆ ◆ ◆

By Thursday afternoon Nathan was tired of all the tests. He had been poked, prodded, scanned, analyzed, and reanalyzed for two and a half days. Now, in the aftermath of a carotid arteriogram, he found himself back in his hospital bed in the research wing, staring at the uninteresting ceiling again.

Because he had been punctured in his femoral artery in his right upper thigh for the test, he was under strict orders to remain on his back, unmoving. Staying on his back was no problem, but muscle spasms seemed to plague his legs after the test. So the nurses finally placed a series of wide Velcro restraints across his legs and lower abdomen to keep him from moving so he wouldn't initiate a hemorrhage from the puncture site.

Nathan's days were made more enjoyable by visits from Paige Hannah, Ryan's daughter, who seemed to have taken a keen interest in his progress. Nathan looked over when he heard her voice.

"Hi, Nathan." He watched her eyes widen. "What's going on here?"

"Hi, Paige. Looks pretty silly, doesn't it? The nurses were afraid I might run off."

She wrinkled her forehead.

"I'm kidding, Paige. They put these straps on to keep me from moving so much after my arteriogram. They said that if I moved, the artery they used in my leg could start bleeding."

"You can move?"

"Just with muscle spasms. Nothing I can control."

She sat quietly a moment. "Did the test hurt?"

"The arteriogram?"

"Yeah."

"I couldn't feel most of it. They made a little incision over my artery and did everything without any anesthesia." He smiled. "Didn't feel a thing, except when they injected the dye in my blood vessels. Then my face felt hot for a few moments, and I felt some pressure."

"Oh." She sat down on a chair beside his bed. She looked at her watch. "My father's still in the O.R. Some kid in a car wreck was messed up pretty bad." She shrugged. "He's supposed to take me out to eat. I'll bet he doesn't show, and I'll end up ordering takeout at home."

"Have you heard anything about the workup? Do you know if your father is going to try the surgery on me?"

She groaned. "I'll be the last to know. My dad doesn't tell me much about his research." She paused. "Communication with his family hasn't always been Dad's strong point."

Nathan nodded. "It's not a strong point with many men, Paige." He blew his breath out slowly. "Me included."

"But you seem so easy to talk to. And you talked so openly with us about your faith in God. I think that's neat."

He wasn't sure how to respond. He was glad Paige admired his faith, but he inwardly cringed at the idea of being an example of how a man should communicate with his family. *If you only knew how bad things were between Abby and me, you wouldn't think my faith was such an example.*

Fortunately Paige kept talking, relieving him from responding. "I wish my father would depend on God like you do. I think the only one he trusts in is himself."

He raised his eyebrows. "I still struggle, Paige." He sighed. "Maybe I always will."

"Me too," she responded before changing the subject. "How's Abby doing? I'll bet she's excited about this. Is she coming up to see you?"

"She's supposed to pick me up tomorrow."

"She seems so sweet. Have you been married long?"

"Seven years." *And it looks like it might not last much longer.*

"She must be a special woman. She seems so supportive."

How would you know? You only saw her one time. "Uh, sure. She takes good care of me," he answered flatly.

They looked up to see Dr. Hannah in the doorway.

"Daddy, you're early!"

"I thought we had a dinner date. I checked in the lab, and Dr. Hopkins told me where I'd find you." He looked at Nathan. "Has she talked your ear off yet?"

"Daddy!"

Nathan smiled. "I'm glad she comes by. If it weren't for Paige, I wouldn't have a single visitor who wasn't wanting to take some blood or run another test on me." He looked at the father and daughter together for a moment. *She must look like her mother.*

Nathan cleared his throat. "Have you made any decisions about my workup? Do I look like a good candidate for your surgery?"

Dr. Hannah looked down at Nathan and picked up his hand. "I still have some analysis to do, Nathan. But what I see looks pretty good. I won't give you a definite answer yet, but we certainly haven't ruled you out." He paused, placing Nathan's hand gently back on the bed.

"Regardless of what we decide, you can be proud of your contribution. Even if all we do are the tests, we'll learn something in the process, even if it's just how to select the best candidate for this surgery. In that way you've already helped immensely." He nodded at Nathan. "You're doing something for your fellowman, and that's reason to feel good about yourself."

Nathan nodded and glanced at Paige. Her cheeks were flushed, and she wouldn't lift her eyes from the floor.

Dr. Hannah looked around. "Well, Paige, shall we go?"

Paige nodded before looking at Nathan. "Bye."

Nathan winked. "See you tomorrow?" He paused. "Maybe you'll even get to see Abby."

Dr. Hannah hesitated at the doorway. "I'd like to see her too. If we decide to offer you a position in our study, she'll need to be completely informed of the process . . . and possible outcomes," he added seriously.

"She should be here at noon."

"OK." Dr. Hannah tipped his head forward slightly, and Paige broke into a wide grin, one that she cut short when her eyes met her father's.

They exited, and Nathan strained to hear their fading conversation.

"Why do you do that?"

"Do what?"

"You know, smile like you've just got to show everyone your molars."

◆　◆　◆

As they drove, Ryan cast a sideways glance at his daughter. "You're awfully quiet."

Paige stared out the window.

Ryan adjusted the radio dial.

"Do we have to listen to *that?*"

He didn't feel like arguing. He turned the radio off and continued in silence.

He heard Paige take a deep breath. *Here it comes.*

"I can't believe you said that to Nathan."

"What?"

"You know, that little pep talk." She imitated his voice. "'You're doing something for your fellowman, and that's reason to feel good about yourself.'"

"What's wrong with that? He needs to hear that. It should encourage him."

She huffed and muttered under her breath.

Ryan snapped on the radio and depressed the accelerator. "Hummph!"

◆   ◆   ◆

That night Nathan tried to make some sense of his tangled thoughts. He had been thankful for the chance to be away, to do something different, even if it meant enduring a myriad of invasive tests. At least he had a chance to get his mind off his troubled marriage. But now, with Abby due in Brighton the following day, he knew he had to think seriously about a response to her confession. They couldn't just coexist without talking about it forever.

He sorted the facts, stacking them and restacking them in his mind, and coming to the same dreary end. *Abby doesn't love me.*

I can't take care of myself. Just look at me . . . I'd be a burden to anyone.

Abby slept with my best friend. So is she right? Did Brian shoot me on purpose? Frustration mounted as Nathan tried to come up with some answers.

He grunted audibly as his mind whirled. As soon as he thought he had it all figured out, his theories seemed to collapse again. *I need real evidence, a witness.*

He tried to start with the basic facts again but was diverted by a single, ugly truth, one he wished he could forget. *Abby cheated on me.*

But I still love her . . . I think.

But a one-sided love will never make a marriage.

She doesn't love me. She gave her love to someone else.

I'm a burden to her now. She's staying with me just because she feels sorry for me, not because she wants to.

So I need to let her go. I'm being selfish to want her to stay.

Adultery! That's solid justification for divorce, right?

Wouldn't it be better for everyone if we just called it quits?

He sighed as bitterness gripped his heart. *If only I could talk to that social worker at Briarfield Manor. She could arrange a place for me to stay or find me some full-time attendants so I wouldn't need to rely on Abby.* He looked helplessly around the room. There was no way for him to even use the phone without a nurse's help. That wouldn't do. He needed some privacy to talk. He would just have to wait for his speakerphone at home.

How should I tell Abby?

She'll put up a fight . . . say that I should stay with her and Mel . . . But she'll only be saying that because she feels obligated . . . out of guilt, not out of love.

So I need to make it easy for her. She needs to be free from me, without feeling guilty. That's what she wants.

So I have to make her believe it's what I want too.

CHAPTER
39

THE FOLLOWING DAY, a nurse wearing green scrubs ushered Nathan into a conference room just off the corridor leading to the hospital research unit. Dr. Hopkins was sitting alone at a white table. Above her head a clock revealed the time. Twelve-thirty.

"Hi, Mr. McAllister. All ready for your exit interview?"

He chuckled nervously. "Sure, uh, I guess."

"Dr. Hannah should be here any minute. Will your wife be attending?"

"She was supposed to be here thirty minutes ago."

"She's probably lost in the hospital maze."

Nathan nodded and stared at the clock. It had a long, slender, red hand that jerked rhythmically with each passing second. To Nathan, sitting alone with the resident, each second seemed an eternity, as if the clock's hand fought against an unseen weight. *Where's Abby?*

The door opened again, and in walked Dr. Hannah and two men in business suits. "Ah, Nathan," Dr. Hannah began, lifting his hand, "I'm glad you're already here. This is Mr. McLaughlin and Mr. Ferguson." He pointed at the two men one at a time. "They're attorneys, and I thought it would be beneficial to have them here as a resource."

Lawyers? Nathan raised his eyebrows. *What are they doing here?*

Just then the door cracked open after a timid knock. Nathan looked through the small opening to see Abby's face.

"Ms. McAllister, you're just in time. Have a seat next to your husband." Dr. Hannah's voice seemed to boom in the small room.

Abby cast a furtive glance at Nathan and mouthed, "Hi" before she looked away.

The chief neurosurgeon made introductions again, sat down, and folded his hands. After a brief pause he began, looking intently into Nathan's eyes. "I'm a goal-oriented individual. I'm a surgeon, so my style is to move straight to the bottom line. My goal is to make you whole again." He exchanged glances with Abby before turning his attention back to Nathan. "If you'll agree to the surgery, I believe I can do just that."

Abby reached over and squeezed Nathan's hand. It was a kind gesture that he couldn't feel, a gesture he could see but not prevent.

"So . . . I'm in?" Nathan replied with hesitation.

"We are willing to give it our best effort."

Nathan smiled and nodded his head emphatically. "OK. OK!"

Abby smiled too and seemed to grip his hand with increased vigor.

Dr. Hannah held up his hand to stifle their enthusiasm. "Before you make a decision, we have a lot of groundwork to cover. We need to explain the procedure . . . and the risks," he added soberly, "to be sure you have realistic expectations." He nodded at the men in suits. "And Mr. McLaughlin and Mr. Ferguson are here to explain the complicated consent forms that will be necessary to enter into this research project. They will also go over the contract that spells out your voluntary obligations and our commitment to handle any medical situations that may arise."

Mr. McLaughlin slapped a heavy document onto the table with a thud.

Nathan and Abby nodded numbly.

"Shall we begin?" Dr. Hannah smiled.

The attorney closest to Abby depressed a button on a handheld tape recorder. "Would you mind if I taped this conversation for our records?"

Nathan glanced at his wife. "Uh . . ."

"It's just routine. I'll have it transcribed for the informed consent document."

"Uh," he responded a second time, finding his throat suddenly dry. "Go ahead."

Nathan's excitement mixed with anxiety as Dr. Hannah droned on through a lengthy explanation of the procedure. He understood the basics but got lost in the theory and detail.

". . . will require that you have a tracheostomy to assist your breathing . . ."

Not a tracheostomy! I hated that. I can't speak with a trach. Nathan grunted his disapproval.

Dr. Hannah frowned. "I know you had one before, and I trust this will only be temporary, but with your weakened respiratory function already, I'm concerned about your ability to breathe without a ventilator after such a long surgery." He paused and winced. "I'm sorry, but it's very necessary."

Nathan stared blankly ahead as the surgeon continued. He heard little until the doctor started talking about the complications.

". . .bleeding . . . dependence on the ventilator . . . stroke . . . infection . . . even death . . ."

Death! I knew that was coming. But I've stared that guy down before.

". . . lung damage . . . pneumonia . . . heart failure . . . pulmonary embolism—that's when a clot forms in a big vein, usually in your legs, and breaks loose to lodge in the heart or the lungs . . ."

The surgeon's voice faded again as the list lengthened. Nathan forced himself to concentrate.

". . . unforeseen complications . . . improper return of nerve function . . . of course we only anticipate a partial return of function . . . we really have no idea how much to expect . . . there is no human precedent . . ."

After an hour's discourse, with additional input from the two attorneys, Dr. Hannah concluded, "I want you to take your time making a decision."

"I wouldn't be here if I hadn't decided, Dr. Hannah. I want to do it."

The neurosurgeon countered, "I still want you to give it some thought. And in the meantime, as long as you are leaning toward saying yes, I want you to work your leg muscles with a functional electrical stimulator like the StimMaster. That way your muscles will be in better shape for retraining."

"Retraining?"

"Learning to walk again."

Abby caught Nathan's eye and winked.

He responded with a dry mouth as the idea of walking again struck him head-on. "Wow."

Nathan inspected the surgeon, whose voice was confident and steady, and whose eyes were bright and honest. *You really believe you can make me walk, don't you?*

Dr. Hannah checked his watch. "I really need to go." He slid a card across to Abby. "Here's my office number. Call when you've made a decision." He looked at Nathan. "In the meantime I'll have my assistant requisition a StimMaster for you to use at home. And don't worry about the cost. We will be taking care of that."

He stood and took a step away from the table. "I suppose I don't need to say it, but I do hope that you will keep this quiet. I think you can understand my desire not to have every spinal cord injury patient in America at our doorstep just yet. I want to release the information to the media only after we have had a success. So please, no talking to anyone who doesn't absolutely need to know. And that means no reporters." He paused. "Perhaps it would be best if you only shared this with your immediate family, and pass this same request along to them."

With that, Dr. Hannah excused himself, the others packed up, and Nathan was left to talk to Abby alone.

◆　◆　◆

Nathan and Abby rode home without speaking, neither knowing how to bridge the icy silence between them.

This trip into Fisher's Retreat stood juxtaposed in Nathan's mind against his return from Briarfield Manor. Then there had been fanfare and praise. Then there was celebration and a band. Now there was only sparse traffic, with no one raving about the special blue van or even looking up to watch their approach.

He watched from the window as they passed the First Presbyterian Church, the Post Office, and the cafe. He saw his father getting into his car in front of the drugstore, but they passed on without a wave, unrecognized and unnoticed.

Once home, he played checkers with Melissa and ate dinner, making small talk about his workup or his upcoming surgery. Abby busied herself with the meal and dishes and with a sunset walk around town.

At 8 Abby returned and put Melissa to bed. She was just coming down the stairs when Nathan heard a car door slam. He moved to the front room to see Joe Gibson's patrol car. "It's Joe," he said before he heard the knock at the door.

Abby opened the door and welcomed him.

"Hi, Abby, Nathan." He removed his hat.

"Hi, chief. What brings you by?"

Joe glanced nervously at Abby. "Do you mind if I sit down?" He walked over to a chair and positioned himself to look at Nathan. "I need to talk to you." He looked back at Abby. "Abby told me about your anonymous phone calls."

Nathan watched Abby's reaction. Her face was tense.

"I haven't told Nate about our conversation, Joe," she responded, clasping her hands together. "There—there were other things we needed to talk out." She widened her eyes at the chief.

Joe leaned forward. "Nate, you should have talked to me." He shook his head and sighed. "Abby tells me you were afraid that I'd be offended if you questioned my investigation."

Nathan winced. "Well, uh—" He stopped and dropped his eyes, staying silent for a moment. "That's not it exactly," he huffed. "Every time I talked to you about my shooting, I got the idea you were suspicious of *me*. I got the idea that you thought I was involved in something illegal." He paused. "Charlie Edwards showed me the drug data you guys compiled. Drug usage went up, up, up, for the ten months prior to my injury." He shrugged. "I guess I just wanted a chance to figure it out for myself . . . without someone who was constantly questioning my loyalty."

"Fair enough," Joe said softly. "Maybe I set you up not to cooperate." He reached into his pocket for a notepad. "But now I want to know what you think. Tell me about the phone calls, and your investigations at the Allen house and out at the Yoders'."

Nathan recounted the events, repeating word for word the phone conversations he'd replayed so many times before. Afterwards Nathan asked, "Didn't you think it was odd that Jonas Yoder sustained a neck fracture? That's not consistent with a closet hanging. It implies something more violent." He paused. "And why would Jonas have bought all those needles if he was planning to kill himself? And how did he hang himself in the back of a dark closet?"

"I thought there was a light in the closet."

"There is . . . an automatic one. It goes on only when the door is open, and Rachel says the door was definitely shut. It's *dark* in there."

"Hmmm. Maybe he tied the rope to the bar, then made a noose, shut the door, and . . ."

"That still doesn't explain the neck fracture. That injury is consistent with an old-time judicial hanging."

"These items *have* bothered me, Nate. But we don't have any proof. And according to the medical examiner, if a person is significantly debilitated, a neck fracture could result from a suicidal hanging." He ran his fingers through his hair. "I guess I thought, what with the boy's diabetes and all, that maybe somehow it was just a simple suicide." He shook his head. "And what's to be gained by spending my efforts to look into it? The family isn't interested in digging up ghosts, the state attorney isn't going to push us to do it, and other than our suspicions I have nothing to go on."

"It makes no sense to think he killed himself. My anonymous caller said I knew that someone killed Jonas. If she's right, then who? And what was the motivation?"

"And the caller said, 'when he shot you,' implying that whoever shot you killed Jonas?"

Nathan nodded.

"And we know who shot you."

"Brian."

The chief sighed. "I don't know, Nate. It doesn't make much sense to think that Brian shot you on purpose. What would motivate him to do that?"

Abby leaned forward and sighed. "You don't have to dance around the question because of me, Joe. I've told Nathan all about Brian and me."

Joe held up his hand. "I've thought about this, Abby. I think you may be beating yourself unnecessarily. I suppose it is a possibility that Brian set Nathan up and ambushed him on purpose, out of jealousy for you, but that's not what Nathan's mysterious caller has implied. The caller implied that Nathan knew something about someone killing Jonas, and when he reported what he knew, he was shot. Is that how you read things, Nate?"

"Pretty much. So what are you saying?"

"Well, just that if Brian shot you on purpose, his relationship with Abby may have had nothing to do with it. Could he have been acting out of a desire to cover up another crime that you'd discovered?"

"Hmm."

"As far as I see it, there are a few possibilities here," the chief responded to his own question. "This whole caller thing is a scam, someone's idea of a joke, or someone's intentional misguidance to get us to suspect Brian of a crime . . . or Brian shot you in an attempt to silence you for something you knew, possibly about Jonas Yoder's death, or . . ." He looked at Abby. "I suppose it's possible that he acted out of jealousy."

Nathan closed his eyes tightly for a moment. "I just have a hard time believing Brian would do any of this. He was my friend, and a good cop."

Abby sighed. "I guess I don't need to remind you that he is capable of living a lie. He lived one to you, and to Laurie."

Nathan looked at his wife. *And you did too.* He turned his attention to his old chief. "What do you make of this, Joe? Do you think I'm in danger? The caller seemed to think so."

"The caller sounds like a scared kid. Someone who is acting out of a lot of guilt over something. I'd doubt if she has a proper read on the situation." He shrugged. "I'd say that as long as you lay low and don't raise waves, you're probably a safe man. But if you get your memory back and are capable of finally telling your personal account of the shooting, you'd be a threat to the guilty party, and then I'd question your safety."

Abby frowned. "So why has Brian been stalking the house?"

"What?"

The anxiety was etched into her expression. "Nathan, I've seen him. Two or three times, at night, passing slowly in his car or sitting just down the street."

"You think he's watching us?"

"Me . . . You . . . I don't know. I just know he scares me. I've told him it's over between us, but I think he still . . ." She dropped her eyes. "He still wants me to be his."

Joe stood and began to pace. "All this time I've had my suspicions that something may not be on the up-and-up within the department. Maybe I've been looking at the wrong person all along." His eyes met Nathan's.

Abby persisted, "So why is Brian watching the house?"

"If you want my opinion, it has more to do with you than it does with Nathan. Nathan's no threat to him as he is. Do you want me to talk to him?"

"No," Nathan and Abby answered together.

She continued, "I can take care of myself. I'd be surprised if he ever tried to hurt me. And if he's watching for a chance to catch Nathan, then talking with him would only clue him in that we're suspicious. And if he thinks Nathan suspects something . . ." She looked at Nathan and lowered her voice. ". . . then Nathan becomes a threat to him and Nathan would be a sitting duck."

"I agree," Nathan added. "It's best not to let Brian have any idea that we're putting this together."

"But unless we can find your caller and establish that she's a credible witness, we'll never go anywhere with this investigation. I have no grounds to put Brian back on suspension or anything."

"If I could only remember . . ." Nathan shook his head, as if hoping to dislodge a thought.

"I'll keep my ears and eyes open and keep looking for your caller." Joe walked to the door. "Until then we'll have to keep this discussion between us." He reached for the door. "By the way, I've told your replacement, Charlie Edwards, about the phone calls and about your thoughts about the open window and the syringes in the Allen house. He's been talking with people up and down that street all week, trying to establish the idea of a witness. He's gotten nowhere."

The door banged, and they were alone.

Abby looked at her watch. "How do you feel?"

"Exhausted."

"Dave should be here soon."

"Great." He pulled his lips back to expose his straight teeth. "I've not had my flossing since Monday."

CHAPTER
40

THE WEEKEND passed in torturously slow, silent hours for Nathan, who sat in his room playing computer games or watching TV. On Sunday he declined going to church, even though Abby was off. He said he wasn't feeling well, and that was true enough, but what he didn't say was that he wasn't anxious to sit in the congregation with everyone looking at his happy little family and commenting on how much they admired his courage to face his disability. He just wanted people to see him for what he was on the inside, but his church acquaintances couldn't seem to get beyond his wheelchair. And if he was strictly honest, he didn't even think people would like the inside of him if they knew what bitterness was there.

By Monday morning he was looking forward to being alone with his speakerphone. Once he was in the chair and Abby was at work and Jim Over had finished with Nathan's morning rituals, Nathan set to work.

His first call was to Dr. Hannah's office. He asked Trish to tell Dr. Hannah that Nathan wanted the surgery. She promised to pass the message along and assured him that the doctor would get back to him soon with an expected surgery date. She told him that his StimMaster would arrive in a few days. She was planning on getting a representative from the company to train his attendants so they could assist him through his workouts.

His second call was to Janice Marsh, the social worker from the

Briarfield Manor, who had worked so hard at getting Nathan back to Fisher's Retreat.

He talked for a few moments with the nursing home operator, who forwarded his call to Janice.

"Social Services, Janice speaking."

"Janice, this is Nathan McAllister calling."

"Nathan! I've been thinking I should call you. How are you getting along?"

He hesitated and cleared his throat. "Well, OK, I guess. That's partly why I called."

"Is everything all right? What can I do for you?"

He paused to listen for Melissa. It sounded like she was occupied with *Sesame Street*. "Things here with Abby aren't going exactly the way I wanted. I was hoping—"

"How about your PCAs?" she interrupted. "Are they working out?"

"They're fine." He sighed weakly. "I want to come back to Briarfield Manor."

"Come back? Why?"

"Things aren't working out with Abby. I, well, she . . . Well, our relationship has changed. It's just not working for us to be together."

"Coping with spinal cord injury is tough, Nathan. It's tough on the patient, but equally as tough on his or her loved ones. Do you want to talk to a counselor? Maybe together with Abby?"

"I didn't call for that, Janice." He paused in frustration, wondering what to tell her, not wanting her to pry into the details. "I want a separation, OK?"

He heard Janice's breath, a deep slow, sigh.

"I had hoped you could secure me a room back at Briarfield. My insurance covered it before, right?"

"Yes, but outpatient home care is preferred. It's less expensive, and it's better for you."

"But I have the disability money, plus my worker's comp and the police benevolence fund . . . and it would only be temporary. I'd only need some time to line up full-time attendant care and give Abby a chance to find somewhere else to live. My place will work fine for me. It's already been modified."

"Nathan, it's only been a few weeks for you at home. It's bound to be a difficult adjustment. Maybe you should give it some more time."

He was prepared for her protests. He knew how she felt about families. "Look, I'm going to have some surgery soon, up at Brighton University. So it's likely that I'll need a place to rehabilitate anyway."

"Surgery? I hope nothing serious. Have you gotten a pressure sore or something?"

"Nothing like that. Just some surgery I need."

"Hmm. I guess I could find a bed if you give me enough time."

"I probably won't need it for a few weeks."

"OK." He could hear her fingers tapping on the desk. "Do you know when you'll be in the hospital?"

"Not yet."

"Why don't you call me when you know specifics? I'll see what I can do."

"Thanks, Janice. I'll let you know." He tapped the top of the speakerphone with his mouthstick.

He sat listening to the sound of Big Bird and Elmo laughing with Oscar the Grouch. The *Sesame Street* cheerfulness contrasted with his own heaviness. He stared through the window.

This feels terrible. But I know I've got to let Abby go.

◆　◆　◆

That night Nathan waited until Melissa was in bed, but before he was out of his chair, to talk to Abby. He wanted to be able to follow her if she walked away, at least on the first level of their home.

Abby was in the kitchen fixing a lunch for Mel and filling the coffeemaker with water, preparations for the next day.

He moved his chair up behind her. "Abby, can we talk?"

He detected a stiffening of her expression. "Sure." She opened the refrigerator and put away the jelly.

"I've been thinking about us."

He watched as she picked up a cloth to clean the counter.

"Do you think you could stop that for a moment to listen?"

He sensed her irritation. She raised her eyebrows and slowly folded the cloth in her hand. For a moment he thought she would throw it at him. Instead, she placed it on the counter and returned his gaze. "OK," she responded, drawing out her words, "I'm listening."

"I'm going back to Briarfield Manor after my surgery."

Abby's hands went to her hips.

"That will give you some time to find another place to live."

She pulled back her head. "Another place? What are you saying?"

"I want you to move out. Let's be honest, Abby. Things are not working between us. This whole disability thing isn't what we bargained for." He met her angry stare and continued, "It's not fair to make me move from here since we've already made all the changes." He nodded toward the automatic door. "Being at Briarfield will give me some time to hire full-time attendants and—"

Abby shook her head. "This isn't about your disability, is it, Nate? Let's be honest, as you say. This is about me, about my affair, isn't it? It's about your inability to forgive."

"Oh, now it's on *me*. My inability to forgive? *I* wasn't unfaithful to *you*."

She huffed, "I just want you to admit your true reasons. We were adapting until I told you about Brian!" She pointed her index finger in his face. "Don't blame your disability for the problems we have. They started long before . . . *this!*" she said, gently kicking the front of his wheelchair.

"Fair enough." This discussion was not going as he'd planned. "Abby, this is best for you. It's what I want. I want you to be free."

She walked to the kitchen table and pulled out a chair. She sat and slumped forward, her elbows on the formica top. "What's changed, Nathan? You know that the church always says no divorce."

He moved his chair to the table. "The church will allow divorce under certain circumstances."

He studied her for a moment. She was bent, folded with her head in her hands.

"I talked to Jim Over about it this morning. He doesn't favor divorce as a solution, but he said that in cases of . . . Well, in cases like ours, there is a biblical out."

"In cases like ours? You told him about my affair?"

"No, I didn't tell him! I only posed a hypothetical question. He doesn't know about our situation."

Abby looked up. Her eyes were moist. "I shouldn't have told you. I thought I was finally doing the right thing by confessing it to you."

He wasn't sure what to say next. He knew she wouldn't agree unless he made a strong argument. He knew she'd want to stay with him—but out of guilt, not out of love. "Abby, this is my decision. I want out." He clenched his jaw.

She began to weep.

Her tears ripped his heart. He didn't want to hurt her. He wanted to comfort her, but . . . "The love is gone, Abby. We shouldn't stay together for the wrong reasons." He didn't want her to cry. "Abby, Abby," he said softly, "you know this is best."

"What if—I—don't want—this?"

"You shouldn't have to stay with someone just because you feel guilty."

"Oh, Nate."

"Do you love me, Abby?"

"Don't ask me that! I'm confused. I don't know!"

He backed his chair away. "I want this, Abby," he said with a forced confidence. "I want a divorce."

Abby stood, wiping her eyes. "Your attendant is going to be here soon. I don't want him to see me like this." With that, she ran from the room, disappearing up the stairs.

In a moment he heard the bedroom door slam.

Nathan shook his head. "It's not like you need to shut the door," he muttered.

He listened to the familiar noises. Water running through the old plumbing. A squeak from their old bed.

He sniffed, fought the urge to cry, and sat unmoving until Dave Borntrager arrived fifteen minutes later to assist him with his nightly needs.

◆ ◆ ◆

Nathan looked at the doorway. He was on his right side in his favorite sleeping position, a position he was forced to use only every third night.

After Dave's departure, he'd heard Abby in the kitchen, but for the first time she did not come in to say good night.

Now he listened to her restless tossing and cringed. *The pain won't last forever, Abs. You'll get over this. Time will heal this wound.*

And you'll be better off without me.

◆　◆　◆

Above him, Abby's tears were offered as a prayer. "I've asked you to forgive me, God. And I've asked Nathan too." She buried her whispered prayer in her pillow.

But can I ever forgive myself?

"I've messed everything up."

I thought I could find a way to love him again . . . until he told me about the phone calls . . . until I learned that I'm the reason for his pain . . . Now when I see him I can't seem to think of anything else.

Maybe Nathan's right. Maybe it's best if we separate. Maybe I can eventually find peace if I don't have to live with the constant reminder of my own sin.

I could move away. Never see Nathan. Never see Brian.

But what about Melissa? She still adores her father. She doesn't seem to see him as disabled. Wouldn't it be best to keep her near him?

She tried to imagine the future. A future separated from Nathan. *What if he's healed? What if the experimental surgery works? Would that make a difference? I wouldn't feel so guilty if he was normal again.*

She continued her prayer with a whispered request. "God, heal Nathan. Please!"

◆　◆　◆

Back in Brighton, Ryan Hannah was pushed from sleep by uncomfortable dreams of failure.

He rose, dropped three antacid tablets onto his tongue, and chewed with a scowl of distaste.

He walked toward the kitchen, pausing at Paige's door to listen to her quiet, regular breaths.

In the kitchen he stumbled over a running shoe that had been discarded in the middle of the floor after his daughter's evening workout. "Oomph!" He kicked the shoe aside and rubbed his ankle.

He opened the refrigerator door, hoping to find something to chase away the chalky taste of the antacid. He found some apple juice and sat down at the kitchen table to drink from the jar.

There, in the quietness of the kitchen, his thoughts turned to his research and the surgery he was planning. He thought about Nathan McAllister and about living life from a wheelchair, without movement or feeling from the neck down. He thought about the value of a life like that, and about Paige's conversation with Elizabeth.

He was struck with another idea. *What would it be like to be paralyzed?* He put down the juice container and tried to relax all his muscles. He flopped his hands to his lap, allowing them to slip off and dangle by his side. He let his legs go limp and took a shallow breath. He held his head up and looked around. *I'm paralyzed.*

He thought about not being able to wipe his chin if he drooled or lift his hand to scratch an itch. Of not being able to eat without help. Or walk. Or feel if his foot were hot or cramped inside a shoe. He looked around the kitchen. *I can't turn on the light. I can't feed myself. I can't lift the juice jar.* He looked at the tissue dispenser on the counter. *I can't cover my sneezes. I can't open the refrigerator door for a snack.*

He felt himself sliding down in the chair and stopped himself with his foot. *Oops. I can't do that if I'm paralyzed.* He grunted and thought how frustrating it would be not to be able to sit unless someone strapped him into position.

He looked up to see Paige plodding toward him, rubbing the sleep from her eyes. He resisted the temptation to lift his hand or change his slouch.

She looked at him curiously. "What's with you?"

He watched her eyes widen as she studied his completely relaxed posture. She picked up the apple juice and sniffed the bottle. "Are you drunk?"

He broke out of his imagined paralysis. "Of course not."

"You woke me up."

"You didn't put your shoes away. I could have twisted my ankle."

She sat at the table. "Sorry. What are you doing up anyway?"

"Sour stomach." He pushed the juice jar back from the edge of the table. "I got up to get a drink, and then I just started thinking." He let his arms fall again. "I was trying to imagine what it must be like to be paralyzed. Like Nathan McAllister. What's life like for him? He's totally dependent on others."

"Life is tough for him, I'm sure." She frowned.

"I'm not sure I'd want to live. If I was paralyzed, I mean. Life wouldn't be worth living." He looked at the apple juice. "I'm thirsty, Paige."

She looked at him blankly. "Help yourself."

"I can't. I'm paralyzed."

"You're weird, Dad."

"Try it, Paige. Just imagine that you're paralyzed. Look around and try to see things from the eyes of someone with a disability like that. If you have an urge, you will likely have to squelch it, unless there is someone nearby who can help you."

"I'm tired, Dad."

"Just try it. Just for a minute."

She yawned and let her arms flop. "I want to go back to bed."

"Can't. You're a quad. You have to wait for me to carry you."

"No way!" She sat back up straight.

"Hey, you can't do that."

She looked at the kitchen clock. "Why are we doing this? It's one o'clock in the morning!"

"I just thought it would be interesting, that's all. It might be good to imagine just how worthless you'd feel if you were disabled."

"Worthless by your measuring stick maybe." She wagged her index finger at him before collecting her running shoes and trudging off, leaving Ryan in the kitchen alone.

CHAPTER
41

THE NEXT MORNING Abby looked through the kitchen door at the cafe to the corner booth where Brian sat across from Charlie and Joe. She caught Marty's eye. "Will you wait on them?"

"You know you can't not talk to Brian forever. It's just too small a town for that." Marty held up her hands in mock surrender and smiled. "Hey, I'll take your table for you. Brian always leaves me a big tip. At least he did the other day when he was entertaining those business suit guys."

"Thanks, Marty."

She watched her friend walk off in the direction of the table, carrying a coffeepot. *I forgot about those men.* She tapped her fingers against her temple and watched as Marty joked with the officers. *I never mentioned those men to Joe. If Brian is really into a drugs operation, those guys could have been involved too.* She looked as Brian smiled at Marty. Abby felt her face flush. *He's so smooth on the outside.*

A few minutes later Marty returned to the kitchen. Other than the officers, the cafe had hit a lull between breakfast and lunch. Marty grumbled, "Cops! All they want is coffee." She pulled a pack of cigarettes from the top of a refrigerator unit. "I need a smoke." She motioned to the door. "Come on, Mr. Knitter can handle things for a few minutes. You look like you could use a break too."

They walked out into the alley behind the cafe, where Abby

leaned against a fence hiding a metal dumpster. She watched as Marty took a long draw on a cigarette. "I thought you quit."

"I did for a while."

Abby shuffled her feet before speaking again. "Nate wants a divorce."

Marty's jaw dropped. "Nate?" She coughed and wiped her mouth with her hand. "Abby, this is great . . . isn't it?" She stared at Abby. "Isn't this what you wanted?"

"It's what I *used* to want." She looked away into the morning sky. "I don't know what I want anymore."

"Why would he want to leave you?"

She bit her lip. "I told him about Brian."

"You told him? Oh, great move. You knew how he would react. I told you that myself, didn't I?" She paused, pulling hard on her cigarette again. "But maybe that's why you told him, huh?"

"I thought you were wrong. I thought he'd changed . . . that he'd be more understanding."

"Understanding? Men are not capable of understanding a confession like that. If you wanted out, you did the right thing. If you wanted to stay, it was a crazy move, girl."

"I thought it was the right thing to do."

"Maybe it was. Now you can get out and be free."

"Ever since he returned, I've felt my heart turning toward him again. He's seemed different. At least that's what I told myself. He even asked me to forgive him for being so jealous in the past." She dropped her eyes to the gravel littered with cigarette butts. "But maybe his reaction to my affair is proof that I was wrong. If he could have forgiven me, we might've had a chance."

"Believe me, no man can take that news. They may say they believe in an open marriage, like my Darryl did, but down inside, they'll always see you as damaged goods once you've cheated on 'em."

Abby looked at her friend in wonder. *We are so different. How did we ever become friends?*

Marty chuckled. "You can live with me if you want. I've told you that before." She paused. "It will be like that summer after your freshman year when your parents went to California."

Abby shook her head. "I can stay where I'm at for now. It's not like we get in each other's way or anything. My bedroom's upstairs; Nate's is downstairs."

"Oh."

"He says he wants to go back to Briarfield Manor after his surgery."

"Surgery?"

Abby cringed. "Yes. It's, well . . . it's supposed to be a secret, but I guess I can tell you." She hesitated and lifted her little finger in the air, in a ritual she and her friends had practiced since high school. It was an oath to secrecy. "Sister pact?"

Marty smiled. "Abby . . ."

"I'm serious."

Marty raised her little finger to mirror Abby's. "Sister pact," she repeated. They linked small fingers and shook.

"OK," Abby began. "I've been dying to tell this to someone anyway. It's so exciting . . ."

◆　◆　◆

Dr. Hannah called with the news the following day: Nathan was scheduled for surgery two weeks from Thursday. He would need to come down on Wednesday morning for a nerve harvest, a procedure by which Dr. Hannah would remove a nerve from Nathan's lower leg to use as a spinal cord graft. The sural nerve, Dr. Hannah explained, would be used for the graft and normally functioned to provide sensation on the lateral surface of the foot. At worst, if the procedure worked, Nathan would have some numbness on the outside of his foot and ankle. Dr. Hannah planned to incubate the nerve in NTTF, the neural tube regenerative factor that he had discovered. After twenty-four hours the nerve would be ready for a grafting attempt.

The next day Nathan's StimMaster arrived, and his PCAs gathered for an intensive training session, learning how to help Nathan through his bicycle workouts.

For the next two weeks Nathan's life centered around a routine of preparing for his surgery. He conscientiously ate healthy, drank plenty of fluids, and faithfully did his StimMaster bicycle ergometer workouts.

He took daily powerchair trips down the street for fresh air and became ultra-compulsive about skin checks for pressure irritations. When he wasn't mentally or physically consumed by his goal, he played games with Melissa or read her stories as she held the books and sat in his lap.

As he did his workouts, he observed Abby looking on, wide-eyed and silent, seemingly fascinated by his leg movements. He detected her watching as he played with Melissa and saw her leaning from the edge of the porch to see down the street when he was out for his powerchair "walks." He noticed her fleeting glances when he sat in front of the TV, and he heard her footsteps in his doorway on many nights, long after he'd gone to bed.

Yes, Abby was watching, and checking, and checking again.

It was at night that Nathan found it most difficult to remain resolved in his decision to separate. It was also at night that he stilled himself enough to hear the Spirit's gentle prompting.

It's not all Abby's fault, Nathan. You are responsible too. Responsible for pushing her away in your distrust.

I love you, Nathan. I forgave you. You need to forgive your wife.

In forgiveness, she will be freed to love.

Nathan looked at the clock. Twelve fifteen. He was too excited to sleep. The next day Abby would be taking him to Brighton for surgery. His mind was filled with a mixture of anxiety and anticipation over the procedure, and sadness from knowing that tonight was the last night he'd spend in the same house with Abby.

Janice had found him a room at Briarfield Manor. When he returned to Fisher's Retreat, he would return to an empty house.

And he hoped he would return walking on his feet.

◆ ◆ ◆

On the floor above, Abby dropped to her knees in what had become a nightly routine.

"Please, God. Bring Nathan back to health," she whispered. "Show me your way."

An uncomfortable feeling nudged her. "Keep Nathan safe during the surgery, God. Dr. Hannah says anything can happen. He could even die." She swallowed hard. "Don't let him die, God."

She rose, gingerly pulled back the curtain, and peered into the night. There, just beyond the second house, she saw a familiar Fisher's Retreat patrol car.

Brian Turner.

The name brought with it a flood of emotion. Guilt. Anger. Mystery. Terror. And passion.

Why does he continue to watch us night after night?

Is he obsessed with me . . . with getting me back? Has he somehow found out about our suspicions? Is he studying our routines, waiting to make a move?

Or have I misjudged him? What if I'm making him out to be something he's not? She thought about the things she loved about him—his laugh, his strong arms, his boyish charm. *Nathan is pushing me away. Could I ever find comfort from Brian's touch again?*

Abby gathered her nightgown around her neck to ward off a sudden chill and tried to push away the fright that escalated each time she saw him. *I need to make sure the automatic door is turned off.*

◆　◆　◆

Nathan heard her footsteps on the stairs and listened as she flipped the lock on the back door. In a moment he sensed her in the room behind him. "Abby?"

"Yes?" She moved closer and came around to sit on his bed. "Trouble sleeping?"

He nodded.

"Are you scared, Nathan?"

"A little."

She touched his hair. "You don't have to do this, you know."

"I know." He moved his head. Her fingers tickled him behind his ear.

"I'm not pushing you to do this. Do you feel that I am?"

"No."

"It won't change the way I feel about you, Nate."

He sighed. "I know." He looked at her. "I talked to Janice Marsh. She found a room for me at Briarfield. They'll start holding it for me in a week and a half. Dr. Hannah thought I would be in the hospital at least ten days, maybe longer."

"Nathan, are you sure this is what you want?"

"Abby, please don't keep asking me that. It's my decision." He felt his throat tighten.

"OK." She withdrew her hand. "Are you all right for the night?"

He nodded and tried not to look at her eyes. He was sure she could see into his soul. *I love you, Abby.*

"OK."

"Abby . . ." he called as her footsteps receded into the hall.

"Yes?" Her footsteps paused.

"I could get my father to take me. You don't have to go to Brighton if you don't want to."

"I'm going with you, Nathan." She paused before adding softly, "As long as that's OK with you. I'm still your friend . . . and I'm still your wife."

"OK."

" Good night, Nate."

"Good night."

CHAPTER
42

THE NEXT MORNING, just after sunrise, Abby dropped Melissa off to stay with Nathan's mother, and she and Nathan headed over North Mountain for Brighton. He had informed his parents of the surgery and, with some forceful prodding, had sworn them to secrecy. They planned to join Abby in the surgery waiting room during the main procedure on Thursday. Marty agreed to keep Melissa while Nathan's parents were in Brighton.

After their arrival, Nathan was checked through hospital registration and assigned a bed in the research unit. He would be the only patient there, cared for by a staff of handpicked neurosurgical intensive care unit nurses. Dr. Hannah had reserved the entire unit for two full weeks, a feat of some magnitude accomplished only with the dean's backing.

At just before 9, Nate's right leg was shaved, and he was taken to the operating room. There he was positioned facedown on a padded black O.R. table and introduced to several nurses and an anesthesiologist, who would monitor him during the procedure, a sural nerve harvest. The surgery did not require anesthesia because of his sensory loss due to his spinal cord injury.

At each stage the nurse or Dr. Hannah would explain what was happening.

"We're scrubbing your leg now to kill any skin germs that might be present."

"These drapes are sterile. We need to cover you up."

He felt his head swimming. He looked for the anesthesiologist but couldn't see because of a blue drape that seemed to hover just above his head.

"Knife . . . there . . . there . . . cautery . . . sponge . . . scissors . . ." Dr. Hannah's voice was calm and mechanical. "The nerve looks good . . . oh, hold his leg . . . a muscle spasm . . ."

Nathan became aware of a sweet, burnt aroma. "What's that smell?"

"Just the cautery, Mr. McAllister. We use it to stop small bleeders."

Nathan sniffed. *Burning flesh? My flesh!* "What's that noise?"

"Just your heart monitor, Mr. McAllister."

He fought the sudden urge to sleep. His lips felt large and heavy. His eyelids weighed a ton. "Are you giv—ing me some—thing?"

"Just a little something to make you relax," the anesthesiologist responded.

The room dimmed and spun. And then there was only darkness.

◆ ◆ ◆

Marty pushed her long black hair beneath the net and walked into the alley to smoke. She looked up to see Brian Turner leaning against a patrol car. She smiled. "Abby's not working today."

He shrugged. "I wasn't looking for her." He stepped toward her, the gravel crunching beneath his feet. "How've *you* been?"

"The same. Nothin' much changes around this place." She lit her cigarette.

"Those things'll kill you."

She frowned. "I know." She could feel his eyes on her before she looked up to see.

"I need to get out of here, do something. I'm free tomorrow. Want to take in a movie down in Carlisle?"

"Can't." She batted her eyes. "I'm keeping Abby's kid."

"Melissa? We can take her along."

"I don't think so. Not unless you want to watch *Bambi*. Nate's pretty strict about what she sees."

He grunted. "Why are you keeping Melissa?"

"Abby and Nate are over in Brighton for his surgery."

"Surgery? What's he got?"

Marty looked down and flinched. "I really shouldn't say. Abby made me swear like it's some huge secret or something."

"Hey, they're my friends too," he said, kicking a stone against the fence.

She pulled on her cigarette and looked at Brian's honest face. He smiled thinly. "OK, I'll tell you what I know. Everyone's going to know in a few days anyway. The way Abby talked, he might walk into the cafe one day just to make everyone drop their teeth."

"What?"

"One of the doctors at the university is working on some experimental surgery to cure spinal cord injuries. Nathan is being operated on tomorrow to remove the bullet and hook his spinal cord together . . ." Her voice trailed. "Or something like that."

"Tomorrow? You're serious?" He dropped his jaw.

"Of course. That's why Abby's not here now. She took Nathan over to Brighton University Hospital."

"You're sure about the bullet? The bullet's going to be removed?" His eyes were bright, flicking from Marty to his patrol car and back.

"Yep." She made a face. "Abby had to tell me all the gory details."

"Who else knows about this?"

"No one. It's supposed to be a secret." She winced, seeing his excitement. "Listen, Brian, I really wasn't supposed to tell. I gave Abby my word."

"Don't worry about it."

Marty finished her smoke and threw the butt on the gravel.

"I could give you a fine for littering."

"And I wouldn't go to the movies with you."

"You said you were busy anyway."

"I did say that, didn't I?" She pushed up the brim of his hat.

"Why didn't Abby take Melissa with her? It seems like Nathan would like that."

"She doesn't want Mel to see him like that. He'll be drugged up, lying there on life support, even more defenseless than usual. It would probably scare the poor child half to death." She made a high-pitched growl. "I know seeing people like that gives *me* the willies. I can't imagine what seeing her father in bed like that would do to a young girl."

Brian muttered, repeating her words, "Even more defenseless than usual. Oh, man." He shook his head before turning on his heels. "I need to get back to patrol."

"I'll take a rain check on the movie."

◆   ◆   ◆

On Wednesday, the evening before Nathan's major surgery, Ryan introduced the surgeons that he'd selected for his team. They stood around Nathan's hospital bed in long, white coats, staunch and unmoving like Roman columns. Abby sat in a chair at his bedside, within the circle of the surgical team.

Dr. Hannah pointed at the man to his right. "This is Dr. Samuel Harrison, a plastic surgeon with expertise in the area of free tissue transfer and microvascular work."

The surgeon was a large man, the tallest of the surgical team, with a solid build, looking like he'd be a fierce opponent on a basketball court. The man had a kind face and nodded to Nathan and smiled without speaking.

The neurosurgeon extended his hand toward the next white-coated professional, a compact man with blond hair hanging in bangs over his forehead. He barely looked old enough to work on Nathan's car, much less his spine. "Working with him is Dr. Evan Jacobs, a general and vascular surgeon."

Dr. Jacobs smiled. "Nice to meet you." He extended his hand to Abby and stroked Nathan's closest arm.

Dr. Hannah pointed to Elizabeth. "And you've already met Dr. Hopkins, one of my neurosurgical residents. She will be assisting me."

Dr. Hopkins tipped her head forward without smiling.

"And this," he added, pointing to a wiry man, the oldest on the team, "is the head of our anesthesiology staff, Dr. Joel Thomas. He will be heading a two-member team that's responsible for your anesthesia.

The other anesthesiologist, Dr. Frank Chalam, you met this morning, during your sural nerve harvest."

Nathan wrinkled his forehead. "I don't remember a thing about my operation this morning."

Dr. Thomas smiled and extended his hand to Abby. "That means my associate did his job well."

Dr. Hannah continued to explain, "Dr. Jacobs will begin the operation."

Nathan watched the two men exchange glances. Evan Jacobs nodded and stepped forward, slipping in front of the others. "I'll begin by performing a tracheostomy so we can have a secure airway during the surgery and later for your recovery," he said mechanically. "I'll also be responsible for dissecting out a piece of your omentum, a fatty apron that hangs off your stomach in your upper abdomen." He pulled down the sheet and gently lifted Nathan's gown to expose his skin. He laid his hand on Nathan's flaccid abdomen, massaging as he talked. "Hmmm. You've had some surgery before."

"My appendix."

"This is a pretty big scar for that."

"They told me it was ruptured."

"Hmmm." The general surgeon looked at Dr. Hannah. Nathan studied the surgeon's face, whose lips twitched ever so slightly, as if they were tempted to frown. Dr. Jacobs turned his attention back to Nathan. "I'll be making an incision here," he said, drawing a line with his finger down Nathan's upper abdomen. "From there I'll mobilize a portion of the omentum. Hopefully it will reach all the way to your neck."

To Nathan's relief, the doctor pulled up the sheet again. Nathan didn't like the word, "hopefully." He swallowed.

Dr. Hannah explained, "The omentum will help support the nerve grafts and will provide an avenue for the ingrowth of new blood vessels to feed the spinal cord in the area of injury."

"What if it doesn't reach?"

"That's what I'm here for," the tall surgeon responded. "If it doesn't reach, we will simply take a portion out of the abdomen, transfer it into the neck, and attach it to an artery and vein in your neck to keep it alive."

"Oh." Nathan nodded, trying to appear to understand.

He watched as Abby gently squeezed his arm.

"If that's necessary," Dr. Hannah interjected, "it will lengthen the operation considerably. In fact, the free tissue transfer will likely consume most of your time in the operating room." He paused. "We will begin the procedure, by necessity, with you on your back, so Evan, uh, Dr. Jacobs can get to the omentum. After he's done, he'll close you up, and we'll turn you facedown, so we can approach your spinal cord from behind. Then Dr. Hopkins and I will extract the bullet, remove the damaged area of your cord, and bridge the gap with the nerve grafts we've prepared, carefully passing them through the omentum."

"Will there be stitches?"

"We'll place a few sutures to hold the grafts in place, but most of the physical joining of the grafts to the spinal cord will be done with a surgical glue. Later, we trust, the grafts will be held in place by the ingrowth or regeneration of nerve tissue between the sural nerve grafts and your spinal cord."

Elizabeth Hopkins folded her arms in front of her lab coat. "The nurses will be bringing you an informed consent document to sign. They'll also ask you to initial a transcript of the recorded conversation of your exit interview that we did a few weeks ago."

Nathan replied numbly, "Sure." His head seemed to be in a cloud.

"OK," Dr. Hannah replied with a clap of his hands, "unless you have any questions, I guess that's it."

The team members dispersed, except for the chairman, Dr. Hannah, who lingered contemplatively at the foot of Nathan's bed. He tapped his finger against a clipboard hanging against a side rail and looked at a graph of Nathan's vital signs. He frowned slightly and sighed.

Nathan observed him, trying to interpret his thoughts. Here was one of the most important men he'd ever met, a brain surgeon on the brink of making medical history. But instead of seeing absolute confidence, Nathan detected anxiety covered by a layer of professional formality.

As he watched, Nathan was struck by an irony. *I'm the patient, about to trust you with my life. You should be comforting me, soothing my fears, and yet . . . . I sense that I should do the same for you.*

"Dr. Hannah?"

The neurosurgeon relaxed his knitted brow. "Oh, uh . . . yes?"

"I'm not afraid to do this."

Dr. Hannah drew his lips tightly together and nodded.

"And I will not fault you if the surgery fails."

"Fails?" His voice was loud, perhaps louder than he'd wished, as a faint color appeared in his cheeks before he continued at a lower volume. "Why . . . of course."

"I'm not placing all of my hopes in this one chance. If it doesn't work, my life is not over."

Dr. Hannah edged closer and sat gingerly on the edge of the bed. "You're a strong man, Nathan."

"As are you." Nathan searched Dr. Hannah's face for understanding. The chairman relaxed, and his shoulders stooped forward. He seemed tired, older than he had first appeared.

"God loves me, Dr. Hannah. Just like I am. And nothing you can do will change that."

Dr. Hannah grunted and reached for Nathan's hand.

Nathan's eyes met Abby's. "It's only since my accident that I've begun to understand . . ."

The surgeon looked down, his eyes on Nathan's unmoving form. "I won't let you down," he responded, rising to his feet again. He pivoted, smoothed the front of his white coat, and exited without another word.

◆ ◆ ◆

An hour later Ryan walked from the hospital into the evening air, hoping to clear his mind of the nagging anxieties he carried about Nathan's surgery.

Am I proceeding too fast? Should I have insisted on doing more animal studies? What if the procedure fails . . . or worse? What if I leave my patient worse off than before?

"First do no harm," he muttered to himself as he walked toward the Dennis Building. It was a phrase he'd learned the first day of his medical school training.

He passed a few students on benches and noted the absence of anyone handing out flyers or carrying signs of protest. He entered and took the elevator to the sixth floor, where he found Elizabeth keeping vigilant watch over the incubating nerve grafts he'd harvested that morning.

"Evening, Elizabeth."

She smiled. "Hi." She pointed to the lab bench. There, within a sterile container, the nerve grafts floated in a sea of oxygenated blood, saline, and several buffers. In addition, they had added the NTTF, the neural tube trophic factor, in a concentration that they'd used in the experiments on Heidi.

He nodded. "Good work."

"This is so exciting," she said, stepping closer to him. "No one will ever forget this, you know that."

He watched her expression change as her eyes met his.

"What's wrong? Are you tense about this?" She lifted her hand toward his face but halted before she touched him, pulling her hand away and looking down.

Was she blushing?

"There's a lot on my mind," he admitted casually.

"You've been working hard."

"We're doing something no one has ever tried. I guess that entitles me to a little apprehension." He lifted his chest. "But not enough that a surgeon would admit."

They smiled together for a moment. Ryan looked beyond his assistant to a cot lying against the far wall. It was made up and turned down, as if Elizabeth had been preparing for sleep.

"You're staying here tonight?"

She nodded and followed his gaze to the bed. "Yes. Just like when I used to watch Heidi." She paused. "I don't want to leave anything to chance. I want to be close to these grafts until we use them tomorrow."

"You need to get some sleep. We have a big day ahead."

"I will. Right here." She sighed and frowned. "You need to relax tonight too."

He knew she was right. The pressure of the research had started to weigh him down. He needed to find a mental escape. He needed to prepare and recoup his energy.

"We're alone." Elizabeth's voice broke into his thoughts of escape.

He observed her as she inched closer. "Yes." He inhaled her perfume. He felt himself being drawn forward. A caution light flashed, and he clenched his jaw and stepped back.

"Alone against the world, I mean. You and I, making neurosurgical history. You know what I mean?"

He forced himself to chuckle. "Right." He shook his head. *I've got to get out of here.* "Well, it looks like you have everything under control here. I'm going home."

He walked out without saying good-bye, still wrestling with his doubts, and further disturbed by his attraction to his young female resident. He chided himself as he walked, shaking his head at his own fragile vulnerability. *Way to go, Ryan. You almost made a pass at her! Elizabeth is a physician entrusted to you to train, not to seduce!*

He sighed and plodded through the open elevator doors as he recalled Paige's suspicions about his relationship with Elizabeth and how vehemently he had denied the possibility of impropriety. *Oh, you were righteous in your denial, weren't you, Ryan? But look at you now. You almost did exactly what Paige accused you of.*

He took a deep breath and blew it out slowly as the elevator descended. *Get a grip, Ryan. You didn't do anything. You're tired. You're under a tremendous amount of pressure . . . but you didn't give in. Give yourself a break.* He allowed the thought to comfort him.

Once he was in his car, he thought again about Nathan McAllister and the words he had spoken. *He has confidence in me.*

What is it about him?

He depressed the accelerator and pulled out of the parking lot. As he did, an empty gnawing pressed for recognition. He thought about the trust that Nathan had expressed and how similar Nathan's words sounded to the ones he'd heard Paige harp on over and over. *Does God love me just like I am, and not because of what I can do? Nathan really seems to believe that.*

I wish I was like Nathan McAllister.

◆ ◆ ◆

The nurse held out a paper for Nathan to sign with the pen in his teeth. "This isn't easy," he said out of the corner of his mouth.

"Don't talk," Abby teased. "You'll slobber on the paper."

He shot a glance at her and saw her smile.

"There," he said, pulling his head back and looking at the finished product. "It looks like I dotted the 'L.' Oh well, it's good enough."

The nurse looked on. "Neater than mine." She pulled the clipboard back to her chest and retrieved the pen from his lips, holding it out between her fingers like it was contaminated. "I'll be in to check on you in a few minutes." She disappeared, leaving the McAllisters alone.

"Nathan . . ." Abby's voice was strained. "I don't like hearing about all the complications. It seems like that's all I've heard for two days."

"It's just routine. They have to tell you those things." His eyes widened. "Can you lower my head a little? I feel like I'm slipping down."

She depressed a button on the railing of the bed.

"That's better." He looked at her. "Abby, it's getting late. You'd better go. You'll need some sleep tonight."

"What about you?"

He smiled. "I'm getting an extra nap tomorrow, remember?"

Abby's hand went to her chin. "Nate, they said you could even *die*. I'm afraid for you. I'm not sure you should do this."

"We've been over this before. I *want* to do it."

"But what if something does happen, Nate? Something unexpected. What if you die?" She halted, but her lips quivered as if she wanted to say more.

"Abby, I—"

"Ever since we started talking about this surgery, I've been haunted by the fact that you could die." She sniffed. "I don't think I could handle it if something happened to you," she said flatly. "Especially now, when there are so many unresolved issues between us."

"Everything is going to be OK, Abby. Nothing bad is going to happen to me." He searched her eyes, longing to reach out, wishing there was some way to turn her heart to him again. "You'll see. I'll get through this, and then we can go on."

"We'll go our separate ways is more like it," she muttered.

"That's what's best, isn't it?"

"Perhaps." She shook her head. "But it feels like such a lie to stay here by your side, appearing to be the perfect little supportive wife, when we both know that things aren't right between us."

"It's not wrong for you to be here supporting me."

She slumped forward. "I know, Nate. I'm sorry." She sighed.

"Go get some rest, Abs. I'll see you in the morning before surgery. They're taking me down at 7. Will you be able to make it?"

She nodded and stood. "Sure."

She touched his face once with her hand and retreated to the doorway. "Nate?" Her silhouette appeared against the light in the hall.

"Yes?"

"I admired what you said to Dr. Hannah tonight. You really believe that, don't you?"

"I'm starting to."

She cleared her throat. "Me too, Nate. Me too."

He watched her go, sensing the heaviness that seemed to dog her, wishing he could make it easier for her, but not knowing how.

He quietly spoke a frustrated prayer. "Help her, God." He pinched his eyes closed and asked for a solution to his wife's pain.

The answer came in a single word: *Forgive.*

He shook his head and held on to his anger and hurt. *I should let her go.*

You're not letting her do anything. You're driving her away. Just as you drove her into Brian's arms before.

Nathan closed his eyes tight, unable to escape the gentle prodding of the Spirit on his conscience.

"Mr. McAllister?" The nurse poked her head in the doorway, interrupting his thoughts. "Dr. Hannah wants us to give you a bowel stimulant tonight, so you'll be ready for surgery bright and early. You didn't get it this morning, did you?"

I should have known. Just when I'm starting to have some serious communion with God, in comes The Bowel Program. "No. I didn't get one this morning."

"Good. I'll be right back."

I can hardly wait.

CHAPTER
43

THE NEXT MORNING Ryan arrived at the hospital at 6:30 and checked the schedule at the O.R. main desk. Room 7 had been reserved for his team for the entire day. He had instructed the case to be posted as a cervical laminectomy, as the schedule was widely distributed throughout the hospital and he couldn't risk the leaks that would go out if he posted the true nature of the case. Everyone on the team agreed to abide by the same code of silence. There would be no media involvement until he decided it was appropriate.

He scanned the list, running his finger down to O.R. 7. "Nathan McAllister, cervical laminectomy." Beside it, in the slot for surgeon, three names were listed: "Hannah, Harrison, Jacobs."

That ought to raise some eyebrows around here, Ryan thought. *People will wonder why I need help from a general surgeon and a plastic surgeon just to do a laminectomy.* He smiled to himself. *Oh well, let them wonder. It's better than having everyone who reads this paper know what we're really doing today.*

◆ ◆ ◆

At a quarter to 7 an orderly came with a stretcher for Nathan.

"I haven't seen Abby yet," he told the nurse. "I don't want to go until I see her."

The orderly looked like a high schooler and had a small crop of hairs on his chin, proudly unshaven. "Dr. Hannah wants the patient in the O.R. by 7. You are Mr. McAllister, aren't you?" he said, looking at his clipboard assignment. "You're on for a cervical laminectomy."

"Cervical what?"

"Never mind," the orderly snapped. "Let me see your armband." He glared at Nathan, who remained motionless. He tapped his foot and raised his voice. "I need to see your arm I.D. bracelet."

Nathan met his gaze. "It's on my arm if you want to see."

"He's paralyzed. You'll have to do it for him," the nurse instructed.

"I want to see my wife."

The nurse frowned. "Did she know when you were to leave?"

"I told her 7."

Mr. Adolescent Chin shook his head. "You need to be down there by 7. Dr. Hannah will have a team waiting."

The nurse, a stocky woman with graying hair, snapped, "Did you bring any help along? Mr. McAllister can't move over by himself, you know."

The orderly looked at his clipboard assignment. "There's no note here like that." He looked at Nathan. "You are the laminectomy patient, aren't you?"

"Lami what?"

The nurse scowled. "Don't worry about that. He's the right patient. Let me get another nurse. We can move him together."

"I don't want to go yet!"

"We'll just get you on the stretcher, Mr. McAllister. You still have a few minutes."

The nurse disappeared and brought back another helper, a tall, slender African-American woman with a tender smile. The orderly pushed the stretcher up against Nathan's hospital bed.

"Let's slide him to the edge. Grab the lift sheet," the older nurse instructed. "On three. One, two, three!" The trio slid Nathan to the edge of the bed. "Again, on three. One, two, three!" They slid him onto the stretcher.

Nathan twisted his head around. *Where's Abby?* He frowned. "I need to see my wife before I go into surgery."

The orderly put up two side rails and released the stretcher brake.

"Please," Nathan pleaded.

The tall nurse locked back on the stretcher brake with a forceful grunt. "Hang on for a minute, Bob. You can't go anywhere without the patient chart anyway." She made eye contact with Nathan and continued, "And it's not ready yet. It will take me a while to do his preoperative check list," she added with a wink.

She started down the list while Bob, the orderly, stroked his chin sprouts.

"Hmmm. Arm I.D. bracelet . . . check," she said, lifting Nathan's arm. "Preoperative orders, foley catheter inserted . . . check. Antibiotic and steroid hanging . . . check," she said as she touched two plastic IV containers hanging above Nathan's head. "Preoperative abdominal and neck shave . . . check."

"Come on, Dr. Hannah is expecting him. The checklist was supposed to have been done before I came," the orderly moaned.

"Let's see," she continued, "now where did I put that consent? I'll just be a minute." She started leafing through the patient records. She smiled tersely at Bob and walked out in the direction of the nursing station. "I'll just be a minute," she called from outside the room.

Bob muttered, "Great."

After a few minutes she brought back the chart and laid it on the stretcher, but just as Bob was ready to leave again, she insisted on checking Nathan's IV, emptying his urinary drainage bag, and reconfirming that Nathan had no known allergies.

Bob started edging the stretcher to the door.

"Please, I need to see my wife before I go."

"Sorry, mister. You'll see her right after you get back to your room. Dr. Hannah does these laminectomies all the time. You'll be back here in no time." He pushed the stretcher forward.

"I'm not the right patient," Nathan yelled. "I'm not having a lami whatever!"

Bob looked confused.

The nurse leaned over and put her lips to Nathan's ear. "That's just what Dr. Hannah put on the schedule to keep everyone from knowing what he was doing." Then she pulled her head back and said, "One final thing. Any dentures?"

"Nope." Nathan showed his teeth. "All mine."

"Jewelry?"

"Only my wedding ring."

"I've gotta take it off. O.R. policy," she explained. "Your hand might swell from the IV fluid, and your ring could get stuck, even cut off the circulation to your finger." She lifted his hand. "I'll give it to your wife." She tugged on the ring. "Hmm. Maybe I'd better get some lotion."

Nathan watched her walk away, appreciating the additional delay. He looked at the clock. The nurse's strategy had used up the better part of seven minutes. But there was still no sign of Abby.

The nurse returned, put lotion on his finger, and gently slid the ring off into her hand. "I'll make sure your wife gets it."

Great. I don't get to see Abby, and all she'll get is an empty room and my wedding band. She'll think I'm sending her another message that our marriage is over.

The nurse looked at the clock. "I guess you're going to have to go now."

"No." Nathan shook his head.

"Finally," Bob grunted, wheeling Nathan through the door and into the hall. He pushed him past the nursing station and tapped an automatic paddle to open the door that led from the research unit and into the main hospital corridor. He turned right and guided the stretcher past the main bank of elevators just as Abby came into view. She was coming out of a stairwell door marked Exit.

"Abby!" Nathan called as he whisked by.

Bob kept pushing.

"Nathan?" Abby jogged up beside him. "Sir?"

"Stop the stretcher, Bob!" Nathan looked at his wife. "They came for me early."

"Well, it's not so early now," the orderly moaned.

"Give me a minute. Please."

Bob sighed and walked to the edge of the hall where he could lean against the wall.

"Abby," he started, "I thought I'd missed you."

"I'm here." She took a deep breath. "One of the elevators wasn't working, so I took the stairs."

His eyes searched hers. "Come here."

She leaned over his face. "I'm here, Nate."

"Abby, I've been wrong." He bit his lower lip. "I'm responsible for what you did. It was me, Abs. It was my fault. Not just yours." He halted and tried to moisten his mouth.

"Nate . . ." she whispered.

"I wanted you to know . . . before I went down. I forgive you, Abby. It's past. OK?"

Bob started whistling.

Her eyes were moist. She leaned even closer. This time he did not turn away. She kissed him, then pulled back and looked in his eyes one more time. She stroked his cheek and kissed him again before trying to find her voice. "Thank you."

Bob jostled the stretcher. "Let's go."

Abby whispered, "I'll be praying, Nate." She patted his shoulder. "And I'll be waiting for you when it's over."

Her face disappeared as Bob pushed the stretcher forward. Nathan closed his eyes in hopes of preserving the memory of her embrace. He could still see her eyes, her lips, her hair, the tenderness of her expression. He held his breath and concentrated. When they put him under, he wanted to sleep with her loveliness on his mind.

◆ ◆ ◆

Forty-five minutes later Dr. Jacobs looked over the sterile drapes at the anesthesiologist. "OK to begin?"

Dr. Thomas glanced at the monitors and nodded. "Go ahead."

"Knife."

The scrub assistant handed the instrument to the surgeon.

Gently, Dr. Jacobs guided the scalpel over the patient's neck, the skin and subcutaneous fat offering little resistance to the razor-sharp blade. Meticulously, he deepened his dissection to the trachea, in preparation for the tracheostomy tube.

Nathan McAllister's surgery had begun.

◆ ◆ ◆

Abby checked the clock on the wall and looked around the crowded waiting room.

People sat in groups of two, three, or four, chatting nervously and unwrapping breakfast biscuits purchased from the hospital cafeteria. She sat alone, waiting for Nathan's parents and clutching the small, golden wedding band a nurse had handed her only moments before.

Please be with Nathan, God.

She sipped coffee from a Styrofoam cup and watched the entrance to the large room.

Help Dr. Hannah and the other surgeons. Keep my husband safe.

Abby slowly uncurled her fingers and looked at the ring in her hand.

Oh, Father, don't let my husband die.

◆ ◆ ◆

Surgeon Evan Jacobs positioned a retractor against the cut edge of the abdominal wall and handed it to an assistant. "Pull." He redirected an overhead light to shine into the right lower abdomen. "Oh man. Adhesions."

Dr. Hannah sat on a stool against the wall, watching and waiting for his time. "What's it look like, Evan?"

"His omentum is plastered to a scar in the right lower abdomen." He grunted. "Scissors." He held out his open palm. "What's left of it, that is. He must have had a nightmare case of appendicitis to cause all this."

Dr. Hannah sighed and stood. "I'll be in my office. Keep me updated, OK? I want to be able to keep his wife informed of the progress."

◆ ◆ ◆

Abby looked up from the tattered copy of *National Geographic* in her hands.

Where are Nathan's parents?

She tried to pay attention to the images of the Amazon jungle but recoiled at the close-up of a feeding python and pushed the magazine away just as a breathless Mark and Sally McAllister arrived.

She stood and received her mother-in-law with a bear hug. "Morning."

"Is he in surgery?" Mark asked.

Abby nodded. "They took him at 7 this morning."

Sally shook her head. "There was fog on the mountain."

"It's OK. I'm glad you're here," Abby responded honestly.

"Blasted parking lot is a mile away," Mark grumbled, looking at his wife as she sat down next to Abby. "Did you see where the doctors get to park? Seems to me they should let the patients and their families park up there."

"At least we made it." Sally took a deep breath. "I'm exhausted already," she said, reaching into a large tote bag. "I brought some breakfast." She retrieved a large sticky-bun from a Tupperware container. "Hungry?"

Abby politely declined.

Mark hoisted a canvas camera bag. "I've got the video cam. I want to record his first steps."

Sally squinted. "It's not like he's going to walk out of the operating room today, Mark."

He huffed, set the bag aside, and reached for a pecan-laden bun. "Well, at least I'm prepared."

"Dr. Hannah said it might take days, maybe even longer before we see any response."

Sally began digging in her tote bag again, this time coming up with a large purple ball of yarn and a crochet hook. She looked like she was settling in for the duration.

Mark wrinkled his nose at the *National Geographic*. "Any *Sports Illustrateds* around here?" He stood and went in search of reading material while Abby sighed and scanned the waiting room crowd.

A young mother corraled a wiggly toddler. A gray-haired woman stood to talk with a young man in a scrub outfit. A Spanish-speaking family clustered in the corner.

"My sister's havin' surgery."

Abby turned her attention to a generous-sized woman sitting across from her on the next row of padded chairs. "Oh."

"Nothin' serious. Dr. Bannister is takin' out her gallbladder. He's usin' the laser." She snorted and took a bite of an egg biscuit. "It's not like it used to be. You should see the scar my surgeon put on me." She drew a line across her ample stomach. "Cut me from here to here," she said loudly.

Abby nodded politely. "Oooh."

"It was awful for a while," she said, lifting the biscuit for another bite. "But worth it. Now I can eat whatever I want."

Abby reached for the magazine. Even the Amazon jungle would be better than thinking about gallstones. A minute later, when she dared to lift her eyes again, she breathed a sigh of relief. The woman had turned her attention to the man on her right as he told her of his aunt who had died from some sort of laser.

She looked at Mark, who was now contented with a sports story, and Sally, who seemed to be busy with her yarn. *I hope you don't make us a purple afghan to go with the orange one you gave us last Christmas.*

Her eyes met briefly with a man in a gray business suit across the room. She squinted for a moment as a vague sense of familiarity passed. *Maybe I've seen him in the hospital before?* His impeccable clothing seemed to attract attention in the casual crowd. The man turned away, then stood and walked out, carrying a rolled newspaper.

Abby sighed, looked at the clock, and wondered how each minute could seem so long.

◆ ◆ ◆

The monitor emitted a bright green glow, Nathan's EKG tracing, revealing his heart rate to be eighty-two beats a minute. A continuous blip provided the background noise as Evan Jacobs continued to work.

"Call Dr. Harrison," the surgeon quipped. "This guy doesn't have enough omentum left to reach his cervical spine."

The circulating nurse responded by picking up the phone. "Shall I open the microvascular instrument set?"

"Absolutely. And you'd better call Dr. Hannah too. It's going to be a long day."

◆ ◆ ◆

Thirty minutes and four magazines later, Dr. Hannah stood in the doorway of the surgical waiting room scanning the crowd.

"Dr. Hannah!" Abby raised her hand to catch his eye.

"Boy, that didn't take him as long as I thought," Mark said as he rose to his feet.

His expression was solemn as he approached. Abby felt her throat tighten. *Something's wrong. He shouldn't be here this soon! Nathan's—*

"Ms. McAllister . . ." Dr. Hannah extended his hand to Abby. "Everything is going fine. Nathan is fine."

Mark stepped forward. "How'd it go? Is he awake?"

Dr. Hannah looked at Abby.

"This is Nathan's father, Mark McAllister."

The surgeon nodded without changing his expression. "We have a lot of work left to do. The surgery is far from complete. Dr. Harrison is just beginning. It looks like a free tissue transfer will be necessary," he continued, focusing his eyes on Abby.

"A what?" Sally questioned, shoving her project aside.

Abby lifted her hand toward Sally and looked at Dr. Hannah. "Nathan's mother."

The surgeon took a deep breath to begin, but Abby interrupted, "I can explain it to them."

"OK." He smiled. "I'll try to give you some more updates as we go. Of course, when my turn comes to operate, I won't be coming in person. I'll have the nurses call a message to the volunteer at the desk." He pointed to a woman in a pink smock behind a counter in the corner of the room.

"Good, sir," Mark snapped with a tip of his head. "Keep us posted."

Abby looked at her father-in-law, fearing for a brief moment that he was going to salute.

Dr. Hannah continued, looking only at Abby. "The messages will have to be brief because details are too often confused by the volunteer. I will merely say, 'things are going well' or 'the patient is stable' or some other such message. But please don't let the vague nature of my updates upset you. It won't mean bad news." He paused, then added, "Be prepared for another six to eight hours of this."

Abby appreciated his concern. "Thank you."

He turned to leave. "I'll be in touch," he said as he retreated from the room.

Mark yawned. "Six to eight hours? I'm taking a walk."

◆ ◆ ◆

Paige lifted another bound volume of the *New England Journal of Medicine* and placed it on the library shelf. She looked up at the thousands of bound volumes and marveled at the enormity of knowledge amassed there. She picked up another book from the cart, weighing it in her hand before whispering to a medical student who was searching the shelf in front of her, "I'll be getting my workout today." She hoisted the book onto the top of a stack.

The medical student, a young man with a dark moustache, nodded. "Really," he whispered.

She continued her work reshelving the books, thinking of her future occupation and the challenges it might hold. Occasionally she paused and prayed.

Lord, be with Nathan McAllister today. Guide my father's hand to heal.

◆ ◆ ◆

Marty picked up the phone on the first ring, walking quickly with the phone into her kitchen so she could hear. "Hello."

"Hi, Marty."

"Abby! I thought it might be you. How's Nate?" Marty covered the phone with her hand to keep Abby from hearing the laughter in the other room.

"Still in surgery. I just thought I'd check in."

She lifted her hand from the mouthpiece briefly. "Wow."

"How's Melissa doing?"

"She's fine. She's watching TV."

The giggling from the den grew louder. Marty covered the phone and frowned.

"It sounds like she's having fun. What's so hilarious?"

"I don't know. You know kids. Anything will set 'em off."

"Yeah."

"Don't worry about us, Abs. Mel's fine."

Abby sounded tired. "OK. I'd better get back to the waiting room. I'll call when Nate's out of surgery."

"OK." Marty clicked off the phone and walked back to the den. "Do you two have to make such a racket while I'm on the phone?"

Melissa looked over from where she was perched on Brian's knee. "But the horsey keeps buckin' me off!"

"Watch out!" he teased as he grabbed her little waist. "The bronco's gonna buck!"

Melissa squealed her delight as Marty watched.

"You'd better hit the dusty trail, cowboy," she said flatly. "I think you'd better get back to work."

"Aw, do you have to go?" Melissa protested.

He made an exaggerated frown. "'Fraid so, partner. Now, how about a kiss for your old horse?"

Marty nudged him toward the door, but not before he received a noisy smack from Melissa.

"Here, watch TV, honey," she instructed as she snapped on the tube.

Brian retreated into the doorway.

"I don't think Abby would like you playing with Melissa," she whispered.

"What's the harm?" He put on his hat. "Besides, from what you tell me about Nate and Abby, the girl's gonna need a father figure around."

"See ya, Brian."

He stepped into the midday sun.

Marty put her hand to her mouth and watched him go. *Abby needs to open her eyes. That man is gorgeous.*

◆ ◆ ◆

For Abby, the hours passed in agonizing slow motion. She refused to leave the waiting room except to use the phone or the bathroom and had only a pack of crackers and a Diet Pepsi for lunch. She accepted only the help of the brief updates from Dr. Hannah's team and a thousand whispered prayers.

Just before five o'clock, the weary but jubilant neurosurgeon stepped into the waiting area with Dr. Hopkins right behind him.

Abby, Mark, and Sally hurried to their feet.

"We're done," Dr. Hannah reported with a nod.

"Nathan is fine," Elizabeth added, squeezing Abby's arm.

"He . . . he's OK?" Abby heaved a sigh and reached for Dr. Hannah's hands. She fought not to cry as her relief erupted to the surface. "Oh, thank you."

"Thank God," Sally gasped. "Thank God."

Abby released the chairman's hands and looked at Elizabeth. "Thank you too."

Elizabeth opened her arms and received Abby in a hug. "It went great," she said quietly. "You should have seen Dr. Hannah. He was magnificent."

Abby sniffed and pulled away. "When can I see him?"

"In an hour or two," Dr. Hannah responded. "I'll have his I.C.U. nurses let you know when he's ready."

Elizabeth pointed toward the hall. "There's another waiting area just outside the research unit. You should wait there."

"Go relax. Get some dinner. Nathan is doing fine."

"When will we know—"

"If it worked?" Dr. Hannah wrinkled his forehead. "I don't honestly know. A few days, maybe a week. We might even see a late return of function." He shrugged and added, "Now the real wait begins."

CHAPTER
44

ABBY REMEMBERED with too much clarity how Nathan appeared after his accident. She remembered the bandages, the swelling, and the tracheostomy. She remembered the ventilator, the monitors and tubes, the sounds, and the smell. So now, as a nurse led her in to see him, she prepared for the worst.

Nathan was lying on his back, with the head of his bed elevated. His eyes were closed, his lips and eyelids puffy, and his chin in need of a shave. He was covered by a thin gown and a sheet over his legs.

Abby tentatively touched his forehead. "Nate, it's me, Abby. I'm here."

He did not respond.

"He's still sedated," the nurse explained. "We'll withdraw the medication in the morning and see if he can breathe without the ventilator."

Abby nodded. "Wouldn't he be more comfortable if you lowered his head?"

"Dr. Hannah wants it this way. He doesn't want too much swelling."

The nurse excused herself, leaving Abby alone with Nathan. She stayed for an hour, until they requested she leave, and she left only after they agreed that they would call her if he awoke. Regretfully, exhausted, she returned to her motel.

The next day Nathan made limited progress and was allowed to breathe without the assistance of the ventilator. He responded to Abby by mouthing words but could not speak because of the tracheostomy tube. She stayed by his side until evening, when she returned to Fisher's Retreat to care for Melissa.

◆ ◆ ◆

By the second day Nathan was hungry and was allowed some liquids to drink. In the evening the nurses deflated the balloon cuff on his tracheostomy tube, to allow air to escape around the tube and into Nathan's throat so he could speak again. Even though his voice was weak, he felt a tremendous relief at being able to communicate more freely.

By Sunday, the third day after his surgery, he was given solid food. But he still couldn't move. He longed for the freedom of his powerchair, but Dr. Hannah wanted him to continue the bed rest so Nathan wouldn't move his neck.

On Sunday evening Abby brought Melissa for a visit.

Melissa sat quietly on her hands on a chair, wide-eyed and timid, apparently afraid of the monitors and other devices she saw there.

"It's OK, sweetheart. These things are just the way the hospital can help Daddy," Abby explained.

"Come up here." Nathan peered at his daughter through narrow slits between swollen eyelids. "You can sit on my bed."

Abby lifted her. "Be careful of Daddy's stomach. He had surgery there."

"Lift the sheet, Abs. She can see my bandage."

"Does it hurt?" Melissa wondered.

Nathan wrinkled his nose at Abby. "I can't feel a thing."

Melissa began pointing to items in the room. "What's this? What's that? What's this?" she asked, always ahead of her parents' attempts at answering.

After a few minutes she seemed bored with her own questions and began to sing. "Somewhere out there, beneaf the pale moonwight . . ."

Nathan laughed. "Where'd you learn that?"

"Brian took me to the movies!"

Abby cringed. Nathan felt his cheeks redden.

"It's not what you think, Nate," Abby said quickly. "And I had nothing to do with it. Marty let her go while I was here with you after your surgery." She held up her hands. "I would have said no if I'd known."

Nathan huffed, "Marty should know better." He felt his anger rising but wanted to be careful with his words in front of Mel.

Abby raised her eyes. "It was rated G," she added timidly.

"Doesn't matter. He shouldn't be spending time with her. She's my daughter!" He bit his tongue.

"Nathan, I agree with you." She captured his eyes. "You hear?" She lowered her voice and locked eyes with Nathan. "He's only doing this to spite me. He knows I wouldn't approve."

He sighed and mumbled, "Marty!" He was silent for a moment before sensing a growing alarm. "Abby, he doesn't know about the surgery, does he?"

"No. Marty swore she wouldn't say anything. She and your parents are the only ones who know." She squinted. "Why should it matter anyway? Everyone is going to find out eventually."

He looked at Melissa, who had retreated to the chair to look at a book she'd brought. "Abby, if Brian knew, he'd try to get the bullet. It's the only solid evidence that links him to the shooting."

"If he shot you accidentally, he won't be concerned about the bullet."

"True, but . . . if it wasn't accidental, he'd definitely go after it. He knows enough about police investigation to try and disturb the chain of evidence."

"He doesn't know about your surgery, Nate," Abby responded.

"Unless Melissa told him . . . while she was at the movies."

"Melissa didn't know about the surgery. I never told her anything except that you were at the hospital, until this morning before we left."

Nathan relaxed a notch at hearing that. "Do me a favor, will you? When you get home, tell Joe Gibson about my operation. Tell him that the bullet should be in the pathology lab at this hospital. That way he can come and sign for the bullet, to protect the chain of evidence from being tampered with."

Abby nodded obediently, leaned forward, and placed her hand against his foot.

Nathan's eyes widened. "Abby, my foot's burning!"

She pulled her hand away.

"Abby, I felt that. When you had your hand pressed on my leg, it *burned*."

She hurriedly tore the covers away. "Move your toes, Nate!"

He closed his eyes and concentrated.

Nothing.

He tried again. "See anything?"

"Nothing. Are you trying to wiggle your toes?"

"I'm trying. Press your hand against my foot again."

Abby stroked his foot. "Feel that?"

"No. Press harder."

Abby squeezed.

"It feels hot. It burns, Abby. *I can feel that!*"

"Oh, God, thank you, God," she mumbled while looking at his foot. "Nathan, look away. Close your eyes. Tell me when I'm squeezing."

He closed his eyes. "Now." He paused. "It's gone—you've stopped."

"Nathan, you *can* feel it!" She jumped from her perch on the end of the bed and looked at the doorway. "I'd better get the nurse." She hesitated, then approached him and placed her hands on his face. "Nathan, Nathan," she blubbered, "you're going to be well!" She kissed him softly on the mouth before momentarily regaining her composure. Then she pivoted and ran from the room. "Nurse," he heard her scream. "Get Dr. Hannah right away!"

◆ ◆ ◆

Abby ran almost blindly into the hall, stumbling into a man in a gray suit before excusing herself and yelling for Nathan's nurse. "He felt me touch him. He can feel! He can feel!"

◆ ◆ ◆

That evening before Abby left, Nathan endured assessment after assessment by the nurses, Dr. Hopkins, and Dr. Hannah, each one in turn testing for the first signs of return of neurologic function. Nathan did not have light touch sense, but he did have the ability to detect deep pressure on his foot and lower leg near the ankle. It certainly didn't feel normal, but the burning sensation, Dr. Hannah assured him, was the sensation of nerves awakening again.

Now as he lay awake, the memory of Dr. Hannah's words remained prominent in his mind. *"It's a hopeful sign. The beginning, Nathan. This must be how it begins."*

As the excitement chased the possibility of sleep far away, he thought about Abby and her response. She had kissed him tenderly as she left, but she failed to say the three words that would fill his soul again.

I forgave her, God. Didn't I? Now I must let her go. The thought still caused his heart to ache.

Nonetheless, he sensed her heart beginning to turn. Could it be that she would love him again? But in the recesses of his mind, in the darkness of his hospital room, he doubted her sincerity. *Is she showing me her affection now only because she believes I will be healed?*

That's not love. She touches me with her lips, but she still holds back her heart.

CHAPTER
45

THE NEXT DAY Nathan ate lunch from the hands of a nurse named Sandy. She was friendly and attentive, but her hands smelled like hospital soap, and the combined smells of food and aseptic iodine made Nathan long to leave the hospital and go home.

Shortly after Sandy left, Elizabeth Hopkins and Ryan and Paige Hannah came by. "Afternoon, Nathan," Dr. Hannah said, lifting Nathan's right hand.

"Hi." He looked at the trio. "What's up now?"

"We'd like to do a few additional sensory tests," Dr. Hannah replied. "Have you noticed any changes since yesterday?"

"Nothing new . . . except when the nurse squeezed my foot today, it seemed like I could feel it even better."

The resident questioned, "What about the nature of what you're feeling? Burning? Hot? Are you beginning to feel deep pressure?"

Nathan tilted his head. "Just the burning, I think. It's like my foot feels warm when it's squeezed."

"Painful?"

"More heat than pain."

Just then Abby stepped cautiously through the doorway. "I hope I'm not interrupting anything."

"Not at all. Come in," Dr. Hannah replied.

"Abby!" Nathan dropped his jaw. "I wasn't expecting you today."

She walked to his bed, alongside Dr. Hannah. "I was too excited to work. Mr. Knitter gave me the day off." She paused and smiled. "Melissa's at your parents' until tomorrow. After yesterday I just had to come back to see if you've made any more progress," she added with a shrug before kissing Nathan on the forehead.

"That's what we've just begun to assess," Dr. Hannah responded, holding out his hand to greet Abby.

He pulled back the sheet to uncover Nathan's legs. He squeezed his right foot. "Feel this?"

Nathan nodded.

"What's it like?"

"Same as yesterday. Feels hot."

The surgeon squeezed Nathan's left foot. "How about this? Do you feel this too?"

"Yes. Ow! That hurt for a moment."

"Pain?"

"Yes, definitely painful. Were you squeezing any harder than the other side?"

Dr. Hannah shook his head. "Wiggle your toes. Just try."

Everyone stared at Nathan's feet. The right great toe twitched ever so slightly.

"I did it. Did you see it?"

"There!" Dr. Hopkins exclaimed. "I saw it move. Just slightly, but it moved."

Dr. Hannah smiled. "Let's see your hands. There are more nerves that help us move our fingers than just about anything else. We may be able to see a response there," he said, lifting Nathan's right hand. "Move your fingers."

Nathan strained. Again there was a subtle twitch, this time in his right index finger.

Abby gasped. "Nate, you moved your finger!"

Nathan laughed with relief. "I sure did!"

"Try the other hand," Paige responded, lifting his left hand in front of him.

He took a deep breath and concentrated, watching his fingers. "I'm trying."

"Hmm. Nothing there yet, at least not that we can see with our eye, but that doesn't mean anything. It still may be too early," Dr. Hannah reported. He looked at Dr. Hopkins. "Could you get me some ice? Ask the nurses for it."

Elizabeth walked toward the door as Dr. Hannah added, "And some warm water. It would be nice to test with something warm."

In a minute she returned with two Styrofoam cups, one with ice and another with warm water. "Close your eyes," Dr. Hannah instructed.

Nathan obeyed. "OK."

Dr. Hannah took a piece of ice and held it in Nathan's palm. "Don't look, Nathan. What am I doing?"

"You're moving my hand. You're waving my fingers." Nathan opened his eyes and watched as Elizabeth and Dr. Hannah exchanged silent glances. He looked down at his hand. It seemed to be in the same place as before, but it *felt* like his fingers were moving.

Dr. Hannah removed the ice and gently cradled Nathan's hand in his own. "Tell me when the sensation of movement goes away."

In a few short moments Nathan spoke. "Now."

Dr. Hannah lifted his hand toward Elizabeth, who handed him the other cup. He dipped Nathan's fingers in the water. "Feel anything?"

"I feel like I'm moving my finger. Like when you put the ice on, but not as intense."

Dr. Hannah lifted Nathan's finger from the water and set Nathan's hand down again. Dr. Hannah scratched his chin. "Hmmm." He stepped back from the bed, cleared his throat, and looked at Nathan. "Well, things are definitely beginning to work. You have some limited ability to move." He paused and looked over at his resident assistant before looking back at Nathan. "And you have some reconnection of your sensory nerves." He shrugged. "I think only time will tell." He retreated an additional two steps.

"Are you encouraged? Is this good news?" Abby pressed.

Dr. Hannah didn't smile. "It is encouraging. But the final outcome may not be determined for many weeks."

With that, he nodded his head and held his hand toward the door, ushering his daughter and Elizabeth ahead of him. "I'll leave you two alone. Good day."

With the trio gone, Abby looked at Nathan. "Well, at least he's encouraged."

"He seemed hesitant to make us very excited. I like what he says, but it's what he doesn't say that bothers me."

She lifted his hand in hers. "Try to squeeze."

His managed only a slight wiggle of his index finger.

Their eyes met. "It's a start, Nate. A good start."

They sat quietly for a few moments before Abby took a deep breath. She seemed to be anxious to speak but instead just sighed in sputtery frustration. When she took another audible breath but didn't speak, Nathan turned his head. "What is it, Abs?"

She looked away. "Janice Marsh left a message on our answering machine this morning. She wants me to call her with an update." Abby scooted her chair away from the bed an inch. "She wants to know if we know your discharge date yet, so she can make final arrangements for a room at Briarfield Manor."

"Hmm. What'd you tell her?"

"I didn't call. I didn't know what to tell her, Nate. For one thing, I truthfully don't know when you're getting out of here." She paused, seemingly hesitant to continue. "And for another, I wasn't sure if that's what you really want."

Nathan didn't know what to say. "Abby, it's not just about what I want."

She lifted her eyes from the floor. "You told me you'd forgiven me, right?"

He nodded. "Yes. And I meant it, Abs."

"Does that mean . . . that you want me to stay?"

He searched her eyes. What was he detecting there? Love? Pity? "Forgiveness means I won't hold the past against you anymore. Whether you stay depends on you."

"Me?"

"I *want* you to stay, Abby. That's what *I* think is best." He looked beyond Abby to the doorway. "But if I love you, I can't hold on to you like before." He sighed weakly. "Forgiveness means that I'm freeing you. I'm letting you go." He shook his hand. "Not controlling, not holding on like before."

Abby coughed. "If you love me . . ."

"Abby, I *love* you. You know that. But it's not been easy to say it over and over, knowing you can't say it in return."

His eye began to itch, and he tried to scratch it with exaggerated winks.

"Is something hurting?"

"My eye itches."

She reached up and rubbed his eyes. "There. Is that better?"

"Yes."

She moved her hand from his eyelids to his cheek, pausing to caress him tenderly. He watched her eyes as she held his face for a moment. "Nathan," she said, "tell me what to do. If you want me to stay with you, I'm willing to stay. Tell me."

He shook his head against her hand. "I can't do that."

"Yes, you can. You used to do it."

"Abby, I *won't*." He nuzzled his cheek against her hand. "I will say this—I don't want you to stay out of sympathy. I don't want you to stay out of guilt."

She nodded quietly and slowly withdrew her hand. He could see in her eyes that she understood. "OK," she responded softly. "OK."

◆ ◆ ◆

Ryan Hannah ran his fingers through his thick, gray hair. "I don't like it."

Paige made a face. "I don't get it, Dad. Why are you upset?"

Elizabeth was slumped forward in a chair opposite Ryan's desk. "At least we know that the NTTF is working."

He sighed. "Maybe too well."

Paige demanded, "Would someone mind telling me what's going on?" She threw up her hands. "Shouldn't we be ecstatic? He's *moving*, isn't he? It may not be much, but it's a start, and—"

"We *are* excited about that, Paige," Ryan began. "But there are thousands of nerve connections to be made, and I'm not convinced that they are all hooking up properly." He held up his hand. "Here in my hand I have special sensory nerves that carry the message of light touch, temperature, pain, even the position of my hand." He closed his eyes. "That's the way I know where my hand is, even if my eyes are closed." He dropped his hand again. "My concern is that some of Nathan's pathways may have gotten mixed up as the nerve connections regenerated. Now when a temperature sensation is initiated in Nathan's hand, his brain is receiving a different kind of message, or maybe a partial or mixed message. When we made his hand cold, his brain told him his hand was moving."

"Maybe it's just the beginning. Maybe it will straighten out," Paige offered.

A knock was followed by the blustery entrance of the dean. "Ryan, why am I always the last to hear the good news around this place?" A broad smile spread across his face. "I hear your quad has return of both sensory and motor function."

"Who told you that?"

"I got it from one of the nurses in the research unit. At least *she* was willing to give me some form of an update, which is more than I've gotten from you." He winked at Ryan. "Why have you been holding out on me? It's time to celebrate."

"It's too early to celebrate. I still have major concerns about our procedure," Ryan responded. "And you aren't the *last* to know. I haven't told this information to anyone."

The dean pulled a sheet of paper from his coat pocket. "I had my secretary draw up a preliminary press release." He held it toward the surgeon.

Ryan nearly snatched it from his hand. "What?" He stared at the page for a moment. "It's too early. We can't say these things."

"It's all true, Ryan. Every word."

Elizabeth began to read over Ryan's shoulder. "Spinal cord surgery reverses paralysis. Dr. E. Ryan Hannah, chairman of the neurosurgical department of Brighton University, has restored motor and sensory function to a complete quadriplegic using an experimental new surgical procedure . . ."

"It may be true," Ryan argued, "but it's premature to give the disabled public any false hopes." He shook his head. "Alan, it's too early to tell whether we have done any long-term good. It's wrong to release the information until we have a few more weeks to see the outcome."

"Wrong?" The dean's face reddened. "What's wrong is not sharing your success!"

"I will report this entire experiment, but using the proper channels, with the news first going out to the neuroscience community where the research can be critiqued and verified. I simply will not tolerate a wide release to the public yet. We may be giving misinformation."

"But your nurses tell me things are going great. He's getting more and more sensation and movement back each hour."

"We need to examine the data closely, Alan. Right now it appears that although we do see a small return of nerve function, the signals may be getting crossed somehow. When we give a deep pressure stimulation in Nathan's foot, his brain is receiving a temperature message."

"You sutured the wrong nerves together?" The dean asked.

"This surgery was done with the assistance of a nerve growth factor that we hoped would stimulate the regrowth of connections with our nerve grafts. We did not actually sew individual nerve cells together. That would be impossible. We were counting on the nerves to find the proper channels on their own."

The dean's jaw sagged. "On their own?"

"Just as they do in the formation stage in the embryo. We hypothesized that by recreating the environment present in the formation stage of the spinal cord with the NTTF, the same incredible process could happen again." Ryan didn't smile. "It was all in the research proposal that you reviewed."

The dean grunted. "Well, maybe it would be prudent to wait a few more days."

Ryan crumpled the sheet in his hand. "What we are seeing is nothing short of miraculous, but we are still a long way from understanding what governs the process. Give us a few more weeks. Then maybe we'll know how it's going to pan out."

The dean shook his head. "A week. I'll give you a week." He turned on his heels and barged out.

Ryan shook his head. "Trish!"

When his assistant appeared in the doorway, he continued, "Take a memo to every nurse in the research unit. Remind them that every aspect of Nathan McAllister's care is confidential and to be discussed with no one outside the unit—and that includes Dr. Alan Pritchard."

◆ ◆ ◆

The nurse held the phone up to the side of Nathan's face as he talked. "Uh, hi, Abby. I guess you're not home yet. I just wanted to call and ask if you could bring something with you the next time you visit. It's a copy of the paper that the Brighton police officer gave me when I was at Briarfield Manor. It has the words 'hurt me' written at the top, and my name and Jonas Yoder's name at the bottom. In all this excitement over the surgery, I keep forgetting to ask Dr. Hannah about the meaning of this paper they found in his lab. Could you get it from my desk? I think it's in a stack of papers beside my computer . . . Uh . . . thanks. Bye."

He looked at the nurse. "I hate answering machines."

She pulled the phone away from his ear. "Me too. I usually hang up."

She looked at her watch. "I'll go check on dinner. It should be coming up soon. Are you hungry?"

"A little. I don't work up much of an appetite just lying here."

"You need to eat so you can heal these surgical wounds." He watched her go. Just as she disappeared through the doorway, a tall man in a gray suit entered and immediately held up a police badge.

"Mr. McAllister?" The man tipped his head forward. "I'm Detective John Feldman, with the State Police. We've been investigating an officer in the Fisher's Retreat P.D.," he reported soberly. "Someone has been giving insider information to facilitate drug traffic in the Apple Valley." He pushed a chair up to the side of Nathan's bed. "I think it's time we had a little chat."

Nathan felt his mouth go dry. He tossed his head back. "Sure."

"The time looks right for our suspect to come into the open," he began. "And we need your cooperation . . ."

◆ ◆ ◆

"Well, I earned my salary today," Brian chuckled as he threw his clipboard on the counter in front of Joe Gibson. "I wrote fourteen citations in one morning, all from the speed trap out on Route 752."

Joe smiled. "Makin' friends, are you?"

"Just doin' my job, chief. And doing it by the book." He poured himself a cup of black coffee. "Where's Marge?"

"Left for home just after noon. Said her gallbladder was acting up or something." He yawned. "Boy, I hope she doesn't need surgery. What would we do around here without her?"

"Really," Brian muttered. He tapped his fingers on the counter. "Say, Joe, ever heard anything about narcoanalysis?"

"Narco what?"

"Narcoanalysis," Brian responded. "You know, truth serum and all that. I read about it in a detective journal. The doctors give this medication, sodium amitol or something, and it helps them unlock repressed memories—traumatic stuff. Some folks are using it to help witnesses remember violent crimes." He laughed. "Weird stuff, huh?"

Joe grunted. "Huh?"

"The thing is," Brian continued, "they give a similar medication to surgery patients as they're putting them to sleep, and some folks are waking up after surgery talking about all sorts of things they'd stuffed away in their subconscious."

"Hmm." Joe continued sorting through a stack of papers.

"It just started me thinking about Nate . . . With his new surgery and all, I wonder what he'll remember about his shooting when they put him out."

Joe's eyes widened. "What are you talking about? What surgery? Nate had surgery?"

"Yep. Marty told me all about it. Some experimental deal. He's been over in Brighton at the University since last week. It's been some big secret, I guess, but from what Marty tells me, he's probably going to be walking again soon, so everyone's going to know."

"No kidding? Why didn't they say something?"

"Like I said, it's some secret experiment. Pretty funky stuff if you ask me. I wouldn't let 'em experiment on me, I can tell you that." He paused. "Anyway, Marty gave me all the nitty-gritty details. She said the docs left the bullet in his neck but tried to hook his spinal cord back together with some sort of bridge or something."

"Have you talked to him?"

"Not yet. But I'm not sure he'd want to see me. Recalling memories of being shot can't be a pleasant experience . . . and since I . . . well, since I was involved I don't think he'd be anxious to talk to me right now."

"You believe that stuff? About the unlocked memories, I mean?"

Brian shrugged. "Hey, all I know is that the article I read made it sound like it's happening to surgery patients all the time." He nodded confidently. "Ever heard of post-op depression? They think it comes from unlocking all sorts of painful memories."

Joe pushed the paper stack aside and picked up his hat. "Nate's over at the University hospital?"

"Yep. He's in some special research unit on the fifth floor." He held up his hand. "But, hey, you didn't hear it from me."

◆ ◆ ◆

As Abby drove into Fisher's Retreat, she spotted Marty walking out of the Post Office. Abby pulled the car over and smiled. "Marty!"

"I thought you were in Brighton."

"I *was* in Brighton," she said with a grimace. "But Nathan and I had a heavy conversation, and I needed to get away and think."

Marty smirked. "Oh." She leaned into the car. "Where's Melissa?"

"She's staying with Nathan's parents tonight. Sally offered to keep her so I could go back over to the hospital."

"You could have asked me."

"You were working when I left. Besides, Nate wasn't any too happy about the last time I left her with you."

Marty frowned. "What did I do?"

"It's not what you did. It's who you let spend time with Melissa."

"Brian? Hey, he offered. And he's great with her. What can it hurt to let him befriend her?" she added with a smirk. "Abby, if you'd just open your eyes, you'd see that he's not such a bad guy. And he could still be a support if you'd let him."

"It won't work." Abby shook her head emphatically. "I don't think being friendly with him is such a good idea right now. He's—well, he scares me."

"Scares you?" Marty smiled. "You're afraid of your own feelings about him, aren't you?"

"No!" Abby felt her cheeks flush.

"Yes, you are! Look at how red you get just talking about him. He still has power over you, and you know it."

"No. No, he doesn't."

"Abby, no one would blame you for—"

"No! He's, he's—"

"He still wants you, Abby. You should see the way he looks at you. I've watched his eyes light up when you—"

"Stop, Marty! I don't think you understand." She lowered her voice as a customer entered the Post Office. "He's obsessed with me. I think he's unpredictable and dangerous."

"Dangerous? Come on, Abs. You're paranoid. He's always been a perfect gentleman."

"He shot my husband. I think that's evidence enough that he's dangerous."

Marty pulled her head back from the open car window. "Just what are you saying, Abby?" She put her hands on her hips. "That was an accident."

Abby felt sick. She'd already said too much, but she didn't want to leave things hanging either. "That's what everyone says, isn't it?" She tapped her fingers on the steering wheel. "But doesn't it seem a bit too neat? Brian's in love with me. Nate's my husband. Brian shoots the only one standing in his way."

Marty's mouth fell open. "What?" she scoffed. "I can't believe you're saying this. Brian isn't like that at all."

"He's obsessed. He won't give up."

"He may be interested in you, but he's not a criminal."

"He's been watching our house . . . at night. Something isn't right." She lowered her voice to a whisper. "Marty, I'm serious—he terrifies me."

"You're taking him wrong. He won't cross a line once you've drawn it. Maybe you're sending him mixed signals."

"I am not."

"You're blushing again."

"That's because you're making me mad."

Her friend sighed and leaned forward against the car. "Look, if it makes you feel any better, I've been trying my best to interest him in *me.* But it seems that he can't stop asking about *you,* about Melissa, even about Nate. But he doesn't come across as angry. I think he's one of the few people around who actually cares about someone other than himself."

"Look who needs to open her eyes. You can't seem to see past his smooth exterior."

"And you can't seem to get beyond your own guilt feelings about your relationship."

Abby looked down. Marty's words stung. Stung with bitterness and with truth. "You may be right, Marty. I feel bad about what I did. But you don't know all the facts about Brian either. He's certainly capable of deception," she added slowly. "I played that game myself."

"Abby, he's not malicious. He's interested in you—he doesn't hide that. But he's also Nate's friend. At least, he *was.* I doubt that Nate would consider him a friend now." She coughed. "Now that you've told Nate all about Brian, that is."

"Nathan is forgiving. At least he says he's forgiven me. But I don't know if he can forgive Brian."

Marty nodded and looked at her watch. "How is Nate?"

"It's so exciting. He's getting back a little more feeling every day. Today he was able to wiggle his index finger."

"Hmm. That's great."

"It's going to take some time, I guess. The surgeons don't seem to say much, but I could tell they're excited too."

"Who wouldn't be? Even Brian was fascinated when he heard about Nathan's surgery. He asked me all sorts of questions. About the bullet—"

"You told him?"

"Well," Marty coughed, "uh, yeah."

"It was a secret, Marty! You promised not to tell. We made a sister pact!"

"Come on, Abby. The way you talk, everyone is going to know soon anyway. He was just asking questions. It *is* interesting stuff, you know."

The realization penetrated Abby like a knife. *Brian knows about the bullet!* Her hand went to her mouth. She'd gotten home so late last night that she hadn't talked to Joe like Nathan had asked. She had promised Nathan that she'd tell Joe so he could collect the bullet for official evidence. But if Brian already knew about the surgery, he might go after the bullet! Her mind raced.

"Abby, what's wrong?"

She focused on Marty's face. "Huh? Brian asked about the bullet? You told him that the bullet was removed?"

Marty shrugged. "He asked me, so I told him. He thought it was cool, I guess."

Abby slammed her hand against the lever on the steering column, shifting the old car into drive. With a sickening feeling in her gut, she looked back at Marty. "I've got to get home."

"You're white as a sheet. Do you feel OK?"

"I'll be all right," she said with a confidence she didn't feel. "I just need to get home."

She pulled away, not thinking to look back or wave. She had one thing in mind: she needed to talk to Joe Gibson, and right away!

In minutes she lurched to a halt in her driveway and ran into the house to the phone. Seeing that the time was after 5 P.M., she decided to call Joe at home. He wouldn't be at the office at this hour. She held the receiver to her ear and listened. One ring. Two. Three. *Come on, Joe. Be home!*

"Hello. Gibsons'." The voice was June's.

"June, it's Abby. I need to talk to Joe."

"Oh, Abby, he left half an hour ago for Buck's Creek. He was in a funk too. Something was bothering him, I could tell. But of course he denied it. You know these officers . . . they never show that anything bothers 'em," she prattled on.

"Uh, yeah, I know the type. Could you tell—"

"I tried to get him to tell me what was bothering him, but *no*, he would just say, 'Nothing,' just like always. Suddenly he jumps up and says he's going fishing . . . wants to think . . . and out the door he goes."

Abby frowned and listened to June complain.

"That man hasn't gone fishin' in months and now all of a sudden—"

"June," Abby interrupted, "I *really* need to talk to him. It's real important. Can you have him call me as soon as he gets in?"

"Abby? Is everything OK? You sound worried."

Abby sighed. "I'm not sure if everything's OK. I just need to talk to Joe."

"I could give you his cell-phone number."

"Actually, I think I have it. He gave it to me already."

"Hmmm."

"When do you expect him?"

"He shouldn't be too long. It's gonna be dark soon."

"Well, I guess I can wait a little while. Just have him call me as soon as he arrives. Uh, better yet, just have him come over. I have to talk to him tonight."

"If it's a police matter, I could get Brian or one of the others to call."

"No!" She put her hand to her mouth. "Uh, I mean, no thanks. I'll wait for Joe. OK?"

"OK, Abby. Calm down. I'll tell him." She paused. "Are you sure there's nothing I can do?"

"I'm sure."

Abby hung the phone up and pressed the Replay button on the answering machine. Nathan's voice was barely audible. *Someone must be holding the phone up to his mouth.*

"Uh, hi, Abby. I guess you're not home yet. I just wanted to call and ask if you could bring something with you the next time you visit. It's a copy of the paper that the Brighton police officer gave me when I was at Briarfield Manor. It has the words 'hurt me' written at the top, and my name and Jonas Yoder's name at the bottom. In all this excitement over the surgery, I keep forgetting to ask Dr. Hannah about the meaning of this paper they found in his lab. Could you get it from my desk? I think it's in a stack of papers beside my computer . . . Uh . . . thanks. Bye."

She stared at the phone. *Nathan, I forgot to talk to Joe about the bullet. I've let you down . . . again.* She fought a feeling of rising panic. *What if I'm too late and Brian has already taken the bullet?* She spoke to herself in a soft, methodical tone. "Be reasonable. You don't know for sure that Brian tried to kill Nathan. There is no reason to panic. Just wait for Joe to call, and he'll take care of the evidence. Brian may not be interested in the bullet at all."

She walked to Nathan's room as she whispered a prayer. "God, help me."

She rifled through a stack of magazines and papers on the desk. One by one she placed aside the literature her husband had collected—reports from the Miami Project to Cure Paralysis, speeches by Christopher Reeves and Joni Eareckson Tada, and other information about disabilities that Nathan had downloaded from the Internet. Finally she found the paper he wanted, a photocopy of the strange message left in Dr. Hannah's lab.

She looked at the uneven print. She mouthed the words as she read, "HuRT ME." At the bottom of the page, in small cursive script, were the names Nathan McAllister and Jonas Yoder. *Why were they linked on this paper?* she wondered, feeling an uneasy foreboding. *Could the same person be responsible for both tragedies?*

Her fingers trembled as she carried the paper back to the kitchen, where she placed it on the table so she'd remember to take it to Nathan.

She unlocked the automatic door and walked onto the back patio, studying the dark, cloudy sky. *It looks like rain. Maybe Joe will come by sooner if it starts to rain*, she hoped.

Abby walked back into the house, noticing how quiet things were without Melissa. It was the first time she'd been completely alone at night since Nathan's accident. The small house felt somehow larger and eerie without anyone else around. A shiver prompted her to pick up the phone again.

Maybe I can find out about the bullet myself. She called Information for the number of Brighton University Hospital. Then she called the hospital operator and asked for Pathology. After eight rings she heard a young, male voice.

"Surgical pathology."

Abby explained who she was and what she wanted and shared her concern that the bullet remain safely in the hands of proper police authorities.

"Ma'am, I'm afraid you'll have to call back when our secretaries are here. I'm a pathology resident, and I just happened to hear the phone."

"Please," she begged.

"Look, I really shouldn't give out information to anyone except the patient. I—"

"Sir, all I'm asking is that you tell me whether the bullet removed from my husband is still in your lab! That's all. I'm not asking for confidential information."

A sigh came over the phone. "Hold on. I guess I can check the logbook."

Abby waited. Waited and paced around the quiet kitchen.

Finally the voice returned. "Ms. McAllister? You can rest easy. That bullet was logged in on the day of your husband's surgery and was released the next morning to the police. I've got the logbook right here. It was signed for by an officer in the Fisher's Retreat Police Department . . . Brian Turner."

The words struck her like a knife.

"Ma'am? Ms. McAllister?"

Abby looked at the phone in disbelief. She was too late!

"Ma'am? Ma'am?"

She heard a huff followed by a click. The resident had hung up.

She dropped the phone onto the counter, her mind trying to make some sense of this new information. She remembered her conversation with Nathan and what he'd said about Brian and the bullet: "*If it wasn't accidental, he'd definitely go after it. He knows enough about police investigation to try and disturb the chain of evidence . . .*"

Does this prove the shooting wasn't an accident?

Abby tried to calm her escalating anxieties. She walked to the front window. Still no Joe Gibson. *Maybe I should call Nathan?* She shook her head. *No. What could he do?*

Just wait for Joe. He'll know what to do.

She walked up the creaky stairs and into her bedroom and stood in front of the mirror. She pulled her hair back from her glistening forehead. *A hot shower will help calm me down.*

She undressed and stepped into the shower, trying to turn her attention to something other than her ruminations about Brian Turner. She thought of Nathan and his recovery and their excitement over the little movement of his index finger and toe. She put her face into the full stream of the water and began to hum, hoping to wash away her stress. She wanted to think of anything except her fear of Brian.

As she shut off the water, she heard a pounding at the front door. *Joe.* She quickly toweled off and grabbed her robe. She gathered it tightly around her and headed down the stairs, relieved to see a familiar Fisher's Retreat patrol car in the driveway through the window. The knocking resumed as she opened the door. "Joe, I—" She gasped as she looked up to see Brian.

His face was sober. "Abby, we need to talk."

She froze for a second before slamming the door. She fumbled with the old chain lock and leaned forward against the doorframe.

"Abby!" He was speaking more loudly now. "I know you can hear me. We need to talk. Please open the door."

"No." Her chin quivered. "No," she said with more authority. "Go away."

"Open the door, Abby. *Please!*"

She could feel her heart in her chest. Slowly she turned the knob and pulled the door open against the chain restraint. She saw the intensity in his eyes. "Go away. It's over, Brian. I don't want to see you again."

"Open the door. We need to talk. There are some things you need to know."

"No."

He put his hand in the opening, reaching his fingers around the door. Abby stepped back.

"Leave me alone." She clutched her robe under her chin and pushed against the door. It didn't budge. She looked through the crack to see his foot braced against the bottom ledge.

"It's time you heard the truth about Nathan's shooting."

She lifted her head to meet his eyes. "I know the truth, Brian."

"It's not what—"

"You need to leave. Now! I've called Joe Gibson. He's on his way over, Brian. And I know about the bullet. I know you took it."

"Abby, it's not what you think!"

"You tried to kill him, didn't you?" She stepped back from the door and then ran forward, bracing her shoulder for the impact. "Get out!"

The door gave way as Brian's fingers disappeared from the opening. "Abby," he shouted. "You need to listen to me! I didn't shoot Nate!"

She twisted the lock on the doorknob.

"That's what I came to tell you."

"You're twisting the evidence!" she yelled to the closed door. "Joe is on his way. Go away." She stumbled from the door toward the kitchen, grabbing the cordless phone and rubbing her shoulder. Then she retreated up the stairs in search of the number of Joe's cell-phone. She found it in her purse and began to dial.

◆ ◆ ◆

June Gibson frowned into the phone. "She sounded awful, Joe. I've never heard Abby so upset. She really wants to talk to you."

Joe muttered a curse.

June pulled the phone back from her ear in surprise. "Joe? What's going on?" She could hear his heavy breathing. "Joe?"

"Nothing's goin' on, June. Nothing, OK? I'll go talk to her." He paused. "I'm sure I won't be home until late."

◆ ◆ ◆

The busy signal made Abby want to scream.

From downstairs she could hear a persistent pounding on the door. Brian's voice was muted but clear. "Abby," he called, "I'm not leaving until you talk to me."

In desperation she opened the closet door and pulled out Nathan's .45 caliber pistol. With trembling hands she loaded the weapon, dropping a bullet onto the floor in her haste. From outside she could hear Brian's voice. It sounded as if he'd made his way around the house and was now standing just below her bedroom window.

"I know you can hear me. Let me in."

Just moments later she heard the automatic door open.

"Abby?" His voice was louder and clearer this time.

She retreated into the closet with the phone and the handgun and quietly closed the door. She lifted the phone and punched 911.

"911 emergency. How may I help you?" The voice was female and strong.

"I'm at 4 Westview Lane. There is a prowler in my house," Abby said in a soft voice.

◆ ◆ ◆

A few moments later Brian Turner's radio crackled. "Fisher's Retreat unit 1. This is dispatch."

He grabbed the radio from the holster on his belt. "Dispatch, this is unit 1."

"I have a 911 caller on the line. She's at 4 Westview Lane and reports a prowler on site. She's hiding in an upstairs bedroom closet."

"I'm on it, dispatch. I'm already on the scene. You can tell your caller to hang up now."

◆ ◆ ◆

A helpless dread settled in Abby's stomach as she heard Brian's radio communication. "No, no," she spoke. "My prowler *is* a police officer!"

The 911 operator continued, "An officer is on site. Try and calm down. Your situation is under control."

Abby threw the phone down in frustration and pushed her back against the wall, hoping to hide herself between the clothing hanging there.

She could hear Brian's footsteps approaching.

"Abby, you have to listen," he called, his voice coming from outside the upstairs bedroom. "I didn't shoot Nate." His footsteps came closer—in the hall, then in the bedroom.

She raised the gun and pointed it at the sliding closet door.

"Abby? We need to talk."

When she saw the door begin to move, she closed her eyes and squeezed the trigger.

CHAPTER
46

FIFTEEN MINUTES LATER, Joe Gibson pulled into the McAllister driveway. Abby's car and Nathan's van sat undisturbed, and the house was
quiet. He knocked on the front door and rang the bell.

"Abby?" He waited. "Abby, it's me, Chief Gibson."

No response. He huffed and walked around the side. A light shone
from a second-floor room. *This is odd.*

He returned to the front and pounded on the door again. He tried
the door, but it was locked. He called out again. "Abby?"

He shook his head and walked across the driveway and around to
the back patio. From there he could see a light in the kitchen, but no
movement inside. As he approached the back glass door, it slid open
automatically. The sudden movement startled him momentarily.
"Abby?" he called more loudly. He stepped into the empty room and
around the table into the den. "Abby?"

With his instinct telling him things weren't right, he reached for
his gun.

"Abby?"

Slowly he ascended the stairs. He followed the light to the bedroom, pushing open the unlatched door with his foot. "Abby, are you
here? I want to help you."

The room was in disarray. He leaned over and picked up a bullet
from the floor before seeing the damage to the wooden closet door.
What's going on?

He made a quick search of the bedroom and bathroom and then through the rest of the house.

Once downstairs, he passed the kitchen table again, this time stopping to examine a solitary piece of paper lying there. He picked it up and read it. "Hurt me," he whispered. His hand began to shake as he read what appeared to be two signatures at the bottom of the page—Nathan McAllister Jonas Yoder.

He looked around the room, his mind racing and his jaw hanging open. He looked back at the paper. *Is this someone's idea of a cruel joke? Or a bad omen? This can't be! Nathan must have remembered!*

He folded the paper hastily and shoved it into his pocket. He returned his gun to its holster and fled the house through the automatic back door.

◆ ◆ ◆

That night Nathan was troubled with increasing burning discomfort in the soles of his feet and the palms of his hands. It made it hard for him to concentrate and next to impossible to sleep. He wanted relief but didn't want his senses to be dulled by medication. It was too important that he stay alert and vigilant.

Just before 11, he looked up to see a familiar form in the doorway. The figure moved forward silently, squinting toward Nathan in the semidarkness.

"Hi, Joe." Nathan would not smile to greet him this time.

"Nate." Joe tipped his head forward.

"How'd you get in here at this hour?"

"Wear a uniform, and you can go anywhere, Nate. You know that." Joe shifted his weight from foot to foot and kept his eyes rotating from Nate to the door. "I just heard about your surgery today. I thought I should come."

Nathan nodded silently.

Joe cleared his throat. "H-have you remembered anything?"

"What are you referring to?"

"Your accident. Brian told me that anesthesia often helps bring out lost memories."

"Are you worried, Joe?"

Joe stayed silent and looked at the door.

"I know all about it, Joe."

The chief's eyes snapped back to Nathan's.

"*You* shot me that day, didn't you?"

Joe began to shake his head with a quick, almost tremor-like movement. "No, Nate. You're wrong. I didn't shoot you."

"It *was* you. The game's up, Joe."

"No," he responded, lifting a syringe from his pocket. "It wasn't me. Lester Fitts grabbed at the gun. I never intended on hurting you, Nate."

Nathan shook his head and spoke by forcing air around his tracheostomy tube, his words barely above a whisper. "You gonna blame Lester for killing Jonas Yoder too?"

Joe's voice began to choke. "I . . . it *was* Lester. I swear. I never told him to kill Jonas, only to make sure he didn't spoil things." He hung his head, staring at the syringe in his hand. "Jonas knew too much. He was starting to talk. He even talked to you."

Joe began to search through the tangle of IV tubing above the bed as Nathan watched. "Are you going to kill me too, Joe? Kill me because I know too much about what you're really up to?" He paused. "When I didn't know, I was safe, huh, Joe?"

"I'm not killing you, Nate. Lester Fitts did that months ago." He fumbled with an IV line, tracing it down to Nathan's right arm. He lifted the syringe of clear liquid and pointed the needle toward an access port leading into the IV. "Look at you, Nate," he seethed. "Your life is worthless now. The way I see it, Lester killed you . . . I'm just putting you out of your misery. I never dreamed it would end this way. Believe me, Nate, I wouldn't have chosen this."

As Joe steadied his hand to plunge the needle into the IV port, Nathan closed his eyes and concentrated. Slowly, and with searing pain, he pulled his hand away.

He watched Joe's eyes widen. "Don't do it, Joe. I'm not the only one who knows."

Joe twitched and looked toward the door.

Nathan continued, "They took the bullet out, Joe. The state police know that you shot me."

"You're lying," he retorted. "Brian told me they didn't remove the bullet." He shoved the needle into the IV port.

"But they have. The bullet's been tested," a tall man in a gray suit said from the doorway. "The bullet removed from Nathan's spinal cord matches others collected from the firing range that came from your gun." He started to present his I.D. badge as three other men joined him.

Joe started for his gun but halted when he saw three weapons trained on his chest.

"Freeze!"

Joe lifted his hands in the air.

"Take this out of my IV," Nathan pleaded.

Detective John Feldman put on a rubber glove and carefully pulled the full syringe from the IV tubing port. He carefully dropped it into an evidence bag as the other state troopers cuffed Joe Gibson and led him away.

"I thought you guys were never coming in," Nathan gasped.

"Didn't mean to scare you, Nathan. We were just outside the doorway all along. And you did great," the detective added.

"Hey, I just said what you told me to."

Nathan listened to the voice in the hallway as Joe Gibson was read his rights.

Detective Feldman smiled. "This almost assures us that we'll get him on an attempted murder charge as well as on the drug charges."

Nathan shook his head. "I never would have believed it."

"Believe it," Feldman responded. "We've been investigating the Fisher's Retreat P.D. for a long time."

Just then Abby appeared in the doorway. Behind her, Brian Turner stood in the hall, seemingly reluctant to enter.

Feldman excused himself as Abby rushed to Nathan's side.

"Abby!"

"Nathan, are you OK?"

He nodded and tried to ignore the worsening pain in his feet. "I didn't expect to see you again today."

"I had to come. Once I heard what was happening, I had to come back."

Nathan craned his neck to look around Abby. "Tell Brian to come in."

Abby turned and motioned. Brian entered solemnly, with his eyes on the floor. He lifted them for a moment. "Hey, Nate."

"You've got some explaining to do, pal," Nathan said softly.

"Nathan, not now," Abby said, grasping Nathan's arm.

"I'm not talking about you, Abby. I'm talking about this police investigation. How long have you been in on this?"

Brian coughed. "A few months. I'm the one who initiated it, Nate. A few weeks before your shooting."

"You?" Nathan frowned. "Why didn't you tell me?"

Brian looked down. "I wasn't sure that you weren't involved. I knew our numbers against the drug traffic looked horrible. I knew someone was helping the other side, but I wasn't sure who. And then when you showed up unarmed in the Allen house, I really had my doubts about you for a while."

"Thanks a lot."

"I'm sorry, Nate."

"How long have you known the truth about the shooting? That you didn't shoot me?"

"A few weeks. All along I had my doubts. I must have gone over the shooting in my mind a thousand times. I can hear the shots I fired as plain now as the day it happened. One shot, two, then a third. I *knew* I'd only fired three shots. Two showed up in Lester Fitts's autopsy report, and another on the wall of the Allen house behind where you were shot. For the longest time I thought that the bullet we extracted from the Allen house was one that went through you." He paused. "Then when Jennifer Hicks came forward with her story, I—"

"Wait a minute! Jennifer Hicks? What story?" Nathan squinted.

"Jennifer Hicks was in the upstairs room at the Allen house the day you were shot. She and Dion had been partying when the fight broke out downstairs. She heard the whole thing."

"What . . . what happened to me?"

"The way she tells it, you must have followed her back from Jonas Yoder's funeral, suspecting some action at the Allen house, based on a tip Jonas had given you before he died. You followed her in but didn't expect to find Joe Gibson and Lester in some sort of financial transaction. She heard you accuse him of killing Jonas Yoder, followed by a lot of yelling. She says she heard Lester screaming, 'Shoot him, shoot him!' before you cried out, 'Ten thirty-three.'"

"My radio code for Mayday," Nathan reflected.

"That's when she heard a shot. Presumably from Joe Gibson's gun."

"Man." Nathan shook his head. "Man oh man."

Abby joined in. "Jennifer Hicks is the one who called you, Nate."

"That's right," Brian continued. "She's been trying to get her life together, off of drugs. But when she saw you on local TV just before you returned, she was confused by your testimony that you believed your shooting was an accident. For the first time she realized that her testimony about the shooting might be important, but she was reluctant to come forward because she was upstairs doing drugs. She was afraid of getting arrested again."

"Why didn't you tell me? If you knew you hadn't shot me, why didn't you let me know?"

"At first when Jennifer came forward, I wasn't sure if I could believe her. She had talked to you but then realized that you really had no memory of the event, and that seemed to frustrate her. She wasn't sure if you were covering for Joe, or if perhaps you might even be part of the drug problem."

Nathan didn't understand. "But when I saw her over at Ashby High, she wouldn't talk to me. She even told Dion not to talk to me."

"That's because at that point she'd come to me and told me about the phone calls, and I instructed her not to talk to you anymore."

"Why, Brian? Why keep me in the dark?"

"Because I realized that your ignorance was your greatest protection. As long as you didn't know anything, you weren't a threat to anyone. The State Police were collecting more data all the time, and then you returned to town and started asking questions. I was afraid your snooping would turn up information that would make you vulnerable. And I didn't really think you could adequately defend yourself."

"Hmmm. What made you believe Jennifer's story?"

"When I came to your house that day and saw your X-ray. Finding out that the bullet was still in you convinced me I really hadn't shot you. Until then I still wasn't sure. I thought the bullet recovered from the Allen house was one that had gone through you."

"What about the police report? Wouldn't that confirm how many shots you'd fired?"

Brian nodded. "But Joe's report said *four* shots had been fired from my gun. I *knew* he'd altered the report, but I couldn't prove it. Not until I had the bullet. Your operation provided the evidence we needed to spring a trap for Joe Gibson."

"What about Jonas Yoder?"

Brian held up his hands. "He was a good kid, from what Jennifer told me. He was always trying to tell the Ashby kids about his religion."

"Why would they let him into their group?"

"They didn't, really. But they used him to get needles. That's all Jennifer kept telling me. He begged the others not to mess with drugs, but he was also so freaked out about losing his father to AIDS that he started his own little needle exchange program. He gave them new needles so they wouldn't have to share."

"So he got in too close with the druggies and found out about Joe Gibson?" Nathan shook his head. "You did his death scene investigation. Weren't you concerned about foul play?"

"I had the same suspicions about his investigations that you did. But at that point I just turned the evidence over to the state police investigators and acted as if I was in agreement with Joe's workup."

"And when I started asking questions about it . . ."

"I convinced Rachel Yoder that giving you information might endanger your life."

"That explains why she refused to cooperate after finally opening up and showing me her son's room. But why not just tell me the truth and get me out of town? It doesn't seem right that you kept me in the dark."

"I knew you wouldn't be in the dark forever, Nate. I was afraid that if you left town, Joe would be alerted to the fact that you knew something. I didn't want to risk Joe running out on us, when we were getting so close to nailing him." He dropped his eyes to the floor again. "I knew Abby wanted me to stay away . . . from her and from you. I thought it was just best if the state police did their investigation with as few people knowing what had really happened as possible. Besides," he added, "I've had your house under almost constant surveillance. If I thought you'd have been safer in the know, I'd have told you myself."

Nathan grimaced as Abby squeezed his arm.

"What's wrong?"

"That hurts. It feels like knives running across my skin when you do that."

Alarm spread across her face. "I barely touched you."

"I know." He pinched his eyes shut as another pain message reached his brain. "I think my nerves are really waking up."

"I'll get your nurse." Abby walked from the room.

Nathan watched as Brian stepped back from the bed. For the first time he noticed a white bandage on Brian's hand. "You injured?"

Brian rubbed his hand. "This? Oh, that's another story altogether." He chuckled. "Abby tried to shoot me when I went to tell her about Joe Gibson."

"What?" Just as Nathan spoke, his legs began a violent contraction, not unlike the muscle spasms he'd had in the past, but this time accompanied by a generalized burning pain. "Ahhh!"

Brian's eyes widened as he retreated from the room. "Nurse!"

In a moment Abby returned with two nurses in tow.

"Mr. McAllister?" the older nurse began. "How would you rate this pain on a scale of 1 to 10?"

"Nine. Eight or 9," Nathan grunted.

"Can't you give him something?" Abby asked.

The younger nurse responded, "Dr. Hannah has ordered morphine to be given as needed. I'll go get it."

Nathan's voice was barely above a whisper. "Maybe you should call him. It seems to be getting worse."

◆ ◆ ◆

That night Abby declined Brian's offer for a return trip to Fisher's Retreat, opting for a cab ride to the Brighton Inn, a motel down the street from the hospital. She wanted to be close to Nathan in case there were any more changes.

Before she slept, she prayed . . . for Nathan, for strength to endure the healing process, for wisdom for his physicians. She prayed for herself too, for understanding and guidance.

She thought about Brian, how she had misjudged him, and how all along he was actually protecting them though she'd thought he was stalking her.

And for a moment she found herself entertaining a desire to be in his arms again. She thought about what Marty had said that very day, about his obvious attraction to her.

"You're afraid of your own feelings about him, aren't you?"

"You should see the way he looks at you."

"He still has power over you, and you know it."

"No." Abby spoke the word out loud, as if to convince herself. She closed her eyes again. "I've made too many wrong choices before, Lord. Help me make the right one this time."

CHAPTER
47

WHEN ABBY returned to Nathan's room the following morning, she found Dr. Hannah and his resident, Dr. Hopkins, hovering over Nathan, talking in hushed tones and looking with concern at his monitors. "Is anything wrong?"

Dr. Hannah extended his hand. "Good morning, Ms. McAllister," he said with a compassionate nod. "We've had a minor setback."

"Setback?"

Nathan looked up. His words were thick and slow. "More spasms, Abby. Painful ones. It's like my body's on fire."

Dr. Hannah explained, "We've had to sedate him quite heavily. We hope it's a temporary problem."

Abby watched as Nathan closed his eyes and began regular breathing.

Elizabeth motioned Abby into the hallway. "This is the first rest he's gotten all night," she whispered.

Just then John Feldman walked up. He gripped Abby's hand firmly. "Morning, Ms. McAllister." He peeked into Nathan's room. "Is this a bad time to talk? I have a few more questions for your husband."

Abby shook her head. "He's been in a lot of pain. He's sleeping now. Could you come back later?"

The detective shuffled his feet. "Uh, sure."

"Maybe I can help you with something?" Abby offered.

He shrugged. "Maybe you can." He pulled a wrinkled sheet of paper from his coat pocket. We found this in Officer Joe Gibson's pocket last night. He said it belonged to Nathan."

Abby took the paper. "It's ours all right. Don't ask me what it means though. I have no idea."

Elizabeth smiled. "I can tell you about it, although I have no idea how Nathan got it. It's a photocopy of a message left in our spinal cord research lab after a break-in by an animal rights group. They call themselves HuRT, which is short for Humans for Responsible Treatment of Animals. They broke into our lab and stole a valuable lab animal. The jerk responsible must have wanted to claim responsibility for the act by leaving us this subtle message—'HuRT ME.'"

"But what about the names at the bottom? Why is Nathan's name there with Jonas Yoder's?" Abby pointed to the paper.

"That's my handwriting. I was collecting names of possible candidates for our research project. I retrieved these names from our state spinal cord injury database. I started with the most recent injuries from the counties close by. These were the only two patients with cervical spinal cord injury within the last six months from the Apple Valley."

"But Jonas Yoder is dead," Abby exclaimed.

"I found that out later," Elizabeth responded. "But that's part of the trouble with the state's database. Names get entered based on information from death certificates as well as from hospital discharge summaries. The only requirement is that the patient have a spinal cord injury." She shrugged. "I had just started collecting names from the database and had copied these two names onto a paper I laid on my desk. The person who broke into the lab must have grabbed this paper in haste to scrawl the message. He must not have noticed the two names I'd written at the bottom."

The detective chuckled.

Abby didn't understand. "What's so funny?"

"It's just that seeing this just about freaked out the police chief. Can you imagine? He felt responsible for both of these people's tragedies, and to see their signatures below the words 'hurt me' was just about enough to send him over the edge. He was certain it was some divine sign or something."

Abby didn't feel like laughing. Just then, with Nathan in such agony, nothing could have seemed funny. Instead she offered a quick smile and looked back into Nathan's room, where she could see Dr. Hannah pacing.

"Have you eaten breakfast?" Elizabeth asked with visible concern.

"No." She didn't take her eyes off her husband's room.

"You'll need your strength. It may be a long day for him. Why don't you eat something while he's sleeping? There's a cafeteria on the main floor."

Abby excused herself and left the research unit, but not before glancing back one more time at her husband's sleeping form.

◆ ◆ ◆

When Abby returned after breakfast, Dr. Hannah greeted her at the doorway and ushered her to Nathan's bedside. Immediately she recognized the rhythmic sound of the ventilator. She looked at her husband's body, now completely still except for the rise and fall of his chest as the ventilator forced air into his lungs.

"We couldn't seem to control the painful muscle spasms," he said in defeat, looking down at Nathan. "Even with the narcotics, his spasms continued relentlessly until we gave him a muscle-paralyzing agent to cease all movement."

"He's paralyzed again?"

"Only temporarily. If we stop this medication," he said, pointing to an IV bag, "his paralysis will wear off and he'll be able to breathe on his own again."

"What can be done?"

"We can only wait and see." The neurosurgery chairman seemed tired. His clothes were wrinkled, and there were dark circles beneath his eyes. "I don't think we should take away the paralyzing agent until tomorrow. We may have to leave him like this for a while, to see if the pain is a transient problem in his spinal cord regeneration."

"The pain may go away?"

"We hope so," the surgeon answered.

"Can he hear me?"

"Yes, but he's deeply sedated. It's like being asleep. He can't respond to you or even open his eyes."

Abby nodded numbly and began a bedside vigil that would eventually stretch into a full week. She left for meals and for sleep, but mostly she sat and prayed, holding Nate's hand or just staying in the room making one-sided conversation about Fisher's Retreat's drug problems or the weather or anything she thought Nathan would like to hear. Occasionally she read to herself or even to Nathan—anything to pass the time and take her mind off her anxieties surrounding Nathan's condition.

Every day Dr. Hannah withdrew the paralyzing agent to check for progress. And every day Nathan's muscle spasms and agonizing pain returned as soon as the medication was taken away. By the fourth day back on the ventilator, they were able to taper off the paralyzing agent by using other muscle relaxants to control Nathan's spasms. Joyfully they discovered that Nathan had the ability to control a few of his larger muscle groups with more regularity, but with the progress came bewildering temperature and position sensations, and also searing pain with almost any leg or arm movement at all. Through it all they kept him nearly asleep through IV narcotics, and for this reason they continued his ventilator support. For his nutrition they fed him a liquid formula, administered through a tube inserted through his nose and into his stomach.

Abby observed it all, and every hour, almost every minute, she prayed for a miracle. And slowly but surely a miracle occurred, but not the miracle for which she prayed, or at least not in the way that she would've answered her own petition. Slowly but surely her heart began to turn.

Hour by hour, as she watched her husband, she was touched by a longing in her soul again.

◆ ◆ ◆

On Monday of the following week, the dreamy delirium that surrounded Nathan lifted. As he emerged, a thousand messages assaulted his brain. His right arm was rising above his head. His right leg was on fire. His left leg bounced on the bed. His toes were twitching. He opened his eyes to study what he felt. *Strange*, he thought, *I'm lying still, but my brain doesn't seem to understand.* He lifted his head and looked at his twitching toes. At least he *felt* like he was twitching his toes. He blinked his eyes. His toes were perfectly still.

He concentrated on lifting his hand but found it impossible to ignore the lancing pain that a minimal effort produced.

Just then he noticed movement to his right. Dr. Hannah was adjusting an IV rate.

"Awake, Nathan?"

He nodded.

"I'm turning down your morphine. I want you clearheaded. Let me know if you have too much pain. I'd like to be able to remove the ventilator so you can communicate with me." The surgeon looked away, not meeting Nathan's gaze. "We have some tough decisions to make."

Over the next hour Nathan's pain increased, and he continued experiencing what he could only describe as hallucinations. First he sensed he was walking, then came flooding warmth, then cold, then pinpricks throughout his chest and arms. When Dr. Hannah stroked his arm, he first felt a gentle touch, then agonizing fire.

"Tell me what you're feeling." Dr. Hannah reached forward and disconnected Nathan's trach from the ventilator tubing. "Here," he said, reaching for an empty syringe, "I'll let the cuff down on your trach tube so you can talk to me."

Nathan's voice was weak, barely above a whisper. "My body's on fire, doc. One second I think my arm's above my head, so I look, and it's still lying flat on the bed. Then I have the sensation that I'm walking, but I know it's a lie. What are you giving me to make these hallucinations?"

The surgeon shook his head. "Nothing, Nathan. You're on no medications right now." He squeezed Nathan's hand.

"Ow!"

"Painful?"

"Like a knife."

Dr. Hannah lifted Nathan's foot into the air. As his leg was moved, it felt first cold, then hot, then experienced pain and pinpricks. "Can you tell I'm moving your leg?"

"Only if I watch. It feels funny, like you're pouring cold water on my leg, then hot, then it's just general pain."

Abby appeared in the doorway. She slowly approached with concern etched on her face. "I came as soon as I heard they were going to take away your morphine." She touched Nathan's cheek. "How do you feel?"

"Crazy. My body keeps telling me things that aren't true."

Dr. Hannah frowned. "I'm afraid my first fears are being confirmed. At first I had hoped that the pain and the weird sensations were signs that the nerves responsible for the feelings were being stimulated as they made new connections in the spinal cord. I hoped that once the connections were firmly established, the weird sensations would quit."

"What's goin' on, Dr. Hannah?"

"I think the nerves in your spinal cord have made new connections, but I don't think the nerves have made the proper connections in every case. A nerve in your arm that used to carry the temperature message needs to link up within your spinal cord with the same kind of nerve or the brain will be given a false message. I'm afraid that your brain is getting a complicated mixed bag of signals. And probably many of the nerves that carry messages from the brain to your arms and legs to produce movement are also linking with the wrong nerves at the level of your spinal cord nerve grafts." He hung his head.

"But he's able to move," Abby responded with optimism. "That's encouraging, isn't it?"

Nathan pinched his eyes tightly shut as another pain message struck. "Ahh. Don't touch my hand," he pleaded with Abby. "It hurts too much."

"Every day I have come by, hoping to find an improvement. And every day I have found evidence of new cord regeneration . . . and new central mis-links that have been formed."

Nathan winced again. "I need the medicine back, Dr. Hannah."

"I know. But giving you the morphine is only a temporary solution."

Abby verbalized what Nathan feared. "What are you saying? This isn't going to get better?"

The surgeon slowly shook his head. "Every day it's getting worse.

Sure, he has some movement, but with every proper new connection comes a host of improper ones. There is no value in being able to move your thumb if your brain doesn't know where in space your thumb is and if with every movement comes another false message about temperature or pain."

"What are you saying?" Nathan whispered.

Dr. Hannah's chin quivered for a second before he looked Nathan in the eye. "I'm saying that we lost. I—I wanted to make you well, but all I've done is put your life at risk with a surgery that has ended up producing more harm than good."

"No, doc. You tried. You did your best. I wanted to do this."

Abby reached for Dr. Hannah's arm. "You haven't lost. This is just the beginning. Why, Nate is just starting to get his movement back."

"No. If we allow this to continue, I'm afraid of the consequences. We've already begun to see fairly significant fluctuations in Nathan's blood pressure. I think that's a result of dysfunction of the nerves that supply his blood vessels. They don't know when to contract or when to expand." He glanced at the cardiac monitor above the bed. "If the pain continues to worsen, we may not be able to withdraw the pain medication, and Nathan will remain on the ventilator, unable to communicate. I think we must make a very tough decision *now*."

Nathan winced. "A decision to . . ."

"To operate and remove the grafts," Dr. Hannah announced solemnly.

"Give up?" Abby bit the knuckle of her index finger.

Dr. Hannah nodded. "I'll be honest with you, Nathan. I won't do anything without your consent. But I have true and legitimate fears about letting things continue as they are. You need to know that you may be gambling with your life." He retreated a step. "And only you can tell me if your life, as it has been in recent months, is worth taking that risk. Maybe there are some things worse than death," he added before clearing his throat. "If we operate again and take down the nerve grafts, there is some risk of causing more damage to the spinal cord a bit higher up. You could end up on a portable respirator for life."

Nathan watched Abby's eyes. What did he see there? Fear? Concern?

"I'll have the nurses give some small amounts of pain medication and monitor your breathing. But if we can't control the pain any other way, we'll have to put you back on the respirator so we can maximally sedate you." He retreated another step. "Why don't you two talk while you have the chance? I want you to make a decision soon . . . if you can." He added, "I will abide by your wishes. But you are the one taking the risk, Nathan, not me." With that, he was gone, leaving Nathan alone with Abby.

He searched her eyes. "What do you want me to do?"

"I want you to live, Nate."

"You want me to walk. You've been so excited over each little success."

"I was excited. I am excited. But you heard what he said—you might even die if things continue as they are. That's too big a price, isn't it, Nate? Getting out of a wheelchair isn't worth your life."

Nate felt his eyes began to tear. "I prayed so hard for healing. I thought this was going to be it. I had dreams of walking home." His eyes met hers. "I had dreams of walking with you on my arm again."

"Maybe God is answering your prayers. But maybe in his timing, not ours."

"Maybe," he whispered before he coughed.

Abby reached over and touched his cheek. "I need you to hear something, Nate. It doesn't matter to me if you walk again. I want to stay with you whether you're healed or whether you spend the rest of your life in a wheelchair. It doesn't matter. I'll stay with you, Nate. I'll stay."

"You shouldn't stay because you have—"

She pressed her finger over his lips. "I'm not done, Nathan McAllister. You didn't let me finish." The corners of her mouth turned up. "I love you, Nathan. I need you." She sniffed. "I—don't—want—you to die."

He searched her eyes. Could it be true? "Abby," he whispered, "God *is* answering my prayers."

As Nathan began to weep, Abby wiped away his tears and snuggled her body against his in the cramped hospital bed. She gently laid her arm across his chest. She whispered, "Am I hurting you?"

"No."

"I want you home, Nathan."

"Abby, Abby," Nathan responded, his voice barely audible above the blipping of his cardiac monitor.

She lowered her lips to his ear. "Will you come home to me?"

He nodded his head. "I—want—to." He grimaced with pain. "If . . . if I make it out of here."

"You're going to make it. *We're* going to make it." She placed her head on his shoulder. "I love you just the way you are."

Nathan watched the ceiling blur with his tears. Slowly, but with a buoyant heart, he whispered, "Please pray—for—me."

He closed his eyes and concentrated on Abby's voice. This time, for the first time, she *didn't* pray for his healing. "Oh, God, help us be a real family again."

CHAPTER
48

THAT NIGHT, after Abby left for Fisher's Retreat, Nathan fought to stay alert through a haze of narcotics. Every few minutes he attempted a small movement only to have agonizing spasms rack his arms and legs.

In spite of the pain Nathan found himself at peace, buoyed by the words Abby had spoken, the affirmation of affection he had prayed for so fervently. Just before eleven o'clock he looked up and focused on Dr. Hannah's face.

"Nathan, how are you feeling?"

He grunted. "Rough. Rough but OK."

"Have you thought about what I asked?"

"I can't *not* think about it." He paused, allowing another wave of fire from his right leg to cool. "I want you to reverse the operation."

"You want to be like before?" The surgeon hung his head.

"Yes."

Dr. Hannah sighed heavily. "I'm sorry, Nathan."

"You gave me a chance and I took it. But I don't want to risk losing my life."

The surgeon's eyes were sad and directed away from Nathan's face, onto his hospital bed. "You would choose to live as a quad rather than to take the risk of continuing our experiment?"

Nathan nodded.

Dr. Hannah raised his eyes to meet Nathan's. "You amaze me. I thought you'd be angry."

"You gave it your best, doc. With no guarantees. Why should I be mad?"

"Because I failed you. You should be angry." He lifted Nathan's hand and cupped it in his own.

Nathan struggled to curl his fingers around the surgeon's thumb. Slowly, painfully, he squeezed. "Hear me, doc. I'm disappointed. I hate not walking. I hate not being able to hold my wife . . . my daughter—" His voice caught in a sob before he continued in a whisper. "But I want to live." He squinted his eyes as a throbbing discomfort passed through his hand.

Dr. Hannah gently laid Nathan's arm on the bed.

Nathan watched as the surgeon turned away. The surgeon lifted his hand to his face before turning around again. "You are a rare man, Nathan. A few weeks ago I thought I would be bringing you to wholeness. But *you* have helped *me*." His shoulders slumped forward in defeat. "If you have no objections, I'll schedule your surgery for tomorrow."

Another pain knifed Nathan, passing through his lower abdomen and quickly into his chest. "OK," he gasped.

The surgeon turned to go.

"Please," Nathan asked, "have the nurse bring more medicine. I'm not sure I can take this anymore."

◆ ◆ ◆

The next afternoon, with Nathan anesthetized, Dr. Hannah reopened his posterior neck incision. With Elizabeth assisting, he quietly dissected down to the spinal cord nerve grafts. The mood was somber, and the communication strictly professional.

"Are you going to remove the omental free flap?" Elizabeth questioned.

"No. It looks healthy enough. Let's leave it in place and just remove the grafts running through it. That way if we ever try again, it will be here if we need it."

Elizabeth nodded.

"Suction."

"Scissors."

"Hold here. There. Hmmm. Let's get the pathologists to look at the ends of this graft. I want to see if they can see the area of new growth."

EPILOGUE

ABBY MCALLISTER'S voice cracked as she yelled her daughter's name for the second time. "Melissa!" She paused from her frenzied packing and tilted her head, listening for the sound of little footsteps.

Nothing. Not the expected creak from the old stairs. No footfalls. Only the crooning of a country singer whose radio sonnet could never darken Abby's mood.

"Mel-iiisssaaaa!"

She dragged the suitcase into the narrow second-floor hallway and began tugging it toward the stairs. Once there, she detoured into Melissa's room.

A threadbare throw rug covered the cool wooden floor. A single bed decorated with pink frilly sheets was pushed against the wall. Its sole occupant was an overstuffed gingerbread man named Willie.

"Mel—!" She stopped short when she looked through the window to see her daughter playing on the swing set in the side yard. With the onset of warmer weather, if Melissa wasn't underfoot, it was a sure bet that Abby could find her playing on the swings.

"I should've known," Abby whispered to herself. She struggled with the heavy window, pulling it up only a few inches before it stopped. She yanked with an audible grunt and managed to coax it open another inch. She lowered her face to the opening.

The spring air gave her a warm greeting. Abby pushed back her short, dark hair and paused to listen as her daughter's voice rose and fell with the swing.

"My dad is the bestest dad," she giggled, looking back at her neighborhood friend, Tommy Evans. "Push higher!"

"Mel! It's time to go. Daddy will be waiting."

Abby watched as her daughter scampered around the house. In a moment she heard the front door open, then Melissa's footsteps on the stairs.

"Are you going on a trip?"

"No," Abby responded as she rested her hand on the suitcase. "Mommy is just moving some things downstairs to her new room." She picked a blade of grass from her daughter's hair. "But I can finish moving this stuff later. Come on, it's time to go get Daddy!"

ACKNOWLEDGMENTS

WITH special thanks to . . .

Steve Heatwole, Bruce Dellinger, Shannon Holland, and Jon Markowitz for sharing their lives with me.

Neurosurgeon Dr. Richard Gillespie, for insights into modern neurosurgical practice.

Warren and Martha Shank, dedicated worshipers of Christ from the Old Order Mennonite Church, for sharing their beliefs and lifestyle with me.

Thanks too to Dayton Chief of Police Buddy Farris for answering my many questions on law enforcement, and deputy Kelly Zander for the insight into the DARE program.

Thanks to Gerard McLean from Electrologic of America, Inc. for helpful information about the StimMaster.

Authors Frank Peretti and Susan Bauer for reviewing the manuscript and making helpful critiques.

The entire Crossway family for their support and vision.

My wife, Kris, my ever-faithful first reader.

Most importantly, credit is due to my loving Heavenly Father. Thank you! Thank you! Thank you!

"Kraus may be to the medical thriller what Tom Clancy is to the techno-thriller." —BOOKSTORE JOURNAL

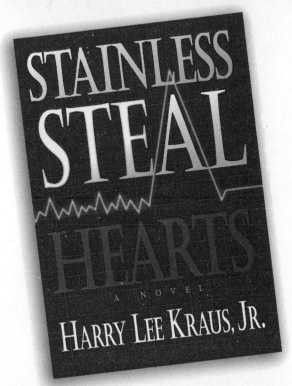

All he wants is to finish his residency and become a surgeon. But the truth has to come out—even if it costs him his career.

Surgical resident Matt Stone and two of his friends have pieced together some strange incidents, and their conclusion is unbelievable—it seems Chief Surgeon Dr. Simons and a local abortionist are involved in some secret research. And when Matt unknowingly gets in the way, Dr. Simons seeks to end Matt's career. Can he and his friends gather enough evidence to expose the experiments before Matt gets suspended from practicing medicine?

A chilling account that must be read because... someday it could be reality!

"A probing and finely detailed story of spiritual warfare on the medical front." —FRANK PERETTI

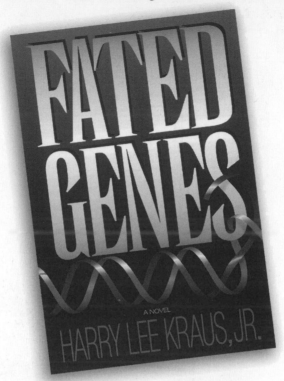

When ambition rules.
When lives are sacrificed for society's good.
When evil is worshipped.
Who dares to stand in the way?

Brad Forrest is a pediatric surgeon who is risking everything to obtain the career opportunity of his dreams.

Web Tyson, head of a prestigious pediatric surgery practice, may be the next Surgeon General of the U.S.—unless someone discovers his secret.

And Lenore Kingsley is using her pharmaceutical company to engage in DNA research in the hopes that her own selfish purposes will be accomplished.

These three personalities collide in a strange chain of events that none of them would have chosen and that none of them may survive. Can anyone make a difference now?

An unforgettable story of passion and power, with spitItual themes that no one should ignore

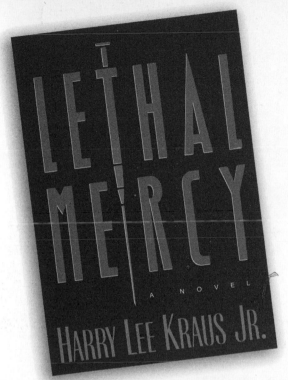

Was it medicine? Mercy? Or murder? For the sake of
his conscience and the community in which
he practices, he has to find out.

When pregnant Sarah Hampton dies suddenly at an alternative cancer treatment facility, an enraged community demands to know
whether her physician-husband assisted her death. Suffering from
traumatic amnesia, Jake would like to know too. He is strongly
against assisted suicide, and yet his wife was suffering such agony—
is it possible?

Hoping to unravel the questions he's not sure he wants answered,
Jake moves to his former hometown. Once there, he receives subtle
and ever more threatening clues from an unidentified stalker. Is a
sinister someone trying to destroy him completely?

Fiction from the heart of today's headlines

"Surgeon Harry Kraus has combined his medical expertise with a gripping tale of modern medical mayhem that will keep you up tonight!" —ANGELA ELWELL HUNT

A high-tech researcher, a caring doctor, a dying young woman. All bear the wounds of darkness. At what cost comes the cure?

The newspapers in and around town are shouting the question: Is he a hero? A murderer? Or a fool? Dr. Seth Berringer is wondering himself. In desperation he tried to take things into his own hands— and now those hands are stained with blood.

He's caught in a cover-up with worldwide scientific and spiritual implications. And only the truth can set him free.

Fiction as real as the dark impulses of the human heart